JANE AUSTEN

MINOR WORKS

THE WHITE HORSE INN AT DORKING

From a drawing by George Scharf I in the British Museum Print Room

The Works of
JANE AUSTEN

VOLUME VI
MINOR WORKS

Now first collected and edited
from the manuscripts
by
R. W. CHAPMAN

*With illustrations from
Contemporary Sources*

LONDON
OXFORD UNIVERSITY PRESS
NEW YORK TORONTO

Oxford University Press, Ely House, London W. 1

GLASGOW   NEW YORK   TORONTO   MELBOURNE   WELLINGTON
CAPE TOWN   IBADAN   NAIROBI   DAR ES SALAAM   LUSAKA   ADDIS ABABA
DELHI   BOMBAY   CALCUTTA   MADRAS   KARACHI   LAHORE   DACCA
KUALA LUMPUR   SINGAPORE   HONG KONG   TOKYO

ISBN 0 19 254706 2

First edition 1954
Reprinted 1958, with revisions 1963, 1965
with further revisions by B. C. Southam 1969, 1972, and 1975

Printed in Great Britain
at the University Press, Oxford
by Vivian Ridler
Printer to the University

PREFACE

THE generous co-operation of Mr. R. A. Austen-Leigh enables me to execute a project long entertained of collecting Jane Austen's minor writings; *Volume the Third*, of which he owns the manuscript, is the last of these to be published. I am indebted also to Mrs. Mowll and A. P. Watt & Son for permission to include *Volume the Second*, first published by Chatto and Windus in 1922 as *Love and Freindship*, and to Mrs. Mowll for a sight of the manuscript.

When Mr. Austen-Leigh's grandfather, James Edward Austen-Leigh, Jane Austen's nephew, was collecting materials for his *Memoir* of his aunt, his half-sister Anna (Mrs. Benjamin Lefroy) discussed with him the propriety of including unpublished pieces. She was not disinclined to the juvenilia, but deprecated any disclosure of what she called the *Betweenities*. In the event Mr. Austen-Leigh yielded to pressure and printed in the second (1871) edition *Lady Susan* and *The Watsons*, adding an account, with quotations, of 'the last work', which came to be known in the family as 'Sanditon'. He printed also the cancelled chapter of *Persuasion*; this I have not included in my collection since it forms an appendix to my edition of the novel.[1]

The *Memoir* with its appendages was familiar to Victorian readers as the sixth volume of Bentley's edition of the novels, in which the lettering on the binding described it as 'Lady Susan'. A brief extract from the juvenilia appeared in the Austen-Leighs' *Life and Letters* in 1913.

These immature or fragmentary fictions call for hardly any comment. The persons named in the *Plan of a Novel*

[1] An exact print of the manuscript, with a record of all its erasures and corrections, is in my separate edition 'Two Chapters of *Persuasion*', Oxford 1926; some copies include a complete facsimile.

and in the *Opinions* on *Mansfield Park* and *Emma* belong
to Jane Austen's biography, and I have identified those
that are obscurely named. Information on many of them
will be found in the indexes to my edition of her *Letters*.
I include the *Opinions*, since the phrasing of some of them,
though not their substance, may be hers.

In my indexes I give (1) real persons and real or fictitious
places, referring to my edition of the *Letters* for those
persons of whom fuller information will be found in the
indexes to that edition; (2) authors and books. This may
be used in connexion with the index of Literary Allusions
in the fifth volume (*Northanger Abbey* and *Persuasion*) of
my edition of the novels. This, in the reprint of 1952,
includes, I believe, almost all such allusions in the novels,
the minor works, and the letters; (3) characters, ignoring
however the juvenilia other than 'Catharine'.

Passages erased in the MSS. of the juvenilia are for the
most part indicated by brackets. Minor corrections, recorded in my separate editions of I and III, are ignored,
as are the very numerous deletions and corrections in the
MSS. of 'The Watsons' and 'Sanditon'; for these I again
refer the student to my separate editions.

1953   R. W. C.

NOTE TO THE REVISED IMPRESSION

THE revisions to this edition are minimal, for two good reasons. Firstly, I have wanted to disturb as little as possible the style of editing and presentation which characterizes so distinctively R. W. Chapman's unobtrusive and scholarly attention to all the writings of Jane Austen. Secondly, the textual and historical points which have arisen since Chapman completed his work are relatively few and scarcely affect our view of Jane Austen's development and output. What we do have is a slightly more precise idea of the chronology of composition and transcription of the juvenilia; this I have tried to present as economically as possible in the appropriate headnotes. The most extensive textual revision is to *Volume the Second*. The text given here is a corrected version of my edition published by the Clarendon Press, 1963. I would like to thank Mr. Darrel Mansell of Dartmouth College for his advice on certain details concerning the sources for 'The History of England'.   B. C. S.

1967

CONTENTS

LIST OF ILLUSTRATIONS

I. The Juvenilia

UNDER this heading are placed Jane Austen's earliest compositions, her childhood writing, covering the period from about 1787 (when she was twelve) to 1793. In the three manuscript notebooks, entitled by Jane Austen herself, there are altogether twenty-seven items, a collection of transcripts which she made over a period of about fifteen or twenty years as a record of her work and for the convenience of reading aloud to the family and friends. The separate manuscripts of the individual items have not survived. Perhaps those originals were destroyed when copies were entered into the notebooks; perhaps they were dispersed among the relatives and friends to whom they were dedicated, later to be lost.

Only four pieces in this collection are dated. Nonetheless, from stylistic and internal evidence it is possible to draw up a tenable order of composition:

1787–90 'Frederic & Elfrida', 'Jack & Alice', 'Edgar & Emma', 'Henry and Eliza', 'Mr. Harley', 'Sir William Mountague', 'Mr. Clifford', 'The beautifull Cassandra', 'Amelia Webster', 'The Visit', 'The Mystery' (all *Volume the First*).

1790 'Love and Friendship', dated June (*Volume the Second*).

1791 'The History of England', dated November, 'Collection of Letters' (both *Volume the Second*).

1792 'Lesley Castle' (*Volume the Second*), 'The three Sisters' (*Volume the First*), 'Evelyn' (*Volume the Third*), 'Catharine', dated August (*Volume the Third*).

1793 'Scraps' (*Volume the Second*), 'Detached pieces', dated June, 'Ode to Pity' (both *Volume the First*).

The factors involved in dating the composition and transcription of this material are discussed in B. C. Southam, *Jane Austen's Literary Manuscripts*, Oxford, 1964.

Volume the First (manuscript in the Bodleian Library, Oxford): the first eleven items are entered in a childish hand and on stylistic evidence can be assigned to the earliest period of Jane Austen's writing, whereas the two dates on the manuscript (see pp. 71, 75), 2nd and 3rd June 1793, belong to the final period of the juvenilia. The text was first edited by R. W. Chapman, Clarendon Press, Oxford, 1933. This edition records the few major manuscript alterations, passages which Jane Austen struck out. For a detailed discussion of the notebook see B. C. Southam, 'The Manuscript of Jane Austen's *Volume the First*', *The Library*, 5th ser., xvii, no. 3 (1962), pp. 231–7.

Volume the Second (manuscript in the possession of Mrs. Rosemary Mowll): the contents of this notebook appear to be compositions dating between 1790 and 1793. The text was first published in 1922 by Chatto & Windus under the title *Love and Freindship*, with an Introduction by G. K. Chesterton; a re-collated text, *Volume the Second*, edited by B. C. Southam, Clarendon Press, Oxford, 1963, contains a full record of Jane Austen's corrections to the manuscript (one of which is to change the original 'ei' to 'ie' in her spelling of Friendship in the title 'Love and Friendship').

Volume the Third (manuscript in the British Museum): the contents of this volume are dated 1792. 'Catharine' was left unfinished by Jane Austen and a continuation was added to the manuscript by her niece Anna Lefroy (see p. 240). 'Evelyn' was also left unfinished and continued by another (unidentified) member of the family (see note to p. 189). The text was first edited by R. W. Chapman, Clarendon Press, Oxford, 1951.

[B. C. S.]

VOLUME THE FIRST

CONTENTS

To Miss Lloyd

MY DEAR MARTHA

As a small testimony of the gratitude I feel for your late generosity to me in finishing my muslin Cloak, I beg leave to offer you this little production of your sincere Freind

THE AUTHOR

FREDERIC

FREDERIC & ELFRIDA

A NOVEL

CHAPTER THE FIRST

THE Uncle of Elfrida was the Father of Frederic; in other words, they were first cousins by the Father's side.

Being both born in one day & both brought up at one school, it was not wonderfull that they should look on each other with something more than bare politeness. They loved with mutual sincerity but were both determined not to transgress the rules of Propriety by owning their attachment, either to the object beloved, or to any one else.

They were exceedingly handsome and so much alike, that it was not every one who knew them apart. Nay even their most intimate freinds had nothing to distinguish them by, but the shape of the face, the colour of the Eye, the length of the Nose & the difference of the complexion.

Elfrida had an intimate freind to whom, being on a visit to an Aunt, she wrote the following Letter.

TO MISS DRUMMOND

DEAR CHARLOTTE

I should be obliged to you, if you would buy me, during your stay with Mrs Williamson, a new & fashionable Bonnet, to suit the complexion of your

E. FALKNOR

Charlotte, whose character was a willingness to oblige every one, when she returned into the Country, brought her

her Freind the wished-for Bonnet, & so ended this little adventure, much to the satisfaction of all parties.

On her return to Crankhumdunberry (of which sweet village her father was Rector) Charlotte was received with the greatest Joy by Frederic & Elfrida, who, after pressing her alternately to their Bosoms, proposed to her to take a walk in a Grove of Poplars which led from the Parsonage to a verdant Lawn enamelled with a variety of variegated flowers & watered by a purling Stream, brought from the Valley of Tempé by a passage under ground.

In this Grove they had scarcely remained above 9 hours, when they were suddenly agreably surprized by hearing a most delightfull voice warble the following stanza.

SONG

That Damon was in love with me
I once thought & beleiv'd
But now that he is not I see,
I fear I was deceiv'd.

———

No sooner were the lines finished than they beheld by a turning in the Grove 2 elegant young women leaning on each other's arm, who immediately on perceiving them, took a different path & disappeared from their sight.

———

CHAPTER THE SECOND

———

As Elfrida & her companions, had seen enough of them to know that they were neither the 2 Miss Greens, nor Mrs Jackson and her Daughter, they could not help expressing their surprise at their appearance; till at length recollecting, that a new family had lately taken a House not far from the Grove, they hastened home, determined to lose
no

no time in forming an acquaintance with 2 such amiable & worthy Girls, of which family they rightly imagined them to be a part.

Agreable to such a determination, they went that very evening to pay their respects to Mrs Fitzroy & her two Daughters. On being shewn into an elegant dressing room, ornamented with festoons of artificial flowers, they were struck with the engaging Exterior & beautifull outside of Jezalinda the eldest of the young Ladies; but e'er they had been many minutes seated, the Wit & Charms which shone resplendent in the conversation of the amiable Rebecca, enchanted them so much that they all with one accord jumped up and exclaimed.

"Lovely & too charming Fair one, notwithstanding your forbidding Squint, your greazy tresses & your swelling Back, which are more frightfull than imagination can paint or pen describe, I cannot refrain from expressing my raptures, at the engaging Qualities of your Mind, which so amply atone for the Horror, with which your first appearance must ever inspire the unwary visitor."

"Your sentiments so nobly expressed on the different excellencies of Indian & English Muslins, & the judicious preference you give the former, have excited in me an admiration of which I can alone give an adequate idea, by assuring you it is nearly equal to what I feel for myself."

Then making a profound Curtesy to the amiable & abashed Rebecca, they left the room & hurried home.

From this period, the intimacy between the Families of Fitzroy, Drummond, and Falknor, daily increased till at length it grew to such a pitch, that they did not scruple to kick one another out of the window on the slightest provocation.

During this happy state of Harmony, the eldest Miss Fitzroy ran off with the Coachman & the amiable Rebecca was asked in marriage by Captain Roger of Buckinghamshire.

Mrs

Mrs Fitzroy did not approve of the match on account of the tender years of the young couple, Rebecca being but 36 & Captain Roger little more than 63. To remedy this objection, it was agreed that they should wait a little while till they were a good deal older.

CHAPTER THE THIRD

In the mean time the parents of Frederic proposed to those of Elfrida, an union between them, which being accepted with pleasure, the wedding cloathes were bought & nothing remained to be settled but the naming of the Day.

As to the lovely Charlotte, being importuned with eagerness to pay another visit to her Aunt, she determined to accept the invitation & in consequence of it walked to Mrs Fitzroys to take leave of the amiable Rebecca, whom she found surrounded by Patches, Powder, Pomatum & Paint with which she was vainly endeavouring to remedy the natural plainness of her face.

"I am come my amiable Rebecca, to take my leave of you for the fortnight I am destined to spend with my aunt. Beleive me this separation is painfull to me, but it is as necessary as the labour which now engages you."

"Why to tell you the truth my Love, replied Rebecca, I have lately taken it into my head to think (perhaps with little reason) that my complexion is by no means equal to the rest of my face & have therefore taken, as you see, to white & red paint which I would scorn to use on any other occasion as I hate art."

Charlotte, who perfectly understood the meaning of her freind's speech, was too good-temper'd & obliging to refuse her, what she knew she wished,—a compliment; & they parted the best freinds in the world.

With

With a heavy heart & streaming Eyes did she ascend the lovely vehicle[1] which bore her from her freinds & home; but greived as she was, she little thought in what a strange & different manner she should return to it.

On her entrance into the city of London which was the place of Mrs Williamson's abode, the postilion, whose stupidity was amazing, declared & declared even without the least shame or Compunction, that having never been informed he was totally ignorant of what part of the Town, he was to drive to.

Charlotte, whose nature we have before intimated, was an earnest desire to oblige every one, with the greatest Condescension & Goodhumour informed him that he was to drive to Portland Place, which he accordingly did & Charlotte soon found herself in the arms of a fond Aunt.

Scarcely were they seated as usual, in the most affectionate manner in one chair, than the Door suddenly opened & an aged gentleman with a sallow face & old pink Coat, partly by intention & partly thro' weakness was at the feet of the lovely Charlotte, declaring his attachment to her & beseeching her pity in the most moving manner.

Not being able to resolve to make any one miserable, she consented to become his wife; where upon the Gentleman left the room & all was quiet.

Their quiet however continued but a short time, for on a second opening of the door a young & Handsome Gentleman with a new blue coat, entered & intreated from the lovely Charlotte, permission to pay to her, his addresses.

There was a something in the appearance of the second Stranger, that influenced Charlotte in his favour, to the full as much as the appearance of the first: she could not account for it, but so it was.

Having therefore agreable to that & the natural turn of her mind to make every one happy, promised to become his Wife the next morning, he took his leave & the two

[1] a post-chaise.

Ladies

Ladies sat down to Supper on a young Leveret, a brace of Partridges, a leash of Pheasants & a Dozen of Pigeons.

CHAPTER THE FOURTH

It was not till the next morning that Charlotte recollected the double engagement she had entered into; but when she did, the reflection of her past folly, operated so strongly on her mind, that she resolved to be guilty of a greater, & to that end threw herself into a deep stream which ran thro' her Aunt's pleasure Grounds in Portland Place.

She floated to Crankhumdunberry where she was picked up & buried; the following epitaph, composed by Frederic Elfrida & Rebecca, was placed on her tomb.

EPITAPH

Here lies our friend who having promis-ed
That unto two she would be marri-ed
Threw her sweet Body & her lovely face
Into the Stream that runs thro' Portland Place.

These sweet lines, as pathetic as beautifull were never read by any one who passed that way, without a shower of tears, which if they should fail of exciting in you, Reader, your mind must be unworthy to peruse them.

Having performed the last sad office to their departed freind, Frederic & Elfrida together with Captain Roger & Rebecca returned to Mrs Fitzroy's at whose feet they threw themselves with one accord & addressed her in the following Manner.

"Madam"

"When the sweet Captain Roger first addressed the amiable Rebecca, you alone objected to their union on
                                                    account

account of the tender years of the Parties. That plea can be no more, seven days being now expired, together with the lovely Charlotte, since the Captain first spoke to you on the subject."

"Consent then Madam to their union & as a reward, this smelling Bottle which I enclose in my right hand, shall be yours & yours forever; I never will claim it again. But if you refuse to join their hands in 3 days time, this dagger which I enclose in my left shall be steeped in your hearts blood."

"Speak then Madam & decide their fate & yours."

Such gentle & sweet persuasion could not fail of having the desired effect. The answer they received, was this.

"My dear young freinds"

"The arguments you have used are too just & too eloquent to be withstood; Rebecca in 3 days time, you shall be united to the Captain."

This speech, than which nothing could be more satisfactory, was received with Joy by all; & peace being once more restored on all sides, Captain Roger intreated Rebecca to favour them with a Song, in compliance with which request having first assured them that she had a terrible cold, she sung as follows.

SONG

When Corydon went to the fair
He bought a red ribbon for Bess,
With which she encircled her hair
& made herself look very fess.

CHAPTER THE FIFTH

At the end of 3 days Captain Roger and Rebecca were united and immediately after the Ceremony set off in the Stage Waggon for the Captains seat in Buckinghamshire.

The

The parents of Elfrida, alltho' they earnestly wished to see her married to Frederic before they died, yet knowing the delicate frame of her mind could ill bear the least exertion & rightly judging that naming her wedding day would be too great a one, forebore to press her on the subject.

Weeks & Fortnights flew away without gaining the least ground; the Cloathes grew out of fashion & at length Capt: Roger & his Lady arrived, to pay a visit to their Mother & introduce to her their beautifull Daughter of eighteen.

Elfrida, who had found her former acquaintance were growing too old & too ugly to be any longer agreable, was rejoiced to hear of the arrival of so pretty a girl as Eleanor with whom she determined to form the strictest freindship.

But the Happiness she had expected from an acquaintance with Eleanor, she soon found was not to be received, for she had not only the mortification of finding herself treated by her as little less than an old woman, but had actually the horror of perceiving a growing passion in the Bosom of Frederic for the Daughter of the amiable Rebecca.

The instant she had the first idea of such an attachment, she flew to Frederic & in a manner truly heroick, spluttered out to him her intention of being married the next Day.

To one in his predicament who possessed less personal Courage than Frederic was master of, such a speech would have been Death; but he not being the least terrified boldly replied.

"Damme Elfrida *you* may be married tomorrow but *I* wont."

This answer distressed her too much for her delicate Constitution. She accordingly fainted & was in such a hurry to have a succession of fainting fits, that she had scarcely patience enough to recover from one before she fell into another.

Tho', in any threatening Danger to his Life or Liberty, Frederic was as bold as brass yet in other respects his heart was as soft as cotton & immediately on hearing of the
dangerous

dangerous way Elfrida was in, he flew to her & finding her
better than he had been taught to expect, was united to
her Forever—.

FINIS

JACK & ALICE

A NOVEL

Is respectfully inscribed to Francis William Austen Esqr Midshipman on board his Majesty's Ship the Perseverance by his obedient humble Servant The Author

CHAPTER THE FIRST

Mr Johnson was once upon a time about 53; in a twelvemonth afterwards he was 54, which so much delighted him
that he was determined to celebrate his next Birthday by
giving a Masquerade to his Children & Freinds. Accordingly on the Day he attained his 55th year tickets were
dispatched to all his Neighbours to that purpose. His
acquaintance indeed in that part of the World were not
very numerous as they consisted only of Lady Williams,
Mr & Mrs Jones, Charles Adams & the 3 Miss Simpsons,
who composed the neighbourhood of Pammydiddle &
formed the Masquerade.

Before I proceed to give an account of the Evening, it
will be proper to describe to my reader, the persons and
Characters of the party introduced to his acquaintance.

Mr & Mrs Jones were both rather tall & very passionate,
but were in other respects, good tempered, wellbehaved
People

People. Charles Adams was an amiable, accomplished & bewitching young Man; of so dazzling a Beauty that none but Eagles could look him in the Face.

Miss Simpson was pleasing in her person, in her Manners & in her Disposition; an unbounded ambition was her only fault. Her second sister Sukey was Envious, Spitefull & Malicious. Her person was short, fat & disagreable. Cecilia (the youngest) was perfectly handsome but too affected to be pleasing.

In Lady Williams every virtue met. She was a widow with a handsome Jointure & the remains of a very handsome face. Tho' Benevolent & Candid, she was Generous & sincere; Tho' Pious & Good, she was Religious & amiable, & Tho Elegant & Agreable, she was Polished & Entertaining.

The Johnsons were a family of Love, & though a little addicted to the Bottle & the Dice, had many good Qualities.

Such was the party assembled in the elegant Drawing Room of Johnson Court, amongst which the pleasing figure of a Sultana was the most remarkable of the female Masks. Of the Males a Mask representing the Sun, was the most universally admired. The Beams that darted from his Eyes were like those of that glorious Luminary tho' infinitely superior. So strong were they that no one dared venture within half a mile of them; he had therefore the best part of the Room to himself, its size not amounting to more than 3 quarters of a mile in length & half a one in breadth. The Gentleman at last finding the feirceness of his beams to be very inconvenient to the concourse by obliging them to croud together in one corner of the room, half shut his eyes by which means, the Company discovered him to be Charles Adams in his plain green Coat, without any mask at all.

When their astonishment was a little subsided their attention was attracted by 2 Domino's who advanced in a horrible Passion; they were both very tall, but seemed in other respects to have many good qualities. "These said

said the witty Charles, these are Mr & Mrs Jones." and so
indeed they were.

No one could imagine who was the Sultana! Till at
length on her addressing a beautifull Flora who was re-
clining in a studied attitude on a couch, with "Oh Cecilia,
I wish I was really what I pretend to be", she was discovered by the never failing genius of Charles Adams, to
be the elegant but ambitious Caroline Simpson, & the
person to whom she addressed herself, he rightly imagined
to be her lovely but affected sister Cecilia.

The Company now advanced to a Gaming Table where
sat 3 Dominos (each with a bottle in their hand) deeply
engaged; but a female in the character of Virtue fled with
hasty footsteps from the shocking scene, whilst a little fat
woman representing Envy, sate alternately on the fore-
heads of the 3 Gamesters. Charles Adams was still as
bright as ever; he soon discovered the party at play to be
the 3 Johnsons, Envy to be Sukey Simpson & Virtue to
be Lady Williams.

The Masks were then all removed & the Company retired to another room, to partake of an elegant & well
managed Entertainment, after which the Bottle being
pretty briskly pushed about by the 3 Johnsons, the whole
party not excepting even Virtue were carried home, Dead
Drunk.

CHAPTER THE SECOND

FOR three months did the Masquerade afford ample subject for conversation to the inhabitants of Pammydiddle;
but no character at it was so fully expatiated on as Charles
Adams. The singularity of his appearance, the beams
which darted from his eyes, the brightness of his Wit, &
the whole *tout ensemble* of his person had subdued the
                                                    hearts

hearts of so many of the young Ladies, that of the six present at the Masquerade but five had returned uncaptivated. Alice Johnson was the unhappy sixth whose heart had not been able to withstand the power of his Charms. But as it may appear strange to my Readers, that so much worth & Excellence as he possessed should have conquered only hers, it will be necessary to inform them that the Miss Simpsons were defended from his Power by Ambition, Envy, & Self-admiration.

Every wish of Caroline was centered in a titled Husband; whilst in Sukey such superior excellence could only raise her Envy not her Love, & Cecilia was too tenderly attached to herself to be pleased with any one besides. As for Lady Williams and Mrs Jones, the former of them was too sensible, to fall in love with one so much her Junior and the latter, tho' very tall & very passionate was too fond of her Husband to think of such a thing.

Yet in spite of every endeavour on the part of Miss Johnson to discover any attachment to her in him; the cold & indifferent heart of Charles Adams still to all appearance, preserved its native freedom; polite to all but partial to none, he still remained the lovely, the lively, but insensible Charles Adams.

One evening, Alice finding herself somewhat heated by wine (no very uncommon case) determined to seek a relief for her disordered Head & Love-sick Heart in the Conversation of the intelligent Lady Williams.

She found her Ladyship at home as was in general the Case, for she was not fond of going out, & like the great Sir Charles Grandison scorned to deny herself when at Home, as she looked on that fashionable method of shutting out disagreeable Visitors, as little less than downright Bigamy.

In spite of the wine she had been drinking, poor Alice was uncommonly out of spirits; she could think of nothing but Charles Adams, she could talk of nothing but him,

&

& in short spoke so openly that Lady Williams soon discovered the unreturned affection she bore him, which excited her Pity & Compassion so strongly that she addressed her in the following Manner.

"I perceive but too plainly my dear Miss Johnson, that your Heart has not been able to withstand the fascinating Charms of this young Man & I pity you sincerely. Is it a first Love ?"

"It is."

"I am still more greived to hear *that*; I am myself a sad example of the Miseries, in general attendant on a first Love & I am determined for the future to avoid the like Misfortune. I wish it may not be too late for you to do the same; if it is not endeavour my dear Girl to secure yourself from so great a Danger. A second attachment is seldom attended with any serious consequences; against *that* therefore I have nothing to say. Preserve yourself from a first Love & you need not fear a second."

"You mentioned Madam something of your having yourself been a sufferer by the misfortune you are so good as to wish me to avoid. Will you favour me with your Life & Adventures ?"

"Willingly my Love."

CHAPTER THE THIRD

"My Father was a gentleman of considerable Fortune in Berkshire; myself & a few more his only Children. I was but six years old when I had the misfortune of losing my Mother & being at that time young & Tender, my father instead of sending me to School, procured an able handed Governess to superintend my Education at Home. My Brothers were placed at Schools suitable to their Ages &

my

my Sisters being all younger than myself, remained still under the Care of their Nurse.

Miss Dickins was an excellent Governess. She instructed me in the Paths of Virtue; under her tuition I daily became more amiable, & might perhaps by this time have nearly attained perfection, had not my worthy Preceptoress been torn from my arms, e'er I had attained my seventeenth year. I never shall forget her last words. 'My dear Kitty she said, Good night t'ye.' I never saw her afterwards" continued Lady Williams wiping her eyes, "She eloped with the Butler the same night."

"I was invited the following year by a distant relation of my Father's to spend the Winter with her in town. Mrs Watkins was a Lady of Fashion, Family & fortune; she was in general esteemed a pretty Woman, but I never thought her very handsome, for my part. She had too high a forehead, Her eyes were too small & she had too much colour."

"How can *that* be?" interrupted Miss Johnson reddening with anger; "Do you think that any one can have too much colour?"

"Indeed I do, & I'll tell you why I do my dear Alice; when a person has too great a degree of red in their Complexion, it gives their face in my opinion, too red a look."

"But can a face my Lady have too red a look?"

"Certainly my dear Miss Johnson & I'll [tell] you why. When a face has too red a look it does not appear to so much advantage as it would were it paler."

"Pray Ma'am proceed in your story."

"Well, as I said before, I was invited by this Lady to spend some weeks with her in town. Many Gentlemen thought her Handsome but in my opinion, Her forehead was too high, her eyes too small & she had too much colour."

"In that Madam as I said before your Ladyship must have been mistaken. Mrs. Watkins could not have too much colour since no one can have too much."

"Excuse

"Excuse me my Love if I do not agree with you in that particular. Let me explain myself clearly; my idea of the case is this. When a Woman has too great a proportion of red in her Cheeks, she must have too much colour."

"But Madam I deny that it is possible for any one to have too great a proportion of red in their Cheeks."

"What my Love not if they have too much colour?"

Miss Johnson was now out of all patience, the more so perhaps as Lady Williams still remained so inflexibly cool. It must be remembered however that her Ladyship had in one respect by far the advantage of Alice; I mean in not being drunk, for heated with wine & raised by Passion, she could have little command of her Temper.

The Dispute at length grew so hot on the part of Alice that, "From Words she almost came to Blows" When Mr Johnson luckily entered & with some difficulty forced her away from Lady Williams, Mrs Watkins & her red cheeks.

CHAPTER THE FOURTH

My Readers may perhaps imagine that after such a fracas, no intimacy could longer subsist between the Johnsons and Lady Williams, but in that they are mistaken for her Ladyship was too sensible to be angry at a conduct which she could not help perceiving to be the natural consequence of inebriety & Alice had too sincere a respect for Lady Williams & too great a relish for her Claret, not to make every concession in her power.

A few days after their reconciliation Lady Williams called on Miss Johnson to propose a walk in a Citron Grove which led from her Ladyship's pigstye to Charles Adams's Horsepond. Alice was too sensible of Lady Williams's kindness in proposing such a walk & too much pleased

with

with the prospect of seeing at the end of it, a Horsepond of Charles's, not to accept it with visible delight. They had not proceeded far before she was roused from the reflection of the happiness she was going to enjoy, by Lady Williams's thus addressing her.

"I have as yet forborn my dear Alice to continue the narrative of my Life from an unwillingness of recalling to your Memory a scene which (since it reflects on you rather disgrace than credit) had better be forgot than remembered."

Alice had already begun to colour up & was beginning to speak, when her Ladyship perceiving her displeasure, continued thus.

"I am afraid my dear Girl that I have offended you by what I have just said; I assure you I do not mean to distress you by a retrospection of what cannot now be helped; considering all things I do not think you so much to blame as many People do; for when a person is in Liquor, there is no answering for what they may do. [a woman (?) in such a situation is particularly off her guard because her head is not strong enough to support intoxication."]¹

"Madam, this is not to be borne; I insist—"

"My dear Girl dont vex yourself about the matter; I assure you I have entirely forgiven every thing respecting it; indeed I was not angry at the time, because as I saw all along, you were nearly dead drunk. I knew you could not help saying the strange things you did. But I see I distress you; so I will change the subject & desire it may never again be mentioned; remember it is all forgot—I will now pursue my story; but I must insist upon not giving you any description of Mrs Watkins; it would only be reviving old stories & as you never saw her, it can be nothing to you, if her forehead *was* too high, her eyes *were* too small, or if she *had* too much colour."

"Again! Lady Williams: this is too much"——

¹ Erased in MS.

So

So provoked was poor Alice at this renewal of the old story, that I know not what might have been the consequence of it, had not their attention been engaged by another object. A lovely young Woman lying apparently in great pain beneath a Citron-tree, was an object too interesting not to attract their notice. Forgetting their own dispute they both with simpathizing tenderness advanced towards her & accosted her in these terms.

"You seem fair Nymph to be labouring under some misfortune which we shall be happy to releive if you will inform us what it is. Will you favour us with your Life & adventures?"

"Willingly Ladies, if you will be so kind as to be seated." They took their places & she thus began.

CHAPTER THE FIFTH

"I AM a native of North Wales & my Father is one of the most capital Taylors in it. Having a numerous family, he was easily prevailed on by a sister of my Mother's who is a widow in good circumstances & keeps an alehouse in the next Village to ours, to let her take me & breed me up at her own expence. Accordingly I have lived with her for the last 8 years of my Life, during which time she provided me with some of the first rate Masters, who taught me all the accomplishments requisite for one of my sex and rank. Under their instructions I learned Dancing, Music, Drawing & various Languages, by which means I became more accomplished than any other Taylor's Daughter in Wales. Never was there a happier creature than I was, till within the last half year—but I should have told you before that the principal Estate in our Neighbourhood belongs to Charles Adams, the owner of the brick House, you see yonder."

"Charles

"Charles Adams!" exclaimed the astonished Alice; "are you acquainted with Charles Adams?"

"To my sorrow madam I am. He came about half a year ago to receive the rents of the Estate I have just mentioned. At that time I first saw him; as you seem ma'am acquainted with him, I need not describe to you how charming he is. I could not resist his attractions;"——

"Ah! who can," said Alice with a deep sigh.

"My aunt being in terms of the greatest intimacy with his cook, determined, at my request, to try whether she could discover, by means of her freind if there were any chance of his returning my affection. For this purpose she went one evening to drink tea with Mrs Susan, who in the course of Conversation mentioned the goodness of her Place & the Goodness of her Master; upon which my Aunt began pumping her with so much dexterity that in a short time Susan owned, that she did not think her Master would ever marry, 'for (said she) he has often & often declared to me that his wife, whoever she might be, must possess, Youth, Beauty, Birth, Wit, Merit, & Money. I have many a time (she continued) endeavoured to reason him out of his resolution & to convince him of the improbability of his ever meeting with such a Lady; but my arguments have had no effect & he continues as firm in his determination as ever.' You may imagine Ladies my distress on hearing this; for I was fearfull that tho' possessed of Youth, Beauty, Wit & Merit, & tho' the probable Heiress of my Aunts House & business, he might think me deficient in Rank, & in being so, unworthy of his hand."

"However I was determined to make a bold push & therefore wrote him a very kind letter, offering him with great tenderness my hand & heart. To this I received an angry & peremptory refusal, but thinking it might be rather the effect of his modesty than any thing else, I pressed him again on the subject. But he never answered any more of my Letters & very soon afterwards left the
Country

Country. As soon as I heard of his departure I wrote to him here, informing him that I should shortly do myself the honour of waiting on him at Pammydiddle, to which I received no answer; therefore choosing to take, Silence for Consent, I left Wales, unknown to my Aunt, & arrived here after a tedious Journey this Morning. On enquiring for his House I was directed thro' this Wood, to the one you there see. With a heart elated by the expected happiness of beholding him I entered it & had proceeded thus far in my progress thro' it, when I found myself suddenly seized by the leg & on examining the cause of it, found that I was caught in one of the steel traps so common in gentlemen's grounds."

"Ah cried Lady Williams, how fortunate we are to meet with you; since we might otherwise perhaps have shared the like misfortune"——

"It is indeed happy for you Ladies, that I should have been a short time before you. I screamed as you may easily imagine till the woods resounded again & till one of the inhuman Wretch's servants came to my assistance & released me from my dreadfull prison, but not before one of my legs was entirely broken."

CHAPTER THE SIXTH

At this melancholy recital the fair eyes of Lady Williams, were suffused in tears & Alice could not help exclaiming,

"Oh! cruel Charles to wound the hearts & legs of all the fair."

Lady Williams now interposed & observed that the young Lady's leg ought to be set without farther delay. After examining the fracture therefore, she immediately began & performed the operation with great skill which was the more wonderfull on account of her having never performed such a one before. Lucy, then arose from the ground

ground & finding that she could walk with the greatest ease, accompanied them to Lady Williams's House at her Ladyship's particular request.

The perfect form, the beautifull face, & elegant manners of Lucy so won on the affections of Alice that when they parted, which was not till after Supper, she assured her that except her Father, Brother, Uncles, Aunts, Cousins & other relations, Lady Williams, Charles Adams & a few dozen more of particular freinds, she loved her better than almost any other person in the world.

Such a flattering assurance of her regard would justly have given much pleasure to the object of it, had she not plainly perceived that the amiable Alice had partaken too freely of Lady Williams's claret.

Her Ladyship (whose discernment was great) read in the intelligent countenance of Lucy her thoughts on the subject & as soon as Miss Johnson had taken her leave, thus addressed her.

"When you are more intimately acquainted with my Alice you will not be surprised, Lucy, to see the dear Creature drink a little too much; for such things happen every day. She has many rare & charming qualities, but Sobriety is not one of them. The whole Family are indeed a sad drunken set. I am sorry to say too that I never knew three such thorough Gamesters as they are, more particularly Alice. But she is a charming girl. I fancy not one of the sweetest tempers in the world; to be sure I have seen her in such passions! However she is a sweet young Woman. I am sure you'll like her. I scarcely know any one so amiable.—Oh! that you could but have seen her the other Evening! How she raved! & on such a trifle too! She is indeed a most pleasing Girl! I shall always love her!"

"She appears by your ladyship's account to have many good qualities", replied Lucy. "Oh! a thousand," answered Lady Williams; tho' I am very partial to her, and perhaps am blinded by my affection, to her real defects."

B   CHAPTER

=====

CHAPTER THE SEVENTH

=====

THE next morning brought the three Miss Simpsons to wait on Lady Williams, who received them with the utmost politeness & introduced to their acquaintance Lucy, with whom the eldest was so much pleased that at parting she declared her sole *ambition* was to have her accompany them the next morning to Bath, whither they were going for some weeks.

"Lucy, said Lady Williams, is quite at her own disposal & if she chooses to accept so kind an invitation, I hope she will not hesitate, from any motives of delicacy on my account. I know not indeed how I shall ever be able to part with her. She never was at Bath & I should think that it would be a most agreable Jaunt to her. Speak my Love, continued she, turning to Lucy, what say you to accompanying these Ladies? I shall be miserable without you— t'will be a most pleasant tour to you—I hope you'll go; if you do I am sure t'will be the Death of me—pray be persuaded"——

Lucy begged leave to decline the honour of accompanying them, with many expressions of gratitude for the extream politeness of Miss Simpson in inviting her.

Miss Simpson appeared much disappointed by her refusal. Lady Williams insisted on her going—declared that she would never forgive her if she did not, and that she should never survive it if she did, & inshort used such persuasive arguments that it was at length resolved she was to go. The Miss Simpsons called for her at ten o'clock the next morning & Lady Williams had soon the satisfaction of receiving from her young freind, the pleasing intelligence of their safe arrival in Bath.

It may now be proper to return to the Hero of this
Novel

Novel, the brother of Alice, of whom I beleive I have scarcely ever had occasion to speak; which may perhaps be partly oweing to his unfortunate propensity to Liquor, which so compleatly deprived him of the use of those faculties Nature had endowed him with, that he never did anything worth mentioning. His Death happened a short time after Lucy's departure & was the natural Consequence of this pernicious practice. By his decease, his sister became the sole inheritress of a very large fortune, which as it gave her fresh Hopes of rendering herself acceptable as a wife to Charles Adams could not fail of being most pleasing to her—& as the effect was Joyfull the Cause could scarcely be lamented.

Finding the violence of her attachment to him daily augment, she at length disclosed it to her Father & desired him to propose a union between them to Charles. Her father consented & set out one morning to open the affair to the young Man. Mr Johnson being a man of few words his part was soon performed & the answer he received was as follows—

"Sir, I may perhaps be expected to appeared [*sic*] pleased at & gratefull for the offer you have made me: but let me tell you that I consider it as an affront. I look upon myself to be Sir a perfect Beauty—where would you see a finer figure or a more charming face. Then, sir I imagine my Manners & Address to be of the most polished kind; there is a certain elegance a peculiar sweetness in them that I never saw equalled & cannot describe—. Partiality aside, I am certainly more accomplished in every Language, every Science, every Art and every thing than any other person in Europe. My temper is even, my virtues innumerable, my self unparalelled. Since such Sir is my character, what do you mean by wishing me to marry your Daughter? Let me give you a short sketch of yourself & of her. I look upon you Sir to be a very good sort of Man in the main; a drunken old Dog to be sure, but that's nothing to me.

Your

Your daughter sir, is neither sufficiently beautifull, sufficiently amiable, sufficiently witty, nor sufficiently rich for me—. I expect nothing more in my wife than my wife will find in me—Perfection. These sir, are my sentiments & I honour myself for having such. One freind I have & glory in having but one—. She is at present preparing my Dinner, but if you choose to see her, she shall come & she will inform you that these have ever been my sentiments."

Mr Johnson was satisfied: & expressing himself to be much obliged to Mr Adams for the characters he had favoured him with of himself & his Daughter, took his leave.

The unfortunate Alice on receiving from her father the sad account of the ill success his visit had been attended with, could scarcely support the disappointment—She flew to her Bottle & it was soon forgot.

CHAPTER THE EIGHTH

WHILE these affairs were transacting at Pammydiddle, Lucy was conquering ever [sic] Heart at Bath. A fortnight's residence there had nearly effaced from her remembrance the captivating form of Charles—The recollection of what her Heart had formerly suffered by his charms & her Leg by his trap, enabled her to forget him with tolerable Ease, which was what she determined to do; & for that purpose dedicated five minutes in every day to the employment of driving him from her remembrance.

Her second Letter to Lady Williams contained the pleasing intelligence of her having accomplished her undertaking to her entire satisfaction; she mentioned in it also an offer of marriage she had received from the Duke of —— an elderly Man of noble fortune whose ill health was the chief inducement of his Journey to Bath. "I am distressed (she continued

continued) to know whether I mean to accept him or not. There are a thousand advantages to be derived from a marriage with the Duke, for besides those more inferior ones of Rank & Fortune it will procure me a home, which of all other things is what I most desire. Your Ladyship's kind wish of my always remaining with you, is noble & generous but I cannot think of becoming so great a burden on one I so much love & esteem. That one should receive obligations only from those we despise, is a sentiment instilled into my mind by my worthy aunt, in my early years, & cannot in my opinion be too strictly adhered to. The excellent woman of whom I now speak, is I hear too much incensed by my imprudent departure from Wales, to receive me again—. I most earnestly wish to leave the Ladies I am now with. Miss Simpson is indeed (setting aside ambition) very amiable, but her 2^d Sister the envious & malvolent Sukey is too disagreable to live with. I have reason to think that the admiration I have met with in the circles of the Great at this Place, has raised her Hatred & Envy; for often has she threatened, & sometimes endeavoured to cut my throat.—Your Ladyship will therefore allow that I am not wrong in wishing to leave Bath, & in wishing to have a home to receive me, when I do. I shall expect with impatience your advice concerning the Duke & am your most obliged

&c. Lucy."

Lady Williams sent her, her opinion on the subject in the following Manner.

"Why do you hesitate my dearest Lucy, a moment with respect to the Duke? I have enquired into his Character & find him to be an unprincipaled, illiterate Man. Never shall my Lucy be united to such a one! He has a princely fortune, which is every day encreasing. How nobly will you spend it!, what credit will you give him in the eyes of all!, How much will he be respected on his Wife's account! But why my dearest Lucy, why will you not at once decide this

this affair by returning to me & never leaving me again? Altho' I admire your noble sentiments with respect to obligations, yet, let me beg that they may not prevent your making me happy. It will to be sure be a great expence to me, to have you always with me—I shall not be able to support it—but what is that in comparison with the happiness I shall enjoy in your society?—'twill ruin me I know—you will not therefore surely, withstand these arguments, or refuse to return to yours most affectionately &c. &c.

C. WILLIAMS"

CHAPTER THE NINTH

WHAT might have been the effect of her Ladyship's advice, had it ever been received by Lucy, is uncertain, as it reached Bath a few Hours after she had breathed her last. She fell a sacrifice to the Envy & Malice of Sukey who jealous of her superior charms took her by poison from an admiring World at the age of seventeen.

Thus fell the amiable & lovely Lucy whose Life had been marked by no crime, and stained by no blemish but her imprudent departure from her Aunts, & whose death was sincerely lamented by every one who knew her. Among the most afflicted of her freinds were Lady Williams, Miss Johnson & the Duke; the 2 first of whom had a most sincere regard for her, more particularly Alice, who had spent a whole evening in her company & had never thought of her since. His Grace's affliction may likewise be easily accounted for, since he lost one for whom he had experienced during the last ten days, a tender affection & sincere regard. He mourned her loss with unshaken constancy for the next fortnight at the end of which time, he gratified the ambition of Caroline Simpson by raising her to the rank

of

of a Dutchess. Thus was she at length rendered compleatly happy in the gratification of her favourite passion. Her sister the perfidious Sukey, was likewise shortly after exalted in a manner she truly deserved, & by her actions appeared to have always desired. Her barbarous Murder was discovered & in spite of every interceding freind she was speedily raised to the Gallows—. The beautifull but affected Cecilia was too sensible of her own superior charms, not to imagine that if Caroline could engage a Duke, she might without censure aspire to the affections of some Prince—& knowing that those of her native Country were cheifly engaged, she left England & I have since heard is at present the favourite Sultana of the great Mogul—.

In the mean time the inhabitants of Pammydiddle were in a state of the greatest astonishment & Wonder, a report being circulated of the intended marriage of Charles Adams. The Lady's name was still a secret. Mr & Mrs Jones imagined it to be, Miss Johnson; but *she* knew better; all *her* fears were centered in his Cook, when to the astonishment of every one, he was publicly united to Lady Williams—

FINIS

EDGAR & EMMA

A TALE

CHAPTER THE FIRST

"I cannot imagine," said Sir Godfrey to his Lady, "why we continue in such deplorable Lodgings as these, in a paltry Market-town, while we have 3 good Houses of our own

own situated in some of the finest parts of England, & perfectly ready to receive us!"

"I'm sure Sir Godfrey," replied Lady Marlow, "it has been much against my inclination that we have staid here so long; or why we should ever have come at all indeed, has been to me a wonder, as none of our Houses have been in the least want of repair."

"Nay my dear," answered Sir Godfrey, "you are the last person who ought to be displeased with what was always meant as a compliment to you; for you cannot but be sensible of the very great inconvenience your Daughters & I have been put to, during the 2 years we have remained crowded in these Lodgings in order to give you pleasure."

"My dear," replied Lady Marlow, "How can you stand & tell such lies, when you very well know that it was merely to oblige the Girls & you, that I left a most commodious House situated in a most delightfull Country & surrounded by a most agreable Neighbourhood, to live 2 years cramped up in Lodgings three pair of stairs high, in a smokey & unwholesome town, which has given me a continual fever & almost thrown me into a Consumption."

As, after a few more speeches on both sides, they could not determine which was the most to blame, they prudently laid aside the debate, & having packed up their Cloathes & paid their rent, they set out the next morning with their 2 Daughters for their seat in Sussex.

Sir Godfrey & Lady Marlow were indeed very sensible people & tho' (as in this instance) like many other sensible People, they sometimes did a foolish thing, yet in general their actions were guided by Prudence & regulated by discretion.

After a Journey of two Days & a half they arrived at Marlhurst in good health & high spirits; so overjoyed were they all to inhabit again a place, they had left with mutual regret for two years, that they ordered the bells to be rung & distributed ninepence among the Ringers.

CHAPTER

CHAPTER THE SECOND

THE news of their arrival being quickly spread throughout the Country, brought them in a few Days visits of congratulation from every family in it.

Amongst the rest came the inhabitants of Willmot Lodge a beautifull Villa not far from Marlhurst. Mr Willmot was the representative of a very ancient Family & possessed besides his paternal Estate, a considerable share in a Lead mine & a ticket in the Lottery. His Lady was an agreable Woman. Their Children were too numerous to be particularly described; it is sufficient to say that in general they were virtuously inclined & not given to any wicked ways. Their family being too large to accompany them in every visit, they took nine with them alternately. When their Coach stopped at Sir Godfrey's door, the Miss Marlow's Hearts throbbed in the eager expectation of once more beholding a family so dear to them. Emma the youngest (who was more particularly interested in their arrival, being attached to their eldest Son) continued at her Dressing-room window in anxious Hopes of seeing young Edgar descend from the Carriage.

Mr & Mrs Willmot with their three eldest Daughters first appeared—Emma began to tremble. Robert, Richard, Ralph, & Rodolphus followed—Emma turned pale. Their two youngest Girls were lifted from the Coach—Emma sunk breathless on a Sopha. A footman came to announce to her the arrival of Company; her heart was too full to contain its afflictions. A confidante was necessary—In Thomas she hoped to experience a faithfull one—for one she must have & Thomas was the only one at Hand. To him she unbosomed herself without restraint & after owning her passion for young Willmot, requested his advice in
                                                              what

what manner she should conduct herself in the melancholy Disappointment under which she laboured.

Thomas, who would gladly have been excused from listening to her complaint, begged leave to decline giving any advice concerning it, which much against her will, she was obliged to comply with.

Having dispatched him therefore with many injunctions of secrecy, she descended with a heavy heart into the Parlour, where she found the good Party seated in a social Manner round a blazing fire.

CHAPTER THE THIRD

EMMA had continued in the Parlour some time before she could summon up sufficient courage to ask Mrs Willmot after the rest of her family; & when she did, it was in so low, so faltering a voice that no one knew she spoke. Dejected by the ill success of her first attempt she made no other, till on Mrs Willmots desiring one of the little Girls to ring the bell for their Carriage, she stepped across the room & seizing the string said in a resolute manner.

"Mrs Willmot, you do not stir from this House till you let me know how all the rest of your family do, particularly your eldest son.'

They were all greatly surprised by such an unexpected address & the more so, on account of the manner in which it was spoken; but Emma, who would not be again disappointed, requesting an answer, Mrs Willmot made the following eloquent oration.

"Our children are all extremely well but at present most of them from home. Amy is with my sister Clayton. Sam at Eton. David with his Uncle John. Jem & Will at Winchester. Kitty at Queen's Square. Ned with his Grandmother. Hetty & Patty in a Convent at Brussells. Edgar at at college, Peter at Nurse, & all the rest (except the nine here) at home."

It was with difficulty that Emma could refrain from tears on hearing of the absence of Edgar; she remained however tolerably composed till the Willmot's were gone when having no check to the overflowings of her greif, she gave free vent to them, & retiring to her own room, continued in tears the remainder of her Life.

FINIS

HENRY AND ELIZA

A NOVEL

Is humbly dedicated to Miss Cooper by her obedient Humble Servant

THE AUTHOR

As Sir George and Lady Harcourt were superintending the Labours of their Haymakers, rewarding the industry of some by smiles of approbation, & punishing the idleness of others, by a cudgel, they perceived lying closely concealed beneath the thick foliage of a Haycock, a beautifull little Girl not more than 3 months old.

Touched with the enchanting Graces of her face & delighted with the infantine tho' sprightly answers she returned to their many questions, they resolved to take her home &, having no Children of their own, to educate her with care & cost.

Being good People themselves, their first & principal care was to incite in her a Love of Virtue & a Hatred of Vice

Vice, in which they so well succeeded (Eliza having a natural turn that way herself) that when she grew up, she was the delight of all who knew her.

Beloved by Lady Harcourt, adored by Sir George & admired by all the World, she lived in a continued course of uninterrupted Happiness, till she had attained her eighteenth year, when happening one day to be detected in stealing a banknote of 50£, she was turned out of doors by her inhuman Benefactors. Such a transition to one who did not possess so noble & exalted a mind as Eliza, would have been Death, but she, happy in the conscious knowledge of her own Excellence, amused herself, as she sate beneath a tree with making & singing the following Lines.

SONG

Though misfortunes my footsteps may ever attend
I hope I shall never have need of a Freind
as an innocent Heart I will ever preserve
and will never from Virtue's dear boundaries
swerve.

Having amused herself some hours, with this song & her own pleasing reflections, she arose & took the road to M. a small market town of which place her most intimate freind kept the red Lion.

To this freind she immediately went, to whom having recounted her late misfortune, she communicated her wish of getting into some family in the capacity of Humble Companion.

Mrs Willson, who was the most amiable creature on earth, was no sooner acquainted with her Desire, than she sate down in the Bar & wrote the following Letter to the Dutchess of F, the woman whom of all others, she most Esteemed.

"To the Dutchess of F."

Receive

Receive into your Family, at my request a young woman of unexceptionable Character, who is so good as to choose your Society in preference to going to Service. Hasten, & take her from the arms of your

SARAH WILSON."

The Dutchess, whose freindship for Mrs Wilson would have carried her any lengths, was overjoyed at such an opportunity of obliging her & accordingly sate out immediately on the receipt of her letter for the red Lion, which she reached the same Evening. The Dutchess of F. was about 45 & a half; Her passions were strong, her freindships firm & her Enmities, unconquerable. She was a widow & had only one Daughter who was on the point of marriage with a young Man of considerable fortune.

The Dutchess no sooner beheld our Heroine than throwing her arms around her neck, she declared herself so much pleased with her, that she was resolved they never more should part. Eliza was delighted with such a protestation of freindship, & after taking a most affecting leave of her dear Mrs Wilson, accompanied her grace the next morning to her seat in Surry.

With every expression of regard did the Dutchess introduce her to Lady Hariet, who was so much pleased with her appearance that she besought her, to consider her as her Sister, which Eliza with the greatest Condescension promised to do.

Mr Cecil, the Lover of Lady Harriet, being often with the family was often with Eliza. A mutual Love took place & Cecil having declared his first, prevailed on Eliza to consent to a private union, which was easy to be effected, as the dutchess's chaplain being very much in love with Eliza himself, would they were certain do anything to oblige her.

The Dutchess & Lady Harriet being engaged one evening to an assembly, they took the opportunity of their absence & were united by the enamoured Chaplain.

When

When the Ladies returned, their amazement was great at finding instead of Eliza the following Note.

"MADAM

We are married & gone.

HENRY & ELIZA CECIL."

Her Grace as soon as she had read the letter, which sufficiently explained the whole affair, flew into the most violent passion & after having spent an agreable half hour, in calling them by all the shocking Names her rage could suggest to her, sent out after them 300 armed Men, with orders not to return without their Bodies, dead or alive; intending that if they should be brought to her in the latter condition to have them put to Death in some torturelike manner, after a few years Confinement.

In the mean time Cecil & Eliza continued their flight to the Continent, which they judged to be more secure than their native Land, from the dreadfull effects of the Dutchess's vengeance, which they had so much reason to apprehend.

In France they remained 3 years, during which time they became the parents of two Boys, & at the end of it Eliza became a widow without any thing to support either her or her Children. They had lived since their Marriage at the rate of 18,000£ a year, of which Mr Cecil's estate being rather less than the twentieth part, they had been able to save but a trifle, having lived to the utmost extent of their Income.

Eliza, being perfectly conscious of the derangement in their affairs, immediately on her Husband's death set sail for England, in a man of War of 55 Guns, which they had built in their more prosperous Days. But no sooner had she stepped on Shore at Dover, with a Child in each hand, than she was seized by the officers of the Dutchess, & conducted by them to a snug little Newgate of their Lady's, which she had erected for the reception of her own private Prisoners.

No

No sooner had Eliza entered her Dungeon than the first thought which occurred to her, was how to get out of it again.

She went to the Door; but it was locked. She looked at the Window; but it was barred with iron; disappointed in both her expectations, she dispaired of effecting her Escape, when she fortunately perceived in a Corner of her Cell, a small saw & Ladder of ropes. With the saw she instantly went to work & in a few weeks had displaced every Bar but one to which she fastened the Ladder.

A difficulty then occurred which for some time, she knew not how to obviate. Her Children were too small to get down the Ladder by themselves, nor would it be possible for her to take them in her arms, when *she* did. At last she determined to fling down all her Cloathes, of which she had a large Quantity, & then having given them strict Charge not to hurt themselves, threw her Children after them. She herself with ease discended by the Ladder, at the bottom of which she had the pleasure of finding her little boys in perfect Health & fast asleep.

Her wardrobe she now saw a fatal necessity of selling, both for the preservation of her Children & herself. With tears in her eyes, she parted with these last reliques of her former Glory, & with the money she got for them, bought others more usefull, some playthings for Her Boys and a gold Watch for herself.

But scarcely was she provided with the above-mentioned necessaries, than she began to find herself rather hungry, & had reason to think, by their biting off two of her fingers, that her Children were much in the same situation.

To remedy these unavoidable misfortunes, she determined to return to her old freinds, Sir George & Lady Harcourt, whose generosity she had so often experienced & hoped to experience as often again.

She had about 40 miles to travel before she could reach their hospitable Mansion, of which having walked 30 with-

out

out stopping, she found herself at the Entrance of a Town, where often in happier times, she had accompanied Sir George & Lady Harcourt to regale themselves with a cold collation at one of the Inns.

The reflections that her adventures since the last time she had partaken of these happy *Junketings*, afforded her, occupied her mind, for some time, as she sate on the steps at the door of a Gentleman's house. As soon as these reflections were ended, she arose & determined to take her station at the very inn, she remembered with so much delight, from the Company of which, as they went in & out, she hoped to receive some Charitable Gratuity.

She had but just taken her post at the Innyard before a Carriage drove out of it, & on turning the Corner at which she was stationed, stopped to give the Postilion an opportunity of admiring the beauty of the prospect. Eliza then advanced to the carriage & was going to request their Charity, when on fixing her Eyes on the Lady, within it, she exclaimed,

"Lady Harcourt!"

To which the lady replied,

"Eliza!"

"Yes Madam it is the wretched Eliza herself."

Sir George, who was also in the Carriage, but too much amazed to speek, was proceeding to demand an explanation from Eliza of the Situation she was then in, when Lady Harcourt in transports of Joy, exclaimed.

"Sir George, Sir George, she is not only Eliza our adopted Daughter, but our real Child."

"Our real Child! What Lady Harcourt, do you mean? You know you never even was with child. Explain yourself, I beseech you."

"You must remember Sir George, that when you sailed for America, you left me breeding."

"I do, I do, go on dear Polly."

"Four months after you were gone, I was delivered of this

this Girl, but dreading your just resentment at her not proving the Boy you wished, I took her to a Haycock & laid her down. A few weeks afterwards, you returned, & fortunately for me, made no enquiries on the subject. Satisfied within myself of the wellfare of my Child, I soon forgot I had one, insomuch that when, we shortly after found her in the very Haycock, I had placed her, I had no more idea of her being my own, than you had, & nothing I will venture to say would have recalled the circumstance to my remembrance, but my thus accidentally hearing her voice, which now strikes me as being the very counterpart of my own Child's."

"The rational & convincing Account you have given of the whole affair, said Sir George, leaves no doubt of her being our Daughter & as such I freely forgive the robbery she was guilty of."

A mutual Reconciliation then took place, & Eliza, ascending the Carriage with her two Children returned to that home from which she had been absent nearly four years.

No sooner was she reinstated in her accustomed power at Harcourt Hall, than she raised an Army, with which she entirely demolished the Dutchess's Newgate, snug as it was, and by that act, gained the Blessings of thousands, & the Applause of her own Heart.

FINIS

THE ADVENTURES OF
MR HARLEY

a short, but interesting Tale, is with all imaginable Respect inscribed to Mr Francis William Austen Midshipman on board his Majestys Ship the Perseverance by his Obedient Servant THE AUTHOR.

MR HARLEY was one of many Children. Destined by his father for the Church & by his Mother for the Sea, desirous of pleasing both, he prevailed on Sir John to obtain for him a Chaplaincy on board a Man of War. He accordingly, cut his Hair and sailed.

In half a year he returned & set-off in the Stage Coach for Hogsworth Green, the seat of Emma. His fellow travellers were, A man without a Hat, Another with two, An old maid & a young Wife.

This last appeared about 17 with fine dark Eyes & an elegant Shape; inshort Mr Harley soon found out, that she was his Emma & recollected he had married her a few weeks before he left England.

FINIS

SIR WILLIAM MOUNTAGUE

an unfinished performance
is humbly dedicated to Charles John
Austen Esqre, by his most obedient humble
Servant

THE AUTHOR

SIR WILLIAM MOUNTAGUE was the son of Sir Henry Mountague, who was the son of Sir John Mountague, a descendant of Sir Christopher Mountague, who was the nephew

nephew of Sir Edward Mountague, whose ancestor was
Sir James Mountague a near relation of Sir Robert Mount-
ague, who inherited the Title & Estate from Sir Frederic
Mountague.

Sir William was about 17 when his Father died, & left
him a handsome fortune, an ancient House & a Park well
stocked with Deer. Sir William had not been long in the
possession of his Estate before he fell in Love with the
3 Miss Cliftons of Kilhoobery Park. These young Ladies
were all equally young, equally handsome, equally rich
& equally amiable—Sir William was equally in Love with
them all, & knowing not which to prefer, he left the Country
& took Lodgings in a small Village near Dover.

In this retreat, to which he had retired in the hope of
finding a shelter from the Pangs of Love, he became
enamoured of a young Widow of Quality, who came for
change of air to the same Village, after the death of a
Husband, whom she had always tenderly loved & now
sincerely lamented.

Lady Percival was young, accomplished & lovely. Sir
William adored her & she consented to become his Wife.
Vehemently pressed by Sir William to name the Day in
which he might conduct her to the Altar, she at length
fixed on the following Monday, which was the first of
September. Sir William was a Shot & could not support
the idea of losing such a Day, even for such a Cause. He
begged her to delay the Wedding a short time. Lady
Percival was enraged & returned to London the next
Morning.

Sir William was sorry to lose her, but as he knew that
he should have been much more greived by the Loss of the
1st of September, his Sorrow was not without a mixture
of Happiness, & his Affliction was considerably lessened
by his Joy.

After staying at the Village a few weeks longer, he left
it & went to a freind's House in Surry. Mr Brudenell was

a

a sensible Man, & had a beautifull Neice with whom Sir William soon fell in love. But Miss Arundel was cruel; she preferred a Mr Stanhope: Sir William shot Mr Stanhope; the lady had then no reason to refuse him; she accepted him, & they were to be married on the 27th of October. But on the 25th Sir William received a visit from Emma Stanhope the sister of the unfortunate Victim of his rage. She begged some recompence, some atonement for the cruel Murder of her Brother. Sir William bade her name her price. She fixed on $\frac{s}{14}$. Sir William offered her himself & Fortune. They went to London the next day & were there privately married. For a fortnight Sir William was compleatly happy, but chancing one day to see a charming young Woman entering a Chariot in Brook Street, he became again most violently in love. On enquiring the name of this fair Unknown, he found that she was the Sister of his old freind Lady Percival, at which he was much rejoiced, as he hoped to have, by his acquaintance with her Ladyship, free access to Miss Wentworth........

FINIS

To Charles John Austen Esqre

Sir,

Your generous patronage of the unfinished tale, I have already taken the Liberty of dedicating to you, encourages me to dedicate to you a second, as unfinished as the first.

I am Sir with every expression
of regard for you & yr noble
Family, your most obed^t
&c. &c. . . .

THE AUTHOR

MEMOIRS

MEMOIRS OF Mr CLIFFORD

AN UNFINISHED TALE

Mr Clifford lived at Bath; & having never seen London, set off one monday morning determined to feast his eyes with a sight of that great Metropolis. He travelled in his Coach & Four, for he was a very rich young Man & kept a great many Carriages of which I do not recollect half. I can only remember that he had a Coach, a Chariot, a Chaise, a Landeau, a Landeaulet, a Phaeton, a Gig, a Whisky, an italian Chair, a Buggy, a Curricle & a wheelbarrow. He had likewise an amazing fine stud of Horses. To my knowledge he had six Greys, 4 Bays, eight Blacks & a poney.

In his Coach & 4 Bays Mr Clifford sate forward about 5 o'clock on Monday Morning the 1st of May for London. He always travelled remarkably expeditiously & contrived therefore to get to Devizes from Bath, which is no less than nineteen miles, the first Day. To be sure he did not get in till eleven at night & pretty tight work it was as you may imagine.

However when he was once got to Devizes he was determined to comfort himself with a good hot Supper and therefore ordered a whole Egg to be boiled for him & his Servants. The next morning he pursued his Journey & in the course of 3 days hard labour reached Overton, where he was seized with a dangerous fever the Consequence of too violent Excercise.

Five months did our Hero remain in this celebrated City under the care of its no less celebrated Physician, who at length compleatly cured him of his troublesome Desease.

As Mr Clifford still continued very weak, his first Day's Journey carried him only to Dean Gate, where he remained a few Days & found himself much benefited by the change of Air.

In

In easy Stages he proceeded to Basingstoke. One day Carrying him to Clarkengreen, the next to Worting, the 3d to the bottom of Basingstoke Hill, & the fourth, to Mr Robins's. . . .

FINIS

THE BEAUTIFULL CASSANDRA

A NOVEL IN TWELVE CHAPTERS

dedicated by permission to Miss Austen.
Dedication.

MADAM

You are a Phoenix. Your taste is refined, your Sentiments are noble, & your Virtues innumerable. Your Person is lovely, your Figure, elegant, & your Form, magestic. Your Manners are polished, your Conversation is rational & your appearance singular. If therefore the following Tale will afford one moment's amusement to you, every wish will be gratified of

Your most obedient
humble servant
THE AUTHOR

CHAPTER THE FIRST

CASSANDRA was the Daughter & the only Daughter of a celebrated Millener in Bond Street. Her father was of noble Birth, being the near relation of the Dutchess of ——'s Butler.

CHAPTER

CHAPTER THE 2ᵈ

WHEN Cassandra had attained her 16ᵗʰ year, she was lovely & amiable & chancing to fall in love with an elegant Bonnet, her Mother had just compleated bespoke by the Countess of ―― she placed it on her gentle Head & walked from her Mother's shop to make her Fortune.

CHAPTER THE 3ᵈ

THE first person she met, was the Viscount of ―― a young Man, no less celebrated for his Accomplishments & Virtues, than for his Elegance & Beauty. She curtseyed & walked on.

CHAPTER THE 4ᵗʰ

SHE then proceeded to a Pastry-cooks where she devoured six ices, refused to pay for them, knocked down the Pastry Cook & walked away.

CHAPTER THE 5ᵗʰ

SHE next ascended a Hackney Coach & ordered it to Hampstead, where she was no sooner arrived than she ordered the Coachman to turn round & drive her back again.

CHAPTER THE 6ᵗʰ

BEING returned to the same spot of the same Street she had sate out from, the Coachman demanded his Pay.

CHAPTER

CHAPTER THE 7th

SHE searched her pockets over again & again; but every search was unsuccessfull. No money could she find. The man grew peremptory. She placed her bonnet on his head & ran away.

CHAPTER THE 8th

THRO' many a street she then proceeded & met in none the least Adventure till on turning a Corner of Bloomsbury Square, she met Maria.

CHAPTER THE 9th

CASSANDRA started & Maria seemed surprised; they trembled, blushed, turned pale & passed each other in a mutual silence.

CHAPTER THE 10th

CASSANDRA was next accosted by her freind the Widow, who squeezing out her little Head thro' her less window, asked her how she did? Cassandra curtseyed & went on.

CHAPTER THE 11th

A QUARTER of a mile brought her to her paternal roof in Bond Street from which she had now been absent nearly 7 hours.

CHAPTER

CHAPTER THE 12th

SHE entered it & was pressed to her Mother's bosom by that worthy Woman. Cassandra smiled & whispered to herself "This is a day well spent."

FINIS

AMELIA WEBSTER

an interesting & well written Tale
is dedicated by Permission
to
Mrs Austen
by
Her humble Servant

THE AUTHOR

Letter the first

TO MISS WEBSTER

MY DEAR AMELIA

You will rejoice to hear of the return of my amiable Brother from abroad. He arrived on thursday, & never did I see a finer form, save that of your sincere freind

MATILDA HERVEY

Letter the 2^d

TO H. BEVERLEY ESQ^{re}

DEAR BEVERLEY

I arrived here last thursday & met with a hearty reception from my Father, Mother & Sisters. The latter are both fine Girls—particularly Maud, who I think would suit you

as

as a Wife well enough. What say you to this? She will
have two thousand Pounds & as much more as you can get.
If you don't marry her you will mortally offend

GEORGE HERVEY

Letter the 3ᵈ

TO MISS HERVEY

DEAR MAUD

.Beleive me I'm happy to hear of your Brother's arrival.
I have a thousand things to tell you, but my paper will
only permit me to add that I am yʳ affecᵗ Freind

AMELIA WEBSTER

Letter the 4ᵗʰ

TO MISS S. HERVEY

DEAR SALLY

I have found a very convenient old hollow oak to put
our Letters in; for you know we have long maintained a
private Correspondence. It is about a mile from my House
& seven from yours. You may perhaps imagine that I
might have made choice of a tree which would have divided
the Distance more equally—I was sensible of this at the
time, but as I considered that the walk would be of benefit
to you in your weak & uncertain state of Health, I preferred it to one nearer your House, & am yʳ faithfull

BENJAMIN BAR

Letter the 5ᵗʰ

TO MISS HERVEY

DEAR MAUD

I write now to inform you that I did not stop at your
house in my way to Bath last Monday.—I have many
things to inform you of besides; but my Paper reminds me
of concluding; & beleive me yʳˢ ever &c.

AMELIA WEBSTER
Letter

Letter the 6th

TO MISS WEBSTER

MADAM   Saturday

An humble Admirer now addresses you.—I saw you lovely Fair one as you passed on Monday last, before our House in your way to Bath. I saw you thro' a telescope, & was so struck by your Charms that from that time to this I have not tasted human food.

GEORGE HERVEY

Letter the 7th

TO JACK

As I was this morning at Breakfast the Newspaper was brought me, & in the list of Marriages I read the following.

"George Hervey Esq[re] to Miss Amelia Webster"
"Henry Beverley Esq[re] to Miss Hervey"
&
"Benjamin Bar Esq[re] to Miss Sarah Hervey".

yours, TOM

FINIS

THE VISIT

A COMEDY IN 2 ACTS

Dedication

To the Rev[d] James Austen

SIR,

The following Drama, which I humbly recommend to your Protection & Patronage, tho' inferior to those celebrated Comedies called "The School for Jealousy" & "The travelled Man", will I hope afford some amusement to so respectable a *Curate* as yourself; which was the end in veiw when it was first composed by your Humble Servant the Author.

Dramatis

Dramatis Personae

Sir Arthur Hampton	Lady Hampton
Lord Fitzgerald	Miss Fitzgerald
Stanly	Sophy Hampton
Willoughby, Sir Arthur's nephew	Cloe Willoughby

The scenes are laid in Lord Fitzgerald's House.

ACT THE FIRST

Scene the first, a Parlour——

enter LORD FITZGERALD & STANLY

STANLY. Cousin your servant.

FITZGERALD. Stanly, good morning to you. I hope you slept well last night.

STANLY. Remarkably well, I thank you.

FITZGERALD. I am afraid you found your Bed too short. It was bought in my Grandmother's time, who was herself a very short woman & made a point of suiting all her Beds to her own length, as she never wished to have any company in the House, on account of an unfortunate impediment in her speech, which she was sensible of being very disagreable to her inmates.

STANLY. Make no more excuses dear Fitzgerald.

FITZGERALD. I will not distress you by too much civility— I only beg you will consider yourself as much at home as in your Father's house. Remember, "The more free, the more Wellcome."

[exit FITZGERALD

STANLY. Amiable Youth!

"Your virtues could he imitate
How happy would be Stanly's fate!"

[exit STANLY
Scene

Scene the 2ᵈ

STANLY & MISS FITZGERALD, *discovered.*

STANLY. What Company is it you expect to dine with you to Day, Cousin?

MISS F. Sir Arthur & Lady Hampton; their Daughter, Nephew & Neice.

STANLY. Miss Hampton & her Cousin are both Handsome, are they not?

MISS F. Miss Willoughby is extreamly so. Miss Hampton is a fine Girl, but not equal to her.

STANLY. Is not your Brother attached to the Latter?

MISS F. He admires her I know, but I beleive nothing more. Indeed I have heard him say that she was the most beautifull, pleasing, & amiable Girl in the world, & that of all others he should prefer her for his Wife. But it never went any farther I'm certain.

STANLY. And yet my Cousin never says a thing he does not mean.

MISS F. Never. From his Cradle he has always been a strict adherent to Truth [He never told a Lie but once, & that was merely to oblige me. Indeed I may truly say there never was such a Brother!][1]
 [Exeunt Severally

End of the First Act.

ACT THE SECOND

Scene the first. The Drawing Room.

Chairs set round in a row. LORD FITZGERALD, MISS FITZGERALD & STANLY *seated.*

Enter a Servant.

SERVANT. Sir Arthur & Lady Hampton. Miss Hampton, Mr & Miss Willoughby.
 [exit SERVANT

[1] Erased in MS.

Enter

Enter the Company.

MISS F. I hope I have the pleasure of seeing your Ladyship
well. Sir Arthur, your servant. Yrs Mr Willoughby.
Dear Sophy, Dear Cloe,—

[*They pay their Compliments alternately.*

MISS F. Pray be seated.

[*They sit*

Bless me! there ought to be 8 Chairs & there are but 6.
However, if your Ladyship will but take Sir Arthur in
your Lap, & Sophy my Brother in hers, I beleive we shall
do pretty well.

LADY H. Oh! with pleasure. . . .

SOPHY. I beg his Lordship would be seated.

MISS F. I am really shocked at crouding you in such a manner, but my Grandmother (who bought all the furniture
of this room) as she had never a very large Party, did
not think it necessary to buy more Chairs than were
sufficient for her own family and two of her particular
freinds.

SOPHY. I beg you will make no apologies. Your Brother is
very light.

STANLY, *aside*) What a cherub is Cloe!

CLOE, *aside*) What a seraph is Stanly!

Enter a Servant.

SERVANT. Dinner is on table.

[*They all rise.*

MISS F. Lady Hampton, Miss Hampton, Miss Willoughby.
STANLY *hands* CLOE, LORD FITZGERALD, SOPHY, WIL-
LOUGHBY, MISS FITZGERALD, *and* SIR ARTHUR, LADY
HAMPTON.

[*Exeunt.*

Scene

Scene the 2^d

The Dining Parlour.

MISS FITZGERALD *at top.* LORD FITZGERALD *at bottom. Company ranged on each side. Servants waiting.*

CLOE. I shall trouble Mr Stanly for a Little of the fried Cowheel & Onion.

STANLY. Oh Madam, there is a secret pleasure in helping so amiable a Lady —.

LADY H. I assure you my Lord, Sir Arthur never touches wine; but Sophy will toss off a bumper I am sure to oblige your Lordship.

LORD F. Elder wine or Mead, Miss Hampton?

SOPHY. If it is equal to you Sir, I should prefer some warm ale with a toast and nutmeg.

LORD F. Two glasses of warmed ale with a toast and nutmeg.

MISS F. I am afraid Mr Willoughby you take no care of yourself. I fear you dont meet with any thing to your liking.

WILLOUGHBY. Oh! Madam, I can want for nothing while there are red herrings on table.

LORD F. Sir Arthur taste that Tripe. I think you will not find it amiss.

LADY H. Sir Arthur never eats Tripe; tis too savoury for him you know my Lord.

MISS F. Take away the Liver & Crow & bring in the suet pudding.

(a short Pause.)

MISS F. Sir Arthur shant I send you a bit of pudding?

LADY H. Sir Arthur never eats suet pudding Ma'am. It is too high a Dish for him.

MISS F. Will no one allow me the honour of helping them? Then John take away the Pudding, & bring the Wine.

[SERVANTS *take away the things and bring in the Bottles & Glasses.*

LORD

LORD F. I wish we had any Desert to offer you. But my
Grandmother in her Lifetime, destroyed the Hothouse
in order to build a receptacle for the Turkies with it's
materials; & we have never been able to raise another
tolerable one.

LADY H. I beg you will make no apologies my Lord.

WILLOUGHBY. Come Girls, let us circulate the Bottle.

SOPHY. A very good notion Cousin; & I will second it with
all my Heart. Stanly you dont drink.

STANLY. Madam, I am drinking draughts of Love from
Cloe's eyes.

SOPHY. That's poor nourishment truly. Come, drink to
her better acquaintance.

[MISS FITZGERALD *goes to a Closet & brings out a bottle*

MISS F. This, Ladies & Gentlemen is some of my dear
Grandmother's own manufacture. She excelled in Goose-
berry Wine. Pray taste it Lady Hampton?

LADY H. How refreshing it is!

MISS F. I should think with your Ladyship's permission,
that Sir Arthur might taste a little of it.

LADY H. Not for Worlds. Sir Arthur never drinks any
thing so high.

LORD F. And now my amiable Sophia condescend to marry
me.

[*He takes her hand & leads her to the front*

STANLY. Oh! Cloe could I but hope you would make me
blessed—

CLOE. I will.

[*They advance.*

MISS F. Since you Willoughby are the only one left, I cannot refuse your earnest solicitations—There is my Hand.

LADY H. And may you all be Happy!

FINIS

THE

THE MYSTERY

AN UNFINISHED COMEDY

Dedication

To the Revᵈ George Austen

Sɪʀ

I humbly solicit your Patronage to the following Comedy, which tho' an unfinished one, is I flatter myself as *complete* a *Mystery* as any of its kind.

> I am Sir your most Humˡᵉ
> Servant
> Tʜᴇ Aᴜᴛʜᴏʀ

THE MYSTERY

A COMEDY

Dramatis Personae

MEN	WOMEN
Colonel Elliott	Fanny Elliott
Sir Edward Spangle	Mrs Humbug
Old Humbug	and
Young Humbug	Daphne
and	
Corydon	

Aᴄᴛ ᴛʜᴇ Fɪʀsᴛ

Scene the 1ˢᵗ

A Garden.

Enter Cᴏʀʏᴅᴏɴ.

ᴄᴏʀʏ.) But Hush! I am interrupted.

> [*Exit* Cᴏʀʏᴅᴏɴ
> *Enter*

Enter OLD HUMBUG *& his* SON, *talking.*

OLD HUM:) It is for that reason I wish you to follow my advice. Are you convinced of its propriety?

YOUNG HUM:) I am Sir, and will certainly act in the manner you have pointed out to me.

OLD HUM:) Then let us return to the House.

[*Exeunt*

Scene the 2ᵈ

A Parlour in HUMBUG'S *House.*

MRS HUMBUG & FANNY, *discovered at work.*

MRS HUM:) You understand me my Love?

FANNY) Perfectly ma'am. Pray continue your narration.

MRS HUM:) Alas! it is nearly concluded, for I have nothing more to say on the Subject.

FANNY) Ah! here's Daphne.

Enter DAPHNE.

DAPHNE) My dear Mrs Humbug how d'ye do? Oh! Fanny t'is all over.

FANNY) Is it indeed!

MRS HUM:) I'm very sorry to hear it.

FANNY) Then t'was to no purpose that I . . . .

DAPHNE) None upon Earth.

MRS HUM:) And what is to become of? . . .

DAPHNE) Oh! thats all settled. (*whispers* MRS HUMBUG)

FANNY) And how is it determined?

DAPHNE) I'll tell you. (*whispers* FANNY)

MRS HUM:) And is he to? . . .

DAPHNE) I'll tell you all I know of the matter. (*whispers* MRS HUMBUG *&* FANNY)

FANNY) Well! now I know everything about it, I'll go [and dress]¹ away.

MRS HUM: ⎫
DAPHNE ⎬ And so will I.   [*Exeunt*
            ⎭

¹ Erased in MS.

Scene

Scene the 3^d

The Curtain rises and discovers SIR EDWARD SPANGLE *reclined in an elegant Attitude on a Sofa, fast asleep.*

Enter COLONEL ELLIOTT.

COLONEL) My Daughter is not here I see . . . there lies Sir Edward . . . Shall I tell him the secret ? . . . No, he'll certainly blab it. . . . But he is asleep and wont hear me. . . . So I'll e'en venture.

[*Goes up to* SIR EDWARD, *whispers him, & Exit*

End of the 1st *Act.*

FINIS

To Edward Austen Esqre

The following unfinished Novel
is respectfully inscribed
by
His obedient hum^{le} serv^t

THE AUTHOR

THE THREE SISTERS

A NOVEL

Letter 1st

MISS STANHOPE TO M^{rs} . . .

MY DEAR FANNY

I am the happiest creature in the World, for I have received an offer of marriage from Mr Watts. It is the first I have ever had & I hardly know how to value it enough. How I will triumph over the Duttons! I do not intend to accept it, at least I beleive not, but as I am not quite

certain

certain I gave him an equivocal answer & left him. And now my dear Fanny I want your Advice whether I should accept his offer or not, but that you may be able to judge of his merits & the situation of affairs I will give you an account of them. He is quite an old Man, about two & thirty, very plain *so* plain that I cannot bear to look at him. He is extremely disagreable & I hate him more than any body else in the world. He has a large fortune & will make great Settlements on me; but then he is very healthy. In short I do not know what to do. If I refuse him he as good as told me that he should offer himself to Sophia and if *she* refused him to Georgiana, & I could not bear to have either of them married before me. If I accept him I know I shall be miserable all the rest of my Life, for he is very ill tempered & peevish extremely jealous, & so stingy that there is no living in the house with him. He told me he should mention the affair to Mama, but I insisted upon it that he did not for very likely she would make me marry him whether I would or no; however probably he *has* before now, for he never does anything he is desired to do. I believe I shall have him. It will be such a triumph to be married before Sophy, Georgiana & the Duttons; And he promised to have a new Carriage on the occasion, but we almost quarrelled about the colour, for I insisted upon its being blue spotted with silver, & he declared it should be a plain Chocolate; & to provoke me more said it should be just as low as his old one. I wont have him I declare. He said he should come again tomorrow & take my final answer, so I believe I must get him while I can. I know the Duttons will envy me & I shall be able to chaprone Sophy & Georgiana to all the Winter Balls. But then what will be the use of that when very likely he wont let me go myself, for I know he hates dancing & [has a great idea of Womens never going from home][1] what he hates himself he has no idea of any other person's liking; & besides he

[1] Erased in MS.

talks

talks a great deal of Women's always Staying at home & such stuff. I beleive I shant have him; I would refuse him at once if I were certain that neither of my Sisters would accept him, & that if they did not, he would not offer to the Duttons. I cannot run such a risk, so, if he will promise to have the Carriage ordered as I like, I will have him, if not he may ride in it by himself for me. I hope you like my determination; I can think of nothing better;

And am your ever Affec^te

MARY STANHOPE

FROM THE SAME TO THE SAME

DEAR FANNY

I had but just sealed my last letter to you when my Mother came up & told me she wanted to speak to me on a very particular subject.

"Ah! I know what you mean; (said I) That old fool Mr Watts has told you all about it, tho' I bid him not. However you shant force me to have him if I dont like it."

"I am not going to force you Child, but only want to know what your resolution is with regard to his Proposals, & to insist upon your making up your mind one way or t'other, that if *you* dont accept him *Sophy* may."

"Indeed (replied I hastily) Sophy need not trouble herself for I shall certainly marry him myself."

"If that is your resolution" (said my Mother) why should you be afraid of my forcing your inclinations?"

"Why, because I have not settled whether I shall have him or not."

"You are the strangest Girl in the World Mary. What you say one moment, you unsay the next. Do tell me once for all, whether you intend to marry Mr Watts or not?"

"Law Mama how can I tell you what I dont know myself?"

"Then I desire you will know, & quickly too, for Mr Watts says he wont be kept in suspense."

"That

"That depends upon me."

"No it does not, for if you do not give him your final answer tomorrow when he drinks Tea with us, he intends to pay his Addresses to Sophy."

"Then I shall tell all the World that he behaved very ill to me."

"What good will that do? Mr Watts has been too long abused by all the World to mind it now."

"I wish I had a Father or a Brother because then they should fight him."

"They would be cunning if they did, for Mr Watts would run away first; & therefore you must & shall resolve either to accept or refuse him before tomorrow evening."

"But why if I don't have him, must he offer to my Sisters?"

"Why! because he wishes to be allied to the Family & because they are as pretty as you are."

"But will Sophy marry him Mama if he offers to her?"

"Most likely. Why should not she? If however she does not choose it, then Georgiana must, for I am determined not to let such an opportunity escape of settling one of my Daughters so advantageously. So, make the most of your time; I leave you to settle the Matter with yourself." And then she went away. The only thing I can think of my dear Fanny is to ask Sophy & Georgiana whether they would have him were he to make proposals to them, & if they say they would not I am resolved to refuse him too, for I hate him more than you can imagine. As for the Duttons if he marries one of *them* I shall still have the triumph of having refused him first. So, adieu my dear Freind—

Y^rs ever M. S.

MISS GEORGIANA STANHOPE TO MISS X X X

My dear Anne   Wednesday

Sophy & I have just been practising a little deceit on our eldest Sister, to which we are not perfectly reconciled, &

yet

yet the circumstances were such that if any thing will excuse it, they must. Our neighbour Mr Watts has made proposals to Mary; Proposals which she knew not how to receive, for tho' she has a particular Dislike to him (in which she is not singular) yet she would willingly marry him sooner than risk his offering to Sophy or me which in case of a refusal from herself, he told her he should do, for you must know the poor Girl considers our marrying before her as one of the greatest misfortunes that can possibly befall her, & to prevent it would willingly ensure herself everlasting Misery by a Marriage with Mr Watts. An hour ago she came to us to sound our inclinations respecting the affair which were to determine hers. A little before she came my Mother had given us an account of it, telling us that she certainly would not let him go farther than our own family for a Wife. "And therefore (said she) If Mary wont have him Sophy must, & if Sophy wont Georgiana *shall.*" Poor Georgiana!—We neither of us attempted to alter my Mother's resolution, which I am sorry to say is generally more strictly kept than rationally formed. As soon as she was gone however I broke silence to assure Sophy that if Mary should refuse Mr Watts I should not expect her to sacrifice *her* happiness by becoming his Wife from a motive of Generosity to me, which I was afraid her Good nature & Sisterly affection might induce her to do.

"Let us flatter ourselves (replied She) that Mary will not refuse him. Yet how can I hope that my Sister may accept a Man who cannot make her happy."

"*He* cannot it is true but his Fortune, his Name, his House, his Carriage will and I have no doubt but that Mary will marry him; indeed why should she not? He is not more than two & thirty; a very proper age for a Man to marry at; He is rather plain to be sure, but then what is Beauty in a Man; if he has but a genteel figure & a sensible looking Face it is quite sufficient."

"This is all very true Georgiana but Mr Watts's figure is unfortunately

unfortunately extremely vulgar & his Countenance is very heavy."

"And then as to his temper; it has been reckoned bad, but may not the World be deceived in their Judgement of it. There is an open Frankness in his Disposition which becomes a Man; They say he is stingy; We'll call that Prudence. They say he is suspicious. *That* proceeds from a warmth of Heart always excusable in Youth, & in short I see no reason why he should not make a very good Husband, or why Mary should not be very happy with him."

Sophy laughed; I continued,

"However whether Mary accepts him or not I am resolved. My determination is made. I never would marry Mr Watts were Beggary the only alternative. So deficient in every respect! Hideous in his person and without one good Quality to make amends for it. His fortune to be sure is good. Yet not so very large! Three thousand a year. What is three thousand a year? It is but six times as much as my Mother's income. It will not tempt me."

"Yet it will be a noble fortune for Mary" said Sophy laughing again.

"For Mary! Yes indeed it will give me pleasure to see *her* in such affluence."

Thus I ran on to the great Entertainment of my Sister till Mary came into the room to appearance in great agitation. She sate down. We made room for her at the fire. She seemed at a loss how to begin & at last said in some confusion

"Pray Sophy have you any mind to be married?"

"To be married! None in the least. But why do you ask me? Are you acquainted with any one who means to make me proposals?"

"I—no, how should I? But may'nt I ask a common question?"

"Not a very *common* one Mary surely." (said I). She paused & after some moments silence went on—

"How

"How should you like to marry Mr Watts Sophy?"

I winked at Sophy & replied for her. "Who is there but must rejoice to marry a man of three thousand a year. [who keeps a postchaise & pair, with silver Harness, a boot before & a window to look out at behind?"][1]

"Very true (she replied) That's very true. So you would have him if he would offer, Georgiana, & would *you* Sophy?"

Sophy did not like the idea of telling a lie & deceiving her Sister; she prevented the first & saved half her conscience by equivocation.

"I should certainly act just as Georgiana would do."

"Well then said Mary with triumph in her Eyes, *I* have had an offer from Mr Watts."

We were of course very much surprised; "Oh! do not accept him said I, and then perhaps he may have me."

In short my scheme took & Mary is resolved to do *that* to prevent our supposed happiness which she would not have done to ensure it in reality. Yet after all my Heart cannot acquit me & Sophy is even more scrupulous. Quiet our Minds my dear Anne by writing & telling us you approve our conduct. Consider it well over. Mary will have real pleasure in being a married Woman, & able to chaprone us, which she certainly shall do, for I think myself bound to contribute as much as possible to her happiness in a State I have made her choose. They will probably have a new Carriage, which will be paradise to her, & if we can prevail on Mr W. to set up his Phaeton she will be too happy. These things however would be no consolation to Sophy or me for domestic Misery. Remember all this & do not condemn us.

Friday.

Last night Mr Watts by appointment drank tea with us. As soon as his Carriage stopped at the Door, Mary went to the Window.

"Would you beleive it Sophy (said she) the old Fool

[1] Erased in MS.

wants

wants to have his new Chaise just the colour of the old one, & hung as low too. But it shant—I *will* carry my point. And if he wont let it be as high as the Duttons, & blue spotted with Silver, I wont have him. Yes I will too. Here he comes. I know he'll be rude; I know he'll be illtempered & wont say one civil thing to me! nor behave at all like a Lover." She then sate down & Mr Watts entered.

"Ladies your most obedient." We paid our Compliments & he seated himself.

"Fine Weather Ladies." Then turning to Mary, "Well Miss Stanhope I hope you have *at last* settled the Matter in your own mind; & will be so good as to let me know whether you will *condescend* to marry me or not".

"I think Sir (said Mary) You might have asked in a genteeler way than that. I do not know whether I *shall* have you if you behave so odd."

"Mary!" (said my Mother) "Well Mama if he will be so cross . . . . "

"Hush, hush, Mary, you shall not be rude to Mr Watts."

"Pray Madam do not lay any restraint on Miss Stanhope by obliging her to be civil. If she does not choose to accept my hand, I can offer it else where, for as I am by no means guided by a particular preference to you above your Sisters it is equally the same to me which I marry of the three." Was there ever such a Wretch! Sophy reddened with anger & I felt *so* spiteful!

"Well then (said Mary in a peevish Accent) I *will* have you if I *must*."

"I should have thought Miss Stanhope that when such Settlements are offered as I have offered to you there can be no great violence done to the inclinations in accepting of them."

Mary mumbled out something, which I who sate close to her could just distinguish to be "What's the use of a great Jointure if Men live forever?" And then audibly "Remember the pinmoney; two hundred a year."

"A

"A hundred and seventy-five Madam."

"Two hundred indeed Sir" said my Mother.

"And Remember I am to have a new Carriage hung as high as the Duttons', & blue spotted with silver; and I shall expect a new saddle horse, a suit of fine lace, and an infinite number of the most valuable Jewels. Diamonds such as never were seen, [Pearls as large as those of the Princess Badroulbadour in the 4th Volume of the Arabian Nights and Rubies, Emeralds, Toppazes, Sapphires, Amythists, Turkeystones, Agate, Beads, Bugles & Garnets][1] and Pearls, Rubies, Emeralds and Beads out of number. You must set up your Phaeton which must be cream coloured with a wreath of silver flowers round it, You must buy 4 of the finest Bays in the Kingdom & you must drive me in it every day. This is not all; You must entirely new furnish your House after my Taste, You must hire two more Footmen to attend me, two Women to wait on me, must always let me do just as I please & make a very good husband."

Here she stopped, I beleive rather out of breath.

"This is all very reasonable Mr Watts for my Daughter to expect."

"And it is very reasonable Mrs Stanhope that your daughter should be disappointed." He was going on but Mary interrupted him "You must build me an elegant Greenhouse & stock it with plants. You must let me spend every Winter in Bath, every Spring in Town, Every Summer in taking some Tour, & every Autumn at a Watering Place, and if we are at home the rest of the year (Sophy & I laughed) You must do nothing but give Balls & Masquerades. You must build a room on purpose & a Theatre to act Plays in. The first Play we have shall be *Which is the Man*, and I will do Lady Bell Bloomer."

"And pray Miss Stanhope (said Mr Watts) What am I to expect from you in return for all this."

"Expect? why you may expect to have me pleased."

[1] Erased in MS.

"It

"It would be odd if I did not. Your expectations Madam are too high for me, & I must apply to Miss Sophy who perhaps may not have raised her's so much."

"You are mistaken Sir in supposing so, (said Sophy) for tho' they may not be exactly in the same Line, yet my expectations are to the full as high as my Sister's; for I expect my Husband to be good tempered & Chearful; to consult my Happiness in all his Actions, & to love me with Constancy & Sincerity."

Mr Watts stared. "These are very odd Ideas truly young Lady. You had better discard them before you marry, or you will be obliged to do it afterwards."

My Mother in the meantime was lecturing Mary who was sensible that she had gone too far, & when Mr Watts was just turning towards me in order I beleive to address me, she spoke to him in a voice half humble, half sulky.

"You are mistaken Mr Watts if you think I was in earnest when I said I expected so much. However I must have a new Chaise."

"Yes Sir, you must allow that Mary has a right to expect that."

"Mrs Stanhope, I *mean* & have always meant to have a new one on my Marriage. But it shall be the colour of my present one."

"I think Mr Watts you should pay my Girl the compliment of consulting her Taste on such Matters."

Mr Watts would not agree to this, & for some time insisted upon its being a Chocolate colour, while Mary was as eager for having it blue with silver Spots. At length however Sophy proposed that to please Mr W. it should be a dark brown & to please Mary it should be hung rather high & have a silver Border. This was at length agreed to, tho' reluctantly on both sides, as each had intended to carry their point entire. We then proceeded to other Matters, & it was settled that they should be married as soon as the Writings could be completed. Mary was very

eager

eager for a Special Licence & Mr Watts talked of Banns A common Licence was at last agreed on. Mary is to have all the Family Jewels which are very inconsiderable I beleive & Mr W. promised to buy her a Saddle horse; but in return she is not to expect to go to Town or any other public place for these three Years. She is to have neither Greenhouse, Theatre or Phaeton; to be contented with one Maid without an additional Footman. It engrossed the whole Evening to settle these affairs; Mr W. supped with us & did not go till twelve. As soon as he was gone Mary exclaimed "Thank Heaven! he's off at last; how I do hate him!" It was in vain that Mama represented to her the impropriety she was guilty of in disliking him who was to be her Husband, for she persisted in declaring her aversion to him & hoping she might never see him again. What a Wedding will this be! Adeiu my dear Anne. Y^r faithfully Sincere

GEORGIANA STANHOPE

FROM THE SAME TO THE SAME

DEAR ANNE   Saturday

Mary eager to have every one know of her approaching Wedding & more particularly desirous of triumphing as she called it over the Duttons, desired us to walk with her this Morning to Stoneham. As we had nothing else to do we readily agreed, & had as pleasant a walk as we could have with Mary whose conversation entirely consisted in abusing the Man she is so soon to marry & in longing for a blue Chaise spotted with Silver. When we reached the Duttons we found the two Girls in the dressing-room with a very handsome Young Man, who was of course introduced to us. He is the son of Sir Henry Brudenell of Leicestershire— [Not related to the Family & even but distantly connected with it. His Sister is married to John Dutton's Wife's Brother. When you have puzzled over this account

a

a little you will understand it.]¹ Mr Brudenell is the handsomest Man I ever saw in my Life; we are all three very
much pleased with him. Mary, who from the moment of
our reaching the Dressing-room had been swelling with the
knowledge of her own importance & with the Desire of
making it known, could not remain long silent on the Subject after we were seated, & soon addressing herself to
Kitty said,

"Dont you think it will be necessary to have all the
Jewels new set?"

"Necessary for what?"

"For What! Why for my appearance."

"I beg your pardon but I really do not understand you.
What Jewels do you speak of, & where is your appearance
to be made?"

"At the next Ball to be sure after I am married."

You may imagine their Surprise. They were at first incredulous, but on our joining in the Story they at last
beleived it. "And who is it to" was of course the first
Question. Mary pretended Bashfulness, & answered in
Confusion her Eyes cast down "to Mr Watts". This also
required Confirmation from us, for that anyone who had
the Beauty & fortune (tho' small yet a provision) of Mary
would willingly marry Mr Watts, could by them scarcely
be credited. The subject being now fairly introduced and
she found herself the object of every one's attention in
company, she lost all her confusion & became perfectly
unreserved & communicative.

"I wonder you should never have heard of it before for
in general things of this Nature are very well known in the
Neighbourhood."

"I assure you said Jemima I never had the least suspicion of such an affair. Has it been in agitation long?"

"Oh! Yes, ever since Wednesday."

They all smiled particularly Mr Brudenell.

¹ Erased in MS.

"You

"You must know Mr Watts is very much in love with me, so that it is quite a match of Affection on his side."

"Not on his only, I suppose" said Kitty.

"Oh! when there is so much Love on one side there is no occasion for it on the other. However I do not much dislike him tho' he is very plain to be sure."

Mr Brudenell stared, the Miss Duttons laughed & Sophy & I were heartily ashamed of our Sister. She went on.

"We are to have a new Postchaise & very likely may set up our Phaeton."

This we knew to be false but the poor Girl was pleased at the idea of persuading the company that such a thing was to be & I would not deprive her of so harmless an Enjoyment. She continued.

"Mr Watts is to present me with the family Jewels which I fancy are very considerable." I could not help whispering Sophy "I fancy not". "These Jewels are what I suppose must be new set before they can be worn. I shall not wear them till the first Ball I go to after my Marriage. If Mrs Dutton should not go to it, I hope you will let me chaprone you; I shall certainly take Sophy & Georgiana."

"You are very good (said Kitty) & since you are inclined to undertake the Care of young Ladies, I should advise you to prevail on Mrs Edgecumbe to let you chaprone her six Daughters which with your two Sisters and ourselves will make your Entrée very respectable."

Kitty made us all smile except Mary who did not understand her Meaning & coolly said that she should not like to chaprone so many. Sophy & I now endeavoured to change the conversation but succeeded only for a few Minutes, for Mary took care to bring back their attention to her & her approaching Wedding. I was sorry for my Sister's sake to see that Mr Brudenell seemed to take pleasure in listening to her account of it, & even encouraged her by his Questions & Remarks, for it was evident that his only Aim was to laugh at her. I am afraid he found her

very

very ridiculous. He kept his Countenance extremely well, yet it was easy to see that it was with difficulty he kept it. At length however he seemed fatigued & Disgusted with her ridiculous Conversation, as he turned from her to us, & spoke but little to her for about half an hour before we left Stoneham. As soon as we were out of the House we all joined in praising the Person & Manners of Mr Brudenell.

We found Mr Watts at home.

"So, Miss Stanhope (said he) you see I am come a courting in a true Lover like Manner."

"Well you need not have *told* me that. I knew why you came very well."

Sophy & I then left the room, imagining of course that we must be in the way, if a Scene of Courtship were to begin. We were surprised at being followed almost immediately by Mary.

"And is your Courting so soon over?" said Sophy.

"Courting! (replied Mary) we have been quarrelling. Watts is such a Fool! I hope I shall never see him again."

"I am afraid you will, (said I) as he dines here to day. But what has been your dispute?"

"Why only because I told him that I had seen a Man much handsomer than he was this Morning, he flew into a great Passion & called me a Vixen, so I only stayed to tell him I thought him a Blackguard & came away."

"Short & sweet; (said Sophy) but pray Mary how will this be made up?"

"He ought to ask my pardon; but if he did, I would not forgive him."

"His Submission then would not be very useful."

When we were dressed we returned to the Parlour where Mama & Mr Watts were in close Conversation. It seems that he had been complaining to her of her Daughter's behaviour, & she had persuaded him to think no more of it. He therefore met Mary with all his accustomed Civility, & except one touch at the Phaeton & another at the Green-

house

house, the Evening went off with great Harmony & Cordiality. Watts is going to Town to hasten the preparations for the Wedding.

I am your affec^{te} Freind G.S.

To Miss Jane Anna Elizabeth Austen

MY DEAR NEICE

Though you are at this period not many degrees removed from Infancy, Yet trusting that you will in time be older, and that through the care of your excellent Parents, You will one day or another be able to read written hand, I dedicate to You the following Miscellanious Morsels, convinced that if you seriously attend to them, You will derive from them very important Instructions, with regard to your Conduct in Life.— If such my hopes should hereafter be realized, never shall I regret the Days and Nights that have been spent in composing these Treatises for your Benefit. I am my dear Neice

Your very Affectionate
Aunt.

June 2^d   THE AUTHOR
  1793

[A FRAGMENT

written to inculcate the practise of Virtue

WE all know that many are unfortunate in their progress through the world, but we do not know all that are so. To seek them out to study their wants, & to leave them unsupplied is the duty, and ought to be the Business of Man. But few have time, fewer still have inclination, and no one has either the one or the other for such employments. Who amidst those that perspire away their Evenings in crouded assemblies can have leisure to bestow a thought on such as sweat under the fatigue of their daily Labour.][1]

[1] Erased in MS.

A

A BEAUTIFUL DESCRIPTION OF THE DIFFERENT EFFECTS OF SENSIBILITY ON DIFFERENT MINDS.

I AM but just returned from Melissa's Bedside, & in my Life tho' it has been a pretty long one, & I have during the course of it been at many Bedsides, I never saw so affecting an object as she exhibits. She lies wrapped in a book muslin bedgown, a chambray gauze shift, and a french net night-cap. Sir William is constantly at her bedside. The only repose he takes is on the Sopha in the Drawing room, where for five minutes every fortnight he remains in an imperfect Slumber, starting up every Moment & exclaiming "Oh! Melissa, Ah! Melissa," then sinking down again, raises his left arm and scratches his head. Poor Mrs Burnaby is beyond measure afflicted. She sighs every now & then, that is about once a week; while the melancholy Charles says every Moment "Melissa how are you?" The lovely Sisters are much to be pitied. Julia is ever lamenting the situation of her friend, while lying behind her pillow & supporting her head—Maria more mild in her greif talks of going to Town next week, & Anna is always recurring to the plea-sures we once enjoyed when Melissa was well.—I am usually at the fire cooking some little delicacy for the unhappy in-valid—Perhaps hashing up the remains of an old Duck, toasting some cheese or making a Curry which are the favourite dishes of our poor friend.—In these situations we were this morning surprised by receiving a visit from Dr Dowkins; "I am come to see Melissa," said he. "How is She?" "Very weak indeed, said the fainting Melissa—"Very weak, replied the punning Doctor, aye indeed it is more than a very *week* since you have taken to your bed—How is your appetite?" "Bad, very bad, said Julia." "That *is* very bad—replied he. Are her spirits good, Madam?" "So poorly Sir that we are obliged to strengthen her with cordials every Minute."—"Well then she receives *Spirits* from your being with her. Does she sleep?" "Scarcely

"Scarcely ever."—"And Ever Scarcely I suppose when she does. Poor thing! Does she think of dieing? "She has not strength to think at all. "Nay then she cannot think to have Strength."

THE GENEROUS CURATE

a moral Tale, setting forth the Advantages of being Generous and a Curate.

In a part little known of the County of Warwick, a very worthy Clergyman lately resided. The income of his living which amounted to about two hundred pound, & the interest of his Wife's fortune which was nothing at all, was entirely sufficient for the Wants & Wishes of a Family who neither wanted or wished for anything beyond what their income afforded them. Mr Williams had been in possession of his living above twenty Years, when this history commences, & his Marriage which had taken place soon after his presentation to it, had made him the father of six very fine Children. The eldest had been placed at the Royal Academy for Seamen at Portsmouth when about thirteen years old, and from thence had been discharged on board of one of the Vessels of a small fleet destined for Newfoundland, where his promising & amiable disposition had procured him many friends among the Natives, & from whence he regularly sent home a large Newfoundland Dog every Month to his family. The second, who was also a Son had been adopted by a neighbouring Clergyman with the intention of educating him at his own expence, which would have been a very desirable Circumstance had the Gentleman's fortune been equal to his generosity, but as he had nothing to support himself and a very large family but a Curacy of fifty pound a year, Young Williams knew nothing more at the age of 18 than what a twopenny Dame's School

in

in the village could teach him. His Character however was perfectly amiable though his genius might be cramped, and he was addicted to no vice, or ever guilty of any fault beyond what his age and situation rendered perfectly excusable. He had indeed sometimes been detected in flinging Stones at a Duck or putting brickbats into his Benefactor's bed; but these innocent efforts of wit were considered by that good Man rather as the effects of a lively imagination, than of anything bad in his Nature, and if any punishment were decreed for the offence it was in general no greater than that the Culprit should pick up the Stones or take the brickbats away.—

FINIS

To Miss Austen, the following Ode to Pity is dedicated, from a thorough knowledge of her pitiful Nature, by her obed[t] hum[le] Serv[t]

THE AUTHOR

ODE TO PITY

1

Ever musing I delight to tread
    The Paths of honour and the Myrtle Grove
Whilst the pale Moon her beams doth shed
        On disappointed Love.
While Philomel on airy hawthorn Bush
    Sings sweet & Melancholy, And the thrush
Converses with the Dove.

Gently

2

Gently brawling down the turnpike road,
   Sweetly noisy falls the Silent Stream—
The Moon emerges from behind a Cloud
   And darts upon the Myrtle Grove her beam.
Ah! then what Lovely Scenes appear,
   The hut, the Cot, the Grot, & Chapel queer,
And eke the Abbey too a mouldering heap,
   Conceal'd by aged pines her head doth rear
And quite invisible doth take a peep.

$$=====$$

END OF THE FIRST VOLUME

$$=====$$

June 3d 1793

VOLUME THE SECOND

=====

Ex dono mei Patris

CONTENTS

To Madame La Comtesse
De Feuillide This Novel is inscribed
by Her obliged Humble Servant The Author

=====

Love and Freindship
a novel
in a series of Letters.

"Deceived in Freindship & Betrayed in Love"

=====

Letter the First
From Isabel to Laura

How often, in answer to my repeated intreaties that you would give my Daughter a regular detail of the Misfortunes and Adventures of your Life, have you said "No, my freind never will I comply with your request till I may be no
longer

longer in Danger of again experiencing such dreadful ones."
Surely that time is now at hand. You are this Day 55. If
a woman may ever be said to be in safety from the determined Perseverance of disagreable Lovers and the cruel
Persecutions of obstinate Fathers, surely it must be at such
a time of Life.

Isabel.

Letter 2d
Laura to Isabel

ALTHO' I cannot agree with you in supposing that I shall
never again be exposed to Misfortunes as unmerited as
those I have already experienced, yet to avoid the imputation of Obstinacy or ill-nature, I will gratify the curiosity
of your daughter; and may the fortitude with which I have
suffered the many Afflictions of my past Life, prove to her
a useful Lesson for the support of those which may befall
her in her own.

Laura

Letter 3d
Laura to Marianne

As the Daughter of my most intimate freind I think you
entitled to that knowledge of my unhappy Story, which
your Mother has so often solicited me to give you.

My Father was a native of Ireland & an inhabitant of
Wales; My Mother was the natural Daughter of a Scotch
Peer by an italian Opera-girl—I was born in Spain & re-
ceived my Education at a Convent in France.

When I had reached my eighteenth Year I was recalled
by my Parents to my paternal roof in Wales. Our mansion
was situated in one of the most romantic parts of the Vale
of Uske. Tho' my Charms are now considerably softened
and somewhat impaired by the Misfortunes I have undergone, I was once beautiful. But lovely as I was the Graces
of

of my Person were the least of my Perfections. Of every accomplishment accustomary to my sex, I was Mistress. When in the Convent, my progress had always exceeded my instructions, my Acquirements had been wonderfull for my Age, and I had shortly surpassed my Masters.

In my Mind, every Virtue that could adorn it was centered ; it was the Rendezvous of every good Quality & of every noble sentiment.

A sensibility too tremblingly alive to every affliction of my Freinds, my Acquaintance and particularly to every affliction of my own, was my only fault, if a fault it could be called. Alas! how altered now! Tho' indeed my own misfortunes do not make less impression on me than they ever did, yet now I never feel for those of an other. My accomplishments too, begin to fade—I can neither sing so well nor Dance so gracefully as I once did—and I have entirely forgot the *Minuet Dela Cour*.

Adeiu.

Laura

Letter 4th
Laura to Marianne

OUR neighbourhood was small, for it consisted only of your mother. She may probably have already told you that being left by her Parents in indigent Circumstances she had retired into Wales on eoconomical motives. There it was, our freindship first commenced. Isabel was then one and twenty—Tho' pleasing both in her Person and Manners (between ourselves) she never possessed the hundredth part of my Beauty or Accomplishments. Isabel had seen the World. She had passed 2 Years at one of the first Boarding schools in London ; had spent a fortnight in Bath & had supped one night in Southampton.

"Beware my Laura (she would often say) Beware of the insipid Vanities and idle Dissipations of the Metropolis of

England;

England ; Beware of the unmeaning Luxuries of Bath &
of the Stinking fish of Southampton."

"Alas! (exclaimed I) how am I to avoid those evils I
shall never be exposed to? What probability is there of
my ever tasting the Dissipations of London, the Luxuries
of Bath or the stinking Fish of Southampton? I who am
doomed to waste my Days of Youth & Beauty in an humble
Cottage in the Vale of Uske."

Ah! little did I then think I was ordained so soon to quit
that humble Cottage for the Deceitfull Pleasures of the
World.

adeiu
Laura

Letter 5th
Laura to Marianne

ONE Evening in December as my Father, my Mother and
myself, were arranged in social converse round our Fireside, we were on a sudden, greatly astonished, by hearing
a violent knocking on the outward Door of our rustic Cot.

My Father started—"What noise is that," (said he.) "It
sounds like a loud rapping at the Door"—(replied my
Mother.) "it does indeed." (cried I.) "I am of your opinion;
(said my Father) it certainly does appear to proceed from
some uncommon violence exerted against our unoffending
Door." "Yes (exclaimed I) I cannot help thinking it must
be somebody who knocks for Admittance."

"That is another point (replied he;) We must not pretend to determine on what motive the person may knock—
tho' that someone *does* rap at the Door, I am partly convinced."

Here, a 2d tremendous rap interrupted my Father in his
speech and somewhat alarmed my Mother and me.

"Had we not better go and see who it is, ? (said she) the
Servants are out." "I think we had." (replied I.) "Certainly,

tainly, (added my Father) by all means." "Shall we go now?" (said my Mother.) "The sooner the better." (answered he). "Oh! let no time be lost." (cried I.)

A third more violent Rap than ever again assaulted our ears. "I am certain there is somebody knocking at the Door." (said my Mother.) "I think there must," (replied my Father) "I fancy the Servants are returned; (said I) I think I hear Mary going to the Door." "I'm glad of it (cried my Father) for I long to know who it is."

I was right in my Conjecture ; for Mary instantly entering the Room, informed us that a young Gentleman & his Servant were at the Door, who had lossed their way, were very cold and begged leave to warm themselves by our fire.

"Wont you admit them?" (said I) "You have no objection, my Dear?" (said my Father.) "None in the World." (replied my Mother.)

Mary, without waiting for any further commands immediately left the room and quickly returned introducing the most beauteous and amiable Youth, I had ever beheld. The servant, She kept to herself.

My natural Sensibility had already been greatly affected by the sufferings of the unfortunate Stranger and no sooner did I first behold him, than I felt that on him the happiness or Misery of my future Life must depend.

adeiu.
Laura.

Letter 6th
Laura to Marianne

THE noble Youth informed us that his name was Lindsay —for particular reasons however I shall conceal it under that of Talbot. He told us that he was the son of an English Baronet, that his Mother had been many years no more and that he had a Sister of the middle size. "My Father (he continued) is a mean and mercenary wretch—it is only
to

to such particular freinds as this Dear Party that I would thus betray his failings. Your Virtues my amiable Polydore (addressing himself to my father) yours Dear Claudia and yours my Charming Laura call on me to repose in you, my Confidence." We bowed. "My Father, seduced by the false glare of Fortune and the Deluding Pomp of Title, insisted on my giving my hand to Lady Dorothea. No never exclaimed I. Lady Dorothea is lovely and Engaging; I prefer no woman to her; but know Sir, that I scorn to marry her in compliance with your wishes. No! Never shall it be said that I obliged my Father,"

We all admired the noble Manliness of his reply. He continued.

"Sir Edward was surprized; he had perhaps little expected to meet with so spirited an opposition to his will. 'Where Edward in the name of wonder (said he) did you pick up this unmeaning Gibberish? You have been studying Novels I suspect.' I scorned to answer: it would have been beneath my Dignity. I mounted my Horse and followed by my faithful William set forwards for my Aunts."

"My Father's house is situated in Bedfordshire, my Aunt's in Middlesex, and tho' I flatter myself with being a tolerable proficienz in Geography, I know not how it happened, but I found myself entering this beautifull Vale which I find is in South Wales, when I had expected to have reached my Aunts."

"After having wandered some time on the Banks of the Uske without knowing which way to go, I began to lament my cruel Destiny in the bitterest and most pathetic Manner. It was now perfectly dark, not a single Star was there to direct my steps, and I know not what might have befallen me had I not at length discerned thro' the solemn Gloom that surrounded me a distant Light, which as I approached it, I discovered to be the chearfull Blaze of your fire. Impelled by the combination of Misfortunes under which I laboured, namely Fear, Cold and Hunger I hesitated

tated not to ask admittance which at length I have gained; and now my Adorable Laura (continued he taking my Hand) when may I hope to receive that reward of all the painfull sufferings I have undergone during the course of my Attachment to you, to which I have ever aspired? Oh! when will you reward me with Yourself?"

"This instant, Dear and Amiable Edward." (replied I.). We were immediately united by my Father, who tho' he had never taken orders had been bred to the Church.

adeiu
Laura.

Letter 7th
Laura to Marianne

WE remained but a few Days after our Marriage, in the Vale of Uske. After taking an affecting Farewell of my father, my Mother and my Isabel, I accompanied Edward to his Aunt's in Middlesex. Philippa received us both with every expression of affectionate Love. My arrival was indeed a most agreable surprize to her as she had not only been totally ignorant of my Marriage with her Nephew, but had never even had the slightest idea of there being such a person in the World.

Augusta, the sister of Edward was on a visit to her when we arrived. I found her exactly what her Brother had described her to be—of the middle size. She received me with equal surprize though not with equal Cordiality, as Philippa. There was a Disagreable Coldness and Forbidding Reserve in her reception of me which was equally Distressing and Unexpected. None of that interesting Sensibility or amiable Simpathy in her Manners and Address to me which should have Distinguished our introduction to each other. Her Language was neither warm, nor affectionate, her expressions of regard were neither animated nor cordial; her arms were not opened to receive me to her Heart, tho' my own were extended to press her to mine.

A

A short Conversation between Augusta and her Brother, which I accidentally overheard encreased my Dislike to her, and convinced me that her Heart was no more formed for the soft ties of Love than for the endearing intercourse of Freindship.

"But do you think that my Father will ever be reconciled to this imprudent connection?" (said Augusta.)

"Augusta (replied the noble Youth) I thought you had a better opinion of me, than to imagine I would so abjectly degrade myself as to consider my Father's Concurrence in any of my Affairs, either of Consequence or concern to me. Tell me Augusta tell me with sincerity; did you ever know me consult his inclinations or follow his Advice in the least trifling Particular since the age of fifteen?"

"Edward (replied she) you are surely too diffident in your own praise. Since you were fifteen only!—My Dear Brother since you were five years old, I entirely acquit you of ever having willingly contributed to the Satisfaction of your Father. But still I am not without apprehensions of your being shortly obliged to degrade yourself in your own eyes by seeking a Support for your Wife in the Generosity of Sir Edward."

"Never, never Augusta will I so demean myself. (said Edward). Support! What Support will Laura want which she can receive from him?"

"Only those very insignificant ones of Victuals and Drink." (answered she.)

"Victuals and Drink! (replied my Husband in a most nobly contemtuous Manner) and dost thou then imagine that there is no other support for an exalted Mind (such as is my Laura's) than the mean and indelicate employment of Eating and Drinking?"

"None that I know of, so efficacious." (returned Augusta).

"And did you then never feel the pleasing Pangs of Love, Augusta? (replied my Edward). Does it appear impossible to your vile and corrupted Palate, to exist on
Love?

Love? Can you not conceive the Luxury of living in every Distress that Poverty can inflict, with the object of your tenderest Affection?"

"You are too ridiculous (said Augusta) to argue with; perhaps however you may in time be convinced that. . . ."

Here I was prevented from hearing the remainder of her Speech, by the Appearance of a very Handsome Young Woman, who was ushered into the Room at the Door of which I had been listening. On hearing her announced by the Name of "Lady Dorothea", I instantly quitted my Post and followed her into the Parlour, for I well remembered that she was the Lady, proposed as a Wife for my Edward by the Cruel and Unrelenting Baronet.

Altho' Lady Dorothea's visit was nominally to Philippa and Augusta, yet I have some reason to imagine that (acquainted with the Marriage and arrival of Edward) to see me was a principal motive to it.

I soon perceived that tho' lovely and Elegant in her Person and tho' Easy and Polite in her Address, she was of that inferior order of Beings with regard to Delicate feeling, tender Sentiments, and refined Sensibility, of which Augusta was one.

She staid but half an hour and neither in the Course of her Visit, confided to me any of her Secret thoughts, nor requested me to confide in her, any of mine. You will easily imagine therefore my Dear Marianne that I could not feel any ardent Affection or very sincere Attachment for Lady Dorothea.

Adeiu
Laura

Letter 8th
Laura to Marianne, in continuation

LADY DOROTHEA had not left us long before another visitor as unexpected a one as her Ladyship, was announced. It
was

was Sir Edward, who informed by Augusta of her Brother's marriage, came doubtless to reproach him for having dared to unite himself to me without his Knowledge. But Edward foreseeing his Design, approached him with heroic fortitude as soon as he entered the Room, and addressed him in the following Manner.

"Sir Edward, I know the motive of your Journey here—You come with the base Design of reproaching me for having entered into an indissoluble engagement with my Laura without your Consent—But Sir, I glory in the Act—. It is my greatest boast that I have incurred the Displeasure of my Father!"

So saying, he took my hand and whilst Sir Edward, Philippa, and Augusta were doubtless reflecting with Admiration on his undaunted Bravery, led me from the Parlour to his Father's Carriage, which yet remained at the Door and in which we were instantly conveyed from the pursuit of Sir Edward.

The Postilions had at first received orders only to take the London road; as soon as we had sufficiently reflected However, we ordered them to Drive to M———. the seat of Edward's most particular freind, which was but a few miles distant.

At M———. we arrived in a few hours; and on sending in our names were immediately admitted to Sophia, the Wife of Edward's freind. After having been deprived during the course of 3 weeks of a real freind (for such I term your Mother) imagine my transports at beholding one, most truly worthy of the Name. Sophia was rather above the middle size ; most elegantly formed. A soft Languor spread over her lovely features, but increased their Beauty. —It was the Charectarestic of her Mind—. She was all Sensibility and Feeling. We flew into each others arms & after having exchanged vows of mutual Friendship for the rest of our Lives, instantly unfolded to each other the most inward Secrets of our Hearts—. We were interrupted in
this

this Delightfull Employment by the entrance of Augustus, (Edward's freind) who was just returned from a solitary ramble.

Never did I see such an affecting Scene as was the meeting of Edward & Augustus.

"My Life! my Soul!" (exclaimed the former) "My Adorable Angel!" (replied the latter) as they flew into each other's arms. It was too pathetic for the feelings of Sophia and myself—We fainted Alternately on a Sofa.

Adeiu

Laura

Letter the 9th
From the Same to the Same

Towards the close of the Day we received the following Letter from Philippa.

"Sir Edward is greatly incensed by your abrupt departure; he has taken back Augusta with him to Bedfordshire. Much as I wish to enjoy again your charming society, I cannot determine to snatch you from that, of such dear & deserving Freinds—When your Visit to them is terminated, I trust you will return to the arms of your"

"Philippa."

We returned a suitable answer to this affectionate Note & after thanking her for her kind invitation assured her that we would certainly avail ourselves of it, whenever we might have no other place to go to. Tho' certainly nothing could to any reasonable Being, have appeared more satisfactory, than so gratefull a reply to her invitation, yet I know not how it was, but she was certainly capricious enough to be displeased with our behaviour and in a few weeks after, either to revenge our Conduct, or releive her own solitude, married a young and illiterate Fortune-hunter. This imprudent Step (tho' we were sensible that it would probably deprive us of that fortune which Philippa had

had ever taught us to expect) could not on our own accounts, excite from our exalted Minds a single sigh; yet fearfull lest it might prove a source of endless misery to the deluded Bride, our trembling Sensibility was greatly affected when we were first informed of the Event. The affectionate Entreaties of Augustus and Sophia that we would for ever consider their House as our Home, easily prevailed on us to determine never more to leave them—. In the Society of my Edward & this Amiable Pair, I passed the happiest moments of my Life: Our time was most delightfully spent, in mutual Protestations of Freindship, and in vows of unalterable Love, in which we were secure from being interrupted, by intruding & disagreable Visitors, as Augustus & Sophia had on their first Entrance in the Neighbourhood, taken due care to inform the surrounding Families, that as their Happiness centered wholly in themselves, they wished for no other society. But alas! my Dear Marianne such Happiness as I then enjoyed was too perfect to be lasting. A most severe & unexpected Blow at once destroyed every Sensation of Pleasure. Convinced as you must be from what I have already told you concerning Augustus & Sophia, that there never were a happier Couple, I need not I imagine inform you that their union had been contrary to the inclinations of their Cruel & Mercenary Parents; who had vainly endeavoured with obstinate Perseverance to force them into a Marriage with those whom they had ever abhorred, but with an Heroic Fortitude worthy to be related & Admired, they had both, constantly refused to submit to such despotic Power.

After having so nobly disentangled themselves from the Shackles of Parental Authority, by a Clandestine Marriage, they were determined never to forfeit the good opinion they had gained in the World, in so doing, by accepting any proposals of reconciliation that might be offered them by their Fathers—to this farther tryal of their noble independance however they never were exposed.

They

They had been married but a few months when our visit to them commenced during which time they had been amply supported by a considerable sum of Money which Augustus had gracefully purloined from his Unworthy father's Escritoire, a few days before his union with Sophia.

By our arrival their Expences were considerably encreased tho' their means for supplying them were then nearly exhausted. But they, Exalted Creatures! scorned to reflect a moment on their pecuniary Distresses & would have blushed at the idea of paying their Debts.—Alas! what was their Reward for such disinterested Behaviour. The beautifull Augustus was arrested and we were all undone. Such perfidious Treachery in the merciless perpetrators of the Deed will shock your gentle nature Dearest Marianne as much as it then affected the Delicate Sensibility of Edward, Sophia, your Laura, & of Augustus himself. To compleat such unparalelled Barbarity we were informed that an Execution in the House would shortly take place. Ah! what could we do but what we did! We sighed & fainted on the Sofa.

Adeiu
Laura

Letter 10th
Laura in continuation

WHEN we were somewhat recovered from the overpowering Effusions of our Grief, Edward desired that we would consider what was the most prudent step to be taken in our unhappy situation while he repaired to his imprisoned freind to lament over his misfortunes. We promised that we would, & he set forwards on his Journey to Town. During his Absence we faithfully complied with his Desire & after the most mature Deliberation, at length agreed that the best thing we could do was to leave the House; of which we every moment expected the Officers of Justice

to

to take possession. We waited therefore with the greatest impatience, for the return of Edward in order to impart to him the result of our Deliberations—. But no Edward appeared—. In vain did we count the tedious Moments of his Absence—in vain did we weep—in vain even did we sigh—no Edward returned—. This was too cruel, too unexpected a Blow to our Gentle Sensibility—. we could not support it—we could only faint—. At length collecting all the Resolution I was Mistress of, I arose & after packing up some necessary Apparel for Sophia & myself, I dragged her to a Carriage I had ordered & instantly we set out for London. As the Habitation of Augustus was within twelve miles of Town, it was not long e'er we arrived there, & no sooner had we entered Holbourn than letting down one of the Front Glasses I enquired of every decent-looking Person that we passed "If they had seen my Edward"?

But as we drove too rapidly to allow them to answer my repeated Enquiries, I gained little, or indeed, no information concerning him. "Where am I to Drive?" said the Postilion. "To Newgate Gentle Youth (replied I), to see Augustus." "Oh! no, no, (exclaimed Sophia) I cannot go to Newgate; I shall not be able to support the sight of my Augustus in so cruel a confinement—my feelings are sufficiently shocked by the *recital*, of his Distress, but to behold it will overpower my Sensibility." As I perfectly agreed with her in the Justice of her Sentiments the Postilion was instantly directed to return into the Country. You may perhaps have been somewhat surprised my Dearest Marianne, that in the Distress I then endured, destitute of any Support, & unprovided with any Habitation, I should never once have remembered my Father & Mother or my paternal Cottage in the Vale of Uske. To account for this seeming forgetfullness I must inform you of a trifling Circumstance concerning them which I have as yet never mentioned—. The death of my Parents a few weeks after my Departure, is the circumstance I allude to. By their decease

decease I became the lawfull Inheritress of their House &
Fortune. But alas! the House had never been their own
& their Fortune had only been an Annuity on their own
Lives. Such is the Depravity of the World! To your
Mother I should have returned with Pleasure, should have
been happy to have introduced to her, my Charming Sophia
& should have with Chearfullness have passed the remainder of my Life in their dear Society in the Vale of Uske,
had not one obstacle to the execution of so agreable a
Scheme, intervened; which was the Marriage & Removal
of your Mother to a Distant part of Ireland.

Adeiu.
Laura.

Letter 11th
Laura in continuation

"I HAVE a Relation in Scotland (said Sophia to me as
we left London) who I am certain would not hesitate in
receiving me." "Shall I order the Boy to drive there?"
said I—but instantly recollecting myself, exclaimed "Alas
I fear it will be too long a Journey for the Horses." Unwilling however to act only from my own inadequate Knowledge of the Strength & Abilities of Horses, I consulted the
Postilion, who was entirely of my Opinion concerning
the Affair. We therefore determined to change Horses at the
next Town & to travel Post the remainder of the Journey.—.
When we arrived at the last Inn we were to stop at, which
was but a few miles from the House of Sophia's Relation,
unwilling to intrude our Society on him unexpected & un-
thought of, we wrote a very elegant & well-penned Note to
him containing an Account of our Destitute & melancholy
Situation, and of our intention to spend some months with
him in Scotland. As soon as we had dispatched this letter,
we immediately prepared to follow it in person & were
stepping into the Carriage for that Purpose when our
Attention

Attention was attracted by the Entrance of a coroneted Coach & 4 into the Inn-yard. A Gentleman considerably advanced in years, descended from it—. At his first Appearance my Sensibility was wonderfully affected & e'er I had gazed at him a 2d time, an instinctive Sympathy whispered to my Heart, that he was my Grandfather.

Convinced that I could not be mistaken in my conjecture I instantly sprang from the Carriage I had just entered, & following the Venerable Stranger into the Room he had been shewn to, I threw myself on my knees before him & besought him to acknowledge me as his Grand Child.—He started, & after having attentively examined my features, raised me from the Ground & throwing his Grand-fatherly arms around my neck, exclaimed, "Acknowledge thee! Yes dear resemblance of my Laurina & my Laurina's Daughter, sweet image of my Claudia & my Claudia's Mother, I do acknowledge thee as the Daughter of the one & the Grandaughter of the other." While he was thus tenderly embracing me, Sophia astonished at my precipitate Departure, entered the Room in search of me—. No sooner had she caught the eye of the venerable Peer, than he exclaimed with every mark of Astonishment—"Another Grandaughter! Yes, yes, I see you are the Daughter of my Laurina's eldest Girl; Your resemblance to the beauteous Matilda sufficiently proclaims it." "Oh.!" replied Sophia, "when I first beheld you the instinct of Nature whispered me that we were in some degree related—But whether Grandfathers, or Grandmothers, I could not pretend to determine." He folded her in his arms, and whilst they were tenderly embracing, the Door of the Apartment opened and a most beautifull Young Man appeared. On perceiving him Lord St. Clair started and retreating back a few paces, with uplifted Hands, said, "Another Grandchild! What an unexpected Happiness is this! to discover in the space of 3 minutes, as many of my Descendants! This, I am certain is Philander the son of my Laurina's

3d Girl the amiable Bertha; there wants now but the presence of Gustavus to compleat the Union of my Laurina's Grand-Children".

"And here he is; (said a Gracefull Youth who that instant entered the room) here is the Gustavus you desire to see. I am the son of Agatha your Laurina's 4th & Youngest Daughter." "I see you are indeed ; replied Lord St. Clair—But tell me (continued he looking fearfully towards the Door) tell me, have I any other Grand-Children in the House." "None my Lord." "Then I will provide for you all without further delay—Here are 4 Banknotes of 50£ each—Take them & remember I have done the Duty of a Grandfather—." He instantly left the Room & immediately afterwards the House.

Adeiu.

Laura.

Letter the 12th
Laura in continuation

You may imagine how greatly we were surprised by the sudden departure of Lord St. Clair. "Ignoble Grand-sire!" exclaimed Sophia. "Unworthy Grandfather!" said I, & instantly fainted in each other's arms. How long we remained in this situation I know not; but when we recovered we found ourselves alone, without either Gustavus, Philander or the Bank-notes. As we were deploring our unhappy fate, the Door of the Apartment opened & "Macdonald" was announced. He was Sophia's cousin. The haste with which he came to our releif so soon after the receipt of our Note, spoke so greatly in his favour that I hesitated not to pronounce him at first sight, a tender & Simpathetic Freind. Alas! he little deserved the name—for though he told us that he was much concerned at our Misfortunes, yet by his own account it appeared that the perusal of them, had neither drawn from him a single sigh, nor induced him

to

to bestow one curse on our vindictive Stars.—. He told Sophia that his Daughter depended on her returning with him to Macdonald-Hall, & that as his Cousin's freind he should be happy to see me there also. To Macdonald-Hall, therefore, we went, and were received with great kindness by Janetta the daughter of Macdonald, & the Mistress of the Mansion. Janetta was then only fifteen; naturally well disposed, endowed with a susceptible Heart, and a simpathetic Disposition, she might, had these amiable Qualities been properly encouraged, have been an ornament to human Nature; but unfortunately her Father possessed not a soul sufficiently exalted to admire so promising a Disposition, and had endeavoured by every means in his power to prevent its encreasing with her Years. He had actually so far extinguished the natural noble Sensibility of her Heart, as to prevail on her to accept an offer from a young man of his Recommendation. They were to be married in a few months, and Graham, was in the House when we arrived. *We* soon saw through his Character.—. He was just such a Man as one might have expected to be the choice of Macdonald. They said he was Sensible, well-informed, and Agreable; we did not pretend to Judge of such trifles, but as we were convinced he had no soul, that he had never read the Sorrows of Werter, & that his Hair bore not the slightest resemblance to Auburn, we were certain that Janetta could feel no affection for him, or at least that she ought to feel none. The very circumstance of his being her father's choice too, was so much in his disfavour, that had he been deserving her, in every other respect yet *that* of itself ought to have been a sufficient reason in the Eyes of Janetta for rejecting him. These considerations we were determined to represent to her in their proper light & doubted not of meeting with the desired success from one naturally so well disposed, whose errors in the Affair had only arisen from a want of proper confidence in her own opinion, & a suitable contempt of her father's father's. We found her indeed all that our warmest wishes could have hoped for; we had no difficulty to convince her that it was impossible she could love Graham, or that it was her duty to disobey her Father; the only thing at which she rather seemed to hesitate was our assertion that she must be attached to some other Person. For some time, she persevered in declaring that she knew no other young Man for whom she had the smallest Affection; but upon explaining the impossibility of such a thing she said that she beleived she *did like* Captain M'Kenzie better than any one she knew besides. This confession satisfied us and after having enumerated the good Qualities of M'Kenzie & assured her that she was violently in love with him, we desired to know whether he had ever in any wise declared his Affection to her.

"So far from having ever declared it, I have no reason to imagine that he has ever felt any for me." said Janetta. "That he certainly adores you (replied Sophia) there can be no doubt—. The Attachment must be reciprocal—. Did he never gaze on you with Admiration—tenderly press your hand—drop an involuntary tear—& leave the room abruptly?" "Never (replied She) that I remember—he has always left the room indeed when his visit has been ended, but has never gone away particularly abruptly or without making a bow". "Indeed my Love (said I) you must be mistaken—: for it is absolutely impossible that he should ever have left you but with Confusion, Despair, & Precipitation—. Consider but for a moment Janetta, & you must be convinced how absurd it is to suppose that he could ever make a Bow, or behave like any other Person." Having settled this Point to our satisfaction, the next we took into consideration was, to determine in what manner we should inform M'Kenzie of the favourable Opinion Janetta entertained of him.—. We at length agreed to acquaint him with it by an anonymous Letter which Sophia drew up in the following Manner.

"Oh!

"Oh! happy Lover of the beautifull Janetta, oh! enviable Possessor of *her* Heart whose hand is destined to another, why do you thus delay a confession of your Attachment to the amiable Object of it? Oh! consider that a few weeks will at once put an end to every flattering Hope that you may now entertain, by uniting the unfortunate Victim of her father's Cruelty to the execrable & detested Graham."

"Alas! why do you thus so cruelly connive at the projected Misery of her & of yourself by delaying to communicate that scheme which had doubtless long possessed your imagination? A secret Union will at once secure the felicity of both."

The amiable M'Kenzie, whose modesty as he afterwards assured us had been the only reason of his having so long concealed the violence of his affection for Janetta, on receiving this Billet flew on the wings of Love to Macdonald-Hall, and so powerfully pleaded his Attachment to her who inspired it, that after a few more private interveiws, Sophia & I experienced the Satisfaction of seeing them depart for Gretna-Green, which they chose for the celebration of their Nuptials, in preference to any other place although it was at a considerable distance from Macdonald-Hall.

Adeiu—

Laura—

Letter the 13th
Laura in Continuation

THEY had been gone nearly a couple of Hours, before either Macdonald or Graham had entertained any suspicion of the affair—. And they might not even then have suspected it, but for the following little Accident. Sophia happening one Day to open a private Drawer in Macdonald's Library with one of her own keys, discovered that it was the Place where he kept his Papers of consequence

&

& amongst them some bank notes of considerable amount. This discovery she imparted to me; and having agreed together that it would be a proper treatment of so vile a Wretch as Macdonald to deprive him of money, perhaps dishonestly gained, it was determined that the next time we should either of us happen to go that way, we would take one or more of the Bank notes from the drawer. This well-meant Plan we had often successfully put in Execution; but alas! on the very day of Janetta's Escape, as Sophia was majestically removing the 5th Bank-note from the Drawer to her own purse, she was suddenly most impertinently interrupted in her employment by the entrance of Macdonald himself, in a most abrupt & precipitate Manner. Sophia (who though naturally all winning sweetness could when occasions demanded it call forth the Dignity of her Sex) instantly put on a most forbiding look, & darting an angry frown on the undaunted Culprit, demanded in a haughty tone of voice "Wherefore her retirement was thus insolently broken in on?" The unblushing Macdonald, without even endeavouring to exculpate himself from the crime he was charged with, meanly endeavoured to reproach Sophia with ignobly defrauding him of his Money. The dignity of Sophia was wounded ; "Wretch (exclaimed she, hastily replacing the Bank-note in the Drawer) how darest thou to accuse me of an Act, of which the bare idea makes me blush?" The base wretch was still unconvinced & continued to upbraid the justly-offended Sophia in such opprobrious Language, that at length he so greatly provoked the gentle sweetness of her Nature, as to induce her to revenge herself on him by informing him of Janetta's Elopement, and of the active Part we had both taken in the Affair. At this period of their Quarrel I entered the Library and was as you may imagine equally offended as Sophia at the ill-grounded Accusations of the malevolent and contemptible Macdonald. "Base Miscreant (cried I) how canst thou thus undauntedly endeavour to sully the
spotless

spotless reputation of such bright Excellence? Why dost
thou not suspect *my* innocence as soon?" "Be satisfied
Madam (replied he) I *do* suspect it, & therefore must desire
that you will both leave this House in less than half an hour."

"We shall go willingly; (answered Sophia) our hearts
have long detested thee, & nothing but our freindship for
thy Daughter could have induced us to remain so long beneath thy roof."

"Your Freindship for my Daughter has indeed been
most powerfully exerted by throwing her into the arms of
an unprincipled Fortune-hunter." (replied he)

"Yes, (exclaimed I) amidst every misfortune, it will
afford us some consolation to reflect that by this one act
of Freindship to Janetta, we have amply discharged every
obligation that we have received from her father."

"It must indeed be a most gratefull reflection, to your
exalted minds." (said he.)

As soon as we had packed up our wardrobe & valuables,
we left Macdonald Hall, & after having walked about a
mile & a half we sate down by the side of a clear limpid
stream to refresh our exhausted limbs. The place was
suited to meditation.—. A Grove of full-grown Elms
sheltered us from the East—. A Bed of full-grown Nettles
from the West—. Before us ran the murmuring brook &
behind us ran the turn-pike road. We were in a mood for
contemplation & in a Disposition to enjoy so beautifull a
spot. A mutual Silence which had for some time reigned
between us, was at length broke by my exclaiming—
"What a lovely Scene! Alas why are not Edward &
Augustus here to enjoy its Beauties with us?".

"Ah! my beloved Laura (cried Sophia) for pity's sake
forbear recalling to my remembrance the unhappy situation of my imprisoned Husband. Alas, what would I not
give to learn the fate of my Augustus! to know if he is still
in Newgate, or if he is yet hung. But never shall I be able
so far to conquer my tender sensibility as to enquire after
him.

him. Oh! do not I beseech you ever let me again hear you repeat his beloved name—. It affects me too deeply—. I cannot bear to hear him mentioned, it wounds my feelings."

"Excuse me my Sophia for having thus unwillingly offended you—" replied I—and then changing the conversation, desired her to admire the Noble Grandeur of the Elms which Sheltered us from the Eastern Zephyr. "Alas! my Laura (returned she) avoid so melancholy a subject, I intreat you.— Do not again wound my Sensibility by Observations on those elms. They remind me of Augustus—. He was like them, tall, magestic—he possessed that noble grandeur which you admire in them."

I was silent, fearfull lest I might any more unwillingly distress her by fixing on any other subject of conversation which might again remind her of Augustus.

"Why do you not speak my Laura?" (said she after a short pause) "I cannot support this silence—you must not leave me to my own reflections; they ever recur to Augustus."

"What a beautifull Sky! (said I) How charmingly is the azure varied by those delicate streaks of white!"

"Oh! my Laura (replied she hastily withdrawing her Eyes from a momentary glance at the sky) do not thus distress me by calling my Attention to an object which so cruelly reminds me of my Augustus's blue sattin Waistcoat striped with white! In pity to your unhappy freind avoid a subject so distressing." What could I do? The feelings of Sophia were at that time so exquisite, & the tenderness she felt for Augustus so poignant that I had not the power to start any other topic, justly fearing that it might in some unforseen manner again awaken all her sensibility by directing her thoughts to her Husband.— Yet to be silent would be cruel; She had intreated me to talk.

From this Dilemma I was most fortunately releived by an accident truly apropos; it was the lucky overturning

of

of a Gentleman's Phaeton, on the road which ran murmuring behind us. It was a most fortunate Accident as it diverted the Attention of Sophia from the melancholy reflections which she had been before indulging. We instantly quitted our seats & ran to the rescue of those who but a few moments before had been in so elevated a situation as a fashionably high Phaeton, but who were now laid low and sprawling in the Dust—. "What an ample subject for reflection on the uncertain Enjoyments of this World, would not that Phaeton & the Life of Cardinal Wolsey afford a thinking Mind!" said I to Sophia as we were hastening to the field of Action.

She had not time to answer me for every thought was now engaged by the horrid Spectacle before us. Two Gentlemen most elegantly attired but weltering in their blood was what first struck our Eyes—we approached—they were Edward & Augustus—Yes dearest Marianne they were our Husbands. Sophia shrieked & fainted on the Ground—I screamed and instantly ran mad—. We remained thus mutually deprived of our Senses some minutes, & on regaining them were deprived of them again—. For an Hour & a Quarter did we continue in this unfortunate Situation—Sophia fainting every moment & I running Mad as often. At length a Groan from the hapless Edward (who alone retained any share of Life) restored us to ourselves—. Had we indeed before imagined that either of them lived, we should have been more sparing of our Greif —but as we had supposed when we first beheld them that they were no more, we knew that nothing could remain to be done but what we were about—. No sooner therefore did we hear my Edward's groan than postponing our Lamentations for the present, we hastily ran to the Dear Youth and kneeling on each side of him implored him not to die—. "Laura (said He fixing his now languid Eyes on me) I fear I have been overturned."

I was overjoyed to find him yet sensible—.

"Oh!

"Oh! tell me Edward (said I) tell me I beseech you before you die, what has befallen you since that unhappy Day in which Augustus was arrested & we were separated—"

"I will" (said he) and instantly fetching a Deep sigh, expired—. Sophia immediately sunk again into a swoon—. *My* Greif was more audible, My voice faltered, My Eyes assumed a vacant Stare, My face became as pale as Death, and my Senses were considerably impaired—.

"Talk not to me of Phaetons (said I, raving in a frantic, incoherent manner)—Give me a violin—. I'll play to him & sooth him in his melancholy Hours—Beware ye gentle Nymphs of Cupid's Thunderbolts, avoid the piercing Shafts of Jupiter—Look at that Grove of Firs—I see a Leg of Mutton—They told me Edward was not Dead; but they deceived me—they took him for a Cucumber—" Thus I continued wildly exclaiming on my Edward's death—. For two Hours did I rave thus madly and should not then have left off, as I was not in the least fatigued, had not Sophia who was just recovered from her swoon, intreated me to consider that Night was now approaching and that the Damps began to fall. "And whither shall we go (said I) to shelter us from either"? "To that white Cottage." (replied she pointing to a neat building which rose up amidst the Grove of Elms & which I had not before observed—) I agreed & we instantly walked to it—we knocked at the door—it was opened by an old Woman; on being requested to afford us a Night's Lodging, she informed us that her House was but small, that she had only two Bed-rooms, but that However we should be wellcome to one of them. We were satisfied & followed the good Woman into the House where we were greatly cheered by the sight of a comfortable fire—. She was a Widow & had only one Daughter, who was then just Seventeen—One of the best of ages; but alas! she was very plain & her name was Bridget. . . . . . Nothing therefore could be expected from her—she could not be supposed to possess either exalted

Ideas,

Ideas, Delicate Feelings or refined Sensibilities—She was nothing more than a mere good-tempered, civil & obliging Young Woman ; as such we could scarcely dislike her—she was only an Object of Contempt—.

Adeiu
Laura—

Letter the 14th
Laura in continuation

ARM yourself my amiable Young Freind with all the philosophy you are Mistress of; summon up all the fortitude you possess, for Alas! in the perusal of the following Pages your sensibility will be most severely tried. Ah! what were the Misfortunes I had before experienced & which I have already related to you, to the one I am now going to inform you of. The Death of my Father, my Mother, and my Husband though almost more than my gentle Nature could support, were trifles in comparison to the misfortune I am now proceeding to relate. The morning after our arrival at the Cottage, Sophia complained of a violent pain in her delicate limbs, accompanied with a disagreable Head-ake. She attributed it to a cold caught by her continued faintings in the open Air as the Dew was falling the Evening before. This I feared was but too probably the case; since how could it be otherwise accounted for that I should have escaped the same indisposition, but by supposing that the bodily Exertions I had undergone in my repeated fits of frenzy, had so effectually circulated & warmed my Blood as to make me proof against the chilling Damps of Night, whereas, Sophia lying totally inactive on the Ground must have been exposed to all their Severity. I was most seriously alarmed by her illness which trifling as it may appear to you, a certain instinctive Sensibility whispered me, would in the End be fatal to her.

Alas! my fears were but too fully justified; she grew
gradually

gradually worse & I daily became more alarmed for her.—
At length she was obliged to confine herself solely to the
Bed allotted us by our worthy Landlady—. Her disorder
turned to a galloping Consumption & in a few Days carried
her off. Amidst all my Lamentations for her (& violent
you may suppose they were) I yet received some consolation in the reflection of my having paid every Attention
to her, that could be offered, in her illness. I had wept over
her every Day—had bathed her sweet face with my tears
& had pressed her fair Hands continually in mine—. "My
beloved Laura (said she to me a few Hours before she died)
take warning from my unhappy End & avoid the imprudent conduct which has occasioned it . . beware of
fainting-fits . . Though at the time they may be refreshing
& Agreable yet beleive me they will in the end, if too often
repeated & at improper seasons, prove destructive to your
Constitution . . . . . My fate will teach you this . . I die a
Martyr to my greif for the loss of Augustus . . . . One
fatal swoon has cost me my Life . . . . Beware of swoons
Dear Laura . . . A frenzy fit is not one quarter so pernicious; it is an exercise to the Body & if not too violent, is
I dare say conducive to Health in its consequences—Run
mad as often as you chuse; but do not faint—".

These were the last words she ever adressed to me . . .
It was her dieing Advice to her afflicted Laura, who has
ever most faithfully adhered to it.

After having attended my lamented freind to her Early
Grave, I immediately (tho' late at night) left the detested
Village in which she died, & near which had expired my
Husband & Augustus. I had not walked many yards from
it before I was overtaken by a Stage-Coach, in which I
instantly took a place, determined to proceed in it to Edinburgh, where I hoped to find some kind pitying Freind who
would receive and comfort me in my Afflictions.

It was so dark when I entered the Coach that I could not
distinguish the Number of my Fellow-travellers; I could
only

only perceive that they were Many. Regardless however of any thing concerning them, I gave myself up to my own sad Reflections. A general Silence prevailed—A Silence, which was by nothing interrupted but by the loud & repeated snores of one of the Party.

"What an illiterate villain must that Man be! (thought I to myself) What a total Want of delicate refinement must he have who can thus shock our senses by such a brutal Noise! He must I am certain be capable of every bad Action! There is no crime too black for such a Character!" Thus reasoned I within myself, & doubtless such were the reflections of my fellow travellers.

At length, returning Day enabled me to behold the unprincipled Scoundrel who had so violently disturbed my feelings. It was Sir Edward the father of my Deceased Husband. By his side, sate Augusta, & on the same seat with me were your Mother & Lady Dorothea. Imagine my Surprise at finding myself thus seated amongst my old Acquaintance. Great as was my astonishment, it was yet increased, when on look out of Windows, I beheld the Husband of Philippa, with Philippa by his side, on the Coach-box, & when on looking behind, I beheld, Philander & Gustavus in the Basket. "Oh! Heavens, (exclaimed I) is it possible that I should so unexpectedly be surrounded by my nearest Relations and Connections"? These words roused the rest of the Party, and every eye was directed to the corner in which I sat. "Oh! my Isabel (continued I throwing myself across Lady Dorothea into her arms) receive once more to your Bosom the unfortunate Laura. Alas! when we last parted in the Vale of Usk, I was happy in being united to the best of Edwards; I had then a Father and a Mother, & had never known misfortunes— But now deprived of every freind but you—".

"What! (interrupted Augusta) is my Brother dead then? Tell us I intreat you what is become of him?" "Yes, cold & insensible Nymph, (replied I) that luckless Swain your Brother,

Brother, is no more, & you may now glory in being the Heiress of Sir Edward's fortune."

Although I had always despised her from the Day I had overheard her conversation with my Edward, yet in civility I complied with hers & Sir Edward's intreaties that I would inform them of the whole melancholy Affair. They were greatly shocked—Even the obdurate Heart of Sir Edward & the insensible one of Augusta, were touched with Sorrow, by the unhappy tale. At the request of your Mother I related to them every other misfortune which had befallen me since we parted. Of the imprisonment of Augustus & the absence of Edward—of our arrival in Scotland—of our unexpected Meeting with our Grandfather and our cousins—of our visit to Macdonald-Hall— of the singular Service we there performed towards Janetta —of her Fathers ingratitude for it . . . . . of his inhuman Behaviour, unaccountable suspicions, & barbarous treatment of us, in obliging us to leave the House . . . . . of our Lamentations on the loss of Edward & Augustus & finally of the melancholy Death of my beloved Companion.

Pity & Surprise were strongly depictured in your Mother's Countenance, during the whole of my narration, but I am sorry to say, that to the eternal reproach of her Sensibility, the latter infinitely predominated. Nay, fault-less as my Conduct had certainly been during the whole Course of my late Misfortunes & Adventures, she pretended to find fault with my Behaviour in many of the situations in which I had been placed. As I was sensible myself, that I had always behaved in a manner which reflected Honour on my Feelings & Refinement, I paid little attention to what she said, & desired her to satisfy my Curiosity by in-forming me how she came there, instead of wounding my spotless reputation with unjustifiable Reproaches. As soon as she had complyed with my wishes in this particular & had given me an accurate detail of every thing that had befallen her since our separation (the particulars of which if you are

not

not already acquainted with, your Mother will give you) I applied to Augusta for the same information respecting herself, Sir Edward & Lady Dorothea.

She told me that having a considerable taste for the Beauties of Nature, her curiosity to behold the delightful scenes it exhibited in that part of the World had been so much raised by Gilpin's Tour to the Highlands, that she had prevailed on her Father to undertake a Tour of Scotland & had persuaded Lady Dorothea to accompany them. That they had arrived at Edinburgh a few days before & from thence had made daily Excursions into the Country around in the Stage Coach they were then in, from one of which Excursions they were at that time returning. My next enquiries were concerning Philippa & her Husband, the latter of whom I learned having spent all her fortune, had recourse for subsistance to the talent in which, he had always most excelled, namely, Driving, & that having sold every thing which belonged to them except their Coach, had converted it into a Stage, & in order to be removed from any of his former Acquaintance, had driven it to Edinburgh from whence he went to Sterling every other Day; That Philippa still retaining her affection for her ungratefull Husband, had followed him to Scotland & generally accompanied him in his little Excursions to Sterling. "It has only been to throw a little money into their Pockets (continued Augusta) that my Father has always travelled in their Coach to veiw the beauties of the Country since our arrival in Scotland—for it would certainly have been much more agreable to us, to visit the Highlands in a Postchaise than merely to travel from Edinburgh to Sterling & from Sterling to Edinburgh every other Day in a crouded & uncomfortable Stage." I perfectly agreed with her in her sentiments on the Affair, & secretly blamed Sir Edward for thus sacrificing his Daughter's pleasure for the sake of a ridiculous old Woman whose folly in marrying so young a Man ought to be punished. His Behaviour however

ever was entirely of a peice with his general Character; for what could be expected from a Man who possessed not the smallest atom of Sensibility, who scarcely knew the meaning of Simpathy, & who actually snored—.

Adeiu

Laura.

Letter the 15th
Laura in continuation

When we arrived at the town where we were to Breakfast, I was determined to speak with Philander & Gustavus, & to that purpose as soon as I left the Carriage, I went to the Basket & tenderly enquired after their Health, expressing my fears of the uneasiness of their Situation. At first they seemed rather confused at my Appearance dreading no doubt that I might call them to account for the money which our Grandfather had left me & which they had unjustly deprived me of, but finding that I mentioned nothing of the Matter, they desired me to step into the Basket as we might there converse with greater ease. Accordingly I entered & whilst the rest of the party were devouring Green tea & buttered toast, we feasted ourselves in a more refined & Sentimental Manner by a confidential Conversation. I informed them of every thing which had befallen me during the course of my Life, and at my request they related to me every incident of theirs.

"We are the sons as you already know, of the two youngest Daughters which Lord St. Clair had by Laurina an italian opera girl. Our mothers could neither of them exactly ascertain who were our fathers; though it is generally beleived that Philander, is the son of one Philip Jones a Bricklayer and that my father was Gregory Staves a Staymaker of Edinburgh. This is however of little consequence, for as our Mothers were certainly never married to either of them, it reflects no Dishonour on our Blood which

is

is of a most ancient & unpolluted kind. Bertha (the Mother
of Philander) & Agatha (my own Mother) always lived together. They were neither of them very rich; their united
fortunes had originally amounted to nine thousand Pounds,
but as they had always lived upon the principal of it, when
we were fifteen it was diminished to nine Hundred. This
nine Hundred, they always kept in a Drawer in one of the
Tables which stood in our common sitting Parlour, for the
Convenience of having it always at Hand. Whether it was
from this circumstance, of its being easily taken, or from a
wish of being independant, or from an excess of Sensibility
(for which we were always remarkable) I cannot now determine, but certain it is that when we had reached our 15th
year, we took the Nine Hundred Pounds & ran away.
Having obtained this prize we were determined to manage
it with eoconomy & not to spend it either with folly or
Extravagance. To this purpose we therefore divided it
into nine parcels, one of which we devoted to Victuals, the
2d to Drink, the 3d to Housekeeping, the 4th to Carriages,
the 5th to Horses, the 6th to Servants, the 7th to Amusements, the 8th to Cloathes & the 9th to Silver Buckles.
Having thus arranged our Expences for two Months (for we
expected to make the nine Hundred Pounds last as long)
we hastened to London & had the good luck to spend it in
7 weeks & a Day which was 6 Days sooner than we had
intended. As soon as we had thus happily disencumbered
ourselves from the weight of so much Money, we began to
think of returning to our Mothers, but accidentally hearing
that they were both starved to death, we gave over the
design & determined to engage ourselves to some strolling
Company of Players, as we had always a turn for the Stage.
Accordingly we offered our services to one & were accepted;
our Company was indeed rather small, as it consisted only
of the Manager his wife & ourselves, but there were fewer
to pay and the only inconvenience attending it was the
Scarcity of Plays which for want of People to fill the
Characters,

Characters, we could perform.—. We did not mind trifles however—. One of our most admired Performances was *Macbeth*, in which we were truly great. The Manager always played *Banquo* himself, his Wife my *Lady Macbeth*. I did the *Three Witches* & Philander acted *all the rest*. To say the truth this tragedy was not only the Best, but the only Play we ever performed; & after having acted it all over England, and Wales, we came to Scotland to exhibit it over the remainder of Great Britain. We happened to be quartered in that very Town, where you came and met your Grandfather—. We were in the Inn-yard when his Carriage entered & perceiving by the Arms to whom it belonged, & knowing that Lord St. Clair was our Grand-father, we agreed to endeavour to get something from him by discovering the Relationship—. You know how well it succeeded—. Having obtained the two Hundred Pounds, we instantly left the Town, leaving our Manager & his wife to act *Macbeth* by themselves, & took the road to Sterling, where we spent our little fortune with great *eclat*. We are now returning to Edinburgh to get some preferment in the Acting way ; & such my Dear Cousin is our History."

I thanked the amiable Youth for his entertaining Narra-tion, & after expressing my Wishes for their Welfare & Happiness, left them in their little Habitation & returned to my other Freinds who impatiently expected me.

My Adventures are now drawing to a close my dearest Marianne; at least for the present.

When we arrived at Edinburgh Sir Edward told me that as the Widow of his Son, he desired I would accept from his Hands of four Hundred a year. I graciously promised that I would, but could not help observing that the unsim-pathetic Baronet offered it more on account of my being the Widow of Edward than in being the refined & Amiable Laura.

I took up my Residence in a romantic Village in the Highlands of Scotland, where I have ever since continued,

&

& where I can uninterrupted by unmeaning Visits, indulge in a melancholy solitude, my unceasing Lamentations for the Death of my Father, my Mother, my Husband & my Freind.

Augusta has been for several Years united to Graham the Man of all others most suited to her; she became acquainted with him during her stay in Scotland.

Sir Edward in hopes of gaining an Heir to his Title & Estate, at the same time married Lady Dorothea—. His wishes have been answered.

Philander & Gustavus, after having raised their reputation by their Performances in the Theatrical Line at Edinburgh, removed to Covent Garden, where they still Exhibit under the assumed names of *Lewis & Quick.*

Philippa has long paid the Debt of Nature, Her Husband however still continues to drive the Stage-Coach from Edinburgh to Sterling :—

Adeiu my Dearest Marianne.

Laura—

Finis

June 13th 1790

LESLEY CASTLE

an unfinished Novel in Letters

To Henry Thomas Austen Esqre.

Sir

I am now availing myself of the Liberty you have frequently honoured me with of dedicating one of my Novels to you. That it is unfinished, I greive ; yet fear that from me, it will always remain so ; that as far as it is carried, it Should be so trifling and so unworthy of you, is another concern to your obliged humble

Servant

The Author

Messrs

Messrs Demand & Co—please to pay Jane Austen Spinster the sum of one hundred guineas on account of your Humbl. Servant.

H T Austen.

£105.   0.   0

———

Letter The first is from Miss Margaret Lesley to Miss Charlotte Lutterell.

Lesley-Castle Janry 3d—1792.

My Brother has just left us. "Matilda (said he at parting) you and Margaret will I am certain take all the care of my dear little one, that she might have received from an indulgent, an affectionate an amiable Mother." Tears rolled down his cheeks as he spoke these words—the remembrance of her, who had so wantonly disgraced the Maternal character and so openly violated the conjugal Duties, prevented his adding anything farther; he embraced his sweet Child and after saluting Matilda & Me hastily broke from us and seating himself in his Chaise, pursued the road to Aberdeen. Never was there a better young Man! Ah! how little did he deserve the misfortunes he has experienced in the Marriage state. So good a Husband to so bad a Wife! for you know my dear Charlotte that the Worthless Louisa left him, her Child & reputation a few weeks ago in company with Danvers &[+] dishonour. Never was there a sweeter face, a finer form, or a less amiable Heart than Louisa owned! Her child already possesses the personal charms of her unhappy Mother! May she inherit from her Father all his mental ones! Lesley is at present but five and twenty, and has already given himself up to melancholy and Despair; what a difference between him and his Father! Sir George is 57 and still remains the Beau, the

+ Rakehelly Dishonour Esqre.

flighty

flighty stripling, the gay Lad and sprightly Youngster, that his Son was really about five years back, and that *he* has affected to appear ever since my remembrance. While our father is fluttering about the streets of London, gay, dissipated, and Thoughtless at the age of 57, Matilda and I continue secluded from Mankind in our old and Mouldering Castle, which is situated two miles from Perth on a bold projecting Rock, and commands an extensive view of the Town and its delightful Environs. But tho' retired from almost all the World, (for we visit no one but the M'Leods, the M'Kenzies, the M'Phersons, the M'Cartneys, the M'donalds, The M'Kinnons, the M'lellans, the M'Kays, the Macbeths and the Macduffs) we are neither dull nor unhappy; on the contrary there never were two more lively, more agreable or more witty Girls, than we are; not an hour in the Day hangs heavy on our hands. We read, we work, we walk and when fatigued with these Employments releive our spirits, either by a lively song, a graceful Dance, or by some smart bon-mot, and witty repartée. We are handsome my dear Charlotte, very handsome and the greatest of our Perfections is, that we are entirely insensible of them ourselves. But why do I thus dwell on myself? Let me rather repeat the praise of our dear little Neice the innocent Louisa, who is at present sweetly smiling in a gentle Nap, as she reposes on the Sofa. The dear Creature is just turned of two years old; as handsome as tho' 2 & 20, as sensible as tho' 2 & 30, and as prudent as tho' 2 & 40. To convince you of this, I must inform you that she has a very fine complexion and very pretty features, that she already knows the two first letters in the Alphabet, and that she never tears her frocks—. If I have not now convinced you of her Beauty, Sense & Prudence, I have nothing more to urge in support of my assertion, and you will therefore have no way of deciding the Affair but by coming to Lesley Castle, and by a personal acquaintance with Louisa, determine for yourself. Ah! my dear Freind,

how

how happy should I be to see you within these venerable
Walls! It is now four years since my removal from School
has separated me from you; that two such tender Hearts,
so closely linked together by the ties of simpathy and
Freindship, should be so widely removed from each other,
is vastly moving. I live in Perthshire, You in Sussex. We
might meet in London, were my Father disposed to carry
me there, and were your Mother to be there at the same
time. We might meet at Bath, at Tunbridge, or anywhere
else indeed, could we but be at the same place together.
We have only to hope that such a period may arrive. My
Father does not return to us till Autumn; my Brother will
leave Scotland in a few Days; he is impatient to travel.
Mistaken Youth! He vainly flatters himself that change of
Air will heal the Wounds of a broken Heart! You will join
with me I am certain my dear Charlotte, in prayers for the
recovery of the unhappy Lesley's peace of Mind, which
must ever be essential to that of your sincere freind
                                                    M. Lesley.

Letter the second
From Miss C. Lutterell to Miss M. Lesley in
answer

                    Glenford   Feb:ry 12
I HAVE a thousand excuses to beg for having so long delayed
thanking you my dear Peggy for your agreable Letter,
which beleive me I should not have deferred doing, had not
every moment of my time during the last five weeks been
so fully employed in the necessary arrangements for my
sisters Wedding, as to allow me no time to devote either
to you or myself. And now what provokes me more than
anything else is that the Match is broke off, and all my
Labour thrown away. Imagine how great the Dissapoint-
ment must be to me, when you consider that after having
                                                    laboured

laboured both by Night and Day, in order to get the Wedding dinner ready by the time appointed, after having roasted Beef, Broiled Mutton, and Stewed Soup enough to last the new-married Couple through the Honey-moon, I had the mortification of finding that I had been Roasting, Broiling and Stewing both the Meat and Myself to no purpose. Indeed my dear Freind, I never remember suffering any vexation equal to what I experienced on last Monday when my Sister came running to me in the Store-room with her face as White as a Whipt syllabub, and told me that Hervey had been thrown from his Horse, had fractured his Scull and was pronounced by his Surgeon to be in the most emminent Danger. "Good God! (said I) you dont say so? Why what in the name of Heaven will become of all the Victuals? We shall never be able to eat it while it is good. However, we'll call in the Surgeon to help us—. I shall be able to manage the Sir-loin myself; my Mother will eat the Soup, and You and the Doctor must finish the rest." Here I was interrupted, by seeing my poor Sister fall down to appearance Lifeless upon one of the Chests, where we keep our Table linen. I immediately called my Mother and the Maids, and at last we brought her to herself again; as soon as ever she was sensible, she expressed a determination of going instantly to Henry, and was so wildly bent on this Scheme, that we had the greatest Difficulty in the World to prevent her putting it in execution; at last however more by Force than Entreaty we prevailed on her to go into her room; we laid her upon the Bed, and she continued for some Hours in the most dreadful Convulsions. My Mother and I continued in the room with her, and when any intervals of tolerable Composure in Eloisa would allow us, we joined in heartfelt lamentations on the dreadful Waste in our provisions which this Event must occasion, and in concerting some plan for getting rid of them. We agreed that the best thing we could do was to begin eating them immediately, and accordingly we ordered

up

up the cold Ham and Fowls, and instantly began our Devouring Plan on them with great Alacrity. We would have persuaded Eloisa to have taken a Wing of a Chicken, but she would not be persuaded. She was however much quieter than she had been; the Convulsions she had before suffered having given way to an almost perfect Insensibility. We endeavoured to rouse her by every means in our power, but to no purpose. I talked to her of Henry. "Dear Eloisa (said I) there's no occasion for your crying so much about such a trifle. (for I was willing to make light of it in order to comfort her) I beg you would not mind it—. You see it does not vex me in the least; though perhaps *I* may suffer most from it after all; for I shall not only be obliged to eat up all the Victuals I have dressed already, but must if Hervey should recover (which however is not very likely) dress as much for you again; or should he die (as I suppose he will) I shall still have to prepare a Dinner for you whenever you marry any one else. So you see that tho' perhaps for the present it may afflict you to think of Henry's sufferings, Yet I dare say he'll die soon, and then his pain will be over and you will be easy, whereas my Trouble will last much longer for work hard as I may, I am certain that the pantry cannot be cleared in less than a fortnight." Thus I did all in my power to console her, but without any effect, and at last as I saw that she did not seem to listen to me, I said no more, but leaving her with my Mother I took down the remains of The Ham & Chicken, and sent William to ask how Hervey did. He was not expected to live many Hours; he died the same day. We took all possible care to break the Melancholy Event to Eloisa in the tenderest manner; yet in spite of every precaution, her Sufferings on hearing it were too violent for her reason, and she continued for many hours in a high Delirium. She is still extremely ill, and her Physicians are greatly afraid of her going into a Decline. We are therefore preparing for Bristol, where we mean to be in the course

of

of the next week. And now my dear Margaret let me talk
a little of your affairs; and in the first place I must inform
you that it is confidently reported, your Father is going
to be married; I am very unwilling to beleive so unpleasing
a report, and at the same time cannot wholly discredit it.
I have written to my freind Susan Fitzgerald, for information concerning it, which as she is at present in Town, she
will be very able to give me. I know not who is the Lady.
I think your Brother is extremely right in the resolution
he has taken of travelling, as it will perhaps contribute to
obliterate from his remembrance, those disagreable Events,
which have lately so much afflicted him—I am happy to
find that tho' secluded from all the World, neither you nor
Matilda are dull or unhappy—that you may never know
what it is to be either is the wish of your sincerely Affectionate   C.L.

P.S. I have this instant received an answer from my
freind Susan, which I enclose to you, and on which you will
make your own reflections.

The enclosed Letter
My dear Charlotte
You could not have applied for information concerning
the report of Sir George Lesleys Marriage, to anyone better
able to give it you than I am. Sir George is certainly
married; I was myself present at the Ceremony, which you
will not be surprised at when I subscribe myself your
                                            Affectionate
                                            Susan Lesley

Letter the third
From Miss Margaret Lesley to Miss C.
Lutterell
Lesley Castle   February the 16th
I *have* made my own reflections on the letter you enclosed
to me, my Dear Charlotte and I will now tell you what
                                                those

those reflections were. I reflected that if by this second
Marriage Sir George should have a second family, our fortunes must be considerably diminushed—that if his Wife
should be of an extravagant turn, she would encourage
him to persevere in that Gay & Dissipated way of Life to
which little encouragement would be necessary, and which
has I fear already proved but too detrimental to his health
and fortune—that she would now become Mistress of those
Jewels which once adorned our Mother, and which Sir
George had always promised us—that if they did not come
into Perthshire I should not be able to gratify my curiosity
of beholding my Mother-in-law, and that if they did,
Matilda would no longer sit at the head of her Father's
table—. These my dear Charlotte were the melancholy
reflections which crouded into my imagination after perus-
ing Susan's letter to you, and which instantly occurred to
Matilda when she had perused it likewise. The same ideas,
the same fears, immediately occupied her Mind, and I know
not which reflection distressed her most, whether the probable Diminution of our Fortunes, or her own Consequence.
We both wish very much to know whether Lady Lesley is
handsome & what is your opinion of her; as you honour
her with the appellation of your freind, we flatter ourselves
that she must be amiable. My Brother is already in Paris.
He intends to quit it in a few Days, and to begin his route
to Italy. He writes in a most chearfull Manner, says that
the air of France has greatly recovered both his Health
and Spirits; that he has now entirely ceased to think of
Louisa with any degree either of Pity or Affection, that he
even feels himself obliged to her for her Elopement, as he
thinks it very good fun to be single again. By this, you
may perceive that he has entirely regained that chearful
Gaiety, and sprightly Wit, for which he was once so remarkable. When he first became acquainted with Louisa
which was little more than three years ago, he was one of
the most lively, the most agreable young Men of the age—.

I

I beleive you never yet heard the particulars of his first
acquaintance with her. It commenced at our cousin Colonel
Drummond's, at whose house in Cumberland he spent the
Christmas, in which he attained the age of two and twenty.
Louisa Burton was the Daughter of a distant Relation of
Mrs. Drummond, who dieing a few Months before in extreme
poverty, left his only Child then about eighteen to the protection of any of his Relations who would protect her. Mrs.
Drummond was the only one who found herself so disposed
—Louisa was therefore removed from a miserable Cottage
in Yorkshire to an elegant Mansion in Cumberland, and
from every pecuniary Distress that Poverty could inflict,
to every elegant Enjoyment that Money could purchase—.
Louisa was naturally ill-tempered and Cunning; but she
had been taught to disguise her real Disposition, under the
appearance of insinuating Sweetness by a father who but
too well knew, that to be married, would be the only chance
she would have of not being starved, and who flattered
himself that with such an extraoidinary share of personal
beauty, joined to a gentleness of Manners, and an engaging
address, she might stand a good chance of pleasing some
young Man who might afford to marry a Girl without a
Shilling. Louisa perfectly entered into her father's schemes
and was determined to forward them with all her care &
attention. By dint of Perseverance and Application, she
had at length so thoroughly disguised her natural disposition under the mask of Innocence, and Softness, as to im-
pose upon every one who had not by a long and constant
intimacy with her discovered her real Character. Such
was Louisa when the hapless Lesley first beheld her at
Drummond-house. His heart which (to use your favourite
comparison) was as delicate as sweet and as tender as a
Whipt-syllabub, could not resist her attractions. In a very
few Days, he was falling in love, shortly afterwards actually
fell, and before he had known her a Month, he had married
her. My Father was at first highly displeased at so hasty

and

and imprudent a connection; but when he found that they did not mind it, he soon became perfectly reconciled to the match. The Estate near Aberdeen which my brother possesses by the bounty of his great Uncle independant of Sir George, was entirely sufficient to support him and my Sister in Elegance & Ease. For the first twelvemonth, no one could be happier than Lesley, and no one more amiable to appearance than Louisa, and so plausibly did She act and so cautiously behave that tho' Matilda and I often spent several weeks together with them, yet we neither of us had any suspicion of her real Disposition. After the birth of Louisa however, which one would have thought would have strengthened her regard for Lesley, the mask she had so long supported was by degrees thrown aside, and as probably she then thought herself secure in the affection of her Husband (which did indeed appear if possible augmented by the birth of his Child) She seemed to take no pains to prevent that affection from ever diminishing. Our visits therefore to Dunbeath, were now less frequent and by far less agreable than they used to be. Our absence was however never either mentioned or lamented by Louisa who in the society of the young Danvers with whom she became acquainted at Aberdeen (he was at one of the Universities there,) felt infinitely happier than in that of Matilda and your freind, tho' there certainly never were pleasanter Girls than we are. You know the sad end of all Lesleys connubial happiness; I will not repeat it—. Adeiu my dear Charlotte; although I have not yet mentioned any thing of the matter, I hope you will do me the justice to believe that I *think* and *feel*, a great deal for your Sisters affliction. I do not doubt but that the healthy air of the Bristol downs, will intirely remove it, by erasing from her Mind the remembrance of Henry.

I am my dear Charlotte yrs ever

ML—.

Letter

Letter the fourth
From Miss C. Lutterell to Miss M. Lesley

Bristol February 27th

MY DEAR PEGGY

I HAVE but just received your letter, which being directed
to Sussex while I was at Bristol was obliged to be forwarded
to me here, & from some unaccountable Delay, has but this
instant reached me—. I return you many thanks for the
account it contains of Lesley's acquaintance, Love & Marriage with Louisa, which has not the less entertained me
for having often been repeated to me before.

I have the satisfaction of informing you that we have
every reason to imagine our pantry is by this time nearly
cleared, as we left particular orders with the Servants to
eat as hard as they possibly could, and to call in a couple
of Chairwomen to assist them. We brought a cold Pigeon
pye, a cold turkey, a cold tongue, and half a dozen Jellies
with us, which we were lucky enough with the help of our
Landlady, her husband, and their three children, to get rid
of, in less than two days after our arrival. Poor Eloisa is
still so very indifferent both in Health & Spirits, that I very
much fear, the air of the Bristol downs, healthy as it is, has
not been able to drive poor Henry from her remembrance.

You ask me whether your new Mother in law is handsome & amiable—I will now give you an exact description
of her bodily and mental charms. She is short, and extremely well-made; is naturally pale, but rouges a good
deal; has fine eyes, and fine teeth, as she will take care to
let you know as soon as she sees you, and is altogether very
pretty. She is remarkably good-tempered when she has
her own way, and very lively when she is not out of humour.
She is naturally extravagant and not very affected; she
never reads anything but the letters she receives from me,
and never writes anything but her answers to them. She
plays, sings & Dances, but has no taste for either, and

E   excells

excells in none, tho' she says she is passionately fond of all. Perhaps you may flatter me so far as to be surprised that one of whom I speak with so little affection should be my particular freind; but to tell you the truth, our freindship arose rather from Caprice on her side than Esteem on mine. We spent two or three days together with a Lady in Berkshire with whom we both happened to be connected—. During our visit, the Weather being remarkably bad, and our party particularly stupid, she was so good as to conceive a violent partiality for me, which very soon settled in a downright Freindship, and ended in an established correspondence. She is probably by this time as tired of me, as I am of her; but as she is too polite and I am too civil to say so, our letters are still as frequent and affectionate as ever, and our Attachment as firm and sincere as when it first commenced.— As she had a great taste for the pleasures of London, and of Brighthelmstone, she will I dare say find some difficulty in prevailing on herself ever to satisfy the curiosity I dare say she feels of beholding you, at the expence of quitting those favourite haunts of Dissipation, for the melancholy tho' venerable gloom of the castle you inhabit. Perhaps however if she finds her health impaired by too much amusement, she may acquire fortitude sufficient to undertake a Journey to Scotland in the hope of its proving at least beneficial to her health, if not conducive to her happiness. Your fears I am sorry to say, concerning your fathers extravagance, your own fortunes, your Mothers Jewels and your Sister's consequence, I should suppose are but too well founded. My freind herself has four thousand pounds, and will probably spend nearly as much every year in Dress and Public places, if she can get it—she will certainly not endeavour to reclaim Sir George from the manner of living to which he has been so long accustomed, and there is therefore some reason to fear that you will be very well off, if you get any fortune at all. The Jewels I should imagine too will un-
doubtedly

doubtedly be hers, & there is too much reason to think that she will reside at her Husbands table in preference to his Daughter. But as so melancholy a subject must necessarily extremely distress you, I will no longer dwell on it—.

Eloisa's indisposition has brought us to Bristol at so unfashionable a season of the year, that we have actually seen but one genteel family since we came. Mr & Mrs Marlowe are very agreable people; the ill health of their little boy occasioned their arrival here; you may imagine that being the only family with whom we can converse, we are of course on a footing of intimacy with them; we see them indeed almost every day, and dined with them yesterday. We spent a very pleasant Day, and had a very good Dinner, tho' to be sure the Veal was terribly under-done, and the Curry had no seasoning. I could not help wishing all dinner-time that I had been at the dressing it—. A brother of Mrs Marlowe, Mr Cleveland is with them at present; he is a good-looking young Man, and seems to have a good deal to say for himself. I tell Eloisa that she should set her cap at him, but she does not at all seem to relish the proposal. I should like to see the girl married and Cleveland has a very good estate. Perhaps you may wonder that I do not consider *myself* as well as my Sister in my matrimonial Projects; but to tell you the truth I never wish to act a more principal part at a Wedding than the superintending and directing the Dinner, and therefore while I can get any of my acquaintance to marry for me, I shall never think of doing it myself, as I very much sus-pect that I should not have so much time for dressing my own Wedding-dinner, as for dressing that of my freinds.

Yrs sincerely
CL.

Letter

Letter the fifth
Miss Margaret Lesley to Miss Charlotte
Lutterell

Lesley-Castle   March 18th

On the same day that I received your last kind letter, Matilda received one from Sir George which was dated from Edinburgh, and informed us that he should do himself the pleasure of introducing Lady Lesley to us on the following evening. This as you may suppose considerably surprised us, particularly as your account of her Ladyship had given us reason to imagine there was little chance of her visiting Scotland at a time that London must be so gay. As it was our business however to be delighted at such a mark of condescension as a visit from Sir George and Lady Lesley, we prepared to return them an answer expressive of the happiness we enjoyed in expectation of such a Blessing, when luckily recollecting that as they were to reach the Castle the next Evening, it would be impossible for my father to receive it before he left Edinburgh, We contented ourselves with leaving them to suppose that we were as happy as we ought to be. At nine in the Evening on the following day, they came, accompanied by one of Lady Lesleys brothers. Her Ladyship perfectly answers the description you sent me of her, except that I do not think her so pretty as you seem to consider her. She has not a bad face, but there is something so extremely unmajestic in her little diminutive figure, as to render her in comparison with the elegant height of Matilda and Myself, an insignificant Dwarf. Her curiosity to see us (which must have been great to bring her more than four hundred miles) being now perfectly gratified, she already begins to mention their return to town, and has desired us to accompany her—. We cannot refuse her request since it is seconded by the commands of our Father, and thirded by the entreaties of Mr Fitzgerald who is certainly one of the most

pleasing

pleasing young Men, I ever beheld, It is not yet determined when we are to go, but when ever we do we shall certainly take our little Louisa with us. Adeiu my dear Charlotte; Matilda unites in best Wishes to You & Eloisa, with your ever

                                                    M L

Letter the sixth
Lady Lesley to Miss Charlotte Lutterell

Lesley-Castle   March 20th

WE arrived here my sweet Freind about a fortnight ago, and I already heartily repent that I ever left our charming House in Portman-Square for such a dismal old weather-beaten Castle as this. You can form no idea sufficiently hideous, of its dungeon-like form. It is actually perched upon a Rock to appearance so totally inaccessible, that I expected to have been pulled up by a rope; and sincerely repented having gratified my curiosity to behold my Daughters at the expence of being obliged to enter their prison in so dangerous & ridiculous a Manner. But as soon as I once found myself safely arrived in the inside of this tremendous building, I comforted myself with the hope of having my spirits revived, by the sight of the two beauti-full Girls, such as the Miss Lesleys had been represented to me, at Edinburgh. But here again, I met with nothing but Disapointment and Surprise. Matilda and Margaret Lesley are two great, tall, out of the way, over-grown Girls, just of a proper size to inhabit a Castle almost as Large in comparison as themselves. I wish my dear Charlotte that you could but behold these Scotch Giants; I am sure they would frighten you out of your wits. They will do very well as foils to myself, so I have invited them to accompany me to London where I hope to be in the course of a fort-night. Besides these two fair Damsels, I found a little humoured Brat here who I believe is some relation to them; they

they told me who she was, and gave me a long rigmerole story of her father and Miss *Somebody* which I have entirely forgot. I hate Scandal and detest Children.—. I have been plagued ever since I came here with tiresome visits from a parcel of Scotch wretches, with terrible hard names; they were so civil, gave me so many invitations, and talked of coming again so soon, that I could not help affronting them. I suppose I shall not see them any more, and yet as a family party we are so stupid, that I do not know what to do with myself. These girls have no Music, but Scotch Airs, no Drawings but Scotch Mountains, and no Books but Scotch Poems—And I hate everything Scotch. In general I can spend half the Day at my toilett with a great deal of pleasure, but why should I dress here, since there is not a creature in the House whom I have any wish to please.—. I have just had a conversation with my Brother in which he has greatly offended me, and which as I have nothing more entertaining to send you I will give you the particulars of. You must know that I have for these 4 or 5 Days past strongly suspected William of entertaining a partiality to my eldest Daughter. I own indeed that had *I* been inclined to fall in love with any woman, I should not have made choice of Matilda Lesley for the object of my passion; for there is nothing I hate so much as a tall Woman: but however there is no accounting for some men's taste and as William is himself nearly six feet high, it is not wonderful that he should be partial to that height. Now as I have a very great Affection for my Brother and should be extremely sorry to see him unhappy, which I suppose he means to be if he cannot marry Matilda, as moreover I know that his Circumstances will not allow him to marry any one without a fortune, and that Matilda's is entirely dependant on her Father, who will neither have his own inclination, nor my permission to give her anything at present, I thought it would be doing a good-natured action by my Brother to let him know as much, in order that

that he might choose for himself, whether to conquer his passion, or Love and Despair. Accordingly finding myself this Morning alone with him in one of the horrid old rooms of this Castle, I opened the cause to him in the following Manner.

"Well my dear William what do you think of these girls? for my part, I do not find them so plain as I expected; but perhaps you may think me partial to the Daughters of my Husband and perhaps you are right—They are indeed so very like Sir George that it is natural to think. ." . . . .

"My Dear Susan (cried he in a tone of the greatest amazement) You do not really think they bear the least resemblance to their Father! He is so very plain!—but I beg your pardon—I had entirely forgotten to whom I was speaking—"

"Oh! pray dont mind me; (replied I) every one knows Sir George is horribly ugly, and I assure you I always thought him a fright."

"You surprise me extremely (answered William) by what you say both with respect to Sir George and his daughters. You cannot think your Husband so deficient in personal Charms as you speak of, nor can you surely see any resemblance between him and the Miss Lesleys who are in my opinion perfectly unlike him & perfectly Handsome."

"If that is your opinion with regard to the Girls it certainly is no proof of their Fathers beauty, for if they are perfectly unlike him and very handsome at the same time, it is natural to suppose that he is very plain."

"By no means, (said he) for what may be pretty in a Woman, may be very unpleasing in a Man."

"But you yourself (replied I) but a few Minutes ago allowed him to be very plain."

"Men are no Judges of Beauty in their own Sex." (said he)

"Neither Men nor Women can think Sir George tolerable."

"Well,

"Well, well, (said he) we will not dispute about *his* Beauty, but your opinion of his *Daughters* is surely very singular, for if I understood you right, you said you did not find them so plain as you expected to do."!

"Why, do *you* find them plainer then?" (said I).

"I can scarcely beleive you to be serious (returned he) when you speak of their persons in so extroidinary a Manner. Do not you think the Miss Lesleys are two very handsome young Women?"

"Lord! No! (cried I) I think them terribly plain!"

"Plain! (replied He) My dear Susan, you cannot really think so! why what single Feature in the face of either of them, can you possibly find fault with?"

"Oh! trust me for that; (replied I). Come I will begin with the eldest—with Matilda. Shall I, William? (I looked as cunning as I could when I said it, in order to shame him.)

"They are so much alike (said he) that I should suppose the faults of one, would be the faults of both."

"Well, then, in the first place, they are both so horribly tall!"

"They are *taller* than you are indeed." (said he with a saucy smile).

"Nay, (said I); I know nothing of that."

"Well, but (he continued) tho' they may be above the common size, their figures are perfectly elegant; and as to their faces, their Eyes are beautifull—."

"I can never think such tremendous knock-me-down figures in the least degree elegant, and as for their eyes, they are so tall that I never could strain my neck enough to look at them."

"Nay, (replied he), I know not whether you may not be in the right in not attempting it, for perhaps they might dazzle you with their Lustre."

"Oh! Certainly." (said I, with the greatest Complacency, for I assure you my dearest Charlotte I was not in the least offended tho' by what followed, one would suppose that William

William was conscious of having given me just cause to be so, for coming up to me and taking my hand, he said) "You must not look so grave Susan; you will make me fear I have offended you!"

"Offended me! Dear Brother, how came such a thought in your head! (returned I) No really! I assure you that I am not in the least surprised at your being so warm an advocate for the Beauty of these girls"—

"Well, but (interrupted William) remember that we have not yet concluded our dispute concerning them. What fault do you find with their complexion?"

"They are so horribly pale."

"They always have a little colour, and after any exercise it is considerably heightened."

"Yes, but if there should ever happen to be any rain in this part of the world, they will never be able to raise more than their common stock—except indeed they amuse themselves with running up & Down these horrid Galleries and Antichambers—"

"Well, (replied my Brother in a tone of vexation, & glancing an impertinent Look at me) if they *have* but little colour, at least, it is all their own."

This was too much my dear Charlotte, for I am certain that he had the impudence by that look, of pretending to suspect the reality of mine. But you I am sure will indicate my character whenever you may hear it so cruelly aspersed, for you can witness how often I have protested against wearing Rouge, and how much I always told you I dislike it. And I assure you that my opinions are still the same.—. Well, not bearing to be so suspected by my Brother, I left the room immediately, and have ever since been in my own Dressing-room writing to you. What a long Letter have I made of it! But you must not expect to receive such from me when I get to Town ; for it is only at Lesley castle, that one has time to write even to a Charlotte Lutterell.—. I was so much vexed by William's Glance, that

I

I could not summon Patience enough, to stay & give him that Advice respecting his Attachment to Matilda which had first induced me from pure Love to him to begin the conversation; and I am now so thoroughly convinced by it, of his violent passion for her, that I am certain he would never hear reason on the Subject, and I shall therefore give myself no more trouble either about him or his favourite. Adeiu my dear Girl—

Yrs Affectionately Susan L.

Letter the seventh
From Miss C. Lutterell to Miss M. Lesley

Bristol the 27th of March.

I HAVE received Letters from You & your Mother-in-Law within this week which have greatly entertained me, as I find by them that you are both downright jealous of each others Beauty. It is very odd that two pretty Women tho' actually Mother & Daughter cannot be in the same House without falling out about their faces. Do be convinced that you are both perfectly handsome and say no more of the Matter. I suppose this Letter must be directed to Portman Square where probably (great as is your affection for Lesley Castle) you will not be sorry to find yourself. In spite of all that People may say about Green fields and the Country I was always of the opinion that London and its Amusements must be very agreable for a while, and should be very happy could my Mother's income allow her to jockey us into its Public-places, during Winter. I always longed particularly to go to Vaux-hall, to see whether the cold Beef there is cut so thin as it is reported, for I have a sly suspicion that few people understand the art of cutting a slice of cold Beef so well as I do: nay it would be hard if I did not know something of the Matter, for it was a part of my Education that I took by far the most pains with. Mama always found me *her* best Scholar, tho' when Papa

was

was alive Eloisa was *his*. Never to be sure were there two
more different Dispositions in the World. We both loved
Reading. *She* preferred Histories, & *I* Receipts. She loved
drawing Pictures, and I drawing Pullets. No one could
sing a better Song than She, and no one make a better Pye
than I.—And so it has always continued since we have
been no longer Children. The only difference is that all
disputes on the superior excellence of our Employments
then so frequent are now no more. We have for many years
entered into an agreement always to admire each other's
works; I never fail listening to *her* Music, & she is as constant in eating *my* pies. Such at least was the case till
Henry Hervey made his appearance in Sussex. Before the
arrival of his Aunt in our neighbourhood where she established herself you know about a twelvemonth ago, his visits
to her had been at stated times, and of equal & settled
Duration; but on her removal to the Hall which is within
a walk from our House, they became both more frequent
& longer. This as you may suppose could not be pleasing
to Mrs Diana who is a professed Enemy to everything which
is not directed by Decorum and Formality, or which bears
the least resemblance to Ease and Good-breeding. Nay so
great was her aversion to her Nephews behaviour that I
have often heard her give such hints of it before his face
that had not Henry at such times been engaged in conversation with Eloisa, they must have caught his Attention
and have very much distressed him. The alteration in my
Sisters behaviour which I have before hinted at, now took
place. The Agreement we had entered into of admiring
each others productions she no longer seemed to regard &
tho' I constantly applauded even every Country-dance,
She play'd, yet not even a pidgeon-pye of my making could
obtain from her a single word of approbation. This was
certainly enough to put any one in a Passion; however,
I was as cool as a Cream-cheese and having formed my
plan & concerted a scheme of Revenge, I was determined
                                                        to

to let her have her own way & not even to make her a single
reproach. My Scheme was to treat her as she treated me,
and tho' she might even draw my own Picture or play
Malbrook (which is the only tune I ever really like) not to
say so much as "Thank you Eloisa;" tho' I had for many
years constantly hollowed whenever she played, *Bravo,
Bravissimo, Encora, Da Capo, allegretto, con expressione,*
and *Poco presto* with many other such outlandish words,
all of them as Eloisa told me expressive of my Admiration;
and so indeed I suppose they are, as I see some of them
in every Page of every Music book, being the Sentiments
I imagine of the Composer.

I executed my Plan with great Punctuality; I can not
say success, for Alas! my silence while she played seemed
not in the least to displease her; on the contrary she actually said to me one day "Well Charlotte, I am very glad
to find that you have at last left off that ridiculous custom
of applauding my Execution on the Harpsichord till you
made *my* head ake, & yourself hoarse. I feel very much
obliged to you for keeping your Admiration to yourself."
I never shall forget the very witty answer I made to this
speech. "Eloisa (said I) I beg you would be quite at your
Ease with respect to all such fears in future, for be assured
that I shall always keep my Admiration to myself, & my
own pursuits & never extend it to yours." This was the
only very severe thing I ever said in my Life; not but that
I have often felt myself extremely satirical but it was the
only time I ever made my feelings public.

I suppose there never were two young people who had a
greater affection for each other than Henry & Eloisa; no,
the Love of your Brother for Miss Burton could not be so
strong tho' it might be more violent. You may imagine
therefore how provoked my Sister must have been to have
him play her such a trick. Poor Girl! she still laments his
Death with undiminushed Constancy, notwithstanding he
has been dead more than six weeks; but some people mind
such

such things more than others. The ill state of Health into
which his Loss has thrown her makes her so weak, & so
unable to support the least exertion, that she has been in
tears all this Morning merely from having taken Leave of
Mrs Marlowe who with Her husband, Brother and Child
are to leave Bristol this Morning. I am sorry to have them
go because they are the only family with whom we have
here any acquaintance, but I never thought of crying; to
be sure Eloisa & Mrs Marlowe have always been more together than with me, and have therefore contracted a kind
of affection for each other, which does not make Tears so
inexcusable in them as they would be in me. The Marlowes
are going to Town; Cleveland accompanies them; as
neither Eloisa nor I could catch him I hope you or Matilda
may have better Luck. I know not when we shall leave
Bristol, Eloisa's Spirits are so low that she is very averse
to moving, and yet is certainly by no means mended by
her residence here. A week or two will I hope determine
our Measures—in the mean time believe me

&c—&c—Charlotte Lutterell

Letter the Eighth
Miss Lutterell to Mrs Marlowe

Bristol   April 4th

I FEEL myself greatly obliged to you my dear Emma for
such a mark of your affection as I flatter myself was conveyed in the proposal you made me of our Corresponding;
I assure you that it will be a great releif to me to write to
you and as long as my Health & Spirits will allow me, you
will find me a very constant Correspondent; I will not say
an entertaining one, for you know my situation sufficiently
not to be ignorant that in me Mirth would be improper &
I know my own Heart too well not to be sensible that it
would be unnatural. You must not expect News for we
see no one with whom we are in the least acquainted, or in
whose

whose proceedings we have any Interest. You must not expect Scandal for by the same rule we are equally debarred either from hearing or inventing it.—You must expect from me nothing but the melancholy effusions of a broken Heart which is ever reverting to the Happiness it once enjoyed and which ill supports its present wretchedness. The Possibility of being able to write, to speak, to you, of my lost Henry will be a Luxury to me, & your Goodness will not I know refuse to read what it will so much releive my Heart to write. I once thought that to have what is in general called a Freind (I mean one of my own Sex to whom I might speak with less reserve than to any other person) independant of my Sister would never be an object of my wishes, but how much was I mistaken! Charlotte is too much engrossed by two confidential Correspondents of that sort, to supply the place of one to me, & I hope you will not think me girlishly romantic, when I say that to have some kind and compassionate Freind who might listen to my Sorrows without endeavouring to console me was what I had for some time wished for, when our acquaintance with you, the intimacy which followed it & the particular affectionate Attention you paid me almost from the first, caused me to entertain the flattering Idea of those attentions being improved on a closer acquaintance into a Freindship which, if you were what my wishes formed you would be the greatest Happiness I could be capable of enjoying. To find that such Hopes are realised is a satisfaction indeed, a satisfaction which is now almost the only one I can ever experience.—I feel myself so languid that I am sure were you with me you would oblige me to leave off writing, & I cannot give you a greater proof of my Affection for you than by acting as I know you would wish me to do, whether Absent or Present. I am my dear Emmas sincere freind

E.L.

Letter

Letter the Ninth
Mrs Marlowe to Miss Lutterell

Grosvenor Street, April 10th

NEED I say my dear Eloisa how wellcome your Letter was to me? I cannot give a greater proof of the pleasure I received from it, or of the Desire I feel that our Correspondence may be regular & frequent than by setting you so good an example as I now do in answering it before the end of the week—. But do not imagine that I claim any merit in being so punctual; on the contrary I assure you, that it is a far greater Gratification to me to write to you, than to spend the Evening either at a Concert or a Ball. Mr Marlowe is so desirous of my appearing at some of the Public places every evening that I do not like to refuse him, but at the same time so much wish to remain at Home, that independant of the Pleasure I experience in devoting any portion of my Time to my Dear Eloisa, yet the Liberty I claim from having a Letter to write of spending an Evening at home with my little Boy, You know me well enough to be sensible, will of itself be a sufficient Inducement (if one is necessary) to my maintaining with Pleasure a Correspondence with you. As to the Subjects of your Letters to me, whether Grave or Merry, if they concern you they must be equally interesting to me; Not but that I think the Melancholy Indulgence of your own Sorrows by repeating them & dwelling on them to me, will only encourage and increase them, and that it will be more prudent in you to avoid so sad a subject; but yet knowing as I do what a soothing & Melancholy Pleasure it must afford you, I cannot prevail on myself to deny you so great an Indulgence, and will only insist on your not expecting me to encourage you in it, by my own Letters; on the contrary I intend to fill them with such lively Wit and enlivening Humour as shall even provoke a Smile in the sweet but sorrowfull Countenance of my Eloisa.

In

In the first place you are to learn that I have met your Sisters three freinds Lady Lesley and her Daughters, twice in Public since I have been here. I know you will be impatient to hear my opinion of the Beauty of three Ladies of whom You have heard so much. Now, as you are too ill & too unhappy to be vain, I think I may venture to inform you that I like none of their faces so well as I do your own. Yet they are all handsome—Lady Lesley indeed I have seen before; her Daughters I beleive would in general be said to have a finer face than her Ladyship, and Yet what with the charms of a Blooming Complexion, a little Affectation and a great deal of Small-talk, (in each of which She is superior to the Young Ladies) she will I dare say gain herself as many Admirers as the more regular features of Matilda, & Margaret. I am sure you will agree with me in saying that they can none of them be of a proper size for real Beauty, when you know that two of them are taller & the other shorter than ourselves. In spite of this Defect (or rather by reason of it) there is something very noble & majestic in the figures of the Miss Lesleys, and something agreably Lively in the Appearance of their pretty little Mother-in-law. But tho' one may be majestic & the other Lively, yet the faces of neither possess that Bewitching Sweetness of my Eloisas, which her present Languor is so far from diminushing. What would my Husband and Brother say of us, if they knew all the fine things I have been saying to you in this Letter. It is very hard that a pretty Woman is never to be told she is so by any one of her own Sex, without that person's being suspected to be either her determined Enemy, or her professed Toad-eater. How much more amiable are women in that particular! one man may say forty civil things to another without our supposing that he is ever paid for it, and provided he does his Duty by our Sex, we care not how Polite he is to his own.

Mrs Lutterell will be so good as to accept my Compliments, Charlotte, my Love, and Eloisa the best wishes for
the

the recovery of her Health & Spirits that can be offered
by her Affectionate Freind

E.Marlowe

I am afraid this Letter will be but a poor Specimen of
my Powers in the Witty Way; and your opinion of them
will not be greatly increased when I assure you that I have
been as entertaining as I possibly could—.

Letter the Tenth
From Miss Margaret Lesley to Miss Charlotte Lutterell

Portman Square   April 13th

MY DEAR CHARLOTTE

WE left Lesley-Castle on the 28th of Last Month, and
arrived Safely in London after a Journey of seven Days;
I had the pleasure of finding your Letter here waiting my
Arrival, for which you have my grateful Thanks. Ah! my
dear Freind I every day more regret the serene and tranquil Pleasures of the Castle we have left, in exchange for
the uncertain & unequal Amusements of this vaunted City.
Not that I will pretend to assert that these uncertain and
unequal Amusements are in the least Degree unpleasing
to me; on the contrary I enjoy them extremely and should
enjoy them even more, were I not certain that every appearance I make in Public but rivetts the Chains of those
unhappy Beings whose Passion it is impossible not to pity,
tho' it is out of my power to return. In short my Dear
Charlotte it is my sensibility for the sufferings of so many
amiable Young Men, my Dislike of the extreme Admiration
I meet with, and my Aversion to being so celebrated both
in Public, in Private, in Papers, & in Printshops, that are
the reasons why I cannot more fully enjoy, the Amusements
so various and pleasing of London. How often have I
wished that I possessed as little personal Beauty as you
do;

do; that my figure were as inelegant; my face as unlovely; and my Appearance as unpleasing as yours! But ah! what little chance is there of so desirable an Event; I have had the Small-pox, and must therefore submit to my unhappy fate.

I am now going to intrust you my dear Charlotte with a secret which has long disturbed the tranquillity of my days, and which is of a kind to require the most inviolable Secrecy from you. Last Monday se'night Matilda & I accompanied Lady Lesley to a Rout at the Honourable Mrs Kickabout's; we were escorted by Mr Fitzgerald who is a very amiable Young Man in the main, tho' perhaps a little singular in his Taste—He is in love with Matilda— We had scarcely paid our Compliments to the Lady of the House and curtseyed to half a Score different people when my Attention was attracted by the appearance of a Young Man the most lovely of his Sex, who at that moment entered the Room with another Gentleman & Lady. From the first moment I beheld him, I was certain that on him depended the future Happiness of my Life. Imagine my surprise when he was introduced to me by the name of Cleveland—I instantly recognised him as the Brother of Mrs Marlowe, and the acquaintance of my Charlotte at Bristol. Mr and Mrs M. were the gentleman & Lady who accompanied him. (You do not think Mrs Marlowe handsome?) The elegant address of Mr Cleveland, his polished Manners and Delightful Bow, at once confirmed my attachment. He did not speak; but I can imagine every thing he would have said, had he opened his Mouth. I can picture to myself the cultivated Understanding, the Noble Sentiments, & elegant Language which would have shone so conspicuous in the conversation of Mr Cleveland. The approach of Sir James Gower (one of my too numerous Admirers) prevented the Discovery of any such Powers, by putting an end to a conversation we had never commenced, and by attracting my attention to himself. But oh! how inferior are the accomplishments of Sir James to those

those of his so greatly envied Rival! Sir James is one of the most frequent of our Visitors, & is almost always of our Parties. We have since often met Mr & Mrs Marlowe but no Cleveland—he is always engaged some where else. Mrs Marlowe fatigues me to Death every time I see her by her tiresome conversations about You & Eloisa. She is so Stupid! I live in the hope of seeing her irrisistable Brother to night, as we are going to Lady Flambeau's, who is I know intimate with the Marlowes. Our party will be Lady Lesley, Matilda, Fitzgerald, Sir James Gower, & myself. We see little of Sir George, who is almost always at the Gaming-table. Ah! my poor Fortune, where art thou by this time? We see more of Lady L. who always makes her appearance (highly rouged) at Dinner-time. Alas! what Delightful Jewels will she be decked in this evening at Lady Flambeau's!; Yet I wonder how she can herself delight in wearing them; surely she must be sensible of the ridiculous impropriety of loading her little diminutive figure with such superfluous ornaments; is it possible that she can not know how greatly superior an elegant simplicity is to the most studied apparel? Would she but present them to Matilda & me, how greatly should we be obliged to her. How becoming would Diamonds be on our fine majestic figures! And how surprising it is that such an Idea should never have occurred to *her*. I am sure if I have reflected in this Manner once, I have fifty times. Whenever I see Lady Lesley dressed in them such reflections immediately come across me. My own Mother's Jewels too! But I will say no more on so melancholy a Subject—Let me entertain you with something more pleasing—Matilda had a letter this Morning from Lesley, by which we have the pleasure of finding he is at Naples has turned Roman-catholic, obtained one of the Pope's Bulls for annulling his 1st Marriage and had since actually married a Neapolitan Lady of great Rank & Fortune. He tells us moreover that much the same sort of affair has

befallen

befallen his first wife the worthless Louisa who is likewise at Naples has turned Roman-catholic, and is soon to be married to a Neapolitan Nobleman of great & Distinguished Merit. He says, that they are at present very good Freinds, have quite forgiven all past errors and intend in future to be very good Neighbours. He invites Matilda & me to pay him a visit in Italy and to bring him his little Louisa whom both her Mother, Step-Mother, and himself are equally desirous of beholding. As to our accepting his invitation, it is at present very uncertain; Lady Lesley advises us to go without loss of time; Fitzgerald offers to escort us there, but Matilda has some doubts of the Propriety of such a Scheme—She owns it would be very agreable. I am certain she likes the Fellow. My Father desires us not to be in a hurry, as perhaps if we wait a few months both he & Lady Lesley will do themselves the pleasure of attending us. Lady Lesley says no, that nothing will ever tempt her to forego the Amusements of Brighthelmstone for a Journey to Italy merely to see our Brother. "No (says the disagreable woman) I have once in my life been fool enough to travel I dont know how many hundred Miles to see two of the Family, and I found it did not answer, so Deuce take me, if ever I am so foolish again." So says her Ladyship, but Sir George still perseveres in saying that perhaps in a Month or two, they may accompany us.

Adeiu my Dear Charlotte—
Yr faithful Margaret Lesley

The History of England from the reign of Henry the 4th to the death of Charles the 1st

By a partial, prejudiced, & ignorant Historian.
To Miss Austen eldest daughter of the Revd George Austen, this Work is inscribed with all due respect by
The Author
N.B. There will be very few Dates in this History.

Henry

Henry the 4th

HENRY the 4th ascended the throne of England much to his own satisfaction in the year 1399, after having prevailed on his cousin & predecessor Richard the 2d, to resign it to him, & to retire for the rest of his Life to Pomfret Castle, where he happened to be murdered. It is to be supposed that Henry was married, since he had certainly four sons, but it is not in my power to inform the Reader who was his Wife. Be this as it may, he did not live for ever, but falling ill, his son the Prince of Wales came and took away the crown; whereupon the King made a long speech, for which I must refer the Reader to Shakespear's Plays, & the Prince made a still longer. Things being thus settled between them the King died, & was succeeded by his son Henry who had previously beat Sir William Gascoigne.

Henry the 5th

THIS Prince after he succeeded to the throne grew quite reformed & Amiable, forsaking all his dissipated Companions, & never thrashing Sir William again. During his reign, Lord Cobham was burnt alive, but I forget what for. His Majesty then turned his thoughts to France, where he went & fought the famous Battle of Agincourt. He afterwards married the King's daughter Catherine, a very agreable Woman by Shakespear's account. In spite of all this however he died, and was succeeded by his son Henry.

Henry the 6th

I CANNOT say much for this Monarch's Sense—Nor would I if I could, for he was a Lancastrian. I suppose you know all about the Wars between him & The Duke of York who was of the right side; If you do not, you had better read
some

some other History, for I shall not be very diffuse in this, meaning by it only to vent my Spleen *against*, & shew my Hatred *to* all those people whose parties or principles do not suit with mine, & not to give information. This King married Margaret of Anjou, a Woman whose distresses & Misfortunes were so great as almost to make me who hate her, pity her. It was in this reign that Joan of Arc lived & made such a *row* among the English. They should not have burnt her—but they did. There were several Battles between the Yorkists & Lancastrians, in which the former (as they ought) usually conquered. At length they were entirely over come; The King was murdered—The Queen was sent home—& Edward the 4th Ascended the Throne.

Edward the 4th

THIS Monarch was famous only for his Beauty & his Courage, of which the Picture we have here given of him, & his undaunted Behaviour in marrying one Woman while he was engaged to another, are sufficient proofs. His wife was Elizabeth Woodville, a Widow, who, poor Woman!, was afterwards confined in a Convent by that Monster of Iniquity & Avarice Henry the 7th. One of Edward's Mistresses was Jane Shore, who has had a play written about her, but it is a tragedy & therefore not worth reading. Having performed all these noble actions, his Majesty died, & was succeeded by his Son.

Edward the 5th

THIS unfortunate Prince lived so little a while that no body had time to draw his picture. He was murdered by his Uncle's Contrivance, whose name was Richard the 3d.

Richard

Richard the 3rd

THE Character of this Prince has been in general very severely treated by Historians, but as he was *York*, I am rather inclined to suppose him a very respectable Man. It has indeed been confidently asserted that he killed his two Nephews & his Wife, but it has also been declared that he did *not* kill his two Nephews, which I am inclined to beleive true; & if this is the case, it may also be affirmed that he did not kill his Wife, for if Perkin Warbeck was really the Duke of York, why might not Lambert Simnel be the Widow of Richard. Whether innocent or guilty, he did not reign long in peace, for Henry Tudor E. of Richmond as great a Villain as ever lived, made a great fuss about getting the Crown & having killed the King at the battle of Bosworth, he succeeded to it.

Henry the 7th

THIS Monarch soon after his accession married the Princess Elizabeth of York, by which alliance he plainly proved that he thought his own right inferior to hers, tho' he pretended to the contrary. By this Marriage he had two sons & two daughters, the elder of which daughters was married to the King of Scotland & had the happiness of being grandmother to one of the first Characters in the World. But of *her*, I shall have occasion to speak more at large in future. The Youngest, Mary, married first the King of France & secondly the D. of Suffolk, by whom she had one daughter, afterwards the Mother of Lady Jane Grey, who tho' inferior to her lovely Cousin the Queen of Scots, was yet an amiable young woman and famous for reading Greek while other people were hunting. It was in the reign of Henry the 7th that Perkin Warbeck & Lambert Simnel before mentioned made their appearance, the former of whom was set in the Stocks, took shelter in Beaulieu
Abbey,

Abbey, & was beheaded with the Earl of Warwick, & the latter was taken into the King's Kitchen. His Majesty died, & was succeeded by his son Henry whose only merit was his not being *quite* so bad as his daughter Elizabeth.

Henry the 8th

It would be an affront to my Readers were I to suppose that they were not as well acquainted with the particulars of this King's reign as I am myself. It will therefore be saving *them* the task of reading again what they have read before, & *myself* the trouble of writing what I do not perfectly recollect, by giving only a slight sketch of the principal Events which marked his reign. Among these may be ranked Cardinal Wolsey's telling the father Abbott of Leicester Abbey that "he was come to lay his bones among them", the reformation in Religion, & the King's riding through the Streets of London with Anna Bullen. It is however but Justice, & my Duty to declare that this amiable Woman was entirely innocent of the Crimes with which she was accused, of which her Beauty, her Elegance, & her Sprightliness were sufficient proofs, not to mention her solemn protestations of Innocence, the weakness of the Charges against her, and the king's Character; all of which add some confirmation, tho' perhaps but slight ones when in comparison with those before alledged in her favour. Tho' I do not profess giving many dates, yet as I think it proper to give some & shall of course make choice of those which it is most necessary for the Reader to know, I think it right to inform him that her letter to the King was dated on the 6th of May. The Crimes & Cruelties of this Prince, were too numerous to be mentioned, (as this history I trust has fully shown;) & nothing can be said in his vindication, but that his abolishing Religious Houses & leaving them to the ruinous depredations of time has been of infinite use to the landscape of England in general, which probably

was

was a principal motive for his doing it, since otherwise why should a Man who was of no Religion himself be at so much trouble to abolish one which had for Ages been established in the Kingdom. His Majesty's 5th wife was the Duke of Norfolk's Neice who, tho' universally acquitted of the crimes for which she was beheaded, has been by many people supposed to have led an abandoned Life before her Marriage—of this however I have many doubts, since she was a relation of that noble Duke of Norfolk who was so warm in the Queen of Scotland's cause, & who at last fell a victim to it. The king's last wife contrived to survive him, but with difficulty effected it. He was succeeded by his only son Edward.

Edward the 6th

As this prince was only nine years old at the time of his Father's death, he was considered by many people as too young to govern, & the late King happening to be of the same opinion, his mother's Brother the Duke of Somerset was chosen Protector of the realm during his minority. This Man was on the whole of a very amiable Character, & is somewhat of a favourite with me, tho' I would by no means pretend to affirm that he was equal to those first of Men Robert Earl of Essex, Delamere, or Gilpin. He was beheaded, of which he might with reason have been proud, had he known that such was the death of Mary Queen of Scotland; but as it was impossible that He should be conscious of what had never happened, it does not appear that he felt particularly delighted with the manner of it. After his decease the Duke of Northumberland had the care of the King & the Kingdom, & performed his trust of both so well that the King died & the Kingdom was left to his daughter in law the Lady Jane Grey, who has been already mentioned as reading Greek. Whether she really understood that language or whether such a Study proceeded
only

only from an excess of vanity for which I beleive she was always rather remarkable, is uncertain. Whatever might be the cause, she preserved the same appearance of knowledge, & contempt of what was generally esteemed pleasure, during the whole of her Life, for she declared herself displeased with being appointed Queen, and while conducting to the Scaffold, she wrote a Sentence in Latin & another in Greek on seeing the dead Body of her Husband accidentally passing that way.

Mary

THIS Woman had the good luck of being advanced to the throne of England, inspite of the superior pretensions, Merit, & *Beauty* of her Cousins Mary Queen of Scotland & Jane Grey. Nor can I pity the Kingdom for the misfortunes they experienced during her Reign, since they fully deserved them, for having allowed her to succeed her Brother—which was a double peice of folly, since they might have foreseen that as she died without Children, she would be succeeded by that disgrace to humanity, that pest of society, Elizabeth. Many were the people who fell Martyrs to the Protestant Religion during her reign; I suppose not fewer than a dozen. She married Philip King of Spain who in her Sister's reign was famous for building Armadas. She died without issue, & then the dreadful moment came in which the destroyer of all comfort, the deceitful Betrayer of trust reposed in her, & the Murderess of her Cousin succeeded to the Throne.

Elizabeth

IT was the peculiar Misfortune of this Woman to have bad Ministers—Since wicked as she herself was, she could not have committed such extensive mischeif, had not these vile & abandoned men connived at, & encouraged her in

her

her crimes. I know that it has by many people been asserted & beleived that Lord Burleigh, Sir Francis Walsingham, & the rest of those who filled the cheif offices of State were deserving, experienced, & able Ministers. But oh! how blinded such Writers & such Readers must be to true Merit, to Merit despised, neglected & defamed, if they can persist in such opinions when they reflect that these Men, these boasted Men were such Scandals to their Country & their Sex as to allow & assist their Queen in confining for the space of nineteen years, a *Woman* who if the claims of Relationship & Merit were no avail, yet as a Queen & as one who condescended to place confidence in her, had every reason to expect Assistance & Protection; and at length in allowing Elizabeth to bring this amiable Woman to an untimely, unmerited, and scandalous Death. Can any one if he reflects but for a moment on this blot, this everlasting blot upon their Understanding & their Character, allow any praise to Lord Burleigh or Sir Francis Walsingham? Oh! what must this bewitching Princess whose only freind was then the Duke of Norfolk, and whose only ones are now Mr Whitaker, Mrs Lefroy, Mrs Knight & myself, who was abandoned by her son, confined by her Cousin, Abused, reproached & villified by all, what must not her most noble mind have suffered when informed that Elizabeth had given orders for her Death! Yet she bore it with a most unshaken fortitude; firm in her Mind; Constant in her Religion; & prepared herself to meet the cruel fate to which she was doomed, with a magnanimity that could alone proceed from conscious Innocence. And yet could you Reader have beleived it possible that some hardened & zealous Protestants have even abused her for that Steadfastness in the Catholic Religion which reflected on her so much credit? But this is a striking proof of *their* narrow Souls & prejudiced Judgements who accuse her. She was executed in the Great Hall at Fortheringay Castle (sacred Place!) on Wednesday the 8th of February 1586—

to

to the everlasting Reproach of Elizabeth, her Ministers, and of England in general. It may not be unnecessary before I entirely conclude my account of this ill-fated Queen, to observe that she had been accused of several crimes during the time of her reigning in Scotland, of which I now most seriously do assure my Reader that she was entirely innocent; having never been guilty of anything more than Imprudencies into which she was betrayed by the openness of her Heart, her Youth, & her Education. Having I trust by this assurance entirely done away every Suspicion & every doubt which might have arisen in the Reader's mind, from what other Historians have written of her, I shall proceed to mention the remaining Events that marked Elizabeth's reign. It was about this time that Sir Francis Drake the first English Navigator who sailed round the World, lived, to be the ornament of his Country & his profession. Yet great as he was, & justly celebrated as a Sailor, I cannot help foreseeing that he will be equalled in this or the next Century by one who tho' now but young, already promises to answer all the ardent & sanguine expectations of his Relations & Freinds, amongst whom I may class the amiable Lady to whom this work is dedicated, & my no less amiable Self.

Though of a different profession, and shining in a different Sphere of Life, yet equally conspicuous in the Character of an *Earl*, as Drake was in that of a *Sailor*, was Robert Devereux Lord Essex. This unfortunate young Man was not unlike in Character to that equally unfortunate one *Frederic Delamere*. The simile may be carried still farther, & Elizabeth the torment of Essex may be compared to the Emmeline of Delamere. It would be endless to recount the misfortunes of this noble & gallant Earl. It is sufficient to say that he was beheaded on the 25th of Febry, after having been Lord Leuitenant of Ireland, after having clapped his hand on his sword, and after performing many other services to his Country. Elizabeth did not

long

long survive his loss, & died *so* miserable that were it not an injury to the memory of Mary I should pity her.

James the 1st

Though this King had some faults, among which & as the most principal, was his allowing his Mother's death, yet considered on the whole I cannot help liking him. He married Anne of Denmark, and had several Children; fortunately for him his eldest son Prince Henry died before his father or he might have experienced the evils which befell his unfortunate Brother.

As I am myself partial to the roman catholic religion, it is with infinite regret that I am obliged to blame the Behaviour of any Member of it; yet Truth being I think very excusable in an Historian, I am necessitated to say that in this reign the roman Catholics of England did not behave like Gentlemen to the protestants. Their Behaviour indeed to the Royal Family & both Houses of Parliament might justly be considered by them as very uncivil, and even Sir Henry Percy tho' certainly the best bred Man of the party, had none of that general politeness which is so universally pleasing, as his Attentions were entirely confined to Lord Mounteagle.

Sir Walter Raleigh flourished in this & the preceeding reign, & is by many people held in great veneration & respect—But as he was an enemy of the noble Essex, I have nothing to say in praise of him, & must refer all those who may wish to be acquainted with the particulars of his Life, to Mr Sheridan's play of the Critic, where they will find many interesting Anecdotes as well of him as of his freind Sir Christopher Hatton.—. His Majesty was of that amiable disposition which inclines to Freindships, & in such points was possessed of a keener penetration in Discovering Merit than many other people. I once heard an excellent Sharade on a Carpet, of which the subject I am now

now on reminds me, and as I think it may afford my Readers some Amusement to *find it out*, I shall here take the liberty of presenting it to them.

SHARADE

My first is what my second was to King James the 1st, and you tread on my whole.

The principal favourites of his Majesty were Car, who was afterwards created Earl of Somerset and whose name may have some share in the above mentioned Sharade, & George Villiers afterwards Duke of Buckingham. On his Majesty's death he was succeeded by his son Charles.

Charles the 1st

THIS amiable Monarch seems born to have suffered Misfortunes equal to those of his lovely Grandmother; Misfortunes which he could not deserve since he was her descendant. Never certainly was there before so many detestable Characters at one time in England as in this period of its History; Never were amiable Men so scarce. The number of them throughout the whole Kingdom amounting only to *five*, besides the inhabitants of Oxford who were always loyal to their King & faithful to his interests. The names of this noble five who never forgot the duty of the Subject, or swerved from their attachment to his Majesty, were as follows,—The King himself, ever stedfast in his own support—Archbishop Laud, Earl of Strafford, Viscount Faulkland & Duke of Ormond who were scarcely less strenuous or zealous in the cause. While the Villains of the time would make too long a list to be written or read; I shall therefore content myself with mentioning the leaders of the Gang. Cromwell, Fairfax, Hampden, & Pym may be considered as the original Causers of all the disturbances Distresses & Civil Wars in which England for many years was embroiled. In this reign as well as in that of Elizabeth, I am obliged in spite of my Attachment to the Scotch, to consider

consider them as equally guilty with the generality of the English, since they dared to think differently from their Sovereign, to forget the Adoration which as *Stuarts* it was their Duty to pay them, to rebel against, dethrone & imprison the unfortunate Mary; to oppose, to deceive, and to sell the no less unfortunate Charles. The Events of this Monarch's reign are too numerous for my pen, and indeed the recital of any Events (except what I make myself) is uninteresting to me; my principal reason for undertaking the History of England being to prove the innocence of the Queen of Scotland, which I flatter myself with having effectually done, and to abuse Elizabeth, tho' I am rather fearful of having fallen short in the latter part of my Scheme.—. As therefore it is not my intention to give any particular account of the distresses into which this King was involved through the misconduct & Cruelty of his Parliament, I shall satisfy myself with vindicating him from the Reproach of Arbitrary & tyrannical Government with which he has often been Charged. This, I feel, is not difficult to be done, for with one argument I am certain of satisfying every sensible & well disposed person whose opinions have been properly guided by a good Education—& this Arguement is that he was a Stuart.

Finis
Saturday Nov: 26th 1791

A COLLECTION OF LETTERS

To Miss Cooper

COUSIN

Conscious of the Charming Character which in every Country, & every Clime in Christendom is Cried, Concerning you, with Caution & Care I Commend to your Charitable Criticism this Clever Collection of Curious Comments, which have been Carefully Culled, Collected & Classed by your Comical Cousin

The Author

A

A Collection of Letters

Letter the first

From A Mother to her freind

My Children begin now to claim all my attention in a different Manner from that in which they have been used to receive it, as they are now arrived at that age when it is necessary for them in some measure to become conversant with the World. My Augusta is 17 & her Sister scarcely a twelve-month younger. I flatter myself that their education has been such as will not disgrace their appearance in the World, & that *they* will not disgrace their Education I have every reason to beleive. Indeed they are sweet Girls—. Sensible yet unaffected—Accomplished yet Easy—. Lively yet Gentle—. As their progress in every thing they have learnt has been always the same, I am willing to forget the difference of age, and to introduce them together into Public. This very Evening is fixed on as their first entrée into life, as we are to drink tea with Mrs Cope & her Daughter. I am glad that we are to meet no one for my Girls sake, as it would be awkward for them to enter too wide a Circle on the very first day. But we shall proceed by degrees—. Tomorrow Mr Stanly's family will drink tea with us, and perhaps the Miss Phillips will meet them. On Tuesday we shall pay Morning-Visits— On Wednesday we are to dine at Westbrook. On Thursday we have Company at home. On Friday we are to be at a private concert at Sir John Wynne's—& on Saturday we expect Miss Dawson to call in the morning,—which will complete my Daughters Introduction into Life. How they will bear so much dissipation I cannot imagine; of their Spirits I have no fear, I only dread their health.

This mighty affair is now happily over, & my Girls *are out.* As the moment approached for our departure, you

can

can have no idea how the sweet Creatures trembled with fear & expectation. Before the Carriage drove to the door, I called them into my dressing-room, & as soon as they were seated thus addressed them. "My dear Girls the moment is now arrived when I am to reap the rewards of all my Anxieties and Labours towards you during your Education. You are this Evening to enter a World in which you will meet with many wonderfull Things; Yet let me warn you against suffering yourselves to be meanly swayed by the Follies & Vices of others, for beleive me my beloved Children that if you do—I shall be very sorry for it." They both assured me that they would ever remember my advice with Gratitude, & follow it with Attention; That they were prepared to find a World full of things to amaze & shock them : but that they trusted their behaviour would never give me reason to repent the Watchful Care with which I had presided over their infancy & formed their Minds—. "With such expectations & such intentions (cried I) I can have nothing to fear from you—& can chearfully conduct you to Mrs Cope's without a fear of your being seduced by her Example or contaminated by her Follies. Come, then my Children (added I) the Carriage is driving to the door, & I will not a moment delay the happiness you are so impatient to enjoy." When we arrived at Warleigh, poor Augusta could hardly breathe, while Margaret was all Life & Rapture. "The long-expected Moment is now arrived (said she) and we shall soon be in the World."— In a few Moments we were in Mrs Cope's parlour—, where with her daughter she sat ready to receive us. I observed with delight the impression my Children made on them—. They were indeed two sweet, elegant-looking Girls, & tho' somewhat abashed from the peculiarity of their Situation, Yet there was an ease in their Manners & Address which could not fail of pleasing—. Imagine my dear Madam how delighted I must have been in beholding as I did, how attentively they observed every

F   object

object they saw, how disgusted with some Things, how enchanted with others, how astonished at all! On the whole however they returned in raptures with the World, its Inhabitants, & Manners.

Yrs Ever—A–F–.

Letter the second
From a Young lady crossed in Love to her freind—

WHY should this last disappointment hang so heavily on my Spirits? Why should I feel it more, why should it wound me deeper than those I have experienced before? Can it be that I have a greater affection for Willoughby than I had for his amiable predecessors? Or is it that our feelings become more acute from being often wounded? I must suppose my dear Belle that this is the Case, since I am not conscious of being more sincerely attached to Willoughby than I was to Neville, Fitzowen, or either of the Crawfords, for all of whom I once felt the most lasting affection that ever warmed a Woman's heart. Tell me then dear Belle why I still sigh when I think of the faithless Edward, or why I weep when I behold his Bride, for too surely this is the case—. My Freinds are all alarmed for me; They fear my declining health; they lament my want of Spirits; they dread the effects of both. In hopes of releiving my Melancholy, by directing my thoughts to other objects, they have invited several of their freinds to spend the Christmas with us. Lady Bridget Dashwood & her Sister-in-Law Miss Jane are expected on Friday; & Colonel Seaton's family will be with us next week. This is all most kindly meant by my Uncle & Cousins; but what can the presence of a dozen indifferent people do to me, but weary & distress me—. I will not finish my Letter till some of our Visitors are arrived.

Friday

Friday Evening—

Lady Bridget came this Morning, and with her, her sweet Sister Miss Jane—. Although I have been acquainted with this charming Woman above fifteen years, Yet I never before observed how lovely she is. She is now about 35, & in spite of sickness, Sorrow and Time is more blooming than I ever saw a Girl of 17. I was delighted with her, the moment she entered the house, & she appeared equally pleased with me, attaching herself to me during the remainder of the day. There is something so sweet, so mild in her Countenance, that she seems more than Mortal. Her Conversation is as bewitching as her appearance—; I could not help telling her how much she engaged my Admiration—. —"Oh! Miss Jane" (said I)—and stopped from an inability at the moment of expressing myself as I could wish—"Oh! Miss Jane" (I repeated)—I could not think of words to suit my feelings—She seemed waiting for my Speech—. I was confused—distressed—. My thoughts were bewildered—and I could only add "How do you do?" She saw & felt for my embarrassment & with admirable presence of mind releived me from it by saying—"My dear Sophia be not uneasy at having exposed Yourself—I will turn the Conversation without appearing to notice it." Oh! how I loved her for her kindness! "Do you ride as much as you used to do?" said she—. "I am advised to ride by my Physician, We have delightful Rides round us, I have a charming horse, am uncommonly fond of the Amusement," replied I quite recovered from my confusion, "& in short I ride a great deal." "You are in the right my Love," said She, Then repeating the following Line which was an extempore & equally adapted to recommend both Riding & Candour—

"Ride where you may, Be Candid where You can," She added, "*I* rode once, but it is many years ago"—She spoke this in so Low & tremulous a Voice, that I was silent— Struck with her Manner of Speaking I could make no reply.

"I

"I have not ridden, continued she fixing her Eyes on my face, since I was married." I was never so surprised— "Married, Ma'am,!" I repeated. "You may well wear that look of astonishment, said she, since what I have said must appear improbable to you—Yet nothing is more true than that I once was married."

"Then why are you called Miss Jane?"

"I married, my Sophia without the consent or know-ledge of my father—the late Admiral Annesley. It was therefore necessary to keep the secret from him & from every one, till some fortunate opportunity might offer of revealing it—. Such an opportunity alas! was but too soon given in the death of my dear Capt Dashwood—Pardon these tears, continued Miss Jane wiping her Eyes, I owe them to my Husband's Memory, He fell my Sophia, while fighting for his Country in America after a most happy Union of seven years—. My Children, two sweet Boys & a Girl, who had constantly resided with my Father & me, passing with him & with every one as the Children of a Brother (tho' I had ever been an only child) had as yet been the Comforts of my Life. But no sooner had I lossed my Henry, than these sweet Creatures fell sick & died—. Conceive dear Sophia what my feelings must have been when as an Aunt I attended my Children to their early Grave—. My Father did not survive them many weeks— He died, poor Good old Man, happily ignorant to his last hour of my Marriage."

"But did you not own it, & assume his name at your husband's death?"

"No ; I could not bring myself to do it; more especially when in my Children, I lost all inducement for doing it. Lady Bridget, and Yourself are the only persons who are in the knowledge of my having ever been either Wife or Mother. As I could not prevail on myself to take the name of Dashwood (a name which after my Henry's death I could never hear without emotion) and as I was conscious

of

of having no right to that of Annesley, I dropt all thoughts of either, & have made it a point of bearing only my Christian one since my Father's death." She paused— "Oh! my dear Miss Jane (said I) how infinitely am I obliged to you for so entertaining a Story! You cannot think how it has diverted me! But have you quite done?"

"I have only to add my dear Sophia, that my Henry's elder Brother dieing about the same time, Lady Bridget became a Widow like myself, and as we had always loved each other in idea from the high Character in which we had ever been spoken of, though we had never met, we determined to live together. We wrote to one another on the same subject by the same post, so exactly did our feelings & our Actions coincide: We both eagerly embraced the proposals we gave & received of becoming one family, and have from that time lived together in the greatest affection."

"And is this all?" said I, "I hope you have not done."

"Indeed I have; and did you ever hear a Story more pathetic?"

"I never did—and it is for that reason it pleases me so much, for when one is unhappy nothing is so delightful to one's sensations as to hear of equal Misery."

"Ah! but my Sophia why *are you* unhappy?"

"Have you not heard Madam of Willoughby's Marriage?" "But my Love why lament *his* perfidy, when you bore so well that of many young Men before?" "Ah! Madam, I was used to it then, but when Willoughby broke his Engagements I had not been dissapointed for half a year." "Poor Girl!" said Miss Jane.

Letter the third
From A young Lady in distress'd Circumstances to her freind.

A FEW days ago I was at a private Ball given by Mr Ashburnham. As my Mother never goes out she entrusted me

to

to the care of Lady Greville who did me the honour of calling for me in her way & of allowing me to sit forwards,
which is a favour about which I am very indifferent
especially as I know it is considered as confering a great
obligation on me. "So Miss Maria (said her Ladyship as
she saw me advancing to the door of the Carriage) you
seem very smart tonight—*My* poor Girls will appear quite
to disadvantage by *you*. I only hope your Mother may not
have distressed herself to set *you* off. Have you got a new
Gown on?"

"Yes Ma'am," replied I with as much indifference as I
could assume.

"Aye, and a fine one too I think—(feeling it, as by her
permission I seated myself by her) I dare say it is all very
smart—But I must own, for you know I always speak my
mind, that I think it was quite a needless peice of expence
—Why could not you have worn your old striped one? It
is not my way to find fault with people because they are
poor, for I always think that they are more to be despised
& pitied than blamed for it, especially if they cannot help
it, but at the same time I must say that in my opinion your
old striped Gown would have been quite fine enough for
its wearer—for to tell you the truth (I always speak my
mind) I am very much afraid that one half of the people
in the room will not know whether you have a Gown on
or not—But I suppose you intend to make your fortune tonight—Well, the sooner the better; & I wish you success."

"Indeed Ma'am I have no such intention.—"

"Who ever heard a Young Lady own that she was a
Fortune-hunter?" Miss Greville laughed, but I am sure
Ellen felt for me.

"Was your Mother gone to bed before you left her?"
said her Ladyship.

"Dear Ma'am" said Ellen, "it is but nine o'clock."

"True Ellen, but Candles cost money, and Mrs Williams
is too wise to be extravagant."

"She

"She was just sitting down to supper Ma'am."

"And what had she got for Supper?" "I did not observe". "Bread & Cheese I suppose." "I should never wish for a better supper", said Ellen. "You have never any reason" replied her Mother, "as a better is always provided for you." Miss Greville laughed excessively, as she constantly does at her Mother's wit.

Such is the humiliating Situation in which I am forced to appear while riding in her Ladyship's Coach—I dare not be impertinent, as my Mother is always admonishing me to be humble & patient if I wish to make my way in the world. She insists on my accepting every invitation of Lady Greville, or you may be certain that I would never enter either her House, or her Coach, with the disagreable certainty I always have of being abused for my Poverty while I am in them.— When we arrived at Ashburnham, it was nearly ten o'clock, which was an hour and a half later than we were desired to be there; but Lady Greville is too fashionable (or fancies herself to be so) to be punctual. The Dancing however was not begun as they waited for Miss Greville. I had not been long in the room before I was engaged to dance by Mr. Bernard but just as we were going to stand up, he recollected that his Servant had got his white Gloves, & immediately ran out to fetch them. In the mean time the Dancing began & Lady Greville in passing to another room went exactly before me.— She saw me & instantly stopping, said to me though there were several people close to us ;

"Hey day, Miss Maria! What cannot you get a partner? Poor Young Lady! I am afraid your new Gown was put on for nothing. But do not despair; perhaps you may get a hop before the Evening is over." So saying, she passed on without hearing my repeated assurance of being engaged, & leaving me very provoked at being so exposed before every one—Mr Bernard however soon returned & by coming to me the moment he entered the room, and

leading

leading me to the Dancers, my Character I hope was cleared
from the imputation Lady Greville had thrown on it, in
the eyes of all the old Ladies who had heard her speech.
I soon forgot all my vexations in the pleasure of dancing
and of having the most agreable partner in the room. As
he is moreover heir to a very large Estate I could see that
Lady Greville did not look very well pleased when she
found who had been his Choice.— She was determined to
mortify me, and accordingly when we were sitting down
between the dances, she came to me with *more* than her
usual insulting importance attended by Miss Mason and
said loud enough to be heard by half the people in the
room, "Pray Miss Maria in what way of business was your
Grandfather? for Miss Mason & I cannot agree whether
he was a Grocer or a Bookbinder " I saw that she wanted
to mortify me and was resolved if I possibly could to
prevent her seeing that her scheme succeeded. "Neither
Madam; he was a Wine Merchant." "Aye, I knew he was
in some such low way—He broke did not he?" "I beleive
not Ma'am." "Did not he abscond?" "I never heard that
he did." "At least he died insolvent?" "I was never told
so before." "Why was not your Father as poor as a Rat?"
"I fancy not;" "Was not he in the Kings Bench once?"
"I never saw him there." *She* gave me *such* a look, &
turned away in a great passion; while I was half delighted
with myself for my impertinence, & half afraid of being
thought too saucy. As Lady Greville was extremely angry
with me, she took no further notice of me all the evening,
and indeed had I been in favour I should have been equally
neglected, as she was got into a party of great folks & she
never speaks to me when she can to any one else. Miss
Greville was with her Mother's party at Supper, but Ellen
preferred staying with the Bernards & me. We had a very
pleasant Dance & as Lady G— slept all the way home, I
had a very comfortable ride.

The next day while we were at dinner Lady Greville's
Coach

Coach stopped at the door, for that is the time of day she generally contrives it should. She sent in a message by the Servant to say that "she should not get out but that Miss Maria must come to the Coach-door, as she wanted to speak to her, and that she must make haste & come immediately—" "What an impertinent Message Mama!" said I— "Go Maria—" replied She—Accordingly I went & was obliged to stand there at her Ladyships pleasure though the Wind was extremely high and very cold.

"Why I think Miss Maria you are not quite so smart as you were last night—But I did not come to examine your dress, but to tell you that you may dine with us the day after tomorrow—Not tomorrow, remember, do not come tomorrow, for we expect Lord and Lady Clermont & Sir Thomas Stanley's family—There will be no occasion for your being very fine for I shant send the Carriage—If it rains you may take an umbrella—" I could hardly help laughing at hearing her give me leave to keep myself dry— "and pray remember to be in time, for I shant wait—I hate my Victuals over-done—But you need not come *before* the time—How does your Mother do—? She is at dinner is not she?" "Yes Ma'am we were in the middle of dinner when your Ladyship came." "I am afraid you find it very cold Maria." said Ellen. "Yes, it is an horrible East wind"—said her Mother—"I assure you I can hardly bear the window down—But you are used to be blown about the wind Miss Maria & that is what has made your Complexion so ruddy & coarse. You young Ladies who cannot often ride in a Carriage never mind what weather you trudge in, or how the wind shews your legs. I would not have *my* Girls stand out of doors as you do in such a day as this. But some sort of people have no feelings either of cold or Delicacy—Well, remember that we shall expect you on Thursday at 5 o'clock—You must tell your Maid to come for you at night—There will be no Moon—and you will have an horrid walk home—My Compts to your
                                                            Mother—

Mother—I am afraid your dinner will be cold—Drive on—" And away she went, leaving me in a great passion with her as she always does.

Maria Williams

Letter the fourth

From a young Lady rather impertinent to her freind.

WE dined yesterday with Mr Evelyn where we were introduced to a very agreable looking Girl his cousin. I was extremely pleased with her appearance, for added to the charms of an engaging face, her manner & voice had something peculiarly interesting in them. So much so, that they inspired me with a great curiosity to know the history of her Life, who were her Parents, where she came from, and what had befallen her, for it was then only known that she was a relation of Mrs Evelyn, and that her name was Grenville. In the evening a favourable opportunity offered to me of attempting at least to know what I wished to know, for every one played at Cards but Mrs Evelyn, My Mother, Dr Drayton, Miss Grenville and myself, and as the two former were engaged in a whispering Conversation, & the Doctor fell asleep, we were of necessity obliged to entertain each other. This was what I wished and being determined not to remain in ignorance for want of asking, I began the Conversation in the following Manner.

"Have you been long in Essex Ma'am?"

"I arrived on Tuesday".

"You came from Derbyshire?"

"No Ma'am!" appearing surprised at my question, "from Suffolk." You will think this a good dash of mine my dear Mary, but you will know that I am not wanting

for

for Impudence when I have any end in veiw. "Are you pleased with the Country Miss Grenville? Do you find it equal to the one you have left?"

"Much superior Ma'am in point of Beauty." She sighed. I longed to know for why.

"But the face of any Country however beautiful" said I, "can be but a poor consolation for the loss of one's dearest Freinds." She shook her head, as if she felt the truth of what I said. My Curiosity was so much raised, that I was resolved at any rate to satisfy it.

"You regret having left Suffolk then Miss Grenville?" "Indeed I do." You were born there I suppose?" "Yes Ma'am I was & passed many happy years there—".

"That is a great comfort—said I—I hope Ma'am that you never spent any *un*happy one's there."

"Perfect Felicity is not the property of Mortals, & no one has a right to expect uninterrupted Happiness—*Some* Misfortunes I have certainly met with—."

"*What* Misfortunes dear Ma'am?" replied I, burning with impatience to know every thing. "*None* Ma'am I hope that have been the effect of any wilfull fault in me." "I dare say not Ma'am, & have no doubt but that any sufferings you may have experienced could arise only from the cruelties of Relations or the Errors of Freinds." She sighed—"You seem unhappy my dear Miss Grenville—Is it in my power to soften your Misfortunes." " *Your* power Ma'am replied she extremely surprised; it is in *no ones* power to make me happy." She pronounced these words in so mournfull & solemn an accent, that for some time I had not courage to reply. I was actually silenced. I recovered myself however in a few moments & looking at her with all the affection I could, "My dear Miss Grenville said I, you appear extremely young—& may probably stand in need of some one's advice whose regard for you, joined to superior Age, perhaps superior Judgement might authorise her to give it—. I am that person, & I now challenge you

to

to accept the offer I make you of my Confidence and Freindship, in return to which I shall only ask for yours—."

"You are extremely obliging Ma'am—said She—& I
am highly flattered by your attention to me—. But I am
in no difficulty, no doubt, no uncertainty of situation in
which any Advice can be wanted. Whenever I am however
continued she brightening into a complaisant smile, I shall
know where to apply."

I bowed, but felt a good deal mortified by such a repulse;
Still however I had not given up my point. I found that
by the appearance of Sentiment & Freindship nothing was
to be gained & determined therefore to renew my Attacks
by Questions & Suppositions. "Do you intend staying
long in this part of England Miss Grenville?"

"Yes Ma'am, some time I beleive."

"But how will Mr & Mrs Grenville bear your Absence?"

"They are neither of them alive Ma'am."

This was an answer I did not expect—I was quite
silenced & never felt so awkward in my Life—.

Letter the fifth

From a Young Lady very much in love to her Freind.

My Uncle gets more stingy, my Aunt more particular, &
I more in love every day. What shall we all be at this rate
by the end of the year! I had this morning the happiness
of receiving the following Letter from my dear Musgrove.

Sackville St: Jan:ry 7th

It is a month to day since I beheld my lovely Henrietta,
& the sacred anniversary must & shall be kept in a manner
becoming the day—by writing to her. Never shall I forget
the moment when her Beauties first broke on my sight—
No time as you well know can erase it from my Memory.

It

It was at Lady Scudamores. Happy Lady Scudamore to live within a mile of the divine Henrietta! When the lovely Creature first entered the room, Oh! what were my sensations? The sight of you was like the sight of a wonderful fine Thing. I started—I gazed at her with Admiration— She appeared every moment more Charming, and the unfortunate Musgrove became a Captive to your Charms before I had time to look about me. Yes Madam, I had the happiness of adoring you, an happiness for which I cannot be too grateful. "What said he to himself is Musgrove allowed to die for Henrietta? Enviable Mortal; and may he pine for her who is the object of universal Admiration, who is adored by a Colonel, & toasted by a Baronet! Adorable Henrietta how beautiful you are! I declare you are quite divine! You are more than Mortal. You are an angel. You are Venus herself. In short Madam you are the prettiest Girl I ever saw in my Life—& her beauty is encreased in her Musgroves Eyes, by permitting him to love her & allowing me to hope. And Ah! Angelic Miss Henrietta Heaven is my Witness how ardently I do hope for the death of your villanous Uncle & his Abandoned Wife, Since my fair one will not consent to be mine till their decease has placed her in affluence above what my fortune can procure—. Though it is an improvable Estate—. Cruel Henrietta to persist in such a resolution! I am at present with my Sister where I mean to continue till my own house which tho' an excellent one is at present somewhat out of repair, is ready to receive me. Amiable princess of my Heart farewell—Of that heart which trembles while it signs itself your most ardent Admirer & devoted humble Serv.t.

T. Musgrove

There is a pattern for a Love-letter Matilda! Did you ever read such a masterpeice of Writing? Such Sense, Such Sentiment, Such purity of Thought, Such flow of Language & such unfeigned Love in one Sheet? No, never

I

I can answer for it, since a Musgrove is not to be met with
by every Girl. Oh! how I long to be with him! I intend
to send him the following in answer to his Letter tomorrow.

My dearest Musgrove—. Words can not express how
happy your Letter made me; I thought I should have cried
for Joy, for I love you better than any body in the World.
I think you the most amiable, & the handsomest Man in
England, & so to be sure you are. I never read so sweet
a Letter in my Life. Do write me another just like it, &
tell me you are in love with me in every other line. I quite
die to see you. How shall we manage to see one another?
for we are so much in love that we cannot live asunder.
Oh! my dear Musgrove you cannot think how impatiently
I wait for the death of my Uncle and Aunt—If they will
not die soon, I beleive I shall run mad, for I get more in
love with you every day of my Life.

How happy your Sister is to enjoy the pleasure of your
Company in her house, and how happy every body in
London must be because you are there. I hope you will be
so kind as to write to me again soon, for I never read such
sweet Letters as yours. I am my dearest Musgrove most
truly & faithfully yours for ever & ever. Henrietta Halton

I hope he will like my answer; it is as good a one as I can
write, though nothing to his; Indeed I had always heard
what a dab he was at a Love-letter. I saw him you know
for the first time at Lady Scudamore's—And when I saw
her Ladyship afterwards she asked me how I liked her
Cousin Musgrove?

"Why upon my word said I, I think he is a very handsome young Man."

"I am glad you think so replied she, for he is distractedly
in love with you."

"Law! Lady Scudamore, said I, how can you talk so
ridiculously?"

"Nay, t'is very true answered She, I assure you, for he
was in love with you from the first moment he beheld you."

"I

"I wish it may be true said I, for that is the only kind of love I would give a farthing for—There is some Sense in being in love at first sight."

"Well, I give you Joy of your conquest, replied Lady Scudamore, and I beleive it to have been a very complete one; I am sure it is not a contemptible one, for my Cousin is a charming young fellow, has seen a great deal of the World, and writes the best Love-letters I ever read."

This made me very happy, and I was excessively pleased with my conquest. However, I thought it proper to give myself a few Airs—So I said to her—

"This is all very pretty Lady Scudamore, but you know that we young Ladies who are Heiresses must not throw ourselves away upon Men who have no fortune at all."

"My dear Miss Halton said She, I am as much convinced of that as you can be, and I do assure you that I should be the last person to encourage your marrying any one who had not some pretentions to expect a fortune with you. Mr Musgrove is so far from being poor that he has an estate of Several hundreds an year which is capable of great Improvement, and an excellent House, though at present it is not quite in repair."

"If that is the case replied I, I have nothing more to say against him, and if as you say he is an informed young Man and can write good Love-letters, I am sure I have no reason to find fault with him for admiring me, tho' perhaps I may not marry him for all that Lady Scudamore."

"You are certainly under no obligation to marry him answered her Ladyship, except that which love himself will dictate to you, for if I am not greatly mistaken you are at this very moment unknown to yourself, cherishing a most tender affection for him."

"Law, Lady Scudamore replied I blushing how can you think of such a thing?"

"Because every look, every word betrays it, answered She; Come my dear Henrietta, consider me as a friend,

and

and be sincere with me—Do not you prefer Mr Musgrove to any man of your acquaintance?"

"Pray do not ask me such questions Lady Scudamore, said I turning away my head, for it is not fit for me to answer them."

"Nay my Love replied she, now you confirm my suspicions. But why Henrietta should you be ashamed to own a well-placed Love, or why refuse to confide in me?"

"I am not ashamed to own it; said I taking Courage. I do not refuse to confide in you or blush to say that I do love your cousin Mr Musgrove, that I am sincerely attached to him, for it is no disgrace to love a handsome Man. If he were plain indeed I might have had reason to be ashamed of a passion which must have been mean since the Object would have been unworthy. But with such a figure & face, & such beautiful hair as your Cousin has, why should I blush to own that such Superior Merit has made an impression on me."

"My sweet Girl (said Lady Scudamore embracing me with great Affection) what a delicate way of thinking you have in these Matters, and what a quick discernment for one of your years! Oh! how I honour you for such Noble Sentiments!"

"Do you Ma'am? said I; You are vastly obliging. But pray Lady Scudamore did your Cousin himself tell you of his Affection for me? I shall like him the better if he did, for what is a Lover without a Confidante?"

"Oh! my Love replied She, you were born for each other. Every word you say more deeply convinces me that your Minds are actuated by the invisible power of simpathy, for your opinions and Sentiments so exactly coincide. Nay, the colour of your Hair is not very different. Yes my dear Girl, the poor despairing Musgrove did reveal to me the story of his Love—. Nor was I surprised at it— I know not how it was, but I had a kind of presentiment that he *would* be in love with you."

"Well, but how did he break it to you?"

"It

"It was not till after supper. We were sitting round the fire together talking on indifferent subjects, though to say the truth the Conversation was cheifly on my side, for he was thoughtful and silent, when on a sudden he interrupted me in the midst of something I was saying, by exclaiming in a most Theatrical tone—

Yes I'm in love I feel it now

And Henrietta Halton has undone me—"

"Oh! What a Sweet Way replied I, of declaring his Passion! To make such a couple of charming Lines about me! What a pity it is that they are not in rhime!"

"I am very glad you like it, answered She; To be sure there was a great deal of Taste in it. And are you in love with her, Cousin? said I. I am very sorry for it, for unexceptionable as you are in every respect, with a pretty Estate capable of Great improvements, and an excellent House tho' somewhat out of repair, Yet who can hope to aspire with success to the adorable Henrietta who has had an offer from a Colonel & been toasted by a Baronet"—

"*That* I have—" cried I. Lady Scudamore continued. "Ah dear Cousin replied he, I am so well convinced of the little Chance I can have of winning her who is adored by thousands, that I need no assurances of yours to make me more thoroughly so. Yet surely neither you or the fair Henrietta herself will deny me the exquisite Gratification of dieing for her, of falling a victim to her Charms. And when I am dead"—continued he—

"Oh Lady Scudamore," said I wiping my eyes, "that such a sweet Creature should talk of dieing!"

"It is an affecting Circumstance indeed," replied Lady Scudamore. "When I am dead said he, Let me be carried & lain at her feet, & perhaps she may not disdain to drop a pitying tear on my poor remains."

"Dear Lady Scudamore interrupted I, say no more on this affecting Subject. I cannot bear it."

"Oh! how I admire the sweet sensibility of your Soul, and

and as I would not for Worlds wound it too deeply, I will be silent."

"Pray go on" said I. She did so.

"And then added he, Ah! Cousin imagine what my transports will be when I feel the dear precious drops trickle on my face! Who would not die to taste such extacy! And when I am interred, may the divine Henrietta bless some happier Youth with her affection, May he be as tenderly attached to her as the hapless Musgrove & while *he* crumbles to dust, May they live an example of Felicity in the Conjugal state!"

Did you ever hear any thing so pathetic? What a charming wish, to be lain at my feet when he was dead! Oh! what an exalted mind he must have to be capable of such a wish! Lady Scudamore went on.

"Ah! my dear Cousin, replied I to him, such noble behaviour as this, must melt the heart of any Woman however obdurate it may naturally be; and could the divine Henrietta but hear your generous wishes for her happiness, all gentle as is her mind, I have not a doubt but that she would pity your affection & endeavour to return it." "Oh! Cousin answered he, do not endeavour to raise my hopes by such flattering Assurances. No, I cannot hope to please this angel of a Woman, and the only thing which remains for me to do, is to die." "True Love is ever desponding replied I, but *I* my dear Tom will give you even greater hopes of conquering this fair one's heart, than I have yet given you, by assuring you that I watched her with the strictest attention during the whole day, and could plainly discover that she cherishes in her bosom though unknown to herself, a most tender affection for you."

"Dear Lady Scudamore cried I, This is more than I ever knew!"

"Did I not say that it was unknown to yourself? I did not, continued I to him, encourage you by saying this at first, that Surprise might render the pleasure Still Greater."

"No

"No Cousin replied he in a languid voice, nothing will convince me that *I* can have touched the heart of Henrietta Halton, and if you are deceived yourself, do not attempt deceiving me." "In short my Love it was the work of some hours for me to persuade the poor despairing Youth that you had really a preference for him; but when at last he could no longer deny the force of my arguments, or discredit what I told him, his transports, his Raptures, his Extacies are beyond my power to describe."

"Oh! the dear Creature, cried I, how passionately he loves me! But dear Lady Scudamore did you tell him that I was totally dependant on my Uncle & Aunt?"

"Yes, I told him every thing."

"And what did he say?"

"He exclaimed with virulence against Uncles & Aunts; Accused the Laws of England for allowing them to possess their Estates when wanted by their Nephews and Neices, and wished *he* were in the House of Commons, that he might reform the Legislature, & rectify all its abuses."

"Oh! the sweet Man! What a spirit he has!" said I.

"He could not flatter himself he added, that the adorable Henrietta would condescend for his sake to resign those Luxuries & that Splendor to which She had been used, and accept only in exchange the Comforts and Elegancies which his limitted Income could afford her, even supposing that his house were in Readiness to receive her. I told him that it could not be expected that she would; it would be doing her an injustice to suppose her capable of giving up the power she now possesses & so nobly uses of doing such extensive Good to the poorer part of her fellow Creatures, merely for the gratification of you and herself."

"To be sure said I, *I* am very Charitable every now and then. And what did Mr Musgrove say to this?"

"He replied that he was under a melancholy Necessity of owning the truth of what I said, and therefore if he should be the happy Creature destined to be the Husband

of

of the Beautiful Henrietta he must bring himself to wait, however impatiently for the fortunate day, when she might be freed from the power of worthless Relations and able to bestow herself on him."

What a noble Creature he is! Oh! Matilda what a fortunate one *I am* who am to be his Wife! My Aunt is calling to me to come & make the pies, So adeiu my dear freind, & beleive me your &c.—H. Halton.

Finis

SCRAPS

To Miss Fanny Catherine Austen

MY DEAR NEICE

As I am prevented by the great distance between Rowling and Steventon from superintending Your Education Myself, the care of which will probably on that account devolve on your Father & Mother, I think it is my particular Duty to prevent your feeling as much as possible the want of my personal instructions, by addressing to You on paper my Opinions & Admonitions on the conduct of Young Women, which you will find expressed in the following pages.—

I am my dear Neice
Your affectionate Aunt
The Author.

The female philosopher—

A LETTER

MY DEAR LOUISA

Your friend Mr Millar called upon us yesterday in his way to Bath, whither he is going for his health; two of his daughters were with him, but the oldest & the three Boys are

are with their Mother in Sussex. Though you have often told me that Miss Millar was remarkably handsome, you never mentioned anything of her Sisters' beauty; yet they are certainly extremely pretty. I'll give you their description.—Julia is eighteen; with a countenance in which Modesty, Sense & Dignity are happily blended, she has a form which at once presents you with Grace, Elegance & Symmetry. Charlotte who is just Sixteen is shorter than her Sister, and though her figure cannot boast the easy dignity of Julia's, yet it has a pleasing plumpness which is in a different way as estimable. She is fair & her face is expressive sometimes of softness the most bewitching, and at others of Vivacity the most striking. She appears to have infinite wit and a good humour unalterable; her conversation during the half hour they set with us, was replete with humorous Sallies, Bonmots & repartees; while the sensible, the amiable Julia uttered Sentiments of Morality worthy of a heart like her own. Mr Millar appeared to answer the character I had always received of him. My Father met him with that look of Love, that social Shake, & cordial kiss which marked his gladness at beholding an old & valued friend from whom thro' various circumstances he had been separated nearly twenty Years. Mr Millar observed (and very justly too) that many events had befallen each during that interval of time, which gave occasion to the lovely Julia for making most sensible reflections on the many changes in their situation which so long a period had occasioned, on the advantages of some, & the disadvantages of others. From this subject she made a short digression to the instability of human pleasures & the uncertainty of their duration, which led her to observe that all earthly Joys must be imperfect. She was proceeding to illustrate this doctrine by examples from the Lives of great Men when the Carriage came to the Door and the amiable Moralist with her Father & Sister was obliged to depart; but not without a promise of spending five or six

months

months with us on their return. We of course mentioned you, and I assure you that ample Justice was done to your Merits by all. "Louisa Clarke (said I) is in general a very pleasant Girl, yet sometimes her good humour is clouded by Peevishness, Envy & Spite. She neither wants Understanding nor is without some pretensions to Beauty, but these are so very trifling, that the value she sets on her personal charms, & the adoration she expects them to be offered are at once a striking example of her vanity, her pride, & her folly." So said I, & to my opinion everyone added weight by the concurrence of their own.

your affe:te

Arabella Smythe

The first Act of a Comedy

Characters

Popgun	Maria
Charles	Pistoletta
Postilion	Hostess
Chorus of Ploughboys	Cook
and	&
Strephon	Chloe

SCENE—AN INN

Enter Hostess, Charles, Maria & Cook

Host:ss to Maria)	If the gentry in the Lion should want beds, shew them number 9.—
Maria)	Yes Mistress.— *exit* Maria—
Host:ss to Cook)	If their Honours in the Moon ask for the bill of fare give it them.
Cook)	I wull, I wull.— *exit* Cook.
Host:ss to Charles)	If their Ladyships in the Sun ring their Bell—answer it.
Charles)	Yes Madam.— *Exeunt* Severally—.

SCENE

Scene changes to the Moon, & discovers
Popgun & Pistoletta.

Pistol:tta)   Pray papa, how far is it to London?

Popgun)   My Girl, my Darling, my favourite of
all my Children, who art the picture of
thy poor Mother, who died two months
ago, with whom I am going to Town
to marry to Strephon, and to whom I
mean to bequeath my whole Estate, it
wants seven Miles.

Scene changes to the Sun—

Enter Chloe & a chorus of ploughboys.

Chloe)   Where am I? At Hounslow. Where
go I? To London—. What to do? To
be married—. Unto whom? Unto
Strephon. Who is he? A Youth.
Then I will Sing a Song.

Song

I go to Town
And when I come down
I shall be married to Streephon
And that to me will be fun.

Chorus)   Be fun, be fun, be fun,
And that to me will be fun.

Enter cook—

Cook)   Here is the bill of fare.

Chloe reads)   2 Ducks, a leg of beef, a stinking partridge, & a tart.— I will have the leg
of beef and the partridge.

                              exit Cook.

And now I will sing another song.

Song

Song

I am going to have my dinner,
After which I shan't be thinner,
I wish I had here Strephon
For he would carve the partridge
    if it should be a tough one.

Chorus)   Tough one, tough one, tough one,
For he would carve the partridge if it
should be a tough one.

Exit Chloe and Chorus.—.

SCENE CHANGES TO THE INSIDE OF THE LION.

Enter Strephon & Postilion.

Streph.)   You drove me from Staines to this
place, from whence I mean to go to
Town to marry Chloe. How much is
your due?

Post.)   Eighteen pence.

Streph.)   Alas, my friend, I have but a bad
guinea with which I mean to support
myself in Town. But I will pawn to
you an undirected Letter that I
received from Chloe.

Post.)   Sir, I accept your offer.

END OF THE FIRST ACT.—

A Letter from a Young Lady, whose feelings
being too Strong for her Judgement led her into
the commission of Errors which her Heart dis-
approved.—

MANY have been the cares & vicissitudes of my past life,
my beloved Ellinor, & the only consolation I feel for their
bitterness

bitterness is that on a close examination of my conduct, I am convinced that I have strictly deserved them. I murdered my father at a very early period of my Life, I have since murdered my Mother, and I am now going to murder my Sister. I have changed my religion so often that at present I have not an idea of any left. I have been a perjured witness in every public tryal for these past twelve Years; and I have forged my own will. In short there is scarcely a crime that I have not committed—But I am now going to reform. Colonel Martin of the Horse guards has paid his Addresses to me, & we are to be married in a few days. As there is something singular in our Courtship, I will give you an account of it. Col: Martin is the second son of the late Sir John Martin who died immensely rich, but bequeathing only one hundred thousand pound a piece to his three younger Children, left the bulk of his fortune, about eight Million to the present Sir Thomas. Upon his small pittance the Colonel lived tolerably contented for nearly four months when he took it into his head to determine on getting the whole of his eldest Brother's Estate. A new will was forged & the Colonel produced it in Court— but nobody would swear to it's being the right Will except himself, & he had sworn so much that nobody beleived him. At that moment I happened to be passing by the door of the Court, and was beckoned in by the Judge who told the Colonel that I was a Lady ready to witness anything for the cause of Justice, & advised him to apply to me. In short the Affair was soon adjusted. The Colonel & I swore to its' being the right will, & Sir Thomas has been obliged to resign all his illgotten Wealth. The Colonel in gratitude waited on me the next day with an offer of his hand—. I am now going to murder my Sister.

Yours Ever.
Anna Parker.

A

A Tour through Wales—
in a Letter from a young Lady—

MY DEAR CLARA

I HAVE been so long on the ramble that I have not till now had it in my power to thank you for your Letter—. We left our dear home on last Monday month; and proceeded on our tour through Wales, which is a principality contiguous to England and gives the title to the Prince of Wales. We travelled on horseback by preference. My Mother rode upon our little pony & Fanny & I walked by her side or rather ran, for my Mother is so fond of riding fast that She galloped all the way. You may be sure that we were in a fine perspiration when we came to our place of resting. Fanny has taken a great many Drawings of the Country, which are very beautiful, tho' perhaps not such exact resemblances as might be wished, from their being taken as she ran along. It would astonish you to see all the Shoes we wore out in our Tour. We determined to take a good Stock with us & therefore each took a pair of our own besides those we set off in. However we were obliged to have them both capped & heelpeiced at Carmarthen, & at last when they were quite gone, Mama was so kind as to lend us a pair of blue Sattin Slippers, of which we each took one and hopped home from Hereford delightfully—

I am your ever affectionate

Elizabeth Johnson.

A Tale.

A GENTLEMAN whose family name I shall conceal, bought a small Cottage in Pembrokeshire about two Years ago. This daring Action was suggested to him by his elder Brother who promised to furnish two rooms & a Closet for him,

him, provided he would take a small house near the Borders of an extensive Forest, and about three Miles from the Sea. Wilhelminus gladly accepted the Offer and continued for some time searching after such a retreat when he was one morning agreably releived from his Suspence by reading this advertisement in a Newspaper.

To be Lett

A Neat Cottage on the borders of an extensive forest & about three Miles from the Sea. It is ready furnished except two rooms & a Closet.

The delighted Wilhelminus posted away immediately to his brother, and shewed him the advertisement. Robertus congratulated him & sent him in his Carriage to take possession of the Cottage. After travelling for three days & six Nights without Stopping, they arrived at the Forest & following a track which led by it's side down a steep Hill over which ten Rivulets meandered, they reached the Cottage in half an hour. Wilhelminus alighted, and after knocking for some time without receiving any answer or hearing any one stir within, he opened the door which was fastened only by a wooden latch & entered a small room, which he immediately perceived to be one of the two that were unfurnished—From thence he proceeded into a Closet equally bare. A pair of Stairs that went out of it led him into a room above, no less destitute, & these apartments he found composed the whole of the House. He was by no means displeased with this discovery, as he had the comfort of reflecting that he should not be obliged to lay out any thing on furniture himself—. He returned immediately to his Brother, who took him next day to every Shop in Town, & bought what ever was requisite to furnish the two rooms & the Closet. In a few days every thing was completed, and Wilhelminus returned to take possession of the Cottage. Robertus accompanied him, with his Lady and amiable Cecelia & her two lovely Sisters Arabella and

Marina

Marina to whom Wilhelminus was tenderly attached, and a large number of Attendants—An ordinary Genius might probably have been embarrassed in endeavouring to accomodate so large a party, but Wilhelminus with admirable presence of mind gave order for the immediate erection of two noble Tents in an open Spot in the Forest adjoining to the house. Their Construction was both simple & elegant—A couple of old blankets, each supported by four sticks, gave a striking proof of that taste for Architecture & that happy ease in overcoming difficulties which were some of Wilhelminus's most striking Virtues.

Finis

End of the Second Volume

VOLUME THE THIRD

====

Jane Austen—May 6th 1792.

CONTENTS

To Miss Mary Lloyd,

The following Novel is by permission
Dedicated,
by her Obed[t] humble Serv[t]

The Author

EVELYN

EVELYN

In a retired part of the County of Sussex there is a village
(for what I know to the Contrary) called Evelyn, perhaps
one of the most beautiful Spots in the south of England.
A Gentleman passing through it on horseback about twenty
years ago, was so entirely of my opinion in this respect,
that he put up at the little Alehouse in it & enquired with
great earnestness whether there were any house to be lett
in the Parish. The Landlady, who as well as every one else
in Evelyn was remarkably amiable, shook her head at this
question, but seemed unwilling to give him any answer.
He could not bear this uncertainty—yet knew not how to
obtain the information he desired. To repeat a question
which had already appear'd to make the good woman uneasy was impossible—. He turned from her in visible
agitation. "What a situation am I in!" said he to himself
as he walked to the window and threw up the sash. He
found himself revived by the Air, which he felt to a much
greater degree when he had opened the window than he
had done before. Yet it was but for a moment—. The
agonizing pain[1] of Doubt & Suspence again weighed down
his Spirits. The good woman who had watched in eager
silence every turn of his Countenance with that benevolence which characterizes the inhabitants of Evelyn, intreated him to tell her the cause of his uneasiness. "Is
there anything Sir in my power to do that may releive
your Greifs—Tell me in what manner I can sooth them, &
beleive me that the freindly balm of Comfort and Assistance shall not be wanting; for indeed Sir I have a simpathetic Soul."

"Amiable Woman (said Mr Gower, affected almost to

[1] idea *erased.*

tears

tears by this generous offer) This Greatness of mind in one
to whom I am almost a Stranger, serves but to make me
the more warmly wish for a house in this sweet village—.
What would I not give to be your Neighbour, to be blessed
with your Acquaintance, and with the farther knowledge
of your virtues! Oh! with what pleasure would I form
myself by such an example! Tell me then, best of Women,
is there no possibility?—I cannot speak—You know my
meaning——."

"Alas! Sir, replied Mrs Willis, there is *none*. Every house
in this village, from the sweetness of the Situation, & the
purity of the Air, in which neither Misery, Illhealth, or Vice
are ever wafted, is inhabited. And yet, (after a short pause)
there is a Family, who tho' warmly attached to the spot,
yet from a peculiar Generosity of Disposition would perhaps be willing to oblige you with[1] their house." He eagerly
caught at this idea, and having gained a direction to the
place,[2] he set off immediately on his walk to it. As he
approached the House, he was delighted with its situation.
It was in the exact centre of a small circular paddock,
which was enclosed by a regular paling, & bordered with
a plantation of Lombardy poplars, & Spruce firs alterna-
tively placed in three rows. A gravel walk ran through
this beautiful Shrubbery, and as the remainder of the paddock was unincumbered with any other Timber, the surface
of it perfectly even & smooth, and grazed by four white
Cows which were disposed at equal distances from each
other, the whole appearance of the place as Mr Gower
entered the Paddock was uncommonly striking. A beauti-
fully-rounded, gravel road without any turn or interruption
led immediately to the house. Mr Gower rang—the Door
was soon opened. "Are M^r & Mrs Webb at home?" "My
Good Sir they are"—replied the Servant; And leading the
way, conducted Mr Gower upstairs into a very elegant
Dressing room, where a Lady rising from her seat, wel-

[1] the remainder of *erased*.   [2] House *erased*.

comed

comed him with all the Generosity which Mrs Willis had attributed to the Family.

"Welcome best of Men—Welcome to this House, & to everything it contains. William, tell your Master of the happiness I enjoy—invite him to partake of it—. Bring up some Chocolate immediately; Spread a Cloth in the dining Parlour, and carry in the venison pasty—. In the mean time let the Gentleman have some sandwiches, and bring in a Basket of Fruit—Send up some Ices and a bason of Soup, and do not forget some Jellies and Cakes." Then turning to Mr Gower, & taking out her purse, "Accept this my good Sir,—. Beleive me you are welcome to everything that is in my power to bestow.—I wish my purse were weightier, but Mr Webb must make up my deficiencies—. I know he has cash in the house to the amount of an hundred pounds, which he shall bring you immediately." Mr Gower felt overpowered by her generosity as he put the purse in his pocket, and from the excess[1] of his Gratitude, could scarcely express himself intelligibly when he accepted her offer of the hundred pounds. Mr Webb soon entered the room, and repeated every protestation of Freindship & Cordiality which his Lady had already made.[2] The Chocolate, The Sandwiches, the Jellies, the Cakes, the Ice, and the Soup soon made their appearance, and Mr Gower having tasted something of all, and pocketted the rest, was conducted into the dining parlour, where he eat a most excellent Dinner & partook of the most exquisite Wines, while M^r and Mrs Webb stood by him still pressing him to eat and drink a little more. "And now my good Sir, said Mr Webb, when Mr Gower's repast was concluded, what else can we do to contribute to your happiness and express the Affection we bear you.[3] Tell us what you wish more to receive, and depend upon our gratitude for the communication of your wishes." "Give me then

---

[1] effusions *erased.*

[2] before expressed *erased.*   [3] for *erased before* you.

your

your house & Grounds; I ask for nothing else." "It is yours,
exclaimed both at once; from this moment it is yours."
The Agreement concluded on and the present accepted
by M͏ʳ Gower, M͏ʳ Webb rang to have the Carriage ordered,
telling William at the same time to call the Young Ladies.

"Best of Men, said M͏ʳˢ Webb, we will not long intrude
upon your Time."

"Make no Apologies dear Madam, replied M͏ʳ Gower,
You are welcome to stay this half hour if you like it."

They both burst forth into raptures of Admiration at his
politeness, which they agreed served only to make their
Conduct appear more inexcusable in trespassing on his time.

The Young Ladies soon entered the room. The eldest of
them was about seventeen, the other, several years younger.
M͏ʳ Gower had no sooner fixed his Eyes on Miss Webb than
he felt that something more was necessary to his happiness
than the house he had just received—M͏ʳˢ Webb introduced
him to her daughter. "Our dear freind M͏ʳ Gower my Love
—He has been so good as to accept of this house, small as
it is, & to promise to keep it for ever." "Give me leave
to assure you Sir, said Miss Webb, that I am highly sensible
of your kindness in this respect, which from the shortness
of my Father's & Mother's acquaintance with you, is more
than usually flattering."

M͏ʳ Gower bowed—"You are too obliging Ma'am—I
assure you that I like the house extremely—and if they
would complete their generosity by giving me their elder
daughter in marriage with a handsome portion, I should
have nothing more to wish for." This compliment brought
a blush into the cheeks of the lovely Miss Webb, who
seemed however to refer herself to her father & Mother.
They looked delighted at each other—At length M͏ʳˢ Webb
breaking silence, said—"We bend under a weight of obligations to you which we can never repay. Take our girl, take
our Maria, and on her must the difficult task fall, of endeavouring to make some return to so much Benefiscence."

Mr Webb added, "Her fortune is but ten thousand pounds, which is almost too small a sum to be offered." This objection however being instantly removed by the generosity of Mr Gower, who declared himself satisfied with the sum mentioned, M^r & Mrs Webb, with their youngest daughter took their leave, and on the next day, the nuptials of their eldest with Mr Gower were celebrated.—This amiable Man now found himself perfectly happy; united to a very lovely and deserving young woman, with an handsome fortune, an elegant house, settled in the village of Evelyn, & by that means enabled to cultivate his acquaintance with Mrs Willis, could he have a wish ungratified?—For some months he found that he could *not*, till one day as he was walking in the Shrubbery with Maria leaning on his arm, they observed a rose full-blown lying on the gravel; it had fallen from a rose tree which with three others had been planted by Mr Webb to give a pleasing variety to the walk. These four Rose trees served also to mark the quarters of the Shrubbery, by which means the Traveller might always know how far in his progress round the Paddock he was got—. Maria stooped to pick up the beautiful flower, and with all her Family Generosity presented it to her Husband. "My dear Frederic, said she, pray take this charming rose." "Rose! exclaimed Mr Gower—. Oh! Maria, of what does not that remind me! Alas my poor Sister, how have I neglected you!" The truth was that Mr Gower was the only son of a very large Family, of which Miss Rose Gower was the thirteenth daughter. This Young Lady whose merits deserved a better fate than she met with, was the darling of her relations—From the clearness of her skin & the Brilliancy of her Eyes, she was fully entitled to all their partial affection. Another circumstance contributed to the general Love they bore her, and that was one of the finest heads of hair in the world. A few Months before her Brother's marriage, her heart had been engaged by the attentions and charms

of

of a young Man whose high rank and expectations seemed to foretell objections from his Family to a match which would be highly desirable to theirs. Proposals were made on the young Man's part, and proper objections on his Father's—He was desired to return from Carlisle where he was with his beloved Rose, to the family seat in Sussex. He was obliged to comply, and the angry father then finding from his Conversation how determined he was to marry no other woman, sent him for a fortnight to the Isle of Wight under the care of the Family Chaplain, with the hope of overcoming his Constancy by Time and Absence in a foreign Country. They accordingly prepared to bid a long adieu to England—The young Nobleman was not allowed to see his Rosa. They set sail—A storm arose which baffled the arts of the Seamen. The Vessel was wrecked on the coast of Calshot and every Soul on board perished. The sad Event soon reached Carlisle, and the beautiful Rose was affected by it, beyond the power of Expression. It was to soften her affliction by obtaining a picture of her unfortunate Lover that her brother undertook a Journey into Sussex, where he hoped that his petition would not be rejected, by the severe yet afflicted Father. When he reached Evelyn he was not many miles from ——— Castle, but the pleasing events which befell him in that place had for a while made him totally forget the object of his Journey & his unhappy Sister. The little incident of the rose however brought everything concerning her to his recollection again, & he bitterly repented his neglect. He returned to the house immediately and agitated by[1] Greif, Apprehension and Shame wrote the following Letter to Rosa.

July 14th——. Evelyn

My dearest Sister

As it is now four months since I left Carlisle, during which period I have not once written to you, You will

[1] with *erased.*

perhaps

perhaps unjustly accuse me of Neglect and Forgetfulness. Alas! I blush when I own the truth of your Accusation.— Yet if you are still alive, do not think too harshly of me, or suppose that I could for a moment forget the situation of my Rose. Beleive me I will forget you no longer, but will hasten as soon as possible to —— Castle if I find by your answer that you are still alive. Maria joins me in every dutiful and affectionate wish, & I am yours sincerely

F. Gower.

He waited in the most anxious expectation for an answer to his Letter, which arrived as soon as the great distance from Carlisle would admit of.—But alas, it came not from[1] Rosa.

Carlisle July 17th

Dear Brother

My Mother has taken the liberty of opening your Letter to poor Rose, as she has been dead these six weeks. Your long absence and continued Silence gave us all great uneasiness and hastened her to the Grave. Your Journey to —— Castle therefore may be spared. You do not tell us where you have been since the time of your quitting Carlisle, nor in any way account for your tedious absence, which gives us some surprise. We all unite in Comp^ts to Maria, & beg to know who she is—.

Y^r affec:^te Sister

M. Gower.

This Letter, by which Mr Gower was obliged to attribute to his own conduct, his Sister's death, was so violent a shock to his feelings, that in spite of his living at Evelyn where Illness was scarcely ever heard of, he was attacked by a fit of the gout, which confining him to his own room afforded an opportunity to Maria of shining in that favourite character of Sir Charles Grandison's, a nurse. No woman could ever appear more amiable than Maria

¹ for *erased.*

did

did under such circumstances, and at last by her unremitting attentions had the pleasure of seeing him gradually recover the use of his feet. It was a blessing by no means lost on him, for he was no sooner in a condition to leave the house, than he mounted his horse, and rode to —— Castle, wishing to find whether his Lordship softened by his Son's death, might have been brought to consent to the match, had both he and Rosa been alive. His amiable Maria followed him with her Eyes till she could see him no longer, and then sinking into her chair overwhelmed with Greif, found that in his absence she could enjoy no comfort.

Mr Gower arrived late in the evening at the castle, which was situated on a woody Eminence commanding a beautiful prospect of the Sea. Mr Gower did not dislike the situation, tho' it was certainly greatly inferior[1] to that of his own house. There was an irregularity in the fall of the ground, and a profusion of old Timber which appeared to him illsuited to the stile of the Castle, for it being a building of a very ancient[2] date, he thought it required the Paddock of Evelyn lodge to form a Contrast, and enliven the structure. The gloomy appearance of the old Castle frowning on him as he followed its' winding approach, struck him with terror. Nor did he think himself safe, till he was introduced into the Drawing room where the Family were assembled to tea. Mr Gower was a perfect stranger to every one in the Circle but tho' he was always timid in the Dark and easily terrified when alone, he did not want that more necessary and more noble courage which enabled him without a Blush to enter a large party of superior Rank, whom he had never seen before, & to take his Seat amongst them with perfect Indifference. The name of Gower was not unknown to Lord ——. He felt distressed & astonished; yet rose and received him with all the politeness of a well-bred Man. Lady —— who felt a deeper sorrow at the loss

---

[1] superior *erased*.   [2] old *erased*.

of

of her Son, than his Lordships harder heart was capable of, could hardly keep her Seat when she found that he was the Brother of her lamented Henry's[1] Rosa. "My Lord said Mr Gower as soon as he was seated, You are perhaps surprised at receiving a visit from a Man whom you could not have the least expectation of seeing here. But my Sister my unfortunate Sister is the real cause of my thus troubling you: That luckless Girl is now no more—and tho' *she* can receive no pleasure from the intelligence, yet for the satisfaction of her Family I wish to know whether the Death of this unhappy Pair has made an impression on your heart sufficiently strong to obtain that consent to their Marriage which in happier circumstances you would not be persuaded to give supposing that they now were both alive." His Lordship seemed lossed in astonishment. Lady —— could not support the mention of her son, and left the room in tears; the rest of the Family remained attentively listening, almost persuaded that Mr Gower was distracted. "Mr Gower, replied his Lordship This is a very odd question—It appears to me that you are supposing an impossibility—No one can more sincerely regret the death of my Son than I have always done, and it gives me great concern to know that Miss Gower's was hastened by his—. Yet to suppose them alive is destroying at once the Motive for a change in my sentiments concerning the affair." "My Lord, replied Mr Gower in anger, I see that you are a most inflexible Man, and that not even the death of your Son can make you wish his future Life happy. I will no longer detain your Lordship. I see, I plainly see that you are a very vile Man—And now I have the honour of wishing all your Lordships, and Ladyships a good Night." He immediately left the room, forgetting in the heat of his Anger the lateness of the hour, which at any other time would have made him tremble, & leaving the whole Company unanimous in their opinion of his being Mad. When

---

[1] *Erasure illegible.*

however

however he had mounted his horse and the great Gates of the Castle had shut him out, he felt an universal tremor through out his whole frame. If we consider his Situation indeed, alone, on horseback, as late in the year as August, and in the day, as nine o'clock, with no light to direct him but that of the Moon almost full, and the Stars which alarmed him by their twinkling, who can refrain from pitying him?—No house within a quarter of a mile, and a Gloomy Castle blackened by the deep shade of Walnuts and Pines, behind him.—He felt indeed almost distracted with his fears, and shutting his Eyes till he arrived at the Village to prevent his seeing either Gipsies or Ghosts, he rode on a full gallop all the way. On his return home, he rang the house-bell, but no one appeared, a second time he rang, but the door was not opened, a third & a fourth with as little success, when observing the dining parlour window open he leapt in, & persued his way through the house till he reached Maria's Dressingroom, where he found all the servants assembled at tea. Surprized at so very unusual a sight, he fainted, on his recovery he found himself on the Sofa, with his wife's maid kneeling by him, chafing his temples with Hungary water—. From her he learned that his beloved Maria had been so much grieved at his departure that she died of a broken heart about 3 hours after his departure.

He then became sufficiently composed to give necessary orders for her funeral which took place the Monday following this being the Saturday—When Mr Gower had settled the order of the procession he set out himself to Carlisle, to give vent to his sorrow in the bosom of his family—He arrived there in high health & spirits, after a delightful journey of 3 days & a $\frac{1}{2}$—What was his surprize on entering the Breakfast parlour to see Rosa his beloved Rosa seated on a Sofa; at the sight of him she fainted & would have fallen had not a Gentleman sitting with his back to the door, started up & saved her from sinking to the ground—

She

She very soon came to herself & then introduced this gentleman to her Brother as her Husband a Mr Davenport—

But my dearest Rosa said the astonished Gower, I thought you were dead & buried. Why my d^r Frederick replied Rosa I wished you to think so, hoping that you would spread the report about the country & it would thus by some means reach —— Castle—By this I hoped some how or other to touch the hearts of its inhabitants. It was not till the day before yesterday that I heard of the death of my beloved Henry which I learned from M^r D—— who concluded by offering me his hand. I accepted it with transport, & was married yesterday—Mr Gower, embraced his sister & shook hands with Mr Davenport, he then took a stroll into the town—As he passed by a public house he called for a pot of beer, which was brought him immediately by his old friend Mrs Willis—

Great was his astonishment at seeing Mrs Willis in Carlisle. But not forgetful of the respect he owed her, he dropped on one knee, & received the frothy cup from her, more grateful to him than Nectar—He instantly made her an offer of his hand & heart, which she graciously condescended to accept, telling him that she was only on a visit to her cousin, who kept the *Anchor* & should be ready to return to Evelyn, whenever he chose—The next morning they were married & immediately proceeded to Evelyn—When he reached home, he recollected that he had never written to M^r & Mrs Webb to inform them of the death of their daughter, which he rightly supposed they knew nothing of, as they never took in any newspapers—He immediately dispatched the following Letter—

Evelyn—Aug^st 19th 1809—

Dearest Madam,

How can words express the poignancy of my feelings! Our Maria, our beloved Maria is no more, she breathed her last

last, on Saturday the 12th of Augst—I see you now in an
agony of grief lamenting not your own, but my loss—Rest
satisfied I am happy, possessed of my lovely Sarah what
more can I wish for?—

I remain

respectfully Yours

F. GOWER

Westgate Buil^{gs} Augst 22^d

GENEROUS, BEST OF MEN

how truly we rejoice to hear of your present welfare
& happiness! & how truly grateful are we for your unexampled generosity in writing to condole with us on the
late unlucky accident which befel our Maria—I have enclosed a draught on our banker for 30 pounds, which M^r
Webb joins with me in entreating you & the aimiable
Sarah to accept—

Your most grateful

ANNE AUGUSTA WEBB

M^r & Mrs Gower resided many years at Evelyn enjoying
perfect happiness the just reward of their virtues. The
only alteration which took place at Evelyn was that M^r &
Mrs Davenport settled there in Mrs Willis's former abode
& were for many years the proprietors of the White Horse
Inn—

CATHARINE

CATHARINE

OR THE BOWER

═══

To Miss Austen

MADAM

Encouraged by your warm patronage of The beautiful Cassandra, and The History of England, which through your generous support, have obtained a place in every library in the Kingdom, and run through threescore Editions, I take the liberty of begging the same Exertions in favour of the following Novel, which I humbly flatter myself, possesses Merit beyond any already published, or any that will ever in future appear, except such as may proceed from the pen of Your Most Grateful Humble Serv[t]

THE AUTHOR

Steventon August 1792—

═══

CATHARINE[1] had the misfortune, as many heroines have had before her, of losing her Parents when she was very young, and of being brought up under the care of a Maiden Aunt, who while she tenderly loved her, watched over her conduct with so scrutinizing a severity, as to make it very doubtful to many people, and to Catharine[1] amongst the rest, whether she loved her or not. She had frequently been deprived of a real pleasure through this jealous Caution,

[1] Kitty, *erased here, stands elsewhere.*

had

had been sometimes obliged to relinquish a Ball because an Officer was to be there, or to dance with a Partner of her Aunt's introduction in preference to one of her own Choice. But her Spirits were naturally good, and not easily depressed, and she possessed such a fund of vivacity and good humour as could only be damped by some serious vexation.—Besides these antidotes against every disappointment, and consolations under them, she had another, which afforded her constant releif in all her misfortunes, and that was a fine shady Bower, the work of her own infantine Labours assisted by those of two young Companions who had resided in the same village—. To this Bower, which terminated a very pleasant and retired walk in her Aunt's Garden, she always wandered whenever anything disturbed her, and it possessed such a charm over her senses, as constantly to tranquillize her mind & quiet her spirits—Solitude & reflection might perhaps have had the same effect in her Bed Chamber, yet Habit had so strengthened the idea which Fancy had first suggested, that such a thought never occurred to Kitty who was firmly persuaded that her Bower alone could restore her to herself. Her imagination was warm, and in her Freindships, as well as in the whole tenure of her Mind, she was enthousiastic. This beloved Bower had been the united work of herself and two amiable Girls, for whom since her earliest Years, she had felt the tenderest regard. They were the daughters of the Clergyman of the Parish with whose Family, while it had continued there, her Aunt had been on the most intimate terms, and the little Girls tho' separated for the greatest part of the Year by the different Modes of their Education, were constantly together during the holidays of the Miss Wynnes; [they were companions in their walks, their Schemes & Amusements, and while the sweetness of their dispositions had prevented any serious Quarrels, the trifling disputes which it was impossible wholly to avoid, had been far from lessening their affection

affection].[1] In those days of happy Childhood, now so often
regretted by Kitty this arbour had been formed, and
separated perhaps for ever from these dear freinds, it
encouraged more than any other place the tender and
Melancholy recollections of hours rendered pleasant by
them, at one [*sic*] so sorrowful, yet so soothing! It was now
two years since the death of Mr Wynne, and the conse-
quent dispersion of his Family who had been left by it
in great distress. They had been reduced to a state of
absolute dependance on some relations, who though very
opulent and very nearly connected with them, had with
difficulty been prevailed on to contribute anything towards
their Support. Mrs Wynne was fortunately spared the
knowledge & participation of their distress, by her release from a painful illness a few months before the death
of her husband.—The eldest daughter had been obliged
to accept the offer of one of her cousins to equip her for
the East Indies, and tho' infinitely against her inclinations
had been necessitated to embrace the only possibility
that was offered to her, of a Maintenance; Yet it was
one, so opposite to all her ideas of Propriety, so contrary to her Wishes, so repugnant to her feelings, that
she would almost have preferred Servitude to it, had
Choice been allowed her—. Her personal Attractions had
gained her a husband as soon as she had arrived at Bengal,
and she had now been married nearly a twelvemonth.
Splendidly, yet unhappily married. United to a Man of
double her own age, whose disposition was not amiable,
and whose Manners were unpleasing, though his Character
was respectable. Kitty had heard twice from her freind
since her marriage, but her Letters were always unsatisfactory, and though she did not openly avow her feelings,
yet every line proved her to be Unhappy. She spoke
with pleasure of nothing, but of those Amusements which
they had shared together and which could return no more,

[1] *Erased.*

and

and seemed to have no happiness in veiw but that of returning to England again. Her sister had been taken by another relation the Dowager Lady Halifax as a companion to her Daughters, and had accompanied her family into Scotland about the same time of Cecilia's leaving England. From Mary therefore Kitty had the power of hearing more frequently, but her Letters were scarcely more comfortable—. There was not indeed that hopelessness of sorrow in her situation as in her sisters; she was not married, and could yet look forward to a change in her circumstances, but situated for the present without any immediate hope of it, in a family where, tho' all were her relations she had no freind, she wrote usually in depressed Spirits, which her separation from her Sister and her Sister's Marriage had greatly contributed to make so.— Divided thus from the two she loved best on Earth, while Cecilia & Mary were still more endeared to her by their loss, everything that brought a remembrance of them was doubly cherished, & the Shrubs they had planted, & the keepsakes they had given were rendered sacred—. The living of Chetwynde was now in the possession of a Mr Dudley, whose Family unlike the Wynnes were productive only of vexation & trouble to Mrs Percival[1] and her Neice. Mr Dudley, who was the Younger Son of a very noble Family, of a Family more famed for their Pride than their opulence, tenacious of his Dignity, and jealous of his rights, was forever quarrelling, if not with Mrs P. herself, with her Steward and Tenants concerning tythes, and with the principal Neighbours themselves concerning the respect & parade, he exacted. His Wife, an ill-educated, untaught woman of ancient family, was proud of that family almost without knowing why, and like him too was haughty and quarrelsome, without considering for what. Their only daughter, who inherited the ignorance, the insolence, & pride of her parents, was from that Beauty of which she

---

[1] *Substituted here and elsewhere for* Peterson.

was

was unreasonably vain, considered by them as an irresistable Creature, and looked up to as the future restorer, by a Splendid Marriage, of the dignity which their reduced Situation and Mr Dudley's being obliged to take orders for a Country Living had so much lessened. They at once despised the Percivals as people of mean family, and envied them as people of fortune. They were jealous of their being more respected than themselves and while they affected to consider them as of no Consequence, were continually seeking to lessen them in the opinion of the Neighbourhood by Scandalous & Malicious reports. Such a family as this, was ill-calculated to console Kitty for the loss of the Wynnes, or to fill up by their Society, those occasionally irksome hours which in so retired a Situation would sometimes occur for want of a Companion. Her aunt was most excessively fond of her, and miserable if she saw her for a moment out of spirits; Yet she lived in such constant apprehension of her marrying imprudently if she were allowed the opportunity of choosing, and was so dissatisfied with her behaviour when she saw her with Young Men, for it was, from her natural disposition remarkably open and unreserved, that though she frequently wished for her Neice's sake, that the Neighbourhood were larger, and that She had used herself to mix more with it, yet the recollection of there being young Men in almost every Family in it, always conquered the Wish. The same fears that prevented Mrs Peterson's joining much in the Society of her Neighbours, led her equally to avoid inviting her relations to spend any time in her House—She had therefore constantly regretted the annual attempt of a distant relation to visit her at Chetwynde, as there was a young Man in the Family of whom she had heard many traits that alarmed her. This Son was however now on his travels, and the repeated solicitations of Kitty, joined to a consciousness of having declined with too little Ceremony the frequent overtures of her Freinds to be admitted, and a real wish to

see

see them herself, easily prevailed on her to press with great Earnestness the pleasure of a visit from them during the Summer. M^r & Mrs Stanley were accordingly to come, and Catharine, in having an object to look forward to, a something to expect that must inevitably releive the dullness of a constant tete a tete with her Aunt, was so delighted, and her spirits so elevated, that for the three or four days immediately preceding their Arrival, she could scarcely fix herself to any employment. In this point Mrs Percival always thought her defective, and frequently complained of a want of Steadiness & perseverance in her occupations, which were by no means congenial to the eagerness of Kitty's Disposition, and perhaps not often met with in any young person. The tediousness too of her Aunt's conversation and the want of agreable Companions greatly increased this desire of Change in her Employments, for Kitty found herself much sooner tired of Reading, Working, or Drawing, in Mrs Peterson's parlour than in her own Arbour, where Mrs Peterson for fear of its being damp never accompanied her.

As her Aunt prided herself on the exact propriety and Neatness with which everything in her Family was conducted, and had no higher Satisfaction than that of knowing her house to be always in complete Order, as her fortune was good, and her Establishment Ample, few were the preparations necessary for the reception of her Visitors. The day of their arrival so long expected, at length came, and the Noise of the Coach & 4 as it drove round the sweep, was to Catherine a more interesting sound, than the Music of an Italian Opera, which to most Heroines is the hight of Enjoyment. M^r and Mrs Stanley were people of Large Fortune & high Fashion. He was a Member of the house of Commons, and they were therefore most agreably necessitated to reside half the Year in Town; where Miss Stanley had been attended by the most capital Masters from the time of her being six years old to the last Spring, which

comprehending

comprehending a period of twelve Years had been dedicated to the acquirement of Accomplishments which were now to be displayed and in a few Years entirely neglected. She was not inelegant in her appearance, rather handsome, and naturally not deficient in Abilities; but those Years which ought to have been spent in the attainment of useful knowledge and Mental Improvement, had been all bestowed in learning Drawing, Italian and Music, more especially the latter, and she now united to these Accomplishments, an Understanding unimproved by reading and a Mind totally devoid either of Taste or Judgement. Her temper was by Nature good, but unassisted by reflection, she had neither patience under Disappointment, nor could sacrifice her own inclinations to promote the happiness of others. All her Ideas were towards the Elegance of her appearance, the fashion of her dress, and the Admiration she wished them to excite. She professed a love of Books without Reading, was Lively without Wit, and generally good humoured without Merit. Such was Camilla Stanley; and Catherine, who was prejudiced by her appearance, and who from her solitary Situation was ready to like anyone, tho' her Understanding and Judgement would not otherwise have been easily satisfied, felt almost convinced when she saw her, that Miss Stanley would be the very companion She wanted, and in some degree make amends for the loss of Cecilia & Mary Wynne. She therefore attached herself to Camilla from the first day of her arrival, and from being the only young People in the house, they were by inclination constant Companions. Kitty was herself a great reader, tho' perhaps not a very deep one, and felt therefore highly delighted to find that Miss Stanley was equally fond of it. Eager to know that their sentiments as to Books were similar, she very soon began questioning her new Acquaintance on the subject; but though She was well read in Modern history herself, she chose rather to speak first of Books of a lighter kind, of Books universally read

read and Admired, [and that have given rise perhaps to more frequent Arguments than any other of the same sort].[1]

"You have read Mrs Smith's Novels, I suppose?" said she to her Companion—. "Oh! Yes, replied the other, and I am quite delighted with them—They are the sweetest things in the world—" "And which do you prefer of them?" "Oh! dear, I think there is no comparison between them—Emmeline is *so much* better than any of the others—" "Many people think so, I know; but there does not appear so great a disproportion in their Merits to *me*; do you think it is better written?" "Oh! I do not know anything about *that*—but it is better in *everything*—Besides, Ethelinde is so long—" "That is a very common Objection I believe, said Kitty, but for my own part, if a book is well written, I always find it too short." "So do I, only I get tired of it before it is finished." "But did not you find the story of Ethelinde very interesting? And the Descriptions of Grasmere, are not the[y] Beautiful?" "Oh! I missed them all, because I was in such a hurry to know the end of it—Then from an easy transition she added, We are going to the Lakes this Autumn, and I am quite Mad with Joy; Sir Henry Devereux has promised to go with us, and that will make it so pleasant, you know—"

"I dare say it will; but I think it is a pity that Sir Henry's powers of pleasing were not reserved for an occasion where they might be more wanted.—However I quite envy you the pleasure of such a Scheme." "Oh! I am quite delighted with the thoughts of it; I can think of nothing else. I assure you I have done nothing for this last Month but plan what Cloathes I should take with me, and I have at last determined to take very few indeed besides my travelling Dress, and so I advise you to do, when ever you go; for I intend in case we should fall in with any races, or stop at Matlock or Scarborough, to have some Things made for the occasion."

[1] *Erased.*

You

"You intend then to go into Yorkshire?"

"I beleive not—indeed I know nothing of the Route, for I never trouble myself about such things. I only know that we are to go from Derbyshire to Matlock and Scarborough, but to which of them first, I neither know nor care—I am in hopes of meeting some particular freinds of mine at Scarborough—Augusta told me in her last Letter that Sir Peter talked of going; but then you know that is so uncertain. I cannot bear Sir Peter, he is such a horrid Creature—"

"He *is*, is he?" said Kitty, not knowing what else to say. "Oh! he is quite Shocking." Here the Conversation was interrupted, and Kitty was left in a painful Uncertainty, as to the particulars of Sir Peter's Character; She knew only that he was Horrid and Shocking, but why, and in what, yet remained to be discovered. She could scarcely resolve what to think of her new Acquaintance; She appeared to be shamefully ignorant as to the Geography of England, if she had understood her right, and equally devoid of Taste and Information. Kitty was however unwilling to decide hastily; she was at once desirous of doing Miss Stanley justice, and of having her own Wishes in her answered; she determined therefore to suspend all Judgement for some time. After Supper, the Conversation turning on the state of Affairs in the political World, M^rs P, who was firmly of opinion that the whole race of Mankind were degenerating, said that for her part, Everything she beleived was going to rack and ruin, all order was destroyed over the face of the World, The house of Commons she heard did not break up sometimes till five in the Morning, and Depravity never was so general before; concluding with a wish that she might live to see the Manners of the People in Queen Elizabeth's reign, restored again. "Well Ma'am, said her Neice, [I beleive you have as good a chance of it as any one else]^1 but I hope you do not mean with the times to restore Queen Eliz^th herself."

1 *Erased.*

Queen

"Queen Elizth, said Mrs Stanley who never hazarded a remark on History that was not well founded, lived to a good old age, and was a very Clever Woman." "True Ma'am, said Kitty; but I do not consider either of those Circumstances as meritorious in herself, and they are very far from making me wish her return, for if she were to come again with the same Abilities and the same good Constitution She might do as much Mischief and last as long as she did before—then turning to Camilla who had been sitting very silent for some time, she added, What do *you* think of Elizabeth Miss Stanley? I hope you will not defend her."

"Oh! dear, said Miss Stanley, I know nothing of Politics, and cannot bear to hear them mentioned." Kitty started at this repulse, but made no answer; that Miss Stanley must be ignorant of what she could not distinguish from Politics she felt perfectly convinced.—She retired to her own room, perplexed in her opinion about her new Acquaintance, and fearful of her being very unlike Cecilia and Mary. She arose the next morning to experience a fuller conviction of this, and every future day encreased it—. She found no variety in her conversation; She received no information from her but in fashions, and no Amusement but in her performance on the Harpsichord; and after repeated endeavours to find her what she wished, she was obliged to give up the attempt and to consider it as fruitless. There had occasionally appeared a something like humour in Camilla which had inspired her with hopes, that she might at least have a natural genius, tho' not an improved one, but these Sparklings of Wit happened so seldom, and were so ill-supported that she was at last convinced of their being merely accidental. All her stock of knowledge was exhausted in a very few Days, and when Kitty had learnt from her, how large their house in Town was, when the fashionable Amusements began, who were the celebrated Beauties and who the best Millener, Camilla

had

had nothing further to teach, except the Characters of any of her Acquaintance as they occurred in Conversation, which was done with equal Ease and Brevity, by saying that the person was either the sweetest Creature in the world, and one of whom she was doatingly fond, or horrid, shocking and not fit to be seen.

As Catherine was very desirous of gaining every possible information as to the Characters of the Halifax Family, and concluded that Miss Stanley must be acquainted with them, as she seemed to be so with every one of any Consequence, she took an opportunity as Camilla was one day enumerating all the people of rank that her Mother visited, of asking her whether Lady Halifax were among the number.

"Oh! Thank you for reminding me of her, She is the sweetest Woman in the world, and one of our most intimate Acquaintances, I do not suppose there is a day passes during the six Months that we are in Town, but what we see each other in the course of it—. And I correspond with all the Girls."

"They *are* then a very pleasant Family? said Kitty. They ought to be so indeed, to allow of such frequent Meetings, or all Conversation must be at end."

"Oh! dear, not at all, said Miss Stanley, for sometimes we do not speak to each other for a month together. We meet perhaps only in Public, and then you know we are often not able to get near enough; but in that case we always nod & smile."

"Which does just as well—. But I was going to ask you whether you have ever seen a Miss Wynne with them?"

"I know who you mean perfectly—she wears a blue hat—. I have frequently seen her in Brook Street, when I have been at Lady Halifax's Balls—She gives one every Month during the Winter—. But only think how good it is in her to take care of Miss Wynne, for she is a very distant relation, and so poor that, as Miss Halifax told me,

her

her Mother was obliged to find her in Cloathes. Is not it
shameful?"

"That she should be so poor? it is indeed, with such
wealthy connexions as the Family have."

"Oh! no; I mean, was not it shameful in Mr Wynne to
leave his Children so distressed, when he had actually the
Living of Chetwynde and two or three Curacies, and only
four Children to provide for—. What would he have done
if he had had ten, as many people have?"

"He would have given them all a good Education and
have left them all equally poor."

"Well I do think there never was so lucky a Family.
Sir George Fitzgibbon you know sent the eldest girl to
India entirely at his own Expence, where they say she is
most nobly married and the happiest Creature in the
World—Lady Halifax you see has taken care of the
youngest and treats her as if she were her Daughter; She
does not go out into Public with her to be sure; but then
she is always present when her Ladyship gives her Balls,
and nothing can be kinder to her than Lady Halifax is; she
would have taken her to Cheltenham last year, if there
had been room enough at the Lodgings, and therefore I
dont think that *she* can have anything to complain of.
Then there are the two Sons; one of them the Bishop of
M—— has got into the Army[1] as a Leiutenant I suppose;
and the other is extremely well off I know, for I have
a notion that somebody puts him to School somewhere in
Wales. Perhaps you knew them when they lived here?"

"Very well, We met as often as your Family and the
Halifaxes do in Town, but as we seldom had any difficulty
in getting near enough to speak, we seldom parted with
merely a Nod & a Smile. They were indeed a most charming Family, and I beleive have scarcely their Equals in
the World; The Neighbours we now have at the Parsonage,
appear to more disadvantage in coming after them."

[1] sent to Sea *erased.*

Oh

"Oh! horrid Wretches! I wonder you can endure them."

"Why, what would you have one do?"

"Oh! Lord, If I were in your place, I should abuse them all day long."

"So I do, but it does no good."

"Well, I declare it is quite a pity that they should be suffered to live. I wish my Father would propose knocking all their Brains out, some day or other when he is in the House. So abominably proud of their Family! And I dare say after all, that there is nothing particular in it."

"Why Yes, I beleive thay *have* reason to value themselves on it, if any body has; for you know he is Lord Amyatt's Brother."

"Oh! I know all that very well, but it is no reason for their being so horrid. I remember I met Miss Dudley last Spring with Lady Amyatt at Ranelagh, and she had such a frightful Cap on, that I have never been able to bear any of them since.—And so you used to think the Wynnes very pleasant?" "You speak as if their being so were doubtful! Pleasant! Oh! they were every thing that could interest and attach. It is not in my power to do Justice to their Merits, tho' not to feel them, I think must be impossible. They have unfitted me for any Society but their own!"

"Well, That is just what I think of the Miss Halifaxes; by the bye, I must write to Caroline tomorrow, and I do not know what to say to her. The Barlows too are just such other sweet Girls; but I wish Augusta's hair was not so dark. I cannot bear Sir Peter—Horrid Wretch! He is *always* laid up with the Gout, which is exceedingly disagreeable to the Family."

"And perhaps not very pleasant to *himself*—. But as to the Wynnes; do you really think them very fortunate?"

"Do I? Why, does not every body? Miss Halifax & Caroline & Maria all say that they are the luckiest Creatures in the World. So does Sir George Fitzgibbon and so do Every body."

That

"That is, Every body who have themselves conferred an obligation on them. But do you call it lucky, for a Girl of Genius & Feeling to be sent in quest of a Husband to Bengal, to be married there to a Man of whose Disposition she has no opportunity of judging till her Judgement is of no use to her, who may be a Tyrant, or a Fool or both for what she knows to the Contrary. Do you call *that* fortunate?"

"I know nothing of all that; I only know that it was extremely good in Sir George to fit her out and pay her Passage, and that she would not have found Many who would have done the same."

"I wish she had not found *one*, said Kitty with great Eagerness, she might then have remained in England and been happy."

"Well, I cannot conceive the hardship of going out in a very agreeable Manner with two or three sweet Girls for Companions, having a delightful voyage to Bengal or Barbadoes or wherever it is, and being married soon after one's arrival to a very charming Man immensely rich—. I see no hardship in all that."

"Your representation of the Affair, said Kitty laughing, certainly gives a very different idea of it from Mine. But supposing all this to be true, still, as it was by no means certain that she would be so fortunate either in her voyage, her Companions, or her husband; in being obliged to run the risk of their proving very different, she undoubtedly experienced a great hardship—. Besides, to a Girl of any Delicacy, the voyage in itself, since the object of it is so universally known, is a punishment that needs no other to make it very severe.'

"I do not see that at all. She is not the first Girl who has gone to the East Indies for a Husband, and I declare I should think it very good fun if I were as poor."

"I beleive you would think very differently *then*. But at least you will not defend her Sister's situation? Dependant

even

even for her Cloathes on the bounty of others, who of course do not pity her, as by your own account, they consider her as very fortunate."

"You are extremely nice upon my word; Lady Halifax is a delightful Woman, and one of the sweetest tempered Creatures in the World; I am sure I have every reason to speak well of her, for we are under most amazing Obligations to her. She has frequently chaperoned me when my Mother has been indisposed, and last Spring she lent me her own horse three times, which was a prodigious favour, for it is the most beautiful Creature that ever was seen, and I am the only person she ever lent it to.

["If so, *Mary Wynne* can receive very little advantage from her having it."][1]

And then, continued she, the Miss Halifaxes are quite delightful. Maria is one of the cleverest Girls that ever were known—Draws in Oils, and plays anything by sight. She promised me one of her Drawings before I left Town, but I entirely forgot to ask her for it. I would give anything to have one." [Why indeed, if Maria will give my Freind a drawing, she can have nothing to complain of, but as she does not write in Spirits, I suppose she has not yet been fortunate enough to be so distinguished.][2] "But was not it very odd, said Kitty, that the Bishop should send Charles Wynne to sea, when he must have had a much better chance of providing for him in the Church, which was the profession that Charles liked best, and the one for which his Father had intended him? The Bishop I know had often promised Mr Wynne a living, and as he never gave him one, I think it was incumbant on him to transfer the promise to his Son."

"I beleive you think he ought to have resigned his Bishopric to him; you seem determined to be dissatisfied with every thing that has been done for them."

"Well, said Kitty, this is a subject on which we shall

[1] *Erased.*   [2] *Erased.*

never

never agree, and therefore it will be useless to continue it
farther, or to mention it again—" She then left the room,
and running out of the House was soon in her dear Bower
where she could indulge in peace all her affectionate Anger
against the relations of the Wynnes, which was greatly
heightened by finding from Camilla that they were in
general considered as having acted particularly well by
them—. She amused herself for some time in Abusing, and
Hating them all, with great spirit, and when this tribute
to her regard for the Wynnes, was paid, and the Bower
began to have its usual influence over her Spirits, she
contributed towards settling them, by taking out a book,
for she had always one about her, and reading—. She had
been so employed for nearly an hour, when Camilla came
running towards her with great Eagerness, and apparently
great Pleasure—. "Oh! my Dear Catherine, said she, half
out of Breath—I have such delightful News for You—But
you shall guess what it is—We are all the happiest Creatures in the World; would you beleive it, the Dudleys have
sent us an invitation to a Ball at their own House—. What
Charming People they are! I had no idea of there being so
much sense in the whole Family—I declare I quite doat
upon them—. And it happens so fortunately too, for I
expect a new Cap from Town tomorrow which will just do
for a Ball—Gold Net—It will be a most angelic thing—
Every Body will be longing for the pattern—" The expectation of a Ball was indeed very agreable intelligence to
Kitty, who fond of Dancing and seldom able to enjoy it,
had reason to feel even greater pleasure in it than her
Freind; for to *her*, it was now no novelty—. Camilla's
delight however was by no means inferior to Kitty's, and
she rather expressed the most of the two. The Cap came
and every other preparation was soon completed; while
these were in agitation the Days passed gaily away, but
when Directions were no longer necessary, Taste could no
longer be displayed, and Difficulties no longer overcome,
the

the short period that intervened before the day of the Ball
hung heavily on their hands, and every hour was too long.
The very few Times that Kitty had ever enjoyed the
Amusement of Dancing was an excuse for *her* impatience,
and an apology for the Idleness it occasioned to a Mind
naturally very Active; but her Freind without such a plea
was infinitely worse than herself. She could do nothing
but wander from the house to the Garden, and from the
Garden to the avenue, wondering when Thursday would
come, which she might easily have ascertained, and count-
ing the hours as they passed which served only to lengthen
them.—. They retired to their rooms in high Spirits on
Wednesday night, but Kitty awoke the next Morning with
a violent Toothake. It was in vain that she endeavoured
at first to deceive herself; her feelings were witnesses too
acute of it's reality; with as little success did she try to
sleep it off, for the pain she suffered prevented her closing
her Eyes—. She then summoned her Maid and with the
Assistance of the Housekeeper, every remedy that the
receipt book or the head of the latter contained, was tried,
but ineffectually; for though for a short time releived by
them, the pain still returned. She was now obliged to give
up the endeavour, and to reconcile herself not only to the
pain of a Toothake, but to the loss of a Ball; and though
she had with so much eagerness looked forward to the day
of its arrival, had received such pleasure in the necessary
preparations, and promised herself so much delight in it,
Yet she was not so totally void of philosophy as many
Girls of her age, might have been in her situation. She
considered that there were Misfortunes of a much greater
magnitude than the loss of a Ball, experienced every day
by some part of Mortality, and that the time might come
when She would herself look back with Wonder and perhaps with Envy on her having known no greater vexation.
By such reflections as these, she soon reasoned herself into
as much Resignation & Patience as the pain she suffered,
would

would allow of, which after all was the greatest Misfortune
of the two, and told the sad story when she entered the
Breakfast room, with tolerable Composure. Mrs Percival
more grieved for her toothake than her Disappointment,
as she feared that it would not be possible to prevent her
Dancing with a *Man* if she went, was eager to try everything that had already been applied to alleviate the pain,
while at the same time She declared it was impossible for
her to leave the House. Miss Stanley who joined to her
concern for her Freind, felt a mixture of Dread lest her
Mother's proposal that they should all remain at home,
might be accepted, was very violent in her sorrow on the
occasion, and though her apprehensions on the subject
were soon quieted by Kitty's protesting that sooner than
allow any one to stay with her, she would herself go, she
continued to lament it with such unceasing vehemence as
at last drove Kitty to her own room. Her Fears for herself
being now entirely dissipated left her more than ever at
leisure to pity and persecute her Freind who tho' safe when
in her own room, was frequently removing from it to some
other in hopes of being more free from pain, and then had
no opportunity of escaping her—.

"To be sure, there never was anything so shocking, said
Camilla; To come on such a day too! For one would not
have minded it you know had it been at *any other* time.
But it always is so. I never was at a Ball in my Life, but
what something happened to prevent somebody from
going! I wish there were no such things as Teeth in the
World; they are nothing but plagues to one, and I dare
say that People might easily invent something to eat with
instead of them; Poor Thing! what pain you are in! I
declare it is quite Shocking to look at you. But you wo'nt
have it out, will you? For Heaven's sake do'nt; for there
is nothing I dread so much. I declare I had rather undergo
the greatest Tortures in the World than have a tooth
drawn. Well! how patiently you do bear it! how can you
be

be so quiet? Lord, if I were in your place I should make
such a fuss, there would be no bearing me. I should torment you to Death."

"So you do, as it is," thought Kitty.

"For my own part, Catherine said Mrs Percival I have
not a doubt but that you caught this toothake by sitting
so much in that Arbour, for it is always damp. I know it
has ruined your Constitution entirely; and indeed I do not
beleive it has been of much service to mine; I sate down in
it last May to rest myself, and I have never been quite well
since—. I shall order John to pull it all down I assure you."

"I know you will not do that Ma'am, said Kitty, as you
must be convinced how unhappy it would make me."

"You talk very ridiculously Child; it is all whim & Nonsense. Why cannot you fancy this room an Arbour?"

"Had this room been built by Cecilia & Mary, I should
have valued it equally Ma'am, for it is not merely the name
of an Arbour, which charms me."

"Why indeed Mrs Percival, said Mrs Stanley, I must
think that Catherine's affection for her Bower is the effect
of a Sensibility that does her Credit. I love to see a Freindship between young Persons and always consider it as a
sure mark of an aimiable affectionate disposition. I have
from Camilla's infancy taught her to think the same, and
have taken great pains to introduce her to young people
of her own age who were likely to be worthy of her regard.
[There is something mighty pretty I think in young Ladies
corresponding with each other, and][1] nothing forms the
taste more than sensible & Elegant Letters—. Lady Halifax thinks just like me—. Camilla corresponds with her
Daughters, and I beleive I may venture to say that they
are none of them *the worse* for it." These ideas were too
modern to suit Mrs Percival who considered a correspondence between Girls as productive of no good, and as the
frequent origin of imprudence & Error by the effect of

[1] *Erased.*

pernicious

pernicious advice and bad Example. She could not therefore refrain from saying that for her part, she had lived fifty Years in the world without having ever had a correspondent, and did not find herself at all the less respectable for it—. Mrs Stanley could say nothing in answer to this, but her Daughter who was less governed by Propriety, said in her thoughtless way, "But who knows what you might have been Ma'am, if you *had* had a Correspondent; perhaps it would have made you quite a different Creature. I declare I would not be without those I have for all the World. It is the greatest delight of my Life, and you cannot think how much their Letters have formed my taste as Mama says, for I hear from them generally every week."

"You received a Letter from Augusta Barlow to day, did not you my Love? said her Mother—. She writes remarkably well I know."

"Oh! Yes Ma'am, the most delightful Letter you ever heard of. She sends me a long account of the new Regency walking dress Lady Susan has given her, and it is so beautiful that I am quite dieing with envy for it."

"Well, I am prodigiously happy to hear such pleasing news of my young freind; I have a high regard for Augusta, and most sincerely partake in the general Joy on the occasion. But does she say nothing else? it seemed to be a long Letter—Are they to be at Scarborough?"

"Oh! Lord, she never once mentions it, now I recollect it; and I entirely forgot to ask her when I wrote last. She says nothing indeed except about the Regency." "She *must* write well thought Kitty, to make a long Letter upon a Bonnet & Pelisse." She then left the room tired of listening to a conversation which tho' it might have diverted her had she been well, served only to fatigue and depress her, while in pain. Happy was it for *her*, when the hour of dressing came, for Camilla satisfied with being surrounded by her Mother and half the Maids in the House did not want her assistance, and was too agreably employed to

want

want her Society. She remained therefore alone in the parlour, till joined by Mr Stanley & her Aunt, who however after a few enquiries, allowed her to continue undisturbed and began their usual conversation on Politics. This was a subject on which they could never agree, for Mr Stanley who considered himself as perfectly qualified by his Seat in the House, to decide on it without hesitation, resolutely maintained that the Kingdom had not for ages been in so flourishing & prosperous a state, and Mrs Percival with equal warmth, tho' perhaps less argument, as vehemently asserted that the whole Nation would speedily be ruined, and everything as she expressed herself be at sixes & sevens. It was not however unamusing to Kitty to listen to the Dispute, especially as she began then to be more free from pain, and without taking any share in it herself, she found it very entertaining to observe the eagerness with which they both defended their opinions, and could not help thinking that Mr Stanley would not feel more disappointed if her Aunt's expectations were fulfilled, than her Aunt would be mortified by their failure. After waiting a considerable time Mrs Stanley & her daughter appeared, and Camilla in high Spirits, & perfect good humour with her own looks, was more violent than ever in her lamentations over her Freind as she practised her scotch Steps about the room—. At length they departed, & Kitty better able to amuse herself than she had been the whole Day before, wrote a long account of her Misfortunes to Mary Wynne. When her Letter was concluded she had an opportunity of witnessing the truth of that assertion which says that Sorrows are lightened by Communication, for her toothake was then so much releived that she began to entertain an idea of following her Freinds to Mr Dudley's. They had been gone an hour, and as every thing relative to her Dress was in complete readiness, She considered that in another hour since there was so little a way to go, She might be there—. They were gone in Mr Stanley's Carriage

and

and therefore She might follow in her Aunt's. As the plan
seemed so very easy to be executed, and promising so much
pleasure, it was after a few Minutes deliberation finally
adopted, and running up stairs, She rang in great haste for
her Maid. The Bustle & Hurry which then ensued for
nearly an hour was at last happily concluded by her finding
herself very well-dressed and in high Beauty. Anne was
then dispatched in the same haste to order the Carriage,
while her Mistress was putting on her gloves, & arranging
the folds of her dress, [and providing herself with Lavender
water].[1] In a few Minutes she heard the Carriage drive up
to the Door, and tho' at first surprised at the expedition
with which it had been got ready, she concluded after a
little reflection that the Men had received some hint of her
intentions beforehand, and was hastening out of the room,
when Anne came running into it in the greatest hurry and
agitation, exclaiming "Lord Ma'am! Here's a Gentleman
in a Chaise and four come, and I cannot for my Life conceive who it is! I happened to be crossing the hall when the
Carriage drove up, and as I knew nobody would be in the
way to let him in but Tom, and he looks so awkward you
know Ma'am, now his hair is just done up, that I was not
willing the gentleman should see him, and so I went to the
door myself. And he is one of the handsomest young Men
you would wish to see; I was almost ashamed of being seen
in my Apron Ma'am, but however he is vastly handsome
and did not seem to mind it at all.—And he asked me
whether the Family were at home; and so I said everybody
was gone out but you Ma'am, for I would not deny you
because I was sure you would like to see him. And then
he asked me whether M[r] and M[rs] Stanley were not here,
and so I said Yes, and then——

"Good Heavens! said Kitty, what can all this mean!
And who can it possibly be! Did you never see him before?
And Did not he tell you his Name?"

[1] *Erased.*

"No

"No Ma'am, he never said anything about it—So then I asked him to walk into the parlour, and he was prodigious agreable, and——

"Whoever he is, said her Mistress, he has made a great impression upon you Nanny—But where did he come from? and what does he want here?

"Oh! Ma'am, I was going to tell you, that I fancy his business is with you; for he asked me whether you were at leisure to see anybody, and desired I would give his Compliments to you, & say he should be very happy to wait on you—However I thought he had better not come up into your Dressing room, especially as everything is in such a litter, so I told him if he would be so obliging as to stay in the parlour, I would run up stairs and tell you he was come, and I dared to say that you would wait upon *him*. Lord Ma'am, I'd lay anything that he is come to ask you to dance with him tonight, & has got his Chaise ready to take you to Mr Dudley's."

Kitty could not help laughing at this idea, & only wished it might be true, as it was very likely that she would be too late for any other partner—"But what, in the name of wonder, can he have to say to me? Perhaps he is come to rob the house—he comes in stile at least; and it will be some consolation for our losses to be robbed by a Gentleman in a Chaise & 4—. What Livery has his Servants?"

"Why that is the most wonderful thing about him Ma'am, for he has not a single servant with him, and came with hack horses; But he is as handsome as a Prince for all that, and has quite the look of one. Do dear Ma'am, go down, for I am sure you will be delighted with him—"

"Well, I beleive I must go; but it is very odd! What can he have to say to me." Then giving one look at herself in the Glass, she walked with great impatience, tho' trembling all the while from not knowing what to expect, down Stairs, and after pausing a moment at the door to gather Courage for opening it, she resolutely entered the room.
The

The Stranger, whose appearance did not disgrace the account she had received of it from her Maid, rose up on her entrance, and laying aside the Newspaper he had been reading, advanced towards her with an air of the most perfect Ease & Vivacity, and said to her, "It is certainly a very awkward circumstance to be thus obliged to introduce myself, but I trust that the necessity of the case will plead my Excuse, and prevent your being prejudiced by it against me—. *Your* name, I need not ask Ma'am—. Miss Percival is too well known to me by description to need any information of that." Kitty, who had been expecting him to tell his own name, instead of hers, and who from having been little in company, and never before in such a situation, felt herself unable to ask it, tho' she had been planning her speech all the way down stairs, was so confused & distressed by this unexpected address that she could only return a slight curtesy to it, and accepted the chair he reached her, without knowing what she did. The gentleman then continued. "You are, I dare say, surprised to see me returned from France so soon, and nothing indeed but business could have brought me to England; a very Melancholy affair has now occasioned it, and I was unwilling to leave it without paying my respects to the Family in Devonshire whom I have so long wished to be acquainted with—." Kitty, who felt much more surprised at his supposing her *to be so*, than at seeing a person in England, whose having ever left it was perfectly unknown to her, still continued silent from Wonder & Perplexity, and her visitor still continued to talk. "You will suppose Madam that I was not the *less* desirous of waiting on you, from your having M^r & Mrs Stanley with you—. I hope they are well? And Mrs Percival how does *she* do?" Then without waiting for an answer he gaily added, "But my dear Miss Percival you are going out I am sure; and I am detaining you from your appointment. How can I ever expect to be forgiven for such injustice! Yet how can I, so circumstanced, forbear

to

to offend! You seem dressed for a Ball? But this is the Land of gaiety I know; I have for many years been desirous of visiting it. You have Dances I suppose at least every week—But where are the rest of your party gone, and what kind Angel in compassion to me, has excluded *you* from it?"

"Perhaps Sir, said Kitty extremely confused by his manner of speaking to her, and highly displeased with the freedom of his Conversation towards one who had never seen him before and did not *now* know his name, "perhaps Sir, you are acquainted with M^r & Mrs Stanley; and your business may be with *them*?"

"You do me too much honour Ma'am, replied he laughing, in supposing me to be acquainted with M^r & Mrs Stanley; I merely know them by sight; very distant relations; only my Father & Mother. Nothing more I assure you."

"Gracious Heaven! said Kitty, are *you* Mr Stanley then? —I beg a thousand pardons—Though really upon recollection I do not know for what—for you never told me your name——"

"I beg your pardon—I made a very fine speech when you entered the room, all about introducing myself; I assure you it was very great for *me*."

"The speech had certainly great Merit, said Kitty smiling; I thought so at the time; but since you never mentioned your name in it, as an *introductory one* it might have been better."

There was such an air of good humour and Gaiety in Stanley, that Kitty, tho' perhaps not authorized to address him with so much familiarity on so short an acquaintance, could not forbear indulging the natural Unreserve & Vivacity of her own Disposition, in speaking to him, as he spoke to her. She was intimately acquainted too with his Family who were her relations, and she chose to consider herself entitled by the connexion to forget how little a while they

had

had known each other. "M^r & Mrs Stanley and your Sister are extremely well, said she, and will I dare say be very much surprised to see you—But I am sorry to hear that your return to England has been occasioned by an unpleasant circumstance."

"Oh, Do'nt talk of it, said he, it is a most confounded shocking affair, & makes me miserable to think of it; But where are my Father & Mother, & your Aunt gone? Oh! Do you know that I met the prettiest little waiting maid in the world, when I came here; she let me into the house; I took her for you at first."

"You did me a great deal of honour, and give me more credit for good nature than I deserve, for I *never* go to the door when any one comes."

"Nay do not be angry; I mean no offence. But tell me, where are you going to so smart? Your carriage is just coming round."

"I am going to a Dance at a Neighbour's, where your Family and my Aunt are already gone."

"Gone, without you! what's the meaning of *that*? But I suppose you are like myself, rather long in dressing."

"I must have been so indeed, if that were the case for they have been gone nearly these two hours; The reason however was not what you suppose—I was prevented going by a pain——

"By a pain! interrupted Stanley, Oh! heavens, that is dreadful indeed! No Matter where the pain was. But my dear Miss Percival, what do you say to my accompanying you? And suppose you were to dance with me too? *I* think it would be very pleasant."

"I can have no objection to either I am sure, said Kitty laughing to find how near the truth her Maid's conjecture had been; on the contrary I shall be highly honoured by both, and I can answer for Your being extremely welcome to the Family who give the Ball."

"Oh! hang them; who cares for that; they cannot turn

me

me out of the house. But I am afraid I shall cut a sad figure among all your Devonshire Beaux in this dusty, travelling apparel, and I have not wherewithal to change it. You can procure me some powder perhaps, and I must get a pair of Shoes from one of the Men, for I was in such a devil of a hurry to leave Lyons that I had not time to have anything pack'd up but some linen." Kitty very readily undertook to procure for him everything he wanted, & telling the footman to shew him into Mr Stanley's dressing room, gave Nanny orders to send in some powder & pomatum, which orders Nanny chose to execute in person. As Stanley's preparations in dressing were confined to such very trifling articles, Kitty of course expected him in about ten minutes; but she found that it had not been merely a boast of vanity in saying that he was dilatory in that respect, as he kept her waiting for him above half an hour, so that the Clock had struck ten before he entered the room and the rest of the party had gone by eight.

"Well, said he as he came in, have not I been very quick? I never hurried so much in my Life before."

"In that case you certainly have, replied Kitty, for all Merit you know is comparative."

"Oh! I knew you would be delighted with me for making so must[1] haste—. But come, the Carriage is ready; so, do not keep me waiting." And so saying he took her by the hand, & led her out of the room. "Why, my dear Cousin, said he when they were seated, this will be a most agreable surprize to everybody to see you enter the room with such a smart Young Fellow as I am—I hope your Aunt won't be alarmed."

"To tell you the truth, replied Kitty, I think the best way to prevent it, will be to send for her, or your Mother before we go into the room, especially as you are a perfect stranger, & must of course be introduced to M^r & Mrs Dudley—"

"Oh! Nonsense, said he; I did not expect *you* to stand

[1] *sic.*

upon

upon such Ceremony; Our acquaintance with each other renders all such Prudery, ridiculous; Besides, if we go in together, we shall be the whole talk of the Country—"

"To *me* replied Kitty, that would certainly be a most powerful inducement; but I scarcely know whether my Aunt would consider it as such—. Women at her time of life, have odd ideas of propriety you know."

"Which is the very thing that you ought to break them of; and why should you object to entering a room with me where all our relations are, when you have done me the honour to admit me without any chaprone into your Carriage? Do not you think your Aunt will be as much offended with you for one, as for the other of these mighty crimes."

"Why really said Catherine, I do not know but that she may; however, it is no reason that I should offend against Decorum a second time, because I have already done it once."

"On the contrary, that is the very reason which makes it impossible for you to prevent it, since you cannot offend for the *first time* again."

"You are very ridiculous, said she laughing, but I am afraid your arguments divert me too much to convince me."

"At least they will convince you that I am very agreable, which after all, is the happiest conviction for me, and as to the affair of Propriety we will let that rest till we arrive at our Journey's end—. This is a monthly Ball I suppose. Nothing but Dancing here—."

"I thought I had told you that it was given by a Mr Dudley—"

"Oh! aye so you did; but why should not Mr Dudley give one every month? By the bye who *is that* Man? Everybody gives Balls now I think; I beleive I must give one myself soon—. Well, but how do you like my Father & Mother? And poor little Camilla too, has not she plagued you to death with the Halifaxes?" Here the Carriage fortunately

fortunately stopped at Mr Dudley's, and Stanley was too
much engaged in handing her out of it, to wait for an
answer, or to remember that what he had said required
one. They entered the small vestibule which Mr Dudley had
raised to the Dignity of a Hall, & Kitty immediately
desired the footman who was leading the way upstairs, to
inform either Mrs Peterson, or Mrs Stanley of her arrival,
& beg them to come to her, but Stanley unused to any
contradiction & impatient to be amongst them, would
neither allow her to wait, or listen to what she said, &
forcibly seizing her arm within his, overpowered her voice
with the rapidity of his own, & Kitty half angry & half
laughing was obliged to go with him up stairs, and could
even with difficulty prevail on him to relinquish her hand
before they entered the room. Mrs Percival was at that
very moment engaged in conversation with a Lady at the
upper end of the room, to whom she had been giving a long
account of her Neice's unlucky disappointment, & the
dreadful pain that she had with so much fortitude, endured
the whole Day—"I left her however, said she, thank
heaven!, a little better, and I hope she has been able to
amuse herself with a book, poor thing! for she must otherwise be very dull. She is probably in bed by this time,
which while she is so poorly, is the best place for her you
know Ma'am." The Lady was going to give her assent to
this opinion, when the Noise of voices on the stairs, and the
footman's opening the door as if for the entrance of Company, attracted the attention of every body in the room;
and as it was in one of those Intervals between the Dances
when every one seemed glad to sit down, Mrs Peterson had
a most unfortunate opportunity of seeing her Neice whom
she had supposed in bed, or amusing herself as the height
of gaity with a book, enter the room most elegantly dressed,
with a smile on her Countenance, and a glow of mingled
Chearfulness & Confusion on her Cheeks, attended by a
young Man uncommonly handsome, and who without any

of

of her Confusion, appeared to have all her vivacity. Mrs Percival colouring with anger & astonishment, rose from her Seat, & Kitty walked eagerly towards her, impatient to account for what she saw appeared wonderful to every body, and extremely offensive to *her*, while Camilla on seeing her Brother ran instantly towards him, and very soon explained who he was by her words & her actions. Mr Stanley, who so fondly doated on his Son, that the pleasure of seeing him again after an absence of three Months prevented his feeling for the time any anger against him for returning to England without his knowledge, received him with equal surprise & delight; and soon comprehending the cause of his Journey, forbore any further conversation with him, as he was eager to see his Mother, & it was necessary that he should be introduced to Mr Dudley's family. This introduction to any one but Stanley would have been highly unpleasant, for they considered their dignity injured by his coming uninvited to their house, & received him with more than their usual haughtiness: But Stanley who with a vivacity of temper seldom subdued, & a contempt of censure not to be overcome, possessed an opinion of his own Consequence, & a perseverance in his own schemes which were not to be damped by the conduct of others, appeared not to perceive it. The Civilities therefore which they coldly offered, he received with a gaiety & ease peculiar to himself, and then attended by his Father & Sister walked into another room where his Mother was playing at Cards, to experience another Meeting, and undergo a repetition of pleasure, surprise, & Explanations. While these were passing, Camilla eager to communicate all she felt to some one who would attend to her, returned to Catherine, & seating herself by her, immediately began—"Well, did you ever know anything so delightful as this? But it always is so; I never go to a Ball in my Life but what something or other happens unexpectedly that is quite charming!"

"A

"A Ball replied Kitty, seems to be a most eventful thing to you—"

"Oh! Lord, it is indeed—But only think of my brother's returning so suddenly—And how shocking a thing it is that has brought him over! I never heard anything so dreadful—!"

"What is it pray that has occasioned his leaving France? I am sorry to find that it is a melancholy event."

"Oh! it is beyond anything you can conceive! His favourite Hunter who was turned out in the park on his going abroad, somehow or other fell ill—No, I beleive it was an accident, but however it was something or other, or else it was something else, and so they sent an Express immediately to Lyons where my Brother was, for they knew that he valued this Mare more than anything else in the World besides; and so my Brother set off directly for England, and without packing up another Coat; I am quite angry with him about it; it was so shocking you know to come away without a change of Cloathes—"

"Why indeed said Kitty, it seems to have been a very shocking affair from beginning to end."

"Oh! it is beyond anything You can conceive! I would rather have had *anything* happen than that he should have lossed that mare."

"Except his coming away without another coat."

"Oh! yes, that has vexed me more than you can imagine.— Well, & so Edward got to Brampton just as the poor Thing was dead; but as he could not bear to remain there *then*, he came off directly to Chetwynde on purpose to see us—. I hope he may not go abroad again."

"Do you think he will not?"

"Oh! dear, to be sure he must, but I wish he may not with all my heart—. You cannot think how fond I am of him! By the bye are not you in love with him yourself?"

"To be sure I am replied Kitty laughing, I am in love with every handsome Man I see."

"That

"That is just like me—*I* am always in love with every handsome Man in the World."

"There you outdo me replied Catherine for I am only in love with those I *do* see." Mrs Percival who was sitting on the other side of her, & who began now to distinguish the words, *Love* & *handsome Man*, turned hastily towards them, & said "What are you talking of Catherine?" To which Catherine immediately answered with the simple artifice of a Child, "Nothing Ma'am." She had already received a very severe lecture from her Aunt on the imprudence of her behaviour during the whole evening; She blamed her for coming to the Ball, for coming in the same Carriage with Edward Stanley, and still more for entering the room with him. For the last-mentioned offence Catherine knew not what apology to give, and tho' she longed in answer to the second to say that she had not thought it would be civil to make Mr Stanley *walk*, she dared not so to trifle with her aunt, who would have been but the more offended by it. The first accusation however she considered as very unreasonable, as she thought herself perfectly justified in coming. This conversation continued till Edward Stanley entering the room came instantly towards her, and telling her that every one waited for *her* to begin the next Dance led her to the top of the room, for Kitty impatient to escape from so unpleasant a Companion, without the least hesitation, or one civil scruple at being so distinguished, immediately gave him her hand, & joyfully left her seat. This Conduct however was highly resented by several young Ladies present, and among the rest by Miss Stanley whose regard for her brother tho' *excessive*, & whose affection for Kitty tho' *prodigious*, were not proof against such an injury to her importance and her peace. Edward had however only consulted his own inclinations in desiring Miss Peterson to begin the Dance, nor had he any reason to know that it was either wished or expected by anyone else in the Party. As an heiress she

was

was certainly of consequence, but her Birth gave her no
other claim to it, for her Father had been a Merchant. It
was this very circumstance which rendered this unfortunate affair so offensive to Camilla, for tho' she would
sometimes boast in the pride of her heart, & her eagerness to be admired that she did not know who her grandfather had been, and was as ignorant of everything relative
to Genealogy as to Astronomy, (and she might have added,
Geography) yet she was really proud of her family &
Connexions, and easily offended if they were treated with
Neglect. "I should not have minded it, said she to her
Mother, if she had been *anybody* else's daughter; but to
see her pretend to be above *me*, when her Father was
only a tradesman, is too bad! It is such an affront to
our whole Family! I declare I think Papa ought to interfere in it, but he never cares about anything but Politics.
If I were Mr Pitt or the Lord Chancellor, he would take
care I should not be insulted, but he never thinks about *me*;
And it is so provoking that *Edward* should let her stand
there. I wish with all my heart that he had never come to
England! I hope she may fall down & break her neck, or
sprain her Ancle." Mrs Stanley perfectly agreed with her
daughter concerning the affair, & tho' with less violence,
expressed almost equal resentment at the indignity. Kitty
in the meantime remained insensible of having given any
one Offence, and therefore unable either to offer an apology,
or make a reparation; her whole attention was occupied by
the happiness she enjoyed in dancing with the most elegant
young Man in the room, and every one else was equally
unregarded. The Evening indeed to *her*, passed off delightfully; he was her partner during the greatest part of it,
and the united attractions that he possessed of Person,
Address & vivacity, had easily gained that preference from
Kitty which they seldom fail of obtaining from every one.
She was too happy to care either for her Aunt's illhumour
which she could not help remarking, or for the Alteration
in

in Camilla's behaviour which forced itself at last on her observation. Her Spirits were elevated above the influence of Displeasure in any one, and she was equally indifferent as to the cause of Camilla's, or the continuance of her Aunt's. Though Mr Stanley could never be really offended by any imprudence or folly in his Son that had given him the pleasure of seeing him, he was yet perfectly convinced that Edward ought not to remain in England, and was resolved to hasten his leaving it as soon as possible; but when he talked to Edward about it, he found him much less disposed towards returning to France, than to accompany them in their projected tour, which he assured his Father would be infinitely more pleasant to him, and that as to the affair of travelling he considered it of no importance, and what might be pursued at any little odd time, when he had nothing better to do. He advanced these objections in a manner which plainly shewed that he had scarcely a doubt of their being complied with, and appeared to consider his father's arguments in opposition to them, as merely given with a veiw to keep up his authority, & such as he should find little difficulty in combating. He concluded at last by saying, as the chaise in which they returned together from Mr Dudley's reached Mrs Percivals, "Well Sir, we will settle this point some other time, and fortunately it is of so little consequence, that an immediate discussion of it is unnecessary." He then got out of the chaise & entered the house without waiting for his Father's reply. It was not till their return that Kitty could account for that coldness in Camilla's behaviour to her, which had been so pointed as to render it impossible to be entirely unnoticed. When however they were seated in the Coach with the two other Ladies, Miss Stanley's indignation was no longer to be suppressed from breaking out into words, & found the following vent.

"Well, I must say *this*, that I never was at a stupider Ball in my Life! But it always is so; I am always disappointed

appointed in them for some reason or other. I wish there were no such things."

"I am sorry Miss Stanley, said Mrs Percival drawing herself up, that you have not been amused; every thing was meant for the best I am sure, and it is a poor encouragement for your Mama to take you to another if you are so hard to be satisfied."

"I do not know what you mean Ma'am about Mama's *taking* me to another. You know I am come out."

"Oh! dear Mrs Percival, said Mrs Stanley, you must not beleive everything that my lively Camilla says, for her spirits are prodigiously high sometimes, and she frequently speaks without thinking. I am sure it is impossible for *any one* to have been at a more elegant or agreable dance, and so she wishes to express herself I am certain."

"To be sure I do, said Camilla very sulkily, only I must say that it is not very pleasant to have any body behave so rude to me as to be quite shocking! I am sure I am not at all offended, and should not care if all the World were to stand above me, but still it is extremely abominable, & what I cannot put up with. It is not that I mind it in the least, for I had just as soon stand at the bottom as at the top all night long, if it was not so very disagreable—. But to have a person come in the middle of the Evening & take everybody's place is what I am not used to, and tho' I do not care a pin about it myself, I assure you I shall not easily forgive or forget it."

This speech which perfectly explained the whole affair to Kitty, was shortly followed on her side by a very submissive apology, for she had too much good Sense to be proud of her family, and too much good Nature to live at variance with any one. The Excuses she made, were delivered with so much real concern for the Offence, and such unaffected Sweetness, that it was almost impossible for Camilla to retain that anger which had occasioned them; She felt indeed most highly gratified to find that no insult

had

had been intended and that Catherine was very far from forgetting the difference in their birth for which she could *now* only pity her, and her good humour being restored with the same Ease in which it had been affected, she spoke with the highest delight of the Evening, & declared that she had never before been at so pleasant a Ball. The same endeavours that had procured the forgiveness of Miss Stanly ensured to her the cordiality of her Mother, and nothing was wanting but M^rs P's good humour to render the happiness of the others complete; but She, offended with Camilla for her affected Superiority, Still more so with her brother for coming to Chetwynde, & dissatisfied with the whole Evening, continued silent & Gloomy and was a restraint on the vivacity of her Companions. She eagerly seized the very first opportunity which the next Morning offered to her of speaking to Mr Stanley on the subject of his son's return, and after having expressed her opinion of its being a very silly affair that he came at all, concluded with desiring him to inform Mr Edward Stanley that it was a rule with her never to admit a young Man into her house as a visitor for any length of time.

"I do not speak Sir, she continued, out of any disrespect to You, but I could not answer it to myself to allow of his stay; there is no knowing what might be the consequence of it, if he were to continue here, for girls nowadays will always give a handsome young Man the preference before any other, tho' for why, I never could discover, for what after all is Youth and Beauty? [Why in fact, it is nothing more than being Young and Handsome—and that][1] It is but a poor substitute for real worth & Merit; Beleive me Cousin that, what ever people may say to the contrary, there is certainly nothing like Virtue for making us what we ought to be, and as to a young Man's, being young & handsome & having an agreable person, it is nothing at all

[1] *erased, and* It *substituted.*

to

to the purpose for he had much better be respectable. I
always *did* think so, and I always *shall*, and therefore you
will oblige me very much by desiring your son to leave
Chetwynde, or I cannot be answerable for what may
happen between him and my Neice. You will be surprised
to hear *me* say it, she continued, lowering her voice, but
truth will out, and I must own that Kitty is one of the
most impudent Girls that ever existed. [Her intimacies
with Young Men are abominable, and it is all the same to
her, who it is, no one comes amiss to her][1] I assure you Sir,
that I have seen her sit and laugh and whisper with a young
Man whom she has not seen above half a dozen times. Her
behaviour indeed is scandalous, and therefore I beg you
will send your Son away immediately, or everything will be
at sixes & sevens." Mr Stanley who from one part of her
Speech had scarcely known to what length her insinuations of
Kitty's impudence were meant to extend, now endeavoured
to quiet her fears on the occasion, by assuring her, that on
every account he meant to allow only of his son's continuing that day with them, and that she might depend on his
being more earnest in the affair from a wish of obliging her.
He added also that he knew Edward to be very desirous
himself of returning to France, as he wisely considered all
time lost that did not forward the plans in which he was
at present engaged, tho' he was but too well convinced of
the contrary himself. His assurance in some degree quieted
M^rs P, & left her tolerably releived of her Cares & Alarms,
& better disposed to behave with civility towards his Son
during the short remainder of his stay at Chetwynde. M^r
Stanley went immediately to Edward, to whom he repeated
the Conversation that had passed between M^rs P & himself,
& strongly pointed out the necessity of his leaving Chetwynde the next day, since his word was already engaged
for it. His son however appeared struck only by the ridiculous apprehensions of Mrs Peterson; and highly delighted

[1] *Erased.*

at

at having occasioned them himself, seemed engrossed alone
in thinking how he might encrease them, without attending
to any other part of his Father's Conversation. Mr Stanley
could get no determinate Answer from him, and tho' he
still hoped for the best, they parted almost in anger on his
side. His Son though by no means disposed to marry, or
any otherwise attached to Miss Percival than as a good
natured lively Girl who seemed pleased with him, took
infinite pleasure in alarming the jealous fears of her Aunt
by his attentions to her, without considering what effect
they might have on the Lady herself. He would always sit
by her when she was in the room, appear dissatisfied if she
left it, and was the first to enquire whether she meant soon
to return. He was delighted with her Drawings, and
enchanted with her performance on the Harpsichord; Everything that she said, appeared to interest him; his Conversation was addressed to her alone, and she seemed to be
the sole object of his attention. That such efforts should
succeed with one so tremblingly alive to every alarm of the
kind as Mrs Percival, is by no means unnatural, and that
they should have equal influence with her Neice whose
imagination was lively, and whose Disposition romantic,
who was already extremely pleased with him, and of
course desirous that he might be so with her, is as little
to be wondered at. Every moment as it added to the conviction of his liking her, made him still more pleasing, and
strengthened in her Mind a wish of knowing him better.
As for Mrs Percival, she was in tortures the whole Day;
Nothing that she had ever felt before on a similar occasion
was to be compared to the sensations which then distracted
her; her fears had never been so strongly, or indeed so
reasonably excited.—Her dislike of Stanly, her anger at her
Neice, her impatience to have them separated conquered
every idea of propriety & Goodbreeding, and though he
had never mentioned any intention of leaving them the
next day, she could not help asking him after Dinner, in
her

her eagerness to have him gone, at what time he meant to set out.

"Oh! Ma'am, replied he, if I am off by twelve at night, you may think yourself lucky; and if I am not, you can only blame yourself for having left so much as the *hour* of my departure to my own disposal." Mrs Percival coloured very highly at this speech, and without addressing herself to any one in particular, immediately began a long harangue on the shocking behaviour of modern young Men, & the wonderful Alteration that had taken place in them, since her time, which she illustrated with many instructive anecdotes of the Decorum & Modesty which had marked the Characters of those whom she had known, when she had been young. This however did not prevent his walking in the Garden with her Neice, without any other companion for nearly an hour in the course of the Evening. They had left the room for that purpose with Camilla at a time when Mrs Peterson had been out of it, nor was it for some time after her return to it, that she could discover where they were. Camilla had taken two or three turns with them in the walk which led to the Arbour, but soon growing tired of listening to a Conversation in which she was seldom invited to join, & from its turning occasionally on Books, very little able to do it, she left them together in the arbour, to wander alone to some other part of the Garden, to eat the fruit, & examine Mrs Peterson's Greenhouse. Her absence was so far from being regretted, that it was scarcely noticed by them, & they continued conversing together on almost every subject, for Stanley seldom dwelt long on any, and had something to say on all, till they were interrupted by her Aunt.

Kitty was by this time perfectly convinced that both in Natural Abilities, & acquired information, Edward Stanley was infinitely superior to his Sister. Her desire of knowing that he was so, had induced her to take every opportunity of turning the Conversation on History and they were very

soon

soon engaged in an historical dispute, for which no one was more calculated than Stanley who was so far from being really of any party, that he had scarcely a fixed opinion on the Subject. He could therefore always take either side, & always argue with temper. In his indifference on all such topics he was very unlike his Companion, whose judgement being guided by her feelings which were eager & warm, was easily decided, and though it was not always infallible, she defended it with a Spirit & Enthuisasm[1] which marked her own reliance on it. They had continued therefore for sometime conversing in this manner on the character of Richard the 3^d, which he was warmly defending when he suddenly seized hold of her hand, and exclaiming with great emotion, "Upon my honour you are entirely mistaken," pressed it passionately to his lips, & ran out of the arbour. Astonished at this behaviour, for which she was wholly unable to account, she continued for a few Moments motionless on the seat where he had left her, and was then on the point of following him up the narrow walk through which he had passed, when on looking up the one that lay immediately before the arbour, she saw her Aunt walking towards her with more than her usual quickness. This explained at once the reason of his leaving her, but his leaving her in such Manner was rendered still more inexplicable by it. She felt a considerable degree of confusion at having been seen by her in such a place with Edward, and at having that part of his conduct, for which she could not herself account, witnessed by one to whom all gallantry was odious. She remained therefore confused and distressed & irresolute, and suffered her Aunt to approach her, without leaving the Arbour. Mrs Percival's looks were by no means calculated to animate the spirits of her Neice, who in silence awaited her accusation, and in silence meditated her Defence. After a few Moments suspence, for Mrs Peterson was too much fatigued to speak immediately, she

¹ *sic.*

began

began with great Anger and Asperity, the following harangue. "Well; *this* is beyond anything I could have supposed. *Profligate* as I *knew* you to be, I was not prepared for such a sight. This is beyond any thing you ever did *before*; beyond any thing I ever heard of in my Life! Such Impudence, I never witnessed before in such a Girl! And this is the reward for all the cares I have taken in your Education; for all my troubles & Anxieties; and Heaven knows how many they have been! All I wished for, was to breed you up virtuously; I never wanted you to play upon the Harpsichord, or draw better than any one else; but I had hoped to see you respectable and good; to see you able & willing to give an example of Modesty and Virtue to the Young people here abouts. I bought you Blair's Sermons, and Cœlebs in Search of a Wife,[1] I gave you the key to my own Library, and borrowed a great many good books of my Neighbours for you, all to this purpose. But I might have spared myself the trouble—Oh! Catherine, you are an abandoned Creature, and I do not know what will become of you. I am glad however, she continued softening into some degree of Mildness, to see that you have some shame for what you have done, and if you are really sorry for it, and your future life is a life of penitence and reformation perhaps you may be forgiven. But I plainly see that every thing is going to sixes & sevens and all order will soon be at an end throughout the Kingdom."

"Not however Ma'am the sooner, I hope, from any conduct of mine, said Catherine in a tone of great humility, for upon my honour I have done nothing this evening that can contribute to overthrow the establishment of the kingdom."

"You are Mistaken Child, replied she; the welfare of every Nation depends upon the virtue of it's individuals, and any one who offends in so gross a manner against

---

[1] Cœlebs *etc. substituted for* Seccar's explanation of the Catechism.

decorum

decorum & propriety is certainly hastening it's ruin. You have been giving a bad example to the World, and the World is but too well disposed to receive such."

"Pardon me Madam, said her Neice; but I *can* have given an Example only to *You*, for You alone have seen the offence. Upon my word however there is no danger to fear from what I have done; Mr Stanley's behaviour has given me as much surprise, as it has done to You, and I can only suppose that it was the effect of his high spirits, authorized in his opinion by our relationship. But do you consider Madam that it is growing very late? Indeed You had better return to the house." This speech as she well knew, would be unanswerable with her Aunt, who instantly rose, and hurried away under so many apprehensions for her own health, as banished for the time all anxiety about her Neice, who walked quietly by her side, revolving within her own Mind the occurrence that had given her Aunt so much alarm. "I am astonished at my own imprudence, said Mrs Percival; How could I be so forgetful as to sit down out of doors at such a time of night. I shall certainly have a return of my rheumatism after it—I begin to feel very chill already. I must have caught a dreadful cold by this time—I am sure of being lain-up all the winter after it—" Then reckoning with her fingers, "Let me see; This is July; the cold weather will soon be coming in— August—September—October—November—December— January—February—March—April—Very likely I may not be tolerable again before May. I must and will have that arbour pulled down—it will be the death of me; who knows *now*, but what I may never recover—Such things *have* happened—My particular freind Miss Sarah Hutchinson's death was occasioned by nothing more—She staid out late one Evening in April, and got wet through for it rained very hard, and never changed her Cloathes when she came home—It is unknown how many people have died in consequence of catching Cold! I do not beleive there

there is a disorder in the World except the Smallpox which does not spring from it." It was in vain that Kitty endeavoured to convince her that her fears on the occasion were groundless; that it was not yet late enough to catch cold, and that even if it were, she might hope to escape any other complaint, and to recover in less than ten Months. Mrs Percival only replied that she hoped she knew more of Ill health than to be convinced in such a point by a Girl who had always been perfectly well, and hurried up stairs leaving Kitty to make her apologies to M^r & Mrs Stanley for going to bed—. Tho' Mrs Percival seemed perfectly satisfied with the goodness of the Apology herself, yet Kitty felt somewhat embarrassed to find that the only one she could offer to their Visitors was that her Aunt had *perhaps* caught cold, for Mrs Peterson charged her to make light of it, for fear of alarming them. M^r & Mrs Stanley however who well knew that their Cousin was easily terrified on that Score, received the account of it with very little surprise, and all proper concern. Edward & his Sister soon came in, & Kitty had no difficulty in gaining an explanation of his Conduct from him, for he was too warm on the subject himself, and too eager to learn its success, to refrain from making immediate Enquiries about it; & She could not help feeling both surprised & offended at the ease & Indifference with which he owned that all his intentions had been to frighten her Aunt by pretending an affection for *her*, a design so very incompatible with that partiality which she had at one time been almost convinced of his feeling for her. It is true that she had not yet seen enough of him to be actually in love with him, yet she felt greatly disappointed that so handsome, so elegant, so lively a young Man should be so perfectly free from any such Sentiment as to make it his principal Sport. There was a Novelty in his character which to *her* was extremely pleasing; his person was uncommonly fine, his Spirits & Vivacity suited to her own, and his Manners at once so animated & insinuating

sinuating, that she thought it must be impossible for him
to be otherwise than amiable, and was ready to give him
Credit for being perfectly so. He knew the powers of them
himself; to them he had often been endebted for his father's
forgiveness of faults which had he been awkward & inelegant would have appeared very serious; to them, even
more than to his person or his fortune, he owed the regard
which almost every one was disposed to feel for him, and
which Young Women in particular were inclined to entertain. Their influence was acknowledged on the present
occasion by Kitty, whose Anger they entirely dispelled,
and whose Chearfulness they had power not only to restore, but to raise—. The Evening passed off as agreably
as the one that had preceded it; they continued talking to
each other, during the cheif part of it, and such was the
power of his Address, & the Brilliancy of his Eyes, that
when they parted for the Night, tho' Catherine had but
a few hours before totally given up the idea, yet she felt
almost convinced again that he was really in love with her.
She reflected on their past Conversation, and tho' it had
been on various & indifferent subjects, and she could not
exactly recollect any speech on his side expressive of such
a partiality, she was still however nearly certain of it's
being so; But fearful of being vain enough to suppose such
a thing without sufficient reason, she resolved to suspend
her final determination on it, till the next day, and more
especially till their parting which she thought would in-
fallibly explain his regard if any he had—. The more she
had seen of him, the more inclined was she to like him, &
the more desirous that he should like *her*. She was convinced of his being naturally very clever and very well
disposed, and that his thoughtlessness & negligence, which
tho' they appeared to *her* as very becoming in *him*, she was
aware would by many people be considered as defects in his
Character, merely proceeded from a vivacity always pleasing in Young Men, & were far from testifying a weak or

vacant

vacant Understanding. Having settled this point within herself, and being perfectly convinced by her own arguments of it's truth, she went to bed in high Spirits, determined to study his Character, and watch his Behaviour still more the next day. She got up with the same good resolutions and would probably have put them in execution, had not Anne informed her as soon as she entered the room that Mr Edward Stanley was already gone. At first she refused to credit the information, but when her Maid assured her that he had ordered a Carriage the evening before to be there at seven o'clock in the Morning and that she herself had actually seen him depart in it a little after eight, she could no longer deny her beleif to it. "And this, thought she to herself blushing with anger at her own folly, this is the affection for me of which I was so certain. Oh! what a silly Thing is Woman! How vain, how unreasonable! To suppose that a young Man would be seriously attached in the course of four & twenty hours, to a Girl who has nothing to recommend her but a good pair of eyes! And he is really gone! Gone perhaps without bestowing a thought on me! Oh! why was not I up by eight o'clock? But it is a proper punishment for my Lazyness & Folly, and I am heartily glad of it. I deserve it all, & ten times more for such insufferable vanity. It will at least be of service to me in that respect; it will teach me in future *not* to think Every Body is in love with me. Yet I *should* like to have seen him before he went, for perhaps it may be many Years before we meet again. By his Manner of leaving us however, he seems to have been perfectly indifferent about it. How very odd, that he should go without giving us Notice of it, or taking leave of any one! But it is just like a Young Man, governed by the whim of the moment, or actuated merely by the love of doing anything oddly! Unaccountable Beings indeed! And Young Women are equally ridiculous! I shall soon begin to think like my Aunt that everything is going to sixes & sevens, and that the whole race of Mankind

are

are degenerating." She was just dressed, and on the point of leaving her room to make her personal enquiries after Mrs Peterson, when Miss Stanley knocked at her door, & on her being admitted began in her Usual Strain a long harangue upon her Father's being so shocking as to make Edward go at all, and upon Edward's being so horrid as to leave them at such an hour in the Morning. "You have no idea, said she, how surprised I was, when he came into my Room to bid me good bye—"

"Have you seen him then, this Morning?" said Kitty.

"Oh Yes! And I was so sleepy that I could not open my eyes. And so he said, Camilla, goodbye to you for I am going away—. I have not time to take leave of any body else, and I dare not trust myself to see Kitty, for then you know I should never get away—"

"Nonsense, said Kitty; he did not say that, or he was in joke if he did."

"Oh! no I assure you he was as much in earnest as he ever was in his life; he was too much out of spirits to joke *then*. And he desired me when we all met at Breakfast to give his Comp^{ts} to your Aunt, and his Love to you, for you was a nice Girl he said, and he only wished it were in his power to be more with You. You were just the Girl to suit him, because you were so lively and good-natured, and he wished with all his heart that you might not be married before he came back, for there was nothing he liked better than being here. Oh! you have no idea what fine things he said about you, till at last I fell asleep and he went away. But he certainly is in love with you—I am sure he is—I have thought so a great while I assure You."

"How can you be so ridiculous? said Kitty smiling with pleasure; I do not beleive him to be so easily affected. But he *did* desire his Love to me then? And wished I might not be married before his return? And said I was a Nice Girl, did he?"

"Oh! dear, Yes, and I assure You it is the greatest praise

praise in his opinion, that he can bestow on any body; I can hardly ever persuade him to call *me* one, tho' I beg him sometimes for an hour together."

"And do You really think that he was sorry to go?"

"Oh! you can have no idea how wretched it made him. He would not have gone this Month, if my Father had not insisted on it; Edward told me so himself yesterday. He said that he wished with all his heart he had never promised to go abroad, for that he repented it more and more every day; that it interfered with all his other schemes, and that since Papa had spoken to him about it, he was more unwilling to leave Chetwynde than ever."

"Did he really say all this? And why would your father insist upon his going? "His leaving England interfered with all his other plans, and his Conversation with Mr Stanley had made him still more averse to it." What can this Mean?" "Why that he is excessively in love with you to be sure; what other plans can he have? And I suppose my father said that if he had not been going abroad, he should have wished him to marry you immediately.—But I must go and see your Aunt's plants—There is one of them that I quite doat on—and two or three more besides—"

"Can Camilla's explanation be true? said Catherine to herself, when her freind had left the room. And after all my doubts and Uncertainties, can Stanley really be averse to leaving England for *my sake* only? "His plans interrupted." And what indeed can his plans be, but towards Marriage? Yet *so soon* to be in love with me!—But it is the effect perhaps only of a warmth of heart which to *me* is the highest recommendation in any one. A Heart disposed to love—And such under the appearance of so much Gaity and Inattention, is Stanly's! Oh! how much does it endear him to me! But he is gone—Gone perhaps for Years—Obliged to tear himself from what he most loves, his happiness is sacrificed to the vanity of his Father! In what anguish he must have left the house! Unable to see

me

me, or to bid me adieu, while I, senseless wretch, was daring to sleep. This, then explained his leaving us at such a time of day—. He could not trust himself to see me—. Charming Young Man! How much must you have suffered! I *knew* that it was impossible for one so elegant, and so well bred, to leave any Family in such a Manner, but for a Motive like this unanswerable." Satisfied, beyond the power of Change, of this, She went in high spirits to her Aunt's apartment, without giving a Moment's recollection on the vanity of Young Women, or the unaccountable conduct of Young Men.

Kitty continued in this state of satisfaction during the remainder of the Stanley's visit—Who took their leave with many pressing invitations to visit them in London, when as Camilla said, she might have an opportunity of becoming acquainted with that sweet girl Augusta Hallifax —Or Rather (thought Kitty,) of seeing my dr Mary Wynn again—Mrs Percival in answer to Mrs Stanley's invitation replied—That she looked upon London as the hot house of Vice where virtue had long been banished from Society & wickedness of every description was daily gaining ground— that Kitty was of herself sufficiently inclined to give way to, & indulge in vicious inclinations—& therefore was the last girl in the world to be trusted in London, as she would be totally unable to withstand temptation——

After the departure of the Stanleys Kitty returned to her usual occupations, but Alas! they had lost their power of pleasing. Her bower alone retained its interest in her feelings, & perhaps that was oweing to the particular remembrance it brought to her mind of Edwd Stanley.

The Summer passed away unmarked by any incident worth narrating, or any pleasure to Catharine save one, which arose from the reciept of a letter from her friend Cecilia now Mrs Lascelles, announcing the speedy return of herself & Husband to England.

A correspondance productive indeed of little pleasure to
either

either party had been established between Camilla & Catharine. The latter had now lost the only satisfaction she had ever received from the letters of Miss Stanley, as that young Lady having informed her Friend of the departure of her Brother to Lyons now never mentioned his name—Her letters seldom contained any Intelligence except a description of some new Article of Dress, an enumeration of various engagements, a panegyric (?) on Augusta Halifax & perhaps a little abuse of the unfortunate Sir Peter—

The Grove, for so was the Mansion of Mrs Percival at Chetwynde denominated was situated w^hin five miles from Exeter, but though that Lady possessed a carriage & horses of her [her] own, it was seldom that Catharine could prevail on her to visit that town for the purpose of shopping, on account of the many Officers perpetually Quartered there & infested the principal Streets—A company of strolling players in their way from some Neighbouring Races having opened a temporary Theatre there, Mrs Percival was prevailed on by her Niece to indulge her by attending the performance once during their stay—Mrs Percival insisted on paying Miss Dudley the compliment of inviting her to join the party, when a new difficulty arose, from the necessity of having some Gentleman to attend them——

Here follows a contribution to Evelyn *by Jane Austen's niece Anna Lefroy.*

ON re entering his circular domain, his round-Robin of perpetual peace; where enjoyment had no end, and calamity no commencement, his spirits became wonderfully composed, and a delicious calm extended itself through every nerve—With his pocket hankerchief (once hemmed by the genius of the too susceptible Rosa) he wiped the morbid moisture from his brow;—then flew to the Boudoir of

of his Maria—And, did *she* not fly to meet her Frederick?
Did she not dart from the Couch on which she had so gracefully reclined, and, bounding like an agile Fawn over the
intervening Foot stool, precipitate herself into his arms?
Does she not, though fainting between every syllable,
breathe forth as it were by installments her Frederick's
adored name? Who is there of perception so obtuse as not
to realize the touching scene? Who, of ear so dull as not
to catch the soft murmur of Maria's voice? Ah! Who?
The heart of every sympathetic reader repeats, Ah, Who?
Vain Echo! Vain sympathy! There is no Meeting—no
Murmur—No Maria—It is not in the power of language
however potent; nor in that of style, however diffuse to
render justice to the astonishment of Mr Gower—Arming
himself with a mahogany ruler which some fatality had
placed on Maria's writing table, and calling repeatedly on
her beloved Name, he rushed forward to examine the
adjacent apartments—In the Dressing room of his lost one
he had the melancholy satisfaction of picking up a curl
paper, and a gust of wind, as he re entered the Boudoir,
swept from the table, & placed at his feet a skein of black
sewing silk—These were the only traces of Maria!! Carefully locking the doors of these now desolate rooms, bury-
ing the key deep in his Waistcoat pocket, & the mystery
of Maria's disappearance yet deeper in his heart of hearts,
Mr Gower left his once happy home, and sought a supper,
and a Bed, at the house of the hospitable Mrs Willis—
There was an oppression on his chest which made him
extremely uncomfortable; he regretted that instead of the
skein of silk carefully wrapped up in the curl paper & placed
beneath his pillow he had not rather swallowed Laudanum
—It would have been, in all probability, more efficacious—
At last, Mr Gower slept a troubled sleep, and in due course
of time he dreamt a troubled dream—He dreamed of Maria,
as how could he less? She stood by his Bed side, in her
Dressing Gown—one hand held an open book, with the
forefinger

forefinger of the other she pointed to this ominous passage
—"Tantôt c'est un vide; qui nous ennuie; tantôt c'est un
poids qui nous oppresse"—The unfortunate Frederick
uttered a deep groan—& as the vision closed the volume he
observed these characters strangely imprinted on the Cover
—Rolandi—Berners Street. *Who* was this dangerous Rolandi? Doubtless a Bravo or a Monk—possibly both—and
what was he to Maria? Vainly he would have dared the
worst, and put the fatal question—the semblance of Maria
raised her monitory finger, and interdicted speech—Yet,
some words she spoke, or seemed to speak her self; M^r
Gower could distinguish only these—Search—Cupboard—
Top shelf—Once more he essayed to speak, but it was all
bewilderment—He heard strange Demon-like Sounds; hiss-
ing and spitting—he smelt an unearthly smell the agony
became unbearable, and he awoke—Maria had vanished;
the Rush light was expiring in the Socket; and the benevolent Mrs Willis entering his room, threw open the shutters,
and in accordance with her own warmth of heart admitted
the full blaze of a Summer morning's Sun—But what found
he on reentering that circle of peace, that round Robin of
perpetual peace

                                        J. A. E. L.

'Lady

CASSANDRA AUSTEN'S NOTE OF THE DATE OF COMPOSITION
OF HER SISTER'S NOVELS

II. 'Lady Susan'

THE title 'Lady Susan' was given to the untitled manuscript by J. E. Austen-Leigh when he first printed the work in the 1871 *Memoir*. The manuscript (now in the Pierpont Morgan Library, New York) is an undated fair copy, almost free from correction and revision. Two of the leaves are watermarked 1805.

R. W. Chapman judged that the work was composed and transcribed about 1805. But the 1871 *Memoir* refers to a family tradition that it was 'an early production' (p. 52); and according to the *Life* it was written about the same time as 'Elinor and Marianne' (the first version of *Sense and Sensibility*), that is about 1795. My study of the juvenilia and the associated manuscripts leads me to judge that 'Lady Susan' was probably written about 1793–4 (see *Literary Manuscripts*, ch. 3). A full record of the manuscript alterations is given in the text of *Lady Susan* edited by R. W. Chapman, Oxford, 1923.   [B. C. S.]

LETTER 1.

Lady Susan Vernon to Mr *Vernon.*

Langford, Dec^r.

My dear Brother

I can no longer refuse myself the pleasure of profitting by your kind invitation when we last parted, of spending some weeks with you at Churchill, & therefore if quite convenient to you & Mrs Vernon to receive me at present, I shall hope within a few days to be introduced to a Sister whom I have so long desired to be acquainted with. My kind friends here are most affectionately urgent with me to prolong my stay, but their hospitable & chearful dispositions lead them too much into society for my present situation & state of mind; & I impatiently look forward to the hour when I shall be admitted into your delightful retirement. I long to be made known to your dear little Children,

in

in whose hearts I shall be very eager to secure an interest.
I shall soon have occasion for all my fortitude, as I am on
the point of separation from my own daughter. The long
illness of her dear Father prevented my paying her that
attention which Duty & affection equally dictated, & I
have but too much reason to fear that the Governess to
whose care I consigned her, was unequal to the charge. I
have therefore resolved on placing her at one of the best
Private Schools in Town, where I shall have an opportunity of leaving her myself, in my way to you. I am determined you see, not to be denied admittance at Churchill.
It would indeed give me most painful sensations to know
that it were not in your power to receive me.

Y^r most obliged & affec: Sister
S. Vernon.

LETTER 2^d.

Lady Susan to Mrs Johnson.

Langford.

You were mistaken my dear Alicia, in supposing me
fixed at this place for the rest of the winter. It greives me
to say how greatly you were mistaken, for I have seldom
spent three months more agreably than those which have
just flown away. At present nothing goes smoothly. The
Females of the Family are united against me. You foretold
how it would be, when I first came to Langford; and Manwaring is so uncommonly pleasing that I was not without
apprehensions myself. I remember saying to myself as I
drove to the House, "I like this Man; pray Heaven no
harm come of it!" But I was determined to be discreet, to
bear in mind my being only four months a widow, & to be
as quiet as possible,—& I have been so; My dear Creature,
I have admitted no one's attentions but Manwaring's, I
have avoided all general flirtation whatever, I have distinguished no Creature besides of all the Numbers resorting

hither

hither, except Sir James Martin, on whom I bestowed a little notice in order to detach him from Miss Manwaring. But if the World could know my motive *there*, they would honour me. I have been called an unkind Mother, but it was the sacred impulse of maternal affection, it was the advantage of my Daughter that led me on; and if that Daughter were not the greatest simpleton on Earth, I might have been rewarded for my Exertions as I ought.— Sir James did make proposals to me for Frederica—but Frederica, who was born to be the torment of my life, chose to set herself so violently against the match, that I thought it better to lay aside the scheme for the present. I have more than once repented that I did not marry him myself, & were he but one degree less contemptibly weak I certainly should, but I must own myself rather romantic in that respect, & that Riches only, will not satisfy me. The event of all this is very provoking. Sir James is gone, Maria highly incensed, and Mrs Manwaring insupportably jealous; so jealous in short, & so enraged against me, that in the fury of her temper I should not be surprised at her appealing to her Guardian if she had the liberty of addressing him—but there your Husband stands my friend, & the kindest, most amiable action of his Life was his throwing her off forever on her Marriage. Keep up his resentment therefore I charge you. We are now in a sad state; no house was ever more altered; the whole family are at war, & Manwaring scarcely dares speak to me. It is time for me to be gone; I have therefore determined on leaving them, & shall spend I hope a comfortable day with you in Town within this week. If I am as little in favour with Mr Johnson as ever, you must come to me at N° 10 Wigmore S^t—but I hope this may not be the case, for as Mr Johnson with all his faults is a Man to whom that great word "Respectable" is always given, & I am known to be so intimate with his wife, his slighting me has an awkward Look. I take Town in my way to that insupportable spot,

a

a Country Village, for I am really going to Churchill. Forgive me my dear friend, it is my last resource. Were there
another place in England open to me, I would prefer it.
Charles Vernon is my aversion, & I am afraid of his wife.
At Churchill however I must remain till I have something
better in veiw. My young Lady accompanies me to Town,
where I shall deposit her under the care of Miss Summers
in Wigmore Street, till she becomes a little more reasonable. She will make good connections there, as the Girls
are all of the best Families. The price is immense, & much
beyond what I can ever attempt to pay.

Adeiu. I will send you a line, as soon as I arrive in
Town.—Yours Ever,

S. VERNON.

LETTER 3.

Mrs *Vernon to Lady De Courcy.*

Churchill.

My dear Mother

I am very sorry to tell you that it will not be in our power
to keep our promise of spending the Christmas with you;
& we are prevented that happiness by a circumstance
which is not likely to make us any amends. Lady Susan
in a letter to her Brother, has declared her intention of
visiting us almost immediately—& as such a visit is in all
probability merely an affair of convenience, it is impossible
to conjecture it's length. I was by no means prepared for
such an event, nor can I now account for her Ladyship's
conduct. Langford appeared so exactly the place for her
in every respect, as well from the elegant & expensive stile
of Living there, as from her particular attachment to M^{rs}
Manwaring, that I was very far from expecting so speedy
a distinction, tho' I always imagined from her increasing
friendship for us since her Husband's death, that we should
at some future period be obliged to receive her. Mr Vernon

I

I think was a great deal too kind to her, when he was in Staffordshire. Her behaviour to him, independant of her general Character, has been so inexcusably artful and un-generous since our Marriage was first in agitation, that no one less amiable & mild than himself could have overlooked it at all; & tho' as his Brother's widow & in narrow circum-stances it was proper to render her pecuniary assistance, I cannot help thinking his pressing invitation to her to visit us at Churchill perfectly unnecessary. Disposed however as he always is to think the best of every one, her display of Greif, & professions of regret, & general resolutions of prudence were sufficient to soften his heart, & make him really confide in her sincerity. But as for myself, I am still unconvinced; & plausibly as her Ladyship has now written, I cannot make up my mind, till I better understand her real meaning in coming to us. You may guess therefore my dear Madam, with what feelings I look forward to her arrival. She will have occasion for all those attractive Powers for which she is celebrated, to gain any share of my regard; & I shall certainly endeavour to guard myself against their influence, if not accompanied by something more substantial. She expresses a most eager desire of being acquainted with me, & makes very gracious mention of my children, but I am not quite weak enough to suppose a woman who has behaved with inattention if not unkind-ness to her own child, should be attached to any of mine. Miss Vernon is to be placed at a school in Town before her Mother comes to us, which I am glad of, for her sake and my own. It must be to her advantage to be separated from her Mother; & a girl of sixteen who has received so wretched an education would not be a very desirable com-panion here. Reginald has long wished I know to see this captivating Lady Susan, & we shall depend on his joining our party soon. I am glad to hear that my Father continues so well, & am, with best Love &c.,

CATH. VERNON,

I

LETTER

LETTER 4.

M^r De Courcy to Mrs Vernon.

Parklands.

My dear Sister

I congratulate you & Mr Vernon on being about to receive into your family, the most accomplished Coquette in
England. As a very distinguished Flirt, I have been always
taught to consider her; but it has lately fallen in my way
to hear some particulars of her conduct at Langford, which
prove that she does not confine herself to that sort of honest
flirtation which satisfies most people, but aspires to the
more delicious gratification of making a whole family
miserable. By her behaviour to Mr Manwaring, she gave
jealousy & wretchedness to his wife, & by her attentions
to a young man previously attached to Mr Manwaring's
sister, deprived an amiable girl of her Lover. I learnt all
this from a Mr Smith now in this neighbourhood—(I have
dined with him at Hurst & Wilford)—who is just come
from Langford, where he was a fortnight in the house with
her Ladyship, & who is therefore well qualified to make
the communication.

What a Woman she must be! I long to see her, & shall
certainly accept your kind invitation, that I may form
some idea of those bewitching powers which can do so
much—engaging at the same time & in the same house the
affections of two Men who were neither of them at liberty
to bestow them—& all this, without the charm of Youth.
I am glad to find that Miss Vernon does not come with her
Mother to Churchill, as she has not even Manners to recommend her, & according to Mr Smith's account, is equally
dull & proud. Where Pride & Stupidity unite, there can be
no dissimulation worthy notice, & Miss Vernon shall be
consigned to unrelenting contempt; but by all that I can
gather, Lady Susan possesses a degree of captivating
Deceit

Deceit which must be pleasing to witness & detect. I shall be with you very soon, & am

your affec. Brother R. DE COURCY.

LETTER 5.

Lady Susan to Mrs Johnson.

Churchill.

I received your note my dear Alicia, just before I left Town, & rejoice to be assured that Mr Johnson suspected nothing of your engagement the evening before; it is un-doubtedly better to deceive him entirely; since he will be stubborn, he must be tricked. I arrived here in safety, & have no reason to complain of my reception from Mr Vernon; but I confess myself not equally satisfied with the behaviour of his Lady. She is perfectly well bred indeed, & has the air of a woman of fashion, but her Manners are not such as can persuade me of her being prepossessed in my favour. I wanted her to be delighted at seeing me—I was as amiable as possible on the occasion—but all in vain —she does not like me. To be sure, when we consider that I *did* take some pains to prevent my Brother-in-law's marrying her, this want of cordiality is not very surprising —& yet it shews an illiberal & vindictive spirit to resent a project which influenced me six years ago, & which never succeeded at last. I am sometimes half disposed to repent that I did not let Charles buy Vernon Castle when we were obliged to sell it, but it was a trying circumstance, espe-cially as the sale took place exactly at the time of his marriage—& everybody ought to respect the delicacy of those feelings, which could not endure that my Husband's Dignity should be lessened by his younger brother's having possession of the Family Estate. Could Matters have been so arranged as to prevent the necessity of our leaving the Castle, could we have lived with Charles & kept him single,

I

I should have been very far from persuading my husband to dispose of it elsewhere; but Charles was then on the point of marrying Miss De Courcy, & the event has justified me. Here are Children in abundance, & what benefit could have accrued to me from his purchasing Vernon? My having prevented it, may perhaps have given his wife an unfavourable impression—but where there is a disposition to dislike a motive will never be wanting; & as to money-matters, it has not with-held him from being very useful to me. I really have a regard for him, he is so easily imposed on!

The house is a good one, the Furniture fashionable, & everything announces plenty & elegance. Charles is very rich I am sure; when a Man has once got his name in a Banking House he rolls in money. But they do not know what to do with their fortune, keep very little company, and never go to Town but on business. We shall be as stupid as possible. I mean to win my Sister in law's heart through her Children; I know all their names already, & am going to attach myself with the greatest sensibility to one in particular, a young Frederic, whom I take on my lap & sigh over for his dear Uncle's sake.

Poor Manwaring!—I need not tell you how much I miss him—how perpetually he is in my Thoughts. I found a dismal letter from him on my arrival here, full of complaints of his wife & sister, & lamentations on the cruelty of his fate. I passed off the letter as his wife's, to the Vernons, & when I write to him, it must be under cover to you.

Yours Ever, S. V.

LETTER 6.

Mrs Vernon to M^r De Courcy.

Churchill.

Well my dear Reginald, I have seen this dangerous creature, & must give you some description of her, tho' I hope

hope you will soon be able to form your own judgement. She is really excessively pretty. However you may chuse to question the allurements of a Lady no longer young, I must for my own part declare that I have seldom seen so lovely a Woman as Lady Susan. She is delicately fair, with fine grey eyes & dark eyelashes; & from her appearance one would not suppose her more than five & twenty, tho' she must in fact be ten years older. I was certainly not disposed to admire her, tho' always hearing she was beautiful; but I cannot help feeling that she possesses an uncommon union of Symmetry, Brilliancy and Grace. Her address to me was so gentle, frank & even affectionate, that if I had not known how much she has always disliked me for marrying Mr Vernon, & that we had never met before, I should have imagined her an attached friend. One is apt I beleive to connect assurance of manner with coquetry, & to expect that an impudent address will necessarily attend an impudent mind; at least I was myself prepared for an improper degree of confidence in Lady Susan; but her Countenance is absolutely sweet, & her voice & manner winningly mild. I am sorry it is so, for what is this but Deceit? Unfortunately one knows her too well. She is clever & agreable, has all that knowledge of the world which makes conversation easy, & talks very well, with a happy command of Language, which is too often used I beleive to make Black appear White. She has already almost persuaded me of her being warmly attached to her daughter, tho' I have so long been convinced of the contrary. She speaks of her with so much tenderness & anxiety, lamenting so bitterly the neglect of her education, which she represents however as wholly unavoidable, that I am forced to recollect how many successive Springs her Ladyship spent in Town, while her daughter was left in Staffordshire to the care of servants or a Governess very little better, to prevent my beleiving whatever she says.

If her manners have so great an influence on my resentful
heart

heart, you may guess how much more strongly they operate on Mr Vernon's generous temper. I wish I could be as well satisfied as he is, that it was really her choice to leave Langford for Churchill; & if she had not staid three months there before she discovered that her friends' manner of Living did not suit her situation or feelings, I might have beleived that concern for the loss of such a Husband as Mr Vernon, to whom her own behaviour was far from unexceptionable, might for a time make her wish for retirement. But I cannot forget the length of her visit to the Manwarings, & when I reflect on the different mode of Life which she led with them, from that to which she must now submit, I can only suppose that the wish of establishing her reputation by following, tho' late, the path of propriety, occasioned her removal from a family where she must in reality have been particularly happy. Your friend Mr Smith's story however cannot be quite true, as she corresponds regularly with Mrs Manwaring; at any rate it must be exaggerated; it is scarcely possible that two men should be so grossly deceived by her at once.

Y^{rs} &c. CATH. VERNON.

LETTER 7.

Lady Susan to Mrs Johnson.

Churchill.

My dear Alicia

You are very good in taking notice of Frederica, & I am grateful for it as a mark of your friendship; but as I cannot have a doubt of the warmth of that friendship, I am far from exacting so heavy a sacrifice. She is a stupid girl, & has nothing to recommend her. I would not therefore on any account have you encumber one moment of your precious time by sending her to Edward S^t, especially as every visit is so many hours deducted from the grand affair

of

of Education, which I really wish to be attended to, while she remains with Miss Summers. I want her to play & sing with some portion of Taste, & a good deal of assurance, as she has *my* hand & arm, & a tolerable voice. *I* was so much indulged in my infant years that I was never obliged to attend to anything, & consequently am without those accomplishments which are now necessary to finish a pretty Woman. Not that I am an advocate for the prevailing fashion of acquiring a perfect knowledge in all the Languages Arts & Sciences; it is throwing time away; to be Mistress of French, Italian, German, Music, Singing, Drawing &c. will gain a Woman some applause, but will not add one Lover to her list. Grace & Manner after all are of the greatest importance. I do not mean therefore that Frederica's acquirements should be more than superficial, & I flatter myself that she will not remain long enough at school to understand anything thoroughly. I hope to see her the wife of Sir James within a twelvemonth. You know on what I ground my hope, & it is certainly a good foundation, for School must be very humiliating to a girl of Frederica's age; and by the bye, you had better not invite her any more on that account, as I wish her to find her situation as unpleasant as possible. I am sure of Sir James at any time, & could make him renew his application by a Line. I shall trouble you meanwhile to prevent his forming any other attachment when he comes to Town; ask him to your House occasionally, & talk to him about Frederica that he may not forget her.

Upon the whole I commend my own conduct in this affair extremely, & regard it as a very happy mixture of circumspection & tenderness. Some Mothers would have insisted on their daughter's accepting so great an offer on the first overture, but I could not answer it to myself to force Frederica into a marriage from which her heart revolted; & instead of adopting so harsh a measure, merely propose to make it her own choice by rendering her
thoroughly

thoroughly uncomfortable till she does accept him. But enough of this tiresome girl.

You may well wonder how I contrive to pass my time here—& for the first week, it was most insufferably dull. Now however, we begin to mend; our party is enlarged by Mrs Vernon's brother, a handsome young Man, who promises me some amusement. There is something about him that rather interests me, a sort of sauciness, of familiarity which I shall teach him to correct. He is lively & seems clever, & when I have inspired him with greater respect for me than his sister's kind offices have implanted, he may be an agreable Flirt. There is exquisite pleasure in subduing an insolent spirit, in making a person pre-determined to dislike, acknowledge one's superiority. I have disconcerted him already by my calm reserve; & it shall be my endeavour to humble the Pride of these self-important De Courcies still lower, to convince Mrs Vernon that her sisterly cautions have been bestowed in vain, & to persuade Reginald that she has scandalously belied me. This project will serve at least to amuse me, & prevent my feeling so acutely this dreadful separation from You & all whom I love. Adeiu.

Yours Ever

S. Vernon.

LETTER 8.

Mrs Vernon to Lady De Courcy.

Churchill.

My dear Mother

You must not expect Reginald back again for some time. He desires me to tell you that the present open weather induces him to accept Mr Vernon's invitation to prolong his stay in Sussex that they may have some hunting together. He means to send for his Horses immediately, & it is impossible to say when you may see him in Kent. I will

not

not disguise my sentiments on this change from you my dear Madam, tho' I think you had better not communicate them to my Father, whose excessive anxiety about Reginald would subject him to an alarm which might seriously affect his health & spirits. Lady Susan has certainly contrived in the space of a fortnight to make my Brother like her. In short, I am persuaded that his continuing here beyond the time originally fixed for his return, is occasioned as much by a degree of fascination towards her, as by the wish of hunting with Mr Vernon, & of course I cannot receive that pleasure from the length of his visit which my Brother's company would otherwise give me. I am indeed provoked at the artifice of this unprincipled Woman. What stronger proof of her dangerous abilities can be given, than this perversion of Reginald's Judgement, which when he entered the house was so decidedly against her? In his last letter he actually gave me some particulars of her behaviour at Langford, such as he received from a Gentleman who knew her perfectly well, which if true must raise abhorrence against her, & which Reginald himself was entirely disposed to credit. His opinion of her I am sure, was as low as of any Woman in England, & when he first came it was evident that he considered her as one entitled neither to Delicacy nor respect, & that he felt she would be delighted with the attentions of any Man inclined to flirt with her.

Her behaviour I confess has been calculated to do away such an idea, I have not detected the smallest impropriety in it,—nothing of vanity, of pretension, of Levity—& she is altogether so attractive, that I should not wonder at his being delighted with her, had he known nothing of her previous to this personal acquaintance; but against reason, against conviction, to be so well pleased with her as I am sure he is, does really astonish me. His admiration was at first very strong, but no more than was natural; & I did not wonder at his being struck by the gentleness & delicacy of her Manners; but when he has mentioned her of late, it

                                                                has

has been in terms of more extraordinary praise, and yesterday he actually said, that he could not be surprised at any effect produced on the heart of Man by such Loveliness & such Abilities; & when I lamented in reply the badness of her disposition, he observed that whatever might have been her errors, they were to be imputed to her neglected Education & early Marriage, & that she was altogether a wonderful Woman.

This tendency to excuse her conduct, or to forget it in the warmth of admiration vexes me; & if I did not know that Reginald is too much at home at Churchill to need an invitation for lengthening his visit, I should regret Mr Vernon's giving him any.

Lady Susan's intentions are of course those of absolute coquetry, or a desire of universal admiration. I cannot for a moment imagine that she has anything more serious in veiw, but it mortifies me to see a young Man of Reginald's sense duped by her at all. I am &c.

CATH. VERNON.

LETTER 9.

Mrs Johnson to Lady Susan.

Edward S^t.

My dearest Friend

I congratulate you on M^r De Courcy's arrival, & advise you by all means to marry him; his Father's Estate is we know considerable, & I beleive certainly entailed. Sir Reginald is very infirm, & not likely to stand in your way long. I hear the young Man well spoken of, & tho' no one can really deserve you my dearest Susan, M^r De Courcy may be worth having. Manwaring will storm of course, but you may easily pacify him. Besides, the most scrupulous point of honour could not require you to wait for *his* emancipation. I have seen Sir James,—he came to Town for a few days last week, & called several times in Edward
Street

Street. I talked to him about you & your daughter, & he is so far from having forgotten you, that I am sure he would marry either of you with pleasure. I gave him hopes of Frederica's relenting, & told him a great deal of her improvements. I scolded him for making Love to Maria Manwaring; he protested that he had been only in joke, & we both laughed heartily at her disappointment, & in short were very agreable. He is as silly as ever.—Yours faithfully

ALICIA.

LETTER 10.

Lady Susan to Mrs Johnson.

Churchill.

I am much obliged to you my dear Friend, for your advice respecting M^r De Courcy, which I know was given with the fullest conviction of it's expediency, tho' I am not quite determined on following it. I cannot easily resolve on anything so serious as Marriage, especially as I am not at present in want of money, & might perhaps till the old Gentleman's death, be very little benefited by the match. It is true that I am vain enough to beleive it within my reach. I have made him sensible of my power, & can now enjoy the pleasure of triumphing over a Mind prepared to dislike me, & prejudiced against all my past actions. His sister too, is I hope convinced how little the ungenerous representations of any one to the disadvantage of another will avail, when opposed to the immediate influence of Intellect and Manner. I see plainly that she is uneasy at my progress in the good opinion of her Brother, & conclude that nothing will be wanting on her part to counteract me; but having once made him doubt the justice of her opinion of me, I think I may defy her.

It has been delightful to me to watch his advances towards intimacy, especially to observe his altered manner in consequence of my repressing by the calm dignity of my deportment

deportment, his insolent approach to direct familiarity. My conduct has been equally guarded from the first, & I never behaved less like a Coquette in the whole course of my Life, tho' perhaps my desire of dominion was never more decided. I have subdued him entirely by sentiment & serious conversation, & made him I may venture to say at least *half* in Love with me, without the semblance of the most common-place flirtation. Mrs Vernon's consciousness of deserving every sort of revenge that it can be in my power to inflict, for her ill-offices, could alone enable her to perceive that I am actuated by any design in behaviour so gentle and unpretending. Let her think & act as she chuses however; I have never yet found that the advice of a Sister could prevent a young Man's being in love if he chose it. We are advancing now towards some kind of confidence, and in short are likely to be engaged in a kind of platonic friendship. On *my* side, you may be sure of it's never being more, for if I were not already as much attached to another person as I can be to any one, I should make a point of not bestowing my affection on a Man who had dared to think so meanly of me.

Reginald has a good figure, & is not unworthy the praise you have heard given him, but is still greatly inferior to our friend at Langford. He is less polished, less insinuating than Manwaring, and is comparatively deficient in the power of saying those delightful things which put one in good humour with oneself & all the world. He is quite agreable enough however, to afford me amusement, & to make many of those hours pass very pleasantly which would be otherwise spent in endeavouring to overcome my sister in law's reserve, & listening to her Husband's insipid talk.

Your account of Sir James is most satisfactory, & I mean to give Miss Frederica a hint of my intentions very soon.— Yours &c.

S. VERNON.

LETTER

LETTER 11.

Mrs Vernon to Lady De Courcy.

I really grow quite uneasy my dearest Mother about Reginald, from witnessing the very rapid increase of Lady Susan's influence. They are now on terms of the most particular friendship, frequently engaged in long conversations together, & she has contrived by the most artful coquetry to subdue his Judgement to her own purposes. It is impossible to see the intimacy between them, so very soon established, without some alarm, tho' I can hardly suppose that Lady Susan's veiws extend to marriage. I wish you could get Reginald home again, under any plausible pretence. He is not at all disposed to leave us, & I have given him as many hints of my Father's precarious state of health, as common decency will allow me to do in my own house. Her power over him must now be boundless, as she has entirely effaced all his former ill-opinion, & persuaded him not merely to forget, but to justify her conduct. Mr Smith's account of her proceedings at Langford, where he accused her of having made Mr Manwaring & a young Man engaged to Miss Manwaring distractedly in love with her, which Reginald firmly beleived when he came to Churchill, is now he is persuaded only a scandalous invention. He has told me so in a warmth of manner which spoke his regret at having ever beleived the contrary himself.

How sincerely do I greive that she ever entered this house! I always looked forward to her coming with uneasiness—but very far was it, from originating in anxiety for Reginald. I expected a most disagreable companion to myself, but could not imagine that my Brother would be in the smallest danger of being captivated by a Woman with whose principles he was so well acquainted, & whose character he so heartily despised. If you can get him away, it will be a good thing.

Y^{rs} affec:^{ly}
CATH. VERNON.

LETTER

LETTER 12.

Sir Reginald De Courcy to his Son.

Parklands.

I know that young Men in general do not admit of any enquiry even from their nearest relations, into affairs of the heart; but I hope my dear Reginald that you will be superior to such as allow nothing for a Father's anxiety, & think themselves privileged to refuse him their confidence & slight his advice. You must be sensible that as an only son & the representative of an ancient Family, your conduct in Life is most interesting to your connections. In the very important concern of Marriage especially, there is everything at stake; your own happiness, that of your Parents, and the credit of your name. I do not suppose that you would deliberately form an absolute engagement of that nature without acquainting your Mother & myself, or at least without being convinced that we should approve your choice; but I cannot help fearing that you may be drawn in by the Lady who has lately attached you, to a Marriage, which the whole of your Family, far & near, must highly reprobate.

Lady Susan's age is itself a material objection, but her want of character is one so much more serious, that the difference of even twelve years becomes in comparison of small account. Were you not blinded by a sort of fascination, it would be ridiculous in me to repeat the instances of great misconduct on her side, so very generally known. Her neglect of her husband, her encouragement of other Men, her extravagance & dissipation were so gross & notorious, that no one could be ignorant of them at the time, nor can now have forgotten them. To our Family, she has always been represented in softened colours by the benevolence of Mr Charles Vernon; and yet in spite of his generous endeavours to excuse her, we know that she did,

from

from the most selfish motives, take all possible pains to
prevent his marrying Catherine.

My Years & increasing Infirmities make me very desirous
my dear Reginald, of seeing you settled in the world. To
the Fortune of your wife, the goodness of my own, will
make me indifferent; but her family & character must be
equally unexceptionable. When your choice is so fixed as
that no objection can be made to either, I can promise you
a ready & chearful consent; but it is my Duty to oppose
a Match, which deep Art only could render probable, and
must in the end make wretched.

It is possible that her behaviour may arise only from
Vanity, or a wish of gaining the admiration of a Man whom
she must imagine to be particularly prejudiced against her;
but it is more likely that she should aim at something
farther. She is poor, & may naturally seek an alliance
which may be advantageous to herself. You know your
own rights, & that it is out of my power to prevent your
inheriting the family Estate. My Ability of distressing you
during my Life, would be a species of revenge to which
I should hardly stoop under any circumstances. I honestly
tell you my Sentiments & Intentions. I do not wish to
work on your Fears, but on your Sense & Affection. It
would destroy every comfort of my Life, to know that
you were married to Lady Susan Vernon. It would be the
death of that honest Pride with which I have hitherto considered my son, I should blush to see him, to hear of him,
to think of him.

I may perhaps do no good, but that of relieving my own
mind, by this Letter; but I felt it my Duty to tell you that
your partiality for Lady Susan is no secret to your friends,
& to warn you against her. I should be glad to hear your
reasons for disbeleiving Mr Smith's intelligence; you had
no doubt of it's authenticity a month ago.

If you can give me your assurance of having no design
beyond enjoying the conversation of a clever woman for

a short period, & of yeilding admiration only to her Beauty
& Abilities without being blinded by them to her faults,
you will restore me to happiness; but if you cannot do this,
explain to me at least what has occasioned so great an
alteration in your opinion of her.

> I am &c.
> REG^d DE COURCY.

LETTER 13.

Lady De Courcy to Mrs Vernon.

Parklands.

My dear Catherine,

Unluckily I was confined to my room when your last
letter came, by a cold which affected my eyes so much as
to prevent my reading it myself, so I could not refuse your
Father when he offered to read it to me, by which means
he became acquainted to my great vexation with all your
fears about your Brother. I had intended to write to
Reginald myself, as soon as my eyes would let me, to point
out as well as I could the danger of an intimate acquaintance with so artful a woman as Lady Susan, to a young
Man of his age & high expectations. I meant moreover to
have reminded him of our being quite alone now, & very
much in need of him to keep up our spirits these long
winter evenings. Whether it would have done any good,
can never be settled now; but I am excessively vexed that
Sir Reginald should know anything of a matter which we
foresaw would make him so uneasy. He caught all your
fears the moment he had read your Letter, and I am sure
has not had the business out of his head since; he wrote
by the same post to Reginald, a long letter full of it all,
& particularly asking for an explanation of what he may
have heard from Lady Susan to contradict the late shocking reports. His answer came this morning, which I shall
enclose to you, as I think you will like to see it; I wish it

was

was more satisfactory, but it seems written with such a determination to think well of Lady Susan, that his assurances as to Marriage &c., do not set my heart at ease. I say all I can however to satisfy your Father, & he is certainly less uneasy since Reginald's letter. How provoking it is my dear Catherine, that this unwelcome Guest of yours, should not only prevent our meeting this Christmas, but be the occasion of so much vexation & trouble. Kiss the dear Children for me. Your affec: Mother

C. DE COURCY.

LETTER 14.

Mr De Courcy to Sir Reginald.

Churchill.

My dear Sir

I have this moment received your Letter, which has given me more astonishment than I ever felt before. I am to thank my Sister I suppose, for having represented me in such a light as to injure me in your opinion, & give you all this alarm. I know not why she should chuse to make herself & her family uneasy by apprehending an Event, which no one but herself I can affirm, would ever have thought possible. To impute such a design to Lady Susan would be taking from her every claim to that excellent understanding which her bitterest Enemies have never denied her; & equally low must sink my pretensions to common sense, if I am suspected of matrimonial veiws in my behaviour to her. Our difference of age must be an insuperable objection, & I entreat you my dear Sir to quiet your mind, & no longer harbour a suspicion which cannot be more injurious to your own peace than to our Understandings.

I can have no veiw in remaining with Lady Susan than to enjoy for a short time (as you have yourself expressed it) the conversation of a Woman of high mental powers.

If

If Mrs Vernon would allow something to my affection for herself & her husband in the length of my visit, she would do more justice to us all; but my Sister is unhappily prejudiced beyond the hope of conviction against Lady Susan. From an attachment to her husband which in itself does honour to both, she cannot forgive those endeavours at preventing their union, which have been attributed to selfishness in Lady Susan. But in this case, as well as in many others, the World has most grossly injured that Lady, by supposing the worst, where the motives of her conduct have been doubtful.

Lady Susan had heard something so materially to the disadvantage of my Sister, as to persuade her that the happiness of Mr Vernon, to whom she was always much attached, would be absolutely destroyed by the Marriage. And this circumstance while it explains the true motive of Lady Susan's conduct, & removes all the blame which has been so lavished on her, may also convince us how little the general report of any one ought to be credited, since no character however upright, can escape the malevolence of slander. If my Sister in the security of retirement, with as little opportunity as inclination to do Evil, could not avoid Censure, we must not rashly condemn those who living in the World & surrounded with temptation, should be accused of Errors which they are known to have the power of committing.

I blame myself severely for having so easily beleived the scandalous tales invented by Charles Smith to the prejudice of Lady Susan, as I am now convinced how greatly they have traduced her. As to Mrs Manwaring's jealousy, it was totally his own invention; & his account of her attaching Miss Manwaring's Lover was scarcely better founded. Sir James Martin had been drawn in by that young Lady to pay her some attention, & as he is a Man of fortune, it was easy to see that *her* veiws extended to Marriage. It is well known that Miss Manwaring is absolutely on the catch for

a

a husband, & no one therefore can pity her, for losing by the superior attractions of another woman, the chance of being able to make a worthy Man completely miserable. Lady Susan was far from intending such a conquest, & on finding how warmly Miss Manwaring resented her Lover's defection, determined, in spite of M^r and Mrs Manwaring's most earnest entreaties, to leave the family. I have reason to imagine that she did receive serious Proposals from Sir James, but her removing from Langford immediately on the discovery of his attachment, must acquit her on that article, with every Mind of common candour. You will, I am sure my dear Sir, feel the truth of this reasoning, & will hereby learn to do justice to the character of a very injured Woman.

I know that Lady Susan in coming to Churchill was governed only by the most honourable & amiable intentions. Her prudence & economy are exemplary, her regard for Mr Vernon equal even to *his* deserts, & her wish of obtaining my sister's good opinion merits a better return than it has received. As a Mother she is unexceptionable. Her solid affection for her Child is shewn by placing her in hands, where her Education will be properly attended to; but because she has not the blind & weak partiality of most Mothers, she is accused of wanting Maternal Tenderness. Every person of Sense however will know how to value & commend her well directed affection, & will join me in wishing that Frederica Vernon may prove more worthy than she has yet done, of her Mother's tender care.

I have now my dear Sir, written my real sentiments of Lady Susan; you will know from this Letter, how highly I admire her Abilities, & esteem her Character; but if you are not equally convinced by my full & solemn assurance that your fears have been most idly created, you will deeply mortify & distress me.—I am &c.

R. De Courcy.

LETTER

LETTER 15.

Mrs Vernon to Lady De Courcy.

Churchill.

My dear Mother

I return you Reginald's letter, & rejoice with all my heart that my Father is made easy by it. Tell him so, with my congratulations; but between ourselves, I must own it has only convinced *me* of my Brother's having no *present* intention of marrying Lady Susan—not that he is in no danger of doing so three months hence. He gives a very plausible account of her behaviour at Langford, I wish it may be true, but his intelligence must come from herself, & I am less disposed to beleive it, than to lament the degree of intimacy subsisting between them, implied by the discussion of such a subject.

I am sorry to have incurred his displeasure, but can expect nothing better while he is so very eager in Lady Susan's justification. He is very severe against me indeed, & yet I hope I have not been hasty in my judgement of her. Poor Woman! tho' I have reasons enough for my dislike, I can not help pitying her at present as she is in real distress, & with too much cause. She had this morning a letter from the Lady with whom she has placed her daughter, to request that Miss Vernon might be immediately removed, as she had been detected in an attempt to run away. Why, or whither she intended to go, does not appear; but as her situation seems to have been unexceptionable, it is a sad thing & of course highly afflicting to Lady Susan.

Frederica must be as much as sixteen, & ought to know better, but from what her Mother insinuates I am afraid she is a perverse girl. She has been sadly neglected however, & her Mother ought to remember it.

Mr Vernon set off for Town as soon as she had determined what should be done. He is if possible to prevail on Miss Summers to let Frederica continue with her, & if he

cannot

cannot succeed, to bring her to Churchill for the present, till some other situation can be found for her. Her Ladyship is comforting herself meanwhile by strolling along the Shrubbery with Reginald, calling forth all his tender feelings I suppose on this distressing occasion. She has been talking a great deal about it to me, she talks vastly well, I am afraid of being ungenerous or I should say she talks *too* well to feel so very deeply. But I will not look for Faults. She may be Reginald's Wife. Heaven forbid it!—but why should I be quicker sighted than anybody else? Mr Vernon declares that he never saw deeper distress than hers, on the receipt of the Letter—& is his Judgement inferior to mine?

She was very unwilling that Frederica should be allowed to come to Churchill, & justly enough, as it seems a sort of reward to Behaviour deserving very differently. But it was impossible to take her any where else, & she is not to remain here long.

"It will be absolutely necessary, said she, as you my dear Sister must be sensible, to treat my daughter with some severity while she is here;—a most painful necessity, but I will endeavour to submit to it. I am afraid I have been often too indulgent, but my poor Frederica's temper could never bear opposition well. You must support & encourage me—You must urge the necessity of reproof, if you see me too lenient."

All this sounds very reasonably. Reginald is so incensed against the poor silly Girl! Surely it is not to Lady Susan's credit that he should be so bitter against her daughter; his idea of her must be drawn from the Mother's description.

Well, whatever may be his fate, we have the comfort of knowing that we have done our utmost to save him. We must commit the event to an Higher Power. Yours Ever &c.

CATH. VERNON.

LETTER

LETTER 16.

Lady Susan to Mrs Johnson.

Churchill.

Never my dearest Alicia, was I so provoked in my life as by a Letter this morning from Miss Summers. That horrid girl of mine has been trying to run away.—I had not a notion of her being such a little Devil before; she seemed to have all the Vernon Milkiness; but on receiving the letter in which I declared my intentions about Sir James, she actually attempted to elope; at least, I cannot otherwise account for her doing it. She meant I suppose to go to the Clarkes in Staffordshire, for she has no other acquaintance. But she *shall* be punished, she *shall* have him. I have sent Charles to Town to make matters up if he can, for I do not by any means want her here. If Miss Summers will not keep her, you must find me out another school, unless we can get her married immediately. Miss S. writes word that she could not get the young Lady to assign any cause for her extraordinary conduct, which confirms me in my own private explanation of it.

Frederica is too shy I think, & too much in awe of me, to tell tales; but if the mildness of her Uncle *should* get anything from her, I am not afraid. I trust I shall be able to make my story as good as her's. If I am vain of anything, it is of my eloquence. Consideration & Esteem as surely follow command of Language, as Admiration waits on Beauty. And here I have opportunity enough for the exercise of my Talent, as the cheif of my time is spent in Conversation. Reginald is never easy unless we are by ourselves, & when the weather is tolerable, we pace the shrubbery for hours together. I like him on the whole very well, he is clever & has a good deal to say, but he is sometimes impertinent & troublesome. There is a sort of ridiculous delicacy about him which requires the fullest explanation of whatever he may have heard to my disadvantage, & is

never

never satisfied till he thinks he has ascertained the beginning & end of everything.

This is *one* sort of Love—but I confess it does not particularly recommend itself to me. I infinitely prefer the tender & liberal spirit of Manwaring, which impressed with the deepest conviction of my merit, is satisfied that whatever I do must be right; & look with a degree of contempt on the inquisitive & doubting Fancies of that Heart which seems always debating on the reasonableness of it's Emotions. Manwaring is indeed beyond compare superior to Reginald—superior in everything but the power of being with me. Poor fellow! he is quite distracted by Jealousy, which I am not sorry for, as I know no better support of Love. He has been teizing me to allow of his coming into this country, & lodging somewhere near me *incog.*—but I forbid anything of the kind. Those women are inexcusable who forget what is due to themselves & the opinion of the World.

S. VERNON.

LETTER 17.

Mrs Vernon to Lady De Courcy.

Churchill.

My dear Mother

Mr Vernon returned on Thursday night, bringing his neice with him. Lady Susan had received a line from him by that day's post informing her that Miss Summers had absolutely refused to allow of Miss Vernon's continuance in her Academy. We were therefore prepared for her arrival, & expected them impatiently the whole evening. They came while we were at Tea, & I never saw any creature look so frightened in my life as Frederica when she entered the room.

Lady Susan who had been shedding tears before & shewing great agitation at the idea of the meeting, received her

with

with perfect self-command, & without betraying the least tenderness of spirit. She hardly spoke to her, & on Frederica's bursting into tears as soon ⟨as⟩ we were seated, took her out of the room & did not return for some time; when she did, her eyes looked very red, & she was as much agitated as before. We saw no more of her daughter.

Poor Reginald was beyond measure concerned to see his fair friend in such distress, & watched her with so much tender solicitude that I, who occasionally caught her observing his countenance with exultation, was quite out of patience. This pathetic representation lasted the whole evening, & so ostentatious & artful a display had entirely convinced me that she did in fact feel nothing.

I am more angry with her than ever since I have seen her daughter. The poor girl looks so unhappy that my heart aches for her. Lady Susan is surely too severe, because Frederica does not seem to have the sort of temper to make severity necessary. She looks perfectly timid, dejected & penitent.

She is very pretty, tho' not so handsome as her Mother, nor at all like her. Her complexion is delicate, but neither so fair, nor so blooming as Lady Susan's—& she has quite the Vernon cast of countenance, the oval face & mild dark eyes, & there is peculiar sweetness in her look when she speaks either to her Uncle or me, for as we behave kindly to her, we have of course engaged her gratitude. Her Mother has insinuated that her temper is untractable, but I never saw a face less indicative of any evil disposition than her's; & from what I now see of the behaviour of each to the other, the invariable severity of Lady Susan, & the silent dejection of Frederica, I am led to beleive as heretofore that the former has no real Love for her daughter & has never done her justice, or treated her affectionately.

I have not yet been able to have any conversation with my neice; she is shy, & I think I can see that some pains are taken to prevent her being much with me. Nothing satisfactory

satisfactory transpires as to her reason for running away. Her kindhearted Uncle you may be sure, was too fearful of distressing her, to ask many questions as they travelled. I wish it had been possible for me to fetch her instead of him; I think I should have discovered the truth in the course of a Thirty mile Journey.

The small Pianoforté has been removed within these few days at Lady Susan's request, into her Dressing room, & Frederica spends great part of the day there; *practising* it is called, but I seldom hear any noise when I pass that way. What she does with herself there I do not know, there are plenty of books in the room, but it is not every girl who has been running wild the first fifteen years of her life, that can or will read. Poor Creature! the prospect from her window is not very instructive, for that room overlooks the Lawn you know with the Shrubbery on one side, where she may see her Mother walking for an hour together, in earnest conversation with Reginald. A girl of Frederica's age must be childish indeed, if such things do not strike her. Is it not inexcusable to give such an example to a daughter? Yet Reginald still thinks Lady Susan the best of Mothers— still condemns Frederica as a worthless girl! He is convinced that her attempt to run away, proceeded from no justifiable cause, & had no provocation. I am sure I cannot say that it *had*, but while Miss Summers declares that Miss Vernon shewed no sign of Obstinacy or Perverseness during her whole stay in Wigmore S^t till she was detected in this scheme, I cannot so readily credit what Lady Susan has made him & wants to make me beleive, that it was merely an impatience of restraint, & a desire of escaping from the tuition of Masters which brought on the plan of an elopement. Oh! Reginald, how is your Judgement enslaved! He scarcely dares even allow her to be handsome, & when I speak of her beauty, replies only that her eyes have no Brilliancy.

Sometimes he is sure that she is deficient in Understand-

ing

ing, & at others that her temper only is in fault. In short when a person is always to deceive, it is impossible to be consistent. Lady Susan finds it necessary for her own justification that Frederica should be to blame, & probably has sometimes judged it expedient to accuse her of ill-nature & sometimes to lament her want of sense. Reginald is only repeating after her Ladyship.

I am &c.
CATH. VERNON.

LETTER 18.

From the same to the same.

Churchill.

My dear Madam

I am very glad to find that my description of Frederica Vernon has interested you, for I do beleive her truly deserving of our regard, & when I have communicated a notion that has recently struck me, your kind impression in her favour will I am sure be heightened. I cannot help fancying that she is growing partial to my brother, I so very often see her eyes fixed on his face with a remarkable expression of pensive admiration! He is certainly very handsome—& yet more—there is an openness in his manner that must be highly prepossessing, & I am sure she feels it so. Thoughtful & pensive in general her countenance always brightens with a smile when Reginald says anything amusing; & let the subject be ever so serious that he may be conversing on, I am much mistaken if a syllable of his uttering, escape her.

I want to make *him* sensible of all this, for we know the power of gratitude on such a heart as his; & could Frederica's artless affection detach him from her Mother, we might bless the day which brought her to Churchill. I think my dear Madam, you would not disapprove of her as

a

a Daughter. She is extremely young to be sure, has had a wretched Education & a dreadful example of Levity in her Mother; but yet I can pronounce her disposition to be excellent, & her natural abilities very good.

Tho' totally without accomplishment, she is by no means so ignorant as one might expect to find her, being fond of books & spending the cheif of her time in reading. Her Mother leaves her more to herself now than she *did*, & I have her with me as much as possible, & have taken great pains to overcome her timidity. We are very good friends, & tho' she never opens her lips before her Mother, she talks enough when alone with me, to make it clear that if properly treated by Lady Susan she would always appear to much greater advantage. There cannot be a more gentle, affectionate heart, or more obliging manners, when acting without restraint. Her little Cousins are all very fond of her.

Y^{rs} affec:^{ly}
CATH. VERNON.

LETTER 19.

Lady Susan to Mrs Johnson.

Churchill.

You will be eager I know to hear something farther of Frederica, & perhaps may think me negligent for not writing before. She arrived with her Uncle last Thursday fortnight, when of course I lost no time in demanding the reason of her behaviour, & soon found myself to have been perfectly right in attributing it to my own letter. The purport of it frightened her so thoroughly that with a mixture of true girlish perverseness & folly, without considering that she could not escape from my authority by running away from Wigmore Street, she resolved on getting out of the house, & proceeding directly by the stage to her
friends

friends the Clarkes, & had really got as far as the length of
two streets in her journey, when she was fortunately miss'd,
pursued, & overtaken.

Such was the first distinguished exploit of Miss Frederica
Susanna Vernon, & if we consider that it was atchieved at
the tender age of sixteen we shall have room for the most
flattering prognostics of her future renown. I am excessively provoked however at the parade of propriety which
prevented Miss Summers from keeping the girl; & it seems
so extraordinary a peice of nicety, considering what are
my daughter's family connections, that I can only suppose
the Lady to be governed by the fear of never getting her
money. Be that as it may however, Frederica is returned on
my hands, and having now nothing else to employ her, is
busy in pursueing the plan of Romance begun at Langford.
She is actually falling in love with Reginald De Courcy.
To disobey her Mother by refusing an unexceptionable offer
is not enough; her affections must likewise be given without
her Mother's approbation. I never saw a girl of her age, bid
fairer to be the sport of Mankind. Her feelings are tolerably
lively, & she is so charmingly artless in their display, as to
afford the most reasonable hope of her being ridiculed &
despised by every Man who sees her.

Artlessness will never do in Love matters, & that girl is
born a simpleton who has it either by nature or affectation.
I am not yet certain that Reginald sees what she is about;
nor is it of much consequence; she is now an object of
indifference to him, she would be one of contempt were he
to understand her Emotions. Her beauty is much admired
by the Vernons, but it has no effect on *him*. She is in high
favour with her Aunt altogether—because she is so little
like myself of course. She is exactly the companion for
Mrs. Vernon, who dearly loves to be first, & to have all
the sense & all the wit of the Conversation to herself;
Frederica will never eclipse her. When she first came, I
was at some pains to prevent her seeing much of her Aunt,
but

but I have since relaxed, as I beleive I may depend on her observing the rules I have laid down for their discourse.

But do not imagine that with all this Lenity, I have for a moment given up my plan of her marriage; No, I am unalterably fixed on that point, tho' I have not yet quite resolved on the manner of bringing it about. I should not chuse to have the business brought forward here, & canvassed by the wise heads of M^r & Mrs Vernon; & I cannot just now afford to go to Town. Miss Frederica therefore must wait a little.

Yours Ever
S. VERNON.

LETTER 20.

Mrs Vernon to Lady De Courcy.

Churchill.

We have a very unexpected Guest with us at present, my dear Mother. He arrived yesterday. I heard a carriage at the door as I was sitting with my children while they dined, & supposing I should be wanted left the Nursery soon afterwards & was half way down stairs, when Frederica as pale as ashes came running up, & rushed by me into her own room. I instantly followed, & asked her what was the matter. "Oh! cried she, he is come, Sir James is come— & what am I to do?" This was no explanation; I begged her to tell me what she meant. At that moment we were interrupted by a knock at the door; it was Reginald, who came by Lady Susan's direction to call Frederica down. "It is Mr. De Courcy, said she, colouring violently, Mama has sent for me, & I must go."

We all three went down together, & I saw my Brother examining the terrified face of Frederica with surprise. In the breakfast room we found Lady Susan & a young Man of genteel appearance, whom she introduced to me by the name of Sir James Martin, the very person, as you may
remember

remember, whom it was said she had been at pains to detach from Miss Manwaring. But the conquest it seems was not designed for herself, or she has since transferred it to her daughter, for Sir James is now desperately in love with Frederica, & with full encouragement from Mama. The poor girl however I am sure dislikes him; and tho' his person & address are very well, he appears both to Mr. Vernon & me a very weak young Man.

Frederica looked so shy, so confused, when we entered the room, that I felt for her exceedingly. Lady Susan behaved with great attention to her Visitor, & yet I thought I could perceive that she had no particular pleasure in seeing him. Sir James talked a good deal, & made many civil excuses to me for the liberty he had taken in coming to Churchill, mixing more frequent laughter with his discourse than the subject required; said many things over and over again, & told Lady Susan three times that he had seen Mᴿˢ Johnson a few Evenings before. He now & then addressed Frederica, but more frequently her Mother. The poor girl sat all this time without opening her lips; her eyes cast down, & her colour varying every instant, while Reginald observed all that passed, in perfect silence.

At length Lady Susan, weary I believe of her situation, proposed walking, & we left the two Gentlemen together to put on our Pelisses.

As we went upstairs Lady Susan begged permission to attend me for a few moments in my Dressing room, as she was anxious to speak with me in private. I led her thither accordingly, & as soon as the door was closed she said, "I was never more surprised in my life than by Sir James's arrival, & the suddenness of it requires some apology to *You* my dear Sister, tho' to *me* as a Mother, it is highly flattering. He is so warmly attached to my daughter that he could exist no longer without seeing her. Sir James is a young Man of an amiable disposition, & excellent character; a little too much of the *Rattle* perhaps, but a year

or

or two will rectify *that*, & he is in other respects so very eligible a Match for Frederica that I have always observed his attachment with the greatest pleasure, & am persuaded that you & my Brother will give the alliance your hearty approbation. I have never before mentioned the likelihood of it's taking place to any one, because I thought that while Frederica continued at school, it had better not be known to exist; but now, as I am convinced that Frederica is too old ever to submit to school confinement, and have therefore begun to consider her union with Sir James as not very distant, I had intended within a few days to acquaint yourself and Mr Vernon with the whole business. I am sure my dear Sister, you will excuse my remaining silent on it so long, & agree with me that such circumstances, while they continue from any cause in suspense, cannot be too cautiously concealed. When you have the happiness of bestowing your sweet little Catherine some years hence on a Man, who in connection & character is alike unexceptionable, you will know what I feel now; tho' Thank Heaven! you cannot have all my reasons for rejoicing in such an Event. Catherine will be amply provided for, & not like my Frederica endebted to a fortunate Establishment for the comforts of Life."

She concluded by demanding my congratulations. I gave them somewhat awkwardly I beleive; for in fact, the sudden disclosure of so important a matter took from me the power of speaking with any clearness. She thanked me however most affectionately for my kind concern in the welfare of herself & her daughter, & then said,

"I am not apt to deal in professions, my dear Mrs Vernon, & I never had the convenient talent of affecting sensations foreign to my heart; & therefore I trust you will beleive me when I declare that much as I had heard in your praise before I knew you, I had no idea that I should ever love you as I now do; & I must farther say that your friendship towards me is more particularly gratifying,

because

because I have reason to beleive that some attempts were made to prejudice you against me. I only wish that They —whoever they are—to whom I am endebted for such kind intentions, could see the terms on which we now are together, & understand the real affection we feel for each other! But I will not detain you any longer. God bless you, for your goodness to me & my girl, & continue to you all your present happiness."

What can one say of such a Woman, my dear Mother?—such earnestness, such solemnity of expression! & yet I cannot help suspecting the truth of everything she said.

As for Reginald, I beleive he does not know what to make of the matter. When Sir James first came, he appeared all astonishment & perplexity. The folly of the young Man, and the confusion of Frederica entirely engrossed him; & tho' a little private discourse with Lady Susan has since had it's effect, he is still hurt I am sure at her allowing of such a Man's attentions to her daughter.

Sir James invited himself with great composure to remain here a few days; hoped we would not think it odd, was aware of it's being very impertinent, but he took the liberty of a relation, & concluded by wishing with a laugh, that he might be really one soon. Even Lady Susan seemed a little disconcerted by this forwardness;—in her heart I am persuaded, she sincerely wishes him gone.

But something must be done for this poor Girl, if her feelings are such as both her Uncle & I beleive them to be. She must not be sacrificed to Policy or Ambition, she must not be even left to suffer from the dread of it. The Girl, whose heart can distinguish Reginald De Courcy, deserves, however he may slight her, a better fate than to be Sir James Martin's wife. As soon as I can get her alone, I will discover the real Truth, but she seems to wish to avoid me. I hope this does not proceed from anything wrong, & that I shall not find out I have thought too well of her. Her behaviour before Sir James certainly speaks the greatest
consciousness

consciousness & Embarrassment; but I see nothing in it more like Encouragement.

Adieu my dear Madam,

Y^{rs} &c.

CATH. VERNON.

LETTER 21.

Miss Vernon to M^r De Courcy.

Sir,

I hope you will excuse this liberty, I am forced upon it by the greatest distress, or I should be ashamed to trouble you. I am very miserable about Sir James Martin, & have no other way in the world of helping myself but by writing to you, for I am forbidden ever speaking to my Uncle or Aunt on the subject; & this being the case, I am afraid my applying to you will appear no better than equivocation, & as if I attended only to the letter & not the spirit of Mama's commands, but if *you* do not take my part, & persuade her to break it off, I shall be half-distracted, for I cannot bear him. No human Being but *you* could have any chance of prevailing with her. If you will therefore have the unspeakable great kindness of taking my part with her, & persuading her to send Sir James away, I shall be more obliged to you than it is possible for me to express. I always disliked him from the first, it is not a sudden fancy I assure you Sir, I always thought him silly & impertinent & disagreable, & now he is grown worse than ever. I would rather work for my bread than marry him. I do not know how to apologise enough for this Letter, I know it is taking so great a liberty, I am aware how dreadfully angry it will make Mama, but I must run the risk. I am Sir, your most Hum^{ble} Servt

F. S. V.

K

LETTER

LETTER 22ᵈ.

Lady Susan to Mʳˢ Johnson.

Churchill.

This is insufferable! My dearest friend, I was never so enraged before, & must releive myself by writing to you, who I know will enter into all my feelings. Who should come on Tuesday but Sir James Martin? Guess my astonishment & vexation—for as you well know, I never wished him to be seen at Churchill. What a pity that you should not have known his intentions! Not content with coming, he actually invited himself to remain here a few days. I could have poisoned him; I made the best of it however, & told my story with great success to Mrs. Vernon who, whatever might be her real sentiments, said nothing in opposition to mine. I made a point also of Frederica's behaving civilly to Sir James, & gave her to understand that I was absolutely determined on her marrying him. She said something of her misery, but that was all. I have for some time been more particularly resolved on the Match, from seeing the rapid increase of her affection for Reginald, & from not feeling perfectly secure that a knowledge of *that* affection might not in the end awaken a return. Contemptible as a regard founded only on compassion, must make them both, in my eyes, I felt by no means assured that such might not be the consequence. It is true that Reginald had not in any degree grown cool towards me; but yet he had lately mentioned Frederica spontaneously & unnecessarily, & once had said something in praise of her person.

He was all astonishment at the appearance of my visitor; and at first observed Sir James with an attention which I was pleased to see not unmixed with jealousy; but un-luckily it was impossible for me really to torment him, as Sir James tho' extremely gallant to me, very soon made

the

the whole party understand that his heart was devoted to my daughter.

I had no great difficulty in convincing De Courcy when we were alone, that I was perfectly justified, all things considered, in desiring the match; & the whole business seemed most comfortably arranged. They could none of them help perceiving that Sir James was no Solomon, but I had positively forbidden Frederica's complaining to Charles Vernon or his wife, & they had therefore no pretence for Interference, though my impertinent Sister I beleive wanted only opportunity for doing so.

Everything however was going on calmly & quietly; & tho' I counted the hours of Sir James's stay, my mind was entirely satisfied with the posture of affairs. Guess then what I must feel at the sudden disturbance of all my schemes, & that too from a quarter, whence I had least reason to apprehend it. Reginald came this morning into my Dressing room, with a very unusual solemnity of countenance, & after some preface informed me in so many words, that he wished to reason with me on the Impropriety & Unkindness of allowing Sir James Martin to address my Daughter, contrary to *her* inclination. I was all amazement. When I found that he was not to be laughed out of his design, I calmly required an explanation, & begged to know by what he was impelled, & by whom commissioned to reprimand me. He then told me, mixing in his speech a few insolent compliments & illtimed expressions of Tenderness to which I listened with perfect indifference, that my daughter had acquainted him with some circumstances concerning herself, Sir James, & me, which gave him great uneasiness.

In short, I found that she had in the first place actually written to him, to request his interference, & that on receiving her Letter he had conversed with her on the subject of it, in order to understand the particulars & assure himself of her real wishes!

I

I have not a doubt but that the girl took this opportunity of making downright Love to him; I am convinced of it, from the manner in which he spoke of her. Much good, may such Love do him! I shall ever despise the Man who can be gratified by the Passion, which he never wished to inspire, nor solicited the avowal of. I shall always detest them both. He can have no true regard for me, or he would not have listened to her; And she, with her little rebellious heart & indelicate feelings to throw herself into the protection of a young Man with whom she had scarcely ever exchanged two words before. I am equally confounded at *her* Impudence & *his* Credulity. How dared he beleive what she told him in my disfavour! Ought he not to have felt assured that I must have unanswerable Motives for all that I had done! Where was his reliance on my Sense or Goodness then; where the resentment which true Love would have dictated against the person defaming me, that person, too, a Chit, a Child, without Talent or Education, whom he had been always taught to despise?

I was calm for some time, but the greatest degree of Forbearance may be overcome; & I hope I was afterwards sufficiently keen. He endeavoured, long endeavoured to soften my resentment, but that woman is a fool indeed who while insulted by accusation, can be worked on by compliments. At length he left me, as deeply provoked as myself, & he shewed his anger *more*. I was quite cool, but he gave way to the most violent indignation. I may therefore expect it will sooner subside; & perhaps his may be vanished for ever, while mine will be found still fresh & implacable.

He is now shut up in his apartment, whither I heard him go, on leaving mine. How unpleasant, one would think, must his reflections be! But some people's feelings are incomprehensible. I have not yet tranquillized myself enough to see Frederica. *She* shall not soon forget the occurrences of this day. She shall find that she has poured forth

forth her tender Tale of Love in vain, & exposed herself forever to the contempt of the whole world, & the severest Resentment of her injured Mother.

Y^{rs} affec:^{ly}
S. VERNON.

LETTER 23.

Mrs Vernon to Lady De Courcy.

Churchill.

Let me congratulate you, my dearest Mother. The affair which has given us so much anxiety is drawing to a happy conclusion. Our prospect is most delightful; & since matters have now taken so favourable a turn, I am quite sorry that I ever imparted my apprehensions to you; for the pleasure of learning that the danger is over, is perhaps dearly purchased by all that you have previously suffered.

I am so much agitated by Delight that I can scarcely hold a pen, but am determined to send you a few lines by James, that you may have some explanation of what must so greatly astonish you, as that Reginald should be returning to Parklands.

I was sitting about half an hour ago with Sir James in the Breakfast parlour, when my Brother called me out of the room. I instantly saw that something was the matter; his complexion was raised, & he spoke with great emotion. You know his eager manner, my dear Madam, when his mind is interested.

"Catherine, said he, I am going home today. I am sorry to leave you, but I must go. It is a great while since I have seen my Father & Mother. I am going to send James forward with my Hunters immediately, if you have any Letter therefore he can take it. I shall not be at home myself till Wednesday or Thursday, as I shall go through London, where I have business. But before I leave you, he continued, speaking in a lower voice & with still greater energy,

I

I must warn you of one thing. Do not let Frederica Vernon be made unhappy by that Martin. He wants to marry her —her Mother promotes the Match—but *she* cannot endure the idea of it. Be assured that I speak from the fullest conviction of the Truth of what I say. I *know* that Frederica is made wretched by Sir James' continuing here. She is a sweet girl, & deserves a better fate. Send him away immediately. *He* is only a fool—but what her Mother can mean, Heaven only knows! Good bye, he added shaking my hand with earnestness—I do not know when you will see me again. But remember what I tell you of Frederica; you *must* make it your business to see justice done her. She is an amiable girl, & has a very superior Mind to what we have ever given her credit for."

He then left me & ran upstairs. I would not try to stop him, for I knew what his feelings must be; the nature of mine as I listened to him, I need not attempt to describe. For a minute or two I remained in the same spot, overpowered by wonder—of a most agreable sort indeed; yet it required some consideration to be tranquilly happy.

In about ten minutes after my return to the parlour, Lady Susan entered the room. I concluded of course that she & Reginald had been quarrelling, & looked with anxious curiosity for a confirmation of my beleif in her face. Mistress of Deceit however she appeared perfectly unconcerned, & after chatting on indifferent subjects for a short time, said to me, "I find from Wilson that we are going to lose M^r De Courcy. Is it true that he leaves Churchill this morning?" I replied that it was. "He told us nothing of all this last night, said she laughing, or even this morning at Breakfast. But perhaps he did not know it himself. Young Men are often hasty in their resolutions—& not more sudden in forming, than unsteady in keeping them. I should not be surprised if he were to change his mind at last, & not go."

She soon afterwards left the room. I trust however my
dear

dear Mother, that we have no reason to fear an alteration of his present plan; things have gone too far. They must have quarrelled, & about Frederica too. Her calmness astonishes me. What delight will be yours in seeing him again, in seeing him still worthy your Esteem, still capable of forming your Happiness!

When I next write, I shall be able I hope to tell you that Sir James is gone, Lady Susan vanquished, & Frederica at peace. We have much to do, but it shall be done. I am all impatience to know how this astonishing change was effected. I finish as I began, with the warmest congratulations.

Y^{rs} Ever,
CATH. VERNON.

LETTER 24.

From the same to the same.

Churchill.

Little did I imagine my dear Mother, when I sent off my last letter, that the delightful perturbation of spirits I was then in, would undergo so speedy, so melancholy a reverse! I never can sufficiently regret that I wrote to you at all. Yet who could have foreseen what has happened? My dear Mother, every hope which but two hours ago made me so happy, is vanished. The quarrel between Lady Susan & Reginald is made up, & we are all as we were before. One point only is gained; Sir James Martin is dismissed. What are we now to look forward to? I am indeed disappointed. Reginald was all but gone; his horse was ordered, & almost brought to the door! Who would not have felt safe?

For half an hour I was in momentary expectation of his departure. After I had sent off my Letter to you, I went to Mr Vernon & sat with him in his room, talking over the whole matter. I then determined to look for Frederica, whom I had not seen since breakfast. I met her on the stairs & saw that she was crying.

"My

"My dear Aunt, said she, he is going, M^r De Courcy is going, & it is all my fault. I am afraid you will be angry, but indeed I had no idea it would end so."

"My Love, replied I, do not think it necessary to apologize to me on that account. I shall feel myself under an obligation to anyone who is the means of sending my brother home; because, (recollecting myself) I know my Father wants very much to see him. But what is it that *you* have done to occasion all this?"

She blushed deeply as she answered, "I was so unhappy about Sir James that I could not help—I have done something very wrong I know—but you have not an idea of the misery I have been in, & Mama had ordered me never to speak to you or my Uncle about it,—&—" "You therefore spoke to my Brother, to engage *his* interference;" said I, wishing to save her the explanation. "No—but I wrote to him. I did indeed. I got up this morning before it was light—I was two hours about it—& when my Letter was done, I thought I never should have courage to give it. After breakfast however, as I was going to my own room I met him in the passage, & then as I knew that everything must depend on that moment, I forced myself to give it. He was so good as to take it immediately; I dared not look at him—& ran away directly. I was in such a fright that I could hardly breathe. My dear Aunt, you do not know how miserable I have been."

"Frederica, said I, you ought to have told *me* all your distresses. You would have found in me a friend always ready to assist you. Do you think that your Uncle & I should not have espoused your cause as warmly as my Brother?"

"Indeed I did not doubt your goodness, said she, colouring again, but I thought that M^r De Courcy could do anything with my Mother; but I was mistaken; they have had a dreadful quarrel about it, & he is going. Mama will never forgive me, & I shall be worse off than ever." "No, you shall not, replied I.—In such a point as this, your Mother's
prohibition

prohibition ought not to have prevented your speaking to
me on the subject. She has no right to make you unhappy,
& she shall *not* do it. Your applying however to Reginald can
be productive only of Good to all parties. I beleive it is
best as it is. Depend upon it that you shall not be made
unhappy any longer."

At that moment, how great was my astonishment at
seeing Reginald come out of Lady Susan's Dressing room.
My heart misgave me instantly. His confusion on seeing
me was very evident. Frederica immediately disappeared.
"Are you going? said I. You will find Mr Vernon in his
own room." "No Catherine, replied he. "I am *not* going.
Will you let me speak to you a moment?"

We went into my room. "I find, continued he, his confusion increasing as he spoke, that I have been acting with
my usual foolish impetuosity. I have entirely misunderstood Lady Susan, & was on the point of leaving the house
under a false impression of her conduct. There has been
some very great mistake—we have been all mistaken I
fancy. Frederica does not know her Mother—Lady Susan
means nothing but her Good—but Frederica will not make
a friend of her. Lady Susan therefore does not always know
what will make her daughter happy. Besides *I* could have
no right to interfere—Miss Vernon was mistaken in applying to me. In short Catherine, everything has gone wrong
—but it is now all happily settled. Lady Susan I beleive
wishes to speak to you about it, if you are at leisure."

"Certainly;" replied I, deeply sighing at the recital of so
lame a story. I made no remarks however, for words would
have been in vain. Reginald was glad to get away, & I
went to Lady Susan; curious indeed to hear her account
of it.

"Did not I tell you, said she with a smile, that your
Brother would not leave us after all?" "You did indeed,
replied I very gravely, but I flattered myself that you
would be mistaken." "I should not have hazarded such

an

an opinion, returned she, if it had not at that moment occurred ⟨to⟩ me, that his resolution of going might be occasioned by a Conversation in which we had been this morning engaged, & which had ended very much to his Dissatisfaction from our not rightly understanding each other's meaning. This idea struck me at the moment, & I instantly determined that an accidental dispute in which I might probably be as much to blame as himself, should not deprive you of your Brother. If you remember, I left the room almost immediately. I was resolved to lose no time in clearing up these mistakes as far as I could. The case was this. Frederica had set herself violently against marrying Sir James"—"And can your Ladyship wonder that she should? cried I with some warmth. Frederica has an excellent Understanding, and Sir James has none." "I am at least very far from regretting it, my dear Sister, said she; on the contrary, I am grateful for so favourable a sign of my Daughter's sense. Sir James is certainly under par— (his boyish manners make him appear the worse)—and had Frederica possessed the penetration, the abilities, which I could have wished in my daughter, or had I even known her to possess so much as she does, I should not have been anxious for the match." "It is odd that you alone should be ignorant of your Daughter's sense." "Frederica never does justice to herself; her manners are shy & childish. She is besides afraid of me; she scarcely loves me. During her poor Father's life she was a spoilt child; the severity which it has since been necessary for me to shew, has entirely alienated her affection; neither has she any of that Brilliancy of Intellect, that Genius, or Vigour of Mind which will force itself forward." "Say rather that she has been unfortunate in her Education." "Heaven knows my dearest Mrs Vernon, how fully I am aware of *that*; but I would wish to forget every circumstance that might throw blame on the memory of one, whose name is sacred with me."

Here she pretended to cry. I was out of patience with
her

her. "But what, said I, was your Ladyship going to tell me about your disagreement with my Brother?" "It originated in an action of my Daughter's, which equally marks her want of Judgement, and the unfortunate Dread of me I have been mentioning. She wrote to M^r De Courcy." "I know she did. You had forbidden her speaking to Mr Vernon or to me on the cause of her distress; what could she do therefore but apply to my Brother?" "Good God! —she exclaimed, what an opinion must you have of me! Can you possibly suppose that I was aware of her unhappiness? that it was my object to make my own child miserable, & that I had forbidden her speaking to you on the subject, from a fear of your interrupting the Diabolical scheme? Do you think me destitute of every honest, every natural feeling? Am I capable of consigning *her* to everlasting Misery, whose welfare it is my first Earthly Duty to promote?" "The idea is horrible. What then was your intention when you insisted on her silence?" "Of what use my dear Sister, could be any application to you, however the affair might stand? Why should I subject you to entreaties, which I refused to attend to myself? Neither for your sake, for hers, nor for my own, could such a thing be desireable. Where my own resolution was taken, I could not wish for the interference, however friendly, of another person. I was mistaken, it is true, but I beleived myself to be right." "But what was this mistake, to which your Ladyship so often alludes? From whence arose so astonishing a misapprehension of your Daughter's feelings? Did not you know that she disliked Sir James?" "I knew that he was not absolutely the Man she would have chosen. But I was persuaded that her objections to him did not arise from any perception of his Deficiency. You must not question me however my dear Sister, too minutely on this point—continued she, taking me affectionately by the hand. I honestly own that there is something to conceal. Frederica makes me very unhappy. Her applying to M^r

De

De Courcy hurt me particularly." "What is it that you mean to infer said I, by this appearance of mystery? If you think your daughter at all attached to Reginald, her objecting to Sir James could not less deserve to be attended to, than if the cause of her objecting had been a consciousness of his folly. And why should your Ladyship at any rate quarrel with my brother for an interference which you must know, it was not in his nature to refuse, when urged in such a manner?"

"His disposition you know is warm, & he came to expostulate with me, his compassion all alive for this ill-used Girl, this Heroine in distress! We misunderstood each other. He beleived me more to blame than I really was; I considered his interference as less excusable than I now find it. I have a real regard for him, & was beyond expression mortified to find it as I thought so ill bestowed. We were both warm, & of course both to blame. His resolution of leaving Churchill is consistent with his general eagerness; when I understood his intention however, & at the same time began to think that we had perhaps been equally mistaken in each other's meaning, I resolved to have an explanation before it were too late. For any Member of your Family I must always feel a degree of affection, & I own it would have sensibly hurt me, if my acquaintance with Mr De Courcy had ended so gloomily. I have now only to say farther, that as I am convinced of Frederica's having a reasonable dislike to Sir James, I shall instantly inform him that he must give up all hope of her. I reproach myself for having ever, tho' so innocently, made her unhappy on that score. She shall have all the retribution in my power to make; if she value her own happiness as much as I do, if she judge wisely & command herself as she ought, she may now be easy. Escuse me, my dearest Sister, for thus trespassing on your time, but I owed it to my own Character; & after this explanation I trust I am in no danger of sinking in your opinion."

I

I could have said "Not much indeed;"—but I left her almost in silence. It was the greatest stretch of Forbearance I could practise. I could not have stopped myself, had I begun. Her assurance, her Deceit—but I will not allow myself to dwell on them; they will strike you sufficiently. My heart sickens within me.

As soon as I was tolerably composed, I returned to the Parlour. Sir James's carriage was at the door, & he, merry as usual, soon afterwards took his leave. How easily does her Ladyship encourage, or dismiss a Lover!

In spite of this release, Frederica still looks unhappy, still fearful perhaps of her Mother's anger, & tho' dreading my Brother's departure jealous, it may be, of his staying. I see how closely she observes him & Lady Susan. Poor Girl, I have now no hope for her. There is not a chance of her affection being returned. He thinks very differently of her, from what he used to do, he does her some justice, but his reconciliation with her Mother precludes every dearer hope.

Prepare my dear Madam, for the worst. The probability of their marrying is surely heightened. He is more securely her's than ever. When that wretched Event takes place, Frederica must wholly belong to us.

I am thankful that my last Letter will precede this by so little, as every moment that you can be saved from feeling a Joy which leads only to disappointment is of consequence.

Y^rs Ever,
Cath. Vernon.

LETTER 25.

Lady Susan to Mrs Johnson.

Churchill.

I call on you dear Alicia, for congratulations. I am again myself;—gay and triumphant. When I wrote to you the

the other day, I was in truth in high irritation, and with ample cause. Nay, I know not whether I ought to be quite tranquil now, for I have had more trouble in restoring peace than I ever intended to submit to. This Reginald has a proud spirit of his own!—a spirit too, resulting from a fancied sense of superior Integrity which is peculiarly insolent. I shall not easily forgive him I assure you. He was actually on the point of leaving Churchill! I had scarcely concluded my last, when Wilson brought me word of it. I found therefore that something must be done, for I did not chuse to have my character at the mercy of a Man whose passions were so violent and resentful. It would have been trifling with my reputation, to allow of his departing with such an impression in my disfavour; in this light, condescension was necessary.

I sent Wilson to say that I desired to speak with him before he went. He came immediately. The angry emotions which had marked every feature when we last parted, were partially subdued. He seemed astonished at the summons, and looked as if half wishing and half fearing to be softened by what I might say.

If my Countenance expressed what I aimed at, it was composed and dignified—and yet with a degree of pensiveness which might convince him that I was not quite happy. "I beg your pardon Sir, for the liberty I have taken in sending to you, said I; but as I have just learnt your intention of leaving this place to-day, I feel it my duty to entreat that you will not on my account shorten your visit here, even an hour. I am perfectly aware that after what has passed between us, it would ill suit the feelings of either to remain longer in the same house. So very great, so total a change from the intimacy of Friendship, must render any future intercourse the severest punishment; & your resolution of quitting Churchill is undoubtedly in unison with our situation & with those lively feelings which I know you to possess. But at the same time, it is not for me to suffer

such

such a sacrifice, as it must be, to leave Relations to whom you are so much attached & are so dear. My remaining here cannot give that pleasure to M^r & Mrs Vernon which your society must; & my visit has already perhaps been too long. My removal therefore, which must at any rate take place soon, may with perfect convenience be hastened; & I make it my particular request that I may not in any way be instrumental in separating a family so affectionately attached to each other. Where *I* go is of no consequence to anyone; of very little to myself; but *you* are of importance to all your connections." Here I concluded, & I hope you will be satisfied with my speech. It's effect on Reginald justifies some portion of vanity, for it was no less favourable than instantaneous. Oh! how delightful it was, to watch the variations of his Countenance while I spoke, to see the struggle between returning Tenderness & the remains of Displeasure. There is something agreable in feelings so easily worked on. Not that I would envy him their possession, nor would for the world have such myself, but they are very convenient when one wishes to influence the passions of another. And yet this Reginald, whom a very few words from me softened at once into the utmost submission, & rendered more tractable, more attached, more devoted than ever, would have left me in the first angry swelling of his proud heart, without deigning to seek an explanation!

Humbled as he now is, I cannot forgive him such an instance of Pride; & am doubtful whether I ought not to punish him, by dismissing him at once after this our reconciliation, or by marrying & teizing him for ever. But these measures are each too violent to be adopted without some deliberation. At present my Thoughts are fluctuating between various schemes. I have many things to compass. I must punish Frederica, & pretty severely too, for her application to Reginald; I must punish him for receiving it so favourably, & for the rest of his conduct. I must torment

my

my Sister-in-law for the insolent triumph of her Look &
Manner since Sir James has been dismissed—for in recon-
ciling Reginald to me, I was not able to save that ill-fated
young Man—& I must make myself amends for the humilia-
tions to which I have stooped within these few days. To
effect all this I have various plans. I have also an idea of
being soon in Town, & whatever may be my determination
as to the rest, I shall probably put *that* project in execution
—for London will be always the fairest field of action,
however my veiws may be directed, & at any rate, I shall
there be rewarded by your society & a little Dissipation
for a ten weeks' penance at Churchill.

I beleive I owe it to my own Character, to complete the
match between my daughter & Sir James, after having so
long intended it. Let me know your opinion on this point.
Flexibility of Mind, a Disposition easily biassed by others,
is an attribute which you know I am not very desirous of
obtaining; nor has Frederica any claim to the indulgence
of her whims, at the expense of her Mother's inclination.
Her idle Love for Reginald too; it is surely my duty to
discourage such romantic nonsense. All things considered
therefore, it seems encumbent on me to take her to Town,
& marry her immediately to Sir James.

When my own will is effected, contrary to his, I shall
have some credit in being on good terms with Reginald,
which at present in fact I have not, for tho' he is still in my
power, I have given up the very article by which our
quarrel was produced, & at best, the honour of victory is
doubtful.

Send me your opinion on all these matters, my dear
Alicia, & let me know whether you can get Lodgings to
suit me within a short distance of you.

Y^r most attached
S. Vernon.

LETTER

LETTER 26.

Mrs Johnson to Lady Susan.

Edward S^t.

I am gratified by your reference, & this is my advice; that you come to Town yourself without loss of time, but that you leave Frederica behind. It would surely be much more to the purpose to get yourself well established by marrying M^r De Courcy, than to irritate him & the rest of his family, by making her marry Sir James. You should think more of yourself, & less of your Daughter. She is not of a disposition to do you credit in the World, & seems precisely in her proper place, at Churchill with the Vernons; but *you* are fitted for Society, and it is shameful to have you exiled from it. Leave Frederica therefore to punish herself for the plague she has given you, by indulging that romantic tender-heartedness which will always ensure her misery enough; & come yourself to Town, as soon as you can.

I have another reason for urging this.

Manwaring came to town last week, & has contrived, in spite of Mr Johnson, to make opportunities of seeing me. He is absolutely miserable about you, & jealous to such a degree of De Courcy, that it would be highly unadvisable for them to meet at present; & yet if you do not allow him to see you here, I cannot answer for his not committing some great imprudence—such as going to Churchill for instance, which would be dreadful. Besides, if you take my advice, & resolve to marry De Courcy, it will be indispensably necessary for you to get Manwaring out of the way, & you only can have influence enough to send him back to his wife.

I have still another motive for your coming. Mr Johnson leaves London next Tuesday. He is going for his health to Bath, where if the waters are favourable to his constitution

&

& my wishes, he will be laid up with the gout many weeks.
During his absence we shall be able to chuse our own
society, & have true enjoyment. I would ask you to Edward S^t but that he once forced from me a kind of promise
never to invite you to my house. Nothing but my being in
the utmost distress for Money, could have extorted it from
me. I can get you however a very nice Drawingroom-
apartment in Upper Seymour S^t, & we may be always
together, there or here, for I consider my promise to M^r
Johnson as comprehending only (at least in his absence)
your not sleeping in the House.

Poor Manwaring gives me such histories of his wife's
jealousy!—Silly Woman, to expect constancy from so
charming a Man! But she was always silly; intolerably
so, in marrying him at all. She, the Heiress of a large
Fortune, he without a shilling! *One* title I know she
might have had, besides Baronets. Her folly in forming
the connection was so great, that tho' Mr Johnson was
her Guardian & I do not in general share his feelings, I
never can forgive her.

Adeiu, Yours, ALICIA.

LETTER 27.

Mrs Vernon to Lady De Courcy.

Churchill.

This Letter my dear Mother, will be brought you by
Reginald. His long visit is about to be concluded at last,
but I fear the separation takes place too late to do us any
good. *She* is going to Town, to see her particular friend,
Mrs Johnson. It was at first her intention that Frederica
should accompany her for the benefit of Masters, but we
over-ruled her there. Frederica was wretched in the idea of
going, & I could not bear to have her at the mercy of her
Mother. Not all the Masters in London could compensate
for the ruin of her comfort. I should have feared too for

her

her health, & for everything in short but her Principles; *there* I beleive she is not to be injured, even by her Mother, or all her Mother's friends; but with those friends (a very bad set I doubt not) she must have mixed, or have been left in total solitude, & I can hardly tell which would have been worse for her. If she is with her Mother moreover, she must alas! in all probability, be with Reginald—& that would be the greatest evil of all.

Here we shall in time be at peace. Our regular employments, our Books & conversation, with Exercise, the Children, & every domestic pleasure in my power to procure her, will, I trust, gradually overcome this youthful attachment. I should not have a doubt of it, were she slighted for any other woman in the world, than her own Mother.

How long Lady Susan will be in Town, or whether she returns here again, I know not. I could not be cordial in my invitation; but if she chuses to come, no want of cordiality on my part will keep her away.

I could not help asking Reginald if he intended being in Town this winter, as soon as I found that her Ladyship's steps would be bent thither; and tho' he professed himself quite undetermined, there there was a something in his Look and voice as he spoke, which contradicted his words. I have done with Lamentation. I look upon the Event as so far decided, that I resign myself to it in despair. If he leaves you soon for London, everything will be concluded.

Yours affec^{ly}

CATH. VERNON.

LETTER 28.

Mrs Johnson to Lady Susan.

Edward S^t.

My dearest Friend,

I write in the greatest distress; the most unfortunate event has just taken place. Mr Johnson has hit on the most

effectual

effectual manner of plaguing us all. He had heard I imagine
by some means or other, that you were soon to be in
London, & immediately contrived to have such an attack
of the Gout, as must at least delay his journey to Bath, if
not wholly prevent it. I am persuaded the Gout is brought
on, or kept off at pleasure; it was the same, when I wanted
to join the Hamiltons to the Lakes; & three years ago when
I had a fancy for Bath, nothing could induce him to have
a Gouty symptom.

I have received yours, & have engaged the Lodgings in
consequence. I am pleased to find that my Letter had so
much effect on you, & that De Courcy is certainly your
own. Let me hear from you as soon as you arrive, & in
particular tell me what you mean to do with Manwaring.
It is impossible to say when I shall be able to see you. My
confinement must be great. It is such an abominable trick,
to be ill here, instead of at Bath, that I can scarcely command
myself at all. At Bath, his old Aunts would have nursed
him, but here it all falls upon me—& he bears pain with
such patience that I have not the common excuse for losing
my temper.

Y^{rs} Ever,
ALICIA.

LETTER 29.

Lady Susan to Mrs Johnson.

Upper Seymour S^t.

My dear Alicia
There needed not this last fit of the Gout to make me
detest Mr Johnson; but now the extent of my aversion is
not to be estimated. To have you confined, a Nurse in his
apartment! My dear Alicia, of what a mistake were you
guilty in marrying a Man of his age!—just old enough to
be formal, ungovernable & to have the Gout—too old to be
agreable, & too young to die.

I

I arrived last night about five, & had scarcely swallowed my dinner when Manwaring made his appearance. I will not dissemble what real pleasure his sight afforded me, nor how strongly I felt the contrast between his person & manners, & those of Reginald, to the infinite disadvantage of the latter. For an hour or two, I was even stagger'd in my resolution of marrying him—& tho' this was too idle & nonsensical an idea to remain long on my mind, I do not feel very eager for the conclusion of my Marriage, or look forward with much impatience to the time when Reginald according to our agreement is to be in Town. I shall probably put off his arrival, under some pretence or other. He must not come till Manwaring is gone.

I am still doubtful at times, as to Marriage. If the old Man would die, I might not hesitate; but a state of dependance on the caprice of Sir Reginald, will not suit the freedom of my spirit; & if I resolve to wait for that event, I shall have excuse enough at present, in having been scarcely ten months a Widow.

I have not given Manwaring any hint of my intention—or allowed him to consider my acquaintance with Reginald as more than the commonest flirtation; & he is tolerably appeased. Adeiu till we meet. I am enchanted with my Lodgings.

Y^{rs} Ever,
S. VERNON.

LETTER 30.

Lady Susan to M^r De Courcy.

Upper Seymour S^t.

I have received your Letter; & tho' I do not attempt to conceal that I am gratified by your impatience for the hour of meeting, I yet feel myself under the necessity of delaying that hour beyond the time originally fixed. Do not think me unkind for such an exercise of my power, or accuse me

of

of Instability, without first hearing my reasons. In the course of my journey from Churchill, I had ample leisure for reflection on the present state of our affairs, & every reveiw has served to convince me that they require a delicacy and cautiousness of conduct, to which we have hitherto been too little attentive. We have been hurried on by our feelings to a degree of Precipitance which ill accords with the claims of our Friends, or the opinion of the World. We have been unguarded in forming this hasty Engagement; but we must not complete the imprudence by ratifying it, while there is so much reason to fear the Connection would be opposed by those Friends on whom you depend.

It is not for us to blame any expectation on your Father's side of your marrying to advantage; where possessions are so extensive as those of your Family, the wish of increasing them, if not strictly reasonable, is too common to excite surprise or resentment. He has a right to require a woman of fortune in his daughter in law, & I am sometimes quarreling with myself for suffering you to form a connection so imprudent. But the influence of reason is often acknowledged too late by those who feel like me.

I have now been but a few months a widow; & however little endebted to my Husband's memory for any happiness derived from him during an Union of some years, I cannot forget that the indelicacy of so early a second marriage, must subject me to the censure of the World, & incur what would be still more insupportable, the displeasure of Mr Vernon. I might perhaps harden myself in time against the injustice of general reproach; but the loss of *his* valued Esteem, I am as you well know, ill fitted to endure; & when to this, may be added the consciousness of having injured you with your Family, how am I to support myself. With feelings so poignant as mine, the conviction of having divided the son from his Parents, would make me, even with *you*, the most miserable of Beings.

It

It will surely therefore be advisable to delay our Union, to delay it till appearances are more promising, till affairs have taken a more favourable turn. To assist us in such a resolution, I feel that absence will be necessary. We must not meet. Cruel as this sentence may appear, the necessity of pronouncing it, which can alone reconcile it to myself, will be evident to you when you have considered our situation in the light in which I have found myself imperiously obliged to place it. You may be, you must be well assured that nothing but the strongest conviction of Duty, could induce me to wound my own feelings by urging a lengthened separation; & of Insensibility to yours, you will hardly suspect me. Again therefore I say that we ought not, we must not yet meet. By a removal for some Months from each other, we shall tranquillize the sisterly fears of Mrs Vernon, who, accustomed herself to the enjoyment of riches, considers Fortune as necessary every where, & whose Sensibilities are not of a nature to comprehend ours.

Let me hear from you soon, very soon. Tell me that you submit to my Arguments, & do not reproach me for using such. I cannot bear reproaches. My spirits are not so high as to need being repressed. I must endeavour to seek amusement abroad, & fortunately many of my Friends are in town—among them, the Manwarings. You know how sincerely I regard both Husband & wife.

I am ever, Faithfully Yours

S. Vernon.

LETTER 31.

Lady Susan to Mrs Johnson.

Upper Seymour S^t.

My dear Friend,

That tormenting creature Reginald is here. My Letter, which was intended to keep him longer in the Country, has

hastened

hastened him to Town. Much as I wish him away however,
I cannot help being pleased with such a proof of attachment. He is devoted to me, heart & soul. He will carry
this note himself, which is to serve as an Introduction to
you, with whom he longs to be acquainted. Allow him to
spend the Evening with you, that I may be in no danger
of his returning here. I have told him that I am not quite
well, & must be alone—& should he call again there might
be confusion, for it is impossible to be sure of servants.
Keep him therefore I entreat you in Edward S^t. You will
not find him a heavy companion, & I allow you to flirt with
him as much as you like. At the same time do not forget
my real interest; say all that you can to convince him that
I shall be quite wretched if he remain here; you know my
reasons—Propriety & so forth. I would urge them more
myself, but that I am impatient to be rid of him, as Manwaring comes within half an hour. Adeiu.

S. V.

LETTER 32.

Mrs Johnson to Lady Susan.

Edward S^t.

My dear Creature,

I am in agonies, & know not what to do, nor what *you*
can do. M^r De Courcy arrived, just when he should not.
Mrs Manwaring had that instant entered the House, &
forced herself into her Guardian's presence, tho' I did not
know a syllable of it till afterwards, for I was out when
both she & Reginald came, or I would have sent him away
at all events; but *she* was shut up with Mr Johnson, while
he waited in the Drawing room for me. She arrived yesterday in pursuit of her Husband; but perhaps you know this
already from himself. She came to this house to entreat
my Husband's interference, & before I could be aware of
it, everything that you could wish to be concealed, was

known

known to him; & unluckily she had wormed out of Manwaring's servant that he had visited you every day since
your being in Town, & had just watched him to your door
herself! What could I do? Facts are such horrid things!
All is by this time known to De Courcy, who is now alone
with Mr Johnson. Do not accuse me; indeed, it was impossible to prevent it. Mr Johnson has for some time
suspected De Courcy of intending to marry you, & would
speak with him alone, as soon as he knew him to be in
the House.

That detestable Mrs Manwaring, who for your comfort,
has fretted herself thinner & uglier than ever, is still here,
& they have been all closeted together. What can be done?
If Manwaring is now with you, he had better be gone. At
any rate I hope he will plague his wife more than ever.
With anxious wishes,

Y^rs faithfully
ALICIA.

LETTER 33.

Lady Susan to Mrs Johnson.

Upper Seymour S^t.

This Eclaircissement is rather provoking. How unlucky
that you should have been from home! I thought myself
sure of you at 7. I am undismayed however. Do not torment yourself with fears on my account. Depend upon it,
I can make my own story good with Reginald. Manwaring
is just gone; he brought me the news of his wife's arrival.
Silly Woman! what does she expect by such Manœuvres?
Yet, I wish she had staid quietly at Langford.

Reginald will be a little enraged at first, but by Tomorrow's Dinner, everything will be well again.

Adeiu.
S. V.

LETTER

LETTER 34.

M^r De Courcy to Lady Susan.

Hotel.

I write only to bid you Farewell. The spell is removed. I see you as you are. Since we parted yesterday, I have received from indisputable authority, such an history of you as must bring the most mortifying conviction of the Imposition I have been under, & the absolute necessity of an immediate & eternal separation from you. You cannot doubt to what I allude; Langford—Langford—that word will be sufficient. I received my information in Mr Johnson's house, from Mrs Manwaring herself.

You know how I have loved you, you can intimately judge of my present feelings; but I am not so weak as to find indulgence in describing them to a woman who will glory in having excited their anguish, but whose affection they have never been able to gain.

R. De Courcy.

LETTER 35.

Lady Susan to M^r De Courcy.

Upper Seymour S^t.

I will not attempt to describe my astonishment on reading the note, this moment received from you. I am bewilder'd in my endeavours to form some rational conjecture of what Mrs Manwaring can have told you, to occasion so extraordinary a change in your sentiments. Have I not explained everything to you with respect to myself which could bear a doubtful meaning, & which the ill-nature of the World had interpreted to my Discredit? What can you *now* have heard to stagger your Esteem for me? Have I ever had a concealment from you? Reginald, you agitate me beyond expression. I cannot suppose that the old story

of

of Mrs Manwaring's jealousy can be revived again, or at
least, be *listened* to again. Come to me immediately, &
explain what is at present absolutely incomprehensible.
Believe me, the single word of *Langford* is not of such
potent intelligence, as to supersede the necessity of more.
If we *are* to part, it will at least be handsome to take your
personal Leave. But I have little heart to jest; in truth,
I am serious enough—for to be sunk, tho' but an hour, in
your opinion, is an humiliation to which I know not how
to submit. I shall count every moment till your arrival.

S. V.

LETTER 36.

M^r De Courcy to Lady Susan.

Hotel.

Why would you write to me? Why do you require particulars? But since it must be so, I am obliged to declare
that all the accounts of your misconduct during the life
& since the death of Mr Vernon which had reached me in
common with the World in general, & gained my entire
beleif before I saw you, but which you by the exertion of
your perverted Abilities had made me resolve to disallow,
have been unanswerably proved to me. Nay, more, I am
assured that a connection, of which I had never before
entertained a thought, has for some time existed, & still
continues to exist between you & the Man, whose family
you robbed of it's Peace, in return for the hospitality with
which you were received into it! That you have corre-
sponded with him ever since your leaving Langford—not
with his wife—but with him—and that he now visits you
every day. Can you, dare you deny it? & all this at the
time when I was an encouraged, an accepted Lover! From
what have I not escaped! I have only to be grateful. Far
from me be all complaint, & every sigh of regret. My own
Folly has endangered me, my Preservation I owe to the
kindness

kindness, the Integrity of another. But the unfortunate Mrs Manwaring, whose agonies while she related the past, seem'd to threaten her reason—how is *she* to be consoled?

After such a discovery as this, you will scarcely affect farther wonder at my meaning in bidding you Adeiu. My Understanding is at length restored, & teaches me no less to abhor the Artifices which had subdued me, than to despise myself for the weakness, on which their strength was founded.

R. DE COURCY.

LETTER 37.

Lady Susan to M^r^ De Courcy.

Upper Seymour S^t^.

I am satisfied—& will trouble you no more when these few Lines are dismissed. The Engagement which you were eager to form a fortnight ago, is no longer compatible with your veiws, & I rejoice to find that the prudent advice of your Parents has not been given in vain. Your restoration to Peace will, I doubt not, speedily follow this act of filial Obedience, & I flatter myself with the hope of surviving *my* share in this disappointment.

S. V.

LETTER 38.

Mrs Johnson to Lady Susan.

Edward S^t^.

I am greived, tho' I cannot be astonished at your rupture with M^r^ De Courcy; he had just informed Mr Johnson of it by letter. He leaves London he says to-day. Be assured that I partake in all your feelings, & do not be angry if I say that our intercourse even by Letter must soon be given up. It makes me miserable—but Mr Johnson vows that

if

if I persist in the connection, he will settle in the country for the rest of his life—& you know it is impossible to submit to such an extremity while any other alternative remains.

You have heard of course that the Manwarings are to part; I am afraid Mrs M. will come home to us again. But she is still so fond of her Husband & frets so much about him that perhaps she may not live long.

Miss Manwaring is just come to Town to be with her Aunt, & they say, that she declares she will have Sir James Martin before she leaves London again. If I were you, I would certainly get him myself. I had almost forgot to give you my opinion of De Courcy, I am really delighted with him, he is full as handsome I think as Manwaring, & with such an open, goodhumoured Countenance that one cannot help loving him at first sight. Mr Johnson & he are the greatest friends in the World. Adeiu, my dearest Susan. I wish matters did not go so perversely. That unlucky visit to Langford! But I dare say you did all for the best, & there is no defying Destiny.

Y^r sincerely attached
ALICIA.

LETTER 39.

Lady Susan to Mrs Johnson.

Upper Seymour S^t.

My dear Alicia

I yeild to the necessity which parts us. Under such circumstances you could not act otherwise. Our friendship cannot be impaired by it; & in happier times, when your situation is as independant as mine, it will unite us again in the same Intimacy as ever. For this I shall impatiently wait; & meanwhile can safely assure you that I never was more at ease, or better satisfied with myself & everything about me, than at the present hour. Your Husband I

abhor

abhor—Reginald I despise—& I am secure of never seeing either again. Have I not reason to rejoice? Manwaring is more devoted to me than ever; & were he at liberty, I doubt if I could resist even Matrimony offered by *him*. This Event, if his wife live with you, it may be in your power to hasten. The violence of her feelings, which must wear her out, may be easily kept in irritation. I rely on your friendship for this. I am now satisfied that I never could have brought myself to marry Reginald; & am equally determined that Frederica never *shall*. To-morrow I shall fetch her from Churchill, & let Maria Manwaring tremble for the consequence. Frederica shall be Sir James's wife before she quits my house. *She* may whimper, & the Vernons may storm; I regard them not. I am tired of submitting my will to the Caprices of others—of resigning my own Judgement in deference to those, to whom I owe no Duty, & for whom I feel no respect. I have given up too much—have been too easily worked on; but Frederica shall now find the difference.

Adeiu, dearest of Friends. May the next Gouty Attack be more favourable. And may you always regard me as unalterably yours

S. VERNON.

LETTER 40.

Lady De Courcy to Mrs Vernon.

Parklands.

My dear Catherine

I have charming news for you, & if I had not sent off my Letter this morning, you might have been spared the vexation of knowing of Reginald's being gone to Town, for he is returned, Reginald is returned, not to ask our consent to his marrying Lady Susan, but to tell us that they are parted forever! He has been only an hour in the House, & I have not been able to learn particulars, for he

is

is so very low, that I have not the heart to ask questions; but I hope we shall soon know all. This is the most joyful hour he has ever given us, since the day of his birth. Nothing is wanting but to have you here, & it is our particular wish & entreaty that you would come to us as soon as you can. You have owed us a visit many long weeks. I hope nothing will make it inconvenient to Mr Vernon, & pray bring all my Grand Children, & your dear Neice is included of course; I long to see her. It has been a sad heavy winter hitherto, without Reginald, & seeing nobody from Churchill; I never found the season so dreary before, but this happy meeting will make us young again. Frederica runs much in my thoughts, & when Reginald has recovered his usual good spirits, (as I trust he soon will) we will try to rob him of his heart once more, & I am full of hopes of seeing their hands joined at no great distance.

Y^r affec: Mother
C. De Courcy.

LETTER 41.

Mrs Vernon to Lady De Courcy.

Churchill.

My dear Madam

Your Letter has surprised me beyond measure. Can it be true that they are really separated—& for ever? I should be overjoyed if I dared depend on it, but after all that I have seen, how can one be secure? And Reginald really with you! My surprise is the greater, because on Wednesday, the very day of his coming to Parklands, we had a most unexpected & unwelcome visit from Lady Susan, looking all chearfulness & good humour, & seeming more as if she were to marry him when she got back to Town, than as if parted from him for ever. She staid nearly two hours, was as affectionate & agreable as ever, & not a syllable, not a hint was dropped of any Disagreement or

coolness

coolness between them. I asked her whether she had seen my Brother since his arrival in Town—not as you may suppose with any doubt of the fact—but merely to see how she looked. She immediately answered without any embarrassment that he had been kind enough to call on her on Monday, but she beleived he had already returned home —which I was very far from crediting.

Your kind invitation is accepted by us with pleasure, & on Thursday next, we & our little ones will be with you. Pray Heaven! Reginald may not be in Town again by that time!

I wish we could bring dear Frederica too, but I am sorry to add that her Mother's errand hither was to fetch her away; & miserable as it made the poor Girl, it was impossible to detain her. I was thoroughly unwilling to let her go, & so was her Uncle; & all that could be urged, we *did* urge. But Lady Susan declared that as she was now about to fix herself in Town for several Months, she could not be easy if her Daughter were not with her, for Masters, &c. Her Manner, to be sure, was very kind & proper—& Mr Vernon beleives that Frederica will now be treated with affection. I wish I could think so too!

The poor girl's heart was almost broke at taking leave of us. I charged her to write to me very often, & to remember that if she were in any distress, we should be always her friends. I took care to see her alone, that I might say all this, & I hope made her a little more comfortable. But I shall not be easy till I can go to Town & judge of her situation myself.

I wish there were a better prospect than now appears, of the Match, which the conclusion of your Letter declares your expectation of. At present it is not very likely.

Y^{rs} &c.
CATH. VERNON.

CONCLUSION

CONCLUSION

This Correspondence, by a meeting between some of the Parties & a separation between the others, could not, to the great detriment of the Post office Revenue, be continued longer. Very little assistance to the State could be derived from the Epistolary Intercourse of Mrs Vernon & her neice, for the former soon perceived by the stile of Frederica's Letters, that they were written under her Mother's inspection, & therefore deferring all particular enquiry till she could make it personally in Town, ceased writing minutely or often.

Having learnt enough in the meanwhile from her open-hearted Brother, of what had passed between him & Lady Susan to sink the latter lower than ever in her opinion, she was proportionably more anxious to get Frederica removed from such a Mother, & placed under her own care; & tho' with little hope of success, was resolved to leave nothing unattempted that might offer a chance of obtaining her Sister in law's consent to it. Her anxiety on the subject made her press for an early visit to London; & Mr Vernon who, as it must have already appeared, lived only to do whatever he was desired, soon found some accomodating Business to call him thither. With a heart full of the Matter, Mrs Vernon waited on Lady Susan, shortly after her arrival in Town; & she was met with such an easy & chearful affection as made her almost turn from her with horror. No remembrance of Reginald, no consciousness of Guilt, gave one look of embarrassment. She was in excellent spirits, & seemed eager to shew at once, by every possible attention to her Brother and Sister, her sense of their kindness, & her pleasure in their society.

Frederica was no more altered than Lady Susan; the same restrained Manners, the same timid Look in the presence of her Mother as heretofore, assured her Aunt of her situation's being uncomfortable, & confirmed her in

L   the

the plan of altering it. No unkindness however on the part of Lady Susan appeared. Persecution on the subject of Sir James was entirely at an end—his name merely mentioned to say that he was not in London; & in all her conversation she was solicitous only for the welfare & improvement of her Daughter, acknowledging in terms of grateful delight that Frederica was now growing every day more & more what a Parent could desire.

Mrs Vernon surprised & incredulous, knew not what to suspect, & without any change in her own veiws, only feared greater difficulty in accomplishing them. The first hope of anything better was derived from Lady Susan's asking her whether she thought Frederica looked quite as well as she had done at Churchill, as she must confess herself to have sometimes an anxious doubt of London's perfectly agreeing with her.

Mrs Vernon encouraging the doubt, directly proposed her Neice's returning with them into the country. Lady Susan was unable to express her sense of such kindness; yet knew not from a variety of reasons how to part with her Daughter; & as, tho' her own plans were not yet wholly fixed, she trusted it would ere long be in her power to take Frederica into the country herself, concluded by declining entirely to profit by such unexampled attention. Mrs Vernon however persevered in the offer of it, & tho' Lady Susan continued to resist, her resistance in the course of a few days seemed somewhat less formidable.

The lucky alarm of an Influenza, decided what might not have been decided quite so soon. Lady Susan's maternal fears were then too much awakened for her to think of anything but Frederica's removal from the risk of infection. Above all Disorders in the World, she most dreaded the influenza for her daughter's constitution. Frederica returned to Churchill with her Uncle & Aunt, & three weeks afterwards Lady Susan announced her being married to Sir James Martin.

Mrs

Mrs Vernon was then convinced of what she had only suspected before, that she might have spared herself all the trouble of urging a removal, which Lady Susan had doubtless resolved on from the first. Frederica's visit was nominally for six weeks; but her Mother, tho' inviting her to return in one or two affectionate Letters, was very ready to oblige the whole Party by consenting to a prolongation of her stay, & in the course of two months ceased to write of her absence, & in the course of two more, to write to her at all.

Frederica was therefore fixed in the family of her Uncle & Aunt, till such time as Reginald De Courcy could be talked, flattered & finessed into an affection for her— which, allowing leisure for the conquest of his attachment to her Mother, for his abjuring all future attachments & detesting the Sex, might be reasonably looked for in the course of a Twelvemonth. Three Months might have done it in general, but Reginald's feelings were no less lasting than lively.

Whether Lady Susan was, or was not happy in her second Choice—I do not see how it can ever be ascertained —for who would take her assurance of it, on either side of the question? The World must judge from Probability. She had nothing against her, but her Husband, & her Conscience.

Sir James may seem to have drawn an harder Lot than mere Folly merited. I leave him therefore to all the Pity that anybody can give him. For myself, I confess that *I* can pity only Miss Manwaring, who coming to Town & putting herself to an expence in Cloathes, which impoverished her for two years, on purpose to secure him, was defrauded of her due by a Woman ten years older than herself.

FINIS

III. Fragments of Novels

'THE WATSONS'

THE title 'The Watsons' was given to the untitled, uncompleted manuscript by J. E. Austen-Leigh when he first printed the work in the 1871 *Memoir*. The manuscript (now divided: the first six leaves in the Pierpont Morgan Library, the remainder the property of the legatees of the late William Austen-Leigh) is an undated first draft, heavily corrected and revised. The leaves are watermarked 1803.

Following the evidence of the watermark, R. W. Chapman dated its composition in that year or soon after. In fact a more precise date can be given. Fanny Lefroy (a granddaughter of Jane's brother, James) recorded that 'Somewhere in 1804 she began "The Watsons", but her father died early in 1805 [27 January] and it was never finished' ('Is it Just?', *Temple Bar*, lxvii (1883), 277). Fanny Lefroy could have heard these details from the family. Cassandra told the nephews and nieces of her sister's plans for the story's continuation (p. 362), and she may then have mentioned the date it was abandoned.

A full record of the manuscript alterations is given in the text of *The Watsons* edited by R. W. Chapman, Oxford, 1927.

[B. C. S.]

THE first winter assembly in the Town of D. in Surry was to be held on Tuesday Octr ye 13th, & it was generally expected to be a very good one; a long list of Country Families was confidently run over as sure of attending, & sanguine hopes were entertained that the Osbornes themselves would be there.—The Edwardes' invitation to the Watsons followed of course. The Edward's were people of fortune who lived in the Town & kept their coach; the

Watsons

Watsons inhabited a village about 3 miles distant, were poor & had no close carriage; & ever since there had been Balls in the place, the former were accustomed to invite the Latter to dress dine & sleep at their House, on every monthly return throughout the winter.—On the present occasion, as only two of Mr W.'s children were at home, & one was always necessary as companion to himself, for he was sickly & had lost his wife, one only could profit by the kindness of their friends; Miss Emma Watson who was very recently returned to her family from the care of an Aunt who had brought her up, was to make her first public appearance in the Neighbourhood; & her eldest sister, whose delight in a Ball was not lessened by a ten years Enjoyment, had some merit in chearfully undertaking to drive her & all her finery in the old chair to D. on the important morn^g.—As they splashed along the dirty Lane Miss Watson thus instructed & cautioned her inexperienc'd sister.—" I dare say it will be a very good Ball, & among so many officers, you will hardly want partners. You will find Mrs Edwards' maid very willing to help you, and I would advise you to ask Mary Edwards's opinion if you are at all at a loss for she has a very good Taste.—If Mr E. does not lose his money at cards, you will stay as late as you can wish for; if he does, he will hurry you home perhaps—but you are sure of some comfortable soup.— I hope you will be in good looks—. I should not be surprised if you were to be thought one of the prettiest girls in the room, there is a great deal in Novelty. Perhaps Tom Musgrave may take notice of you—but I would advise you by all means not to give him any encouragement. He generally pays attention to every new girl, but he is a great flirt & never means anything serious." " I think I have heard you speak of him before, said Emma. Who is he ? " " A young Man of very good fortune, quite independant, & remarkably agreable, an universal favourite wherever he goes. Most of the girls hereabouts are in love with him, or have been

been. I believe I am the only one among them that have escaped with a whole heart, and yet I was the first he paid attention to, when he came into this Country, six years ago; and very great attention indeed did he pay me. Some people say that he has never seemed to like any girl so well since, tho' he is always behaving in a particular way to one or another."—

"And how came *your* heart to be the only cold one?"— said Emma smiling. "There was a reason for that— replied Miss W. changing colour.—I have not been very well used Emma among them, I hope you will have better luck."—"Dear Sister, I beg your pardon, if I have unthinkingly given you pain."—"When first we knew Tom Musgrave, continued Miss W. without seeming to hear her, I was very much attached to a young Man of the name of Purvis a particular friend of Robert's, who used to be with us a great deal. Every body thought it would have been a Match." A sigh accompanied these words, which Emma respected in silence—but her sister after a short pause went on—"You will naturally ask why it did not take place, & why he is married to another Woman, while I am still single.—But you must ask him—not me—you must ask Penelope.—Yes Emma, Penelope was at the bottom of it all.—She thinks everything fair for a Husband; I trusted her, she set him against me, with a veiw of gaining him herself, & it ended in his discontinuing his visits & soon after marrying somebody else.—Penelope makes light of her conduct, but *I* think such Treachery very bad. It has been the ruin of my happiness. I shall never love any Man as I loved Purvis. I do not think Tom Musgrave should be named with him in the same day."—"You quite shock me by what you say of Penelope—said Emma. Could a sister do such a thing?—Rivalry, Treachery between sisters!—I shall be afraid of being acquainted with her— but I hope it was not so. Appearances were against her"— "You do not know Penelope.—There is nothing she w^d not

not

not do to get married—she would as good as tell you so
herself.—Do not trust her with any secrets of your own,
take warning by me, do not trust her; she has her good
qualities, but she has no Faith, no Honour, no Scruples,
if she can promote her own advantage.—I wish with all
my heart she was well married. I declare I had rather have
her well-married than myself."—"Than yourself!—Yes I
can suppose so. A heart, wounded like yours can have little
inclination for Matrimony."—"Not much indeed—but you
know we must marry.—I could do very well single for my
own part—A little Company, & a pleasant Ball now & then,
would be enough for me, if one could be young for ever,
but my Father cannot provide for us, & it is very bad to
grow old & be poor & laughed at.—I have lost Purvis, it
is true but very few people marry their first Loves. I should
not refuse a man because he was not Purvis—. Not that
I can ever quite forgive Penelope."—Emma shook her
head in acquiescence.—"Penelope however has had her
Troubles—continued Miss W.—she was sadly disappointed
in Tom Musgrave, who afterwards transferred his attentions from me to her, & whom she was very fond of; but he
never means anything serious, & when he had trifled with
her long enough, he began to slight her for Margaret, &
poor Penelope was very wretched—. And since then, she
has been trying to make some match at Chichester; she
wont tell us with whom, but I beleive it is a rich old D^r
Harding, Uncle to the friend she goes to see;—& she has
taken a vast deal of trouble about him & given up a great
deal of Time to no purpose as yet.—When she went away
the other day she said it should be the last time.—I suppose you did not know what her particular Business was
at Chichester—nor guess at the object that could take her
away, from Stanton just as you were coming home after
so many years absence."—"No indeed, I had not the
smallest suspicion of it. I considered her engagement to
Mrs Shaw just at that time as very unfortunate for me.

I

I had hoped to find all my sisters at home; to be able to make an immediate friend of each."—"I suspect the D^r to have an attack of the Asthma,—& that she was hurried away on that account—the Shaws are quite on her side.— At least I believe so—but she tells me nothing. She professes to keep her own counsel; she says, & truly enough, that "too many Cooks spoil the Broth".—"I am sorry for her anxieties, said Emma,—but I do not like her plans or her opinions. I shall be afraid of her.—She must have too masculine & bold a temper.—To be so bent on Marriage— to pursue a Man merely for the sake of situation—is a sort of thing that shocks me; I cannot understand it. Poverty is a great Evil, but to a woman of Education & feeling it ought not, it cannot be the greatest.—I would rather be Teacher at a school (and I can think of nothing worse) than marry a Man I did not like."—"I would rather do any thing than be Teacher at a school—said her sister. *I* have been at school, Emma, & know what a Life they lead; *you* never have.—I should not like marrying a disagreable Man any more than yourself,—but I do not think there *are* many very disagreable Men;—I think I could like any good humoured Man with a comfortable Income.—I suppose my Aunt brought you up to be rather refined." "Indeed I do not know.—My conduct must tell you how I have been brought up. I am no judge of it myself. I cannot compare my Aunt's method with any other persons, because I know no other."—But I can see in a great many things that you are very refined. I have observed it ever since you came home, & I am afraid it will not be for your happiness. Penelope will laugh at you very much." "*That* will not be for my happiness I am sure.—If my opinions are wrong, I must correct them—if they are above my situation, I must endeavour to conceal them.—But I doubt whether Ridicule,—Has Penelope much wit?"—"Yes— she has great spirits, & never cares what she says."—"Margaret is more gentle I imagine?"—"Yes—especially in
company

company; she is all gentleness & mildness when anybody is by.—But she is a little fretful & perverse among ourselves.—Poor creature! she is possessed with the notion of Tom Musgrave's being more seriously in love with her, than he ever was with any body else, & is always expecting him to come to the point. This is the second time within this twelvemonth that she has gone to spend a month with Robert and Jane on purpose to egg him on, by her absence —but I am sure she is mistaken, & that he will no more follow her to Croydon now than he did last March.—He will never marry unless he can marry somebody very great; Miss Osborne perhaps, or something in that stile.—" "Your account of this Tom Musgrave, Elizabeth, gives me very little inclination for his acquaintance." "You are afraid of him, I do not wonder at you."—"No indeed—I dislike & despise him."—"Dislike & Despise Tom Musgrave! No, *that* you never can. I defy you not to be delighted with him if he takes notice of you.—I hope he will dance with you—& I dare say he will, unless the Osbornes come with a large party, & then he will not speak to any body else.—" "He seems to have most engaging manners! —said Emma.—Well, we shall see how irresistable Mr Tom Musgrave & I find each other.—I suppose I shall know him as soon as I enter the Ball-room; he *must* carry some of his Charm in his face."—"You will not find him in the Ballroom I can tell you, You will go early that Mrs Edwards may get a good place by the fire, & he never comes till late; & if the Osbornes are coming, he will wait in the Passage, & come in with them.—I should like to look in upon you Emma. If it was but a good day with my Father, I w^d wrap myself up, & James should drive me over, as soon as I had made Tea for him; & I should be with you by the time the Dancing began." "What! would you come late at night in this Chair?"—"To be sure I would.—There, I said you were very refined;—& *that*'s an instance of it." —Emma for a moment made no answer—at last she said—

"I

"I wish Elizabeth, you had not made a point of my going to this Ball, I wish you were going instead of me. Your pleasure would be greater than mine. I am a stranger here, & know nobody but the Edwardses; my Enjoyment therefore must be very doubtful. Yours among all your acquaintance w^d be certain.—It is not too late to change. Very little apology cd. be requisite to the Edwardes, who must be more glad of your company than of mine, & I sh^d most readily return to my Father; & should not be at all afraid to drive this quiet old Creature, home. Your Cloathes I would undertake to find means of sending to you."—"My dearest Emma cried Eliz: warmly—do you think I would do such a thing?—Not for the Universe—but I shall never forget your goodnature in proposing it. You must have a sweet temper indeed;—I never met with any thing like it!—And w^d you really give up the Ball, that I might be able to go to it!—Beleive me Emma, I am not so selfish as that comes to. No, tho' I am nine years older than you are, I would not be the means of keeping you from being seen.—You are very pretty, & it would be very hard that you should not have as fair a chance as we have all had, to make your fortune.—No Emma, whoever stays at home this winter, it shan't be you. I am sure I sh^d never have forgiven the person who kept me from a Ball at 19." Emma expressed her gratitude, & for a few minutes they jogged on in silence.—Elizabeth first spoke.—"You will take notice who Mary Edwards dances with."—"I will remember her partners if I can—but you know they will be all strangers to me." "Only observe whether she dances with Capt. Hunter, more than once; I have my fears in that quarter. Not that her Father or Mother like officers, but if she does you know, it is all over with poor Sam.— And I have promised to write him word who she dances with." "Is Sam. attached to Miss Edwardes?"—"Did not you know *that*?"—"How should I know it? How should I know in Shropshire, what is passing of that nature in Surry

Surry ?—It is not likely that circumstances of such delicacy should make any part of the scanty communication which passed between you & me for the last 14 years." "I wonder I never mentioned it when I wrote. Since you have been at home, I have been so busy with my poor Father and our great wash that I have had no leisure to tell you anything—but indeed I concluded you knew it all.—He has been very much in love with her these two years, & it is a great disappointment to him that he cannot always get away to our Balls—but Mr Curtis won't often spare him, & just now it is a sickly time at Guilford—" "Do you suppose Miss Edwardes inclined to like him?" "I am afraid not: You know she is an only Child, & will have at least ten thousand pounds."—"But still she may like our Brother." "Oh! no—. The Edwardes look much higher. Her Father & Mother w^d never consent to it. Sam is only a Surgeon you know.—Sometimes I think she does like him. But Mary Edwardes is rather prim & reserved; I do not always know what she w^d be at."—"Unless Sam feels on sure grounds with the Lady herself, It seems a pity to me that he should be encouraged to think of her at all."— "A young Man must think of somebody. said Eliz:—& why should not he be as lucky as Robert, who has got a good wife & six thousand pounds?" "We must not all expect to be individually lucky replied Emma. The Luck of one member of a Family is Luck to all.—" "Mine is all to come I am sure—said Eliz: giving another sigh to the remembrance of Purvis.—I have been unlucky enough, & I cannot say much for you, as my Aunt married again so foolishly.—Well—you will have a good Ball I dare say. The next turning will bring us to the Turnpike. You may see the Church Tower over the hedge, & the White Hart is close by it.—I shall long to know what you think of Tom Musgrave." Such were the last audible sounds of Miss Watson's voice, before they passed thro' the Turnpike gate & entered on the pitching of the Town—the jumbling & noise

noise of which made farther Conversation most thoroughly
undesirable.—The old Mare trotted heavily on, wanting
no direction of the reins to take the right Turning, & making only one Blunder, in proposing to stop at the Milleners,
before she drew up towards Mr Edward's door.—M^r E.
lived in the best house in the Street, & the best in the
place, if Mr Tomlinson the Banker might be indulged in
calling his newly erected House at the end of the Town
with a Shrubbery & sweep in the Country.—Mr E.s House
was higher than most of its neighbours with two windows
on each side the door, the windows guarded by posts and
chain, the door approached by a flight of stone steps.—
"Here we are—said Eliz:—as the Carriage ceased moving
—safely arrived;—& by the Market Clock, we have been
only five & thirty minutes coming.—which I think is doing
pretty well, tho' it would be nothing for Penelope.—Is
not it a nice Town?—The Edwards' have a noble house
you see, & they live quite in stile. The door will be
opened by a Man in Livery with a powder'd head, I can
tell you."

Emma had seen the Edwardses only one morn^g at
Stanton, they were therefore all but Strangers to her, &
tho' her spirits were by no means insensible to the expected
joys of the Evening, she felt a little uncomfortable in the
thought of all that was to precede them. Her conversation
with Eliz: too giving her some very unpleasant feelings,
with respect to her own family, had made her more open to
disagreable impressions from any other cause, & increased
her sense of the awkwardness of rushing into Intimacy
on so slight an acquaintance.—There was nothing in the
manners of M^{rs} or Miss Edwardes to give immediate change
to these Ideas;—the Mother tho' a very freindly woman,
had a reserved air, & a great deal of formal Civility—& the
daughter, a genteel looking girl of 22, with her hair in
papers, seemed very naturally to have caught something
of the stile of the Mother who had brought her up.—Emma

was

was soon left to know what they could be, by Eliz.'s being obliged to hurry away—& some very, very languid remarks on the probable Brilliancy of the Ball, were all that broke at intervals a silence of half an hour before they were joined by the Master of the house.—Mr Edwards had a much easier, & more communicative air than the Ladies of the Family; he was fresh from the Street, & he came ready to tell what ever might interest.—After a cordial reception of Emma, he turned to his daughter with "Well Mary, I bring you good news.—The Osbornes will certainly be at the Ball tonight.—Horses for two Carriages are ordered from the White Hart, to be at Osborne Castle by 9.—" "I am glad of it—observed Mrs E., because their coming gives a credit to our Assemblies. The Osbornes being known to have been at the first Ball, will dispose a great many people to attend the second.—It is more than they deserve, for in fact they add nothing to the pleasure of the Evening, they come so late, & go so early;—but Great People have always their charm."—Mr Edwards proceeded to relate every other little article of news which his morning's lounge had supplied him with, & they chatted with greater briskness, till Mrs E.'s moment for dressing arrived, & the young Ladies were carefully recommended to lose no time.— Emma was shewn to a very comfortable apartment, & as soon as·Mrs E.'s civilities could leave her to herself, the happy occupation, the first Bliss of a Ball began.—The girls, dressing in some measure together, grew unavoidably better acquainted; Emma found in Miss E.— the shew of good sense, a modest unpretending mind, & a great wish of obliging—& when they returned to the parlour where Mrs E. was sitting respectably attired in one of the two Sattin gowns which went thro' the winter, & a new cap from the Milliners, they entered it with much easier feelings & more natural smiles than they had taken away.—Their dress was now to be examined; Mrs Edwards acknowledged herself too old-fashioned to approve of every modern

extravagance

extravagance however sanctioned—& tho' complacently
veiwing her daughter's good looks, w^d give but a qualified
admiration; & Mr E. not less satisfied with Mary, paid some
Compliments of good humoured Gallantry to Emma at her
expence.—The discussion led to more intimate remarks,
& Miss Edwardes gently asked Emma if she were not often
reckoned very like her youngest brother.—Emma thought
she could perceive a faint blush accompany the question, &
there seemed something still more suspicious in the manner
in which Mr E. took up the subject.—" You are paying Miss
Emma no great compliment I think Mary, said he hastily—.
Mr Sam Watson is a very good sort of young Man, & I dare
say a very clever Surgeon, but his complexion has been
rather too much exposed to all weathers, to make a likeness
to him very flattering." Mary apologized in some confusion. "She had not thought a strong Likeness at all incompatible with very different degrees of Beauty.—There
might be resemblance in Countenance; & the complexion,
& even the features be very unlike."—"I know nothing of
my Brother's Beauty, said Emma, for I have not seen him
since he was 7 years old—but my father reckons us alike."
'Mr Watson!—cried Mr Edwardes, Well, you astonish
me.—There is not the least likeness in the world; Y^r
brother's eyes are grey, yours are brown, He has a long
face, & a wide mouth.—My dear, do *you* perceive the least
resemblance?"—"Not the least.—Miss Emma Watson
puts me very much in mind of her eldest Sister, & sometimes I see a look of Miss Penelope—& once or twice there
has been a glance of Mr Robert—but I cannot perceive any
likeness to Mr Samuel." "I see the likeness between her &
Miss Watson, replied Mr E.—, very strongly—but I am not
sensible of the others.—I do not much think she is like any
of the Family *but* Miss Watson; but I am very sure there
is no resemblance between her & Sam."—

This matter was settled, & they went to Dinner.—" Your
Father, Miss Emma, is one of my oldest friends—said M^r
Edwardes

Edwardes, as he helped her to wine, when they were drawn round the fire to enjoy their Desert,—We must drink to his better health.—It is a great concern to me I assure you that he should be such an Invalid.—I know nobody who likes a game of cards in a social way, better than he does; & very few people that play a fairer rubber.—It is a thousand pities that he should be so deprived of the pleasure. For now we have a quiet little Whist club that meets three times a week at the White Hart, & if he c^d but have his health, how much he w^d enjoy it." "I dare say he would Sir—& I wish with all my heart he were equal to it." "Your Club w^d be better fitted for an Invalid, said Mrs E. if you did not keep it up so late."—This was an old greivance.— "So late, my dear, what are you talking of; cried the Husband with sturdy pleasantry—. We are always at home before Midnight. They would laugh at Osborne Castle to hear you call *that* late; they are but just rising from dinner at midnight."—"That is nothing to the purpose.—retorted the Lady calmly. The Osbornes are to be no rule for us. You had better meet every night, & break up two hours sooner." So far, the subject was very often carried;—but M^r & Mrs Edwards were so wise as never to pass that point; & Mr Edwards now turned to something else.—He had lived long enough in the Idleness of a Town to become a little of a Gossip, & having some curiosity to know more of the Circumstances of his young Guest than had yet reached him, he began with, "I think Miss Emma, I remember your Aunt very well about 30 years ago; I am pretty sure I danced with her in the old rooms at Bath, the year before I married—. She was a very fine woman then— but like other people I suppose she is grown somewhat older since that time.—I hope she is likely to be happy in her second choice."

"I hope so, I beleive so, Sir—said Emma in some agitation.—" "Mr Turner had not been dead a great while I think? "About 2 years Sir." "I forget what her name is

now

now?"—"O'brien." "Irish! Ah! I remember—& she is
gone to settle in Ireland.—I do not wonder that you should
not wish to go with her into *that* Country Miss Emma—
but it must be a great deprivation to her, poor Lady!—
After bringing you up like a Child of her own."—"I was not
so ungrateful Sir, said Emma warmly, as to wish to be any
where but with her.—It did not suit them, it did not suit
Capt. O'brien that I sh^d be of the party."—"Captain!—
repeated Mrs E. the Gentleman is in the army then?" "Yes
Ma'am."—"Aye—there is nothing like your officers for
captivating the Ladies, Young or Old.—There is no resisting a Cockade my dear."—"I hope there is."—said M^rs E.
gravely, with a quick glance at her daughter;—and Emma
had just recovered from her own perturbation in time to
see a blush on Miss E.'s cheek, & in remembering what
Elizabeth had said of Capt. Hunter, to wonder & waver
between his influence & her brother's.—

"Elderly Ladies should be careful how they make a
second choice." observed Mr Edwardes.—"Carefulness—
Discretion—should not be confined to Elderly Ladies, or
to a second choice added his wife. It is quite as necessary
to young Ladies in their first."—"Rather more so, my
dear—replied he, because young Ladies are likely to feel
the effects of it longer. When an old Lady plays the fool,
it is not in the course of nature that she should suffer from
it many years." Emma drew her hand across her eyes—&
Mrs Edwards on perceiving it, changed the subject to one
of less anxiety to all.—

With nothing to do but to expect the hour of setting
off, the afternoon was long to the two young Ladies; & tho'
Miss Edwards was rather discomposed at the very early
hour which her mother always fixed for going, that early
hour itself was watched for with some eagerness.—The
entrance of the Tea things at 7 o'clock was some releif—
& luckily M^r & Mrs Edwards always drank a dish extraordinary, & ate an additional muffin when they were going
to

to sit up late, which lengthened the ceremony almost to
the wished for moment. At a little before 8, the Tomlinsons carriage was heard to go by, which was the constant
signal for Mrs Edwards to order hers to the door; & in
a very few minutes, the party were transported from the
quiet warmth of a snug parlour, to the bustle, noise &
draughts of air of the broad Entrance-passage of an Inn.—
Mrs Edwards carefully guarding her own dress, while she
attended with yet greater Solicitude to the proper security
of her young Charges' Shoulders & Throats, led the way
up the wide staircase, while no sound of a Ball but the first
Scrape of one violin, blessed the ears of her followers, &
Miss Edwards on hazarding the anxious enquiry of whether
there were many people come yet was told by the Waiter
as she knew she should, that "Mr Tomlinson's family were
in the room." In passing along a short gallery to the
Assembly-room, brilliant in lights before them, they were
accosted by a young Man in a morning dress & Boots, who
was standing in the doorway of a Bedchamber, apparently
on purpose to see them go by.—"Ah! M^{rs} E— how do you
do?—How do you do Miss E.?—he cried, with an easy air;
—You are determined to be in good time I see, as usual.—
The Candles are but this moment lit"—"I like to get a good
seat by the fire you know, Mr Musgrave." replied M^{rs} E.
"I am this moment going to dress, said he—I am waiting
for my stupid fellow.—We shall have a famous Ball, The
Osbornes are certainly coming; you may depend upon *that*
for I was with Ld Osborne this morn^g—"

The party passed on—M^{rs} E's sattin gown swept along
the clean floor of the Ball-room, to the fireplace at the
upper end, where one party only were formally seated,
while three or four Officers were lounging together, passing
in & out from the adjoining card-room.—A very stiff
meeting between these near neighbours ensued—& as soon
as they were all duely placed again, Emma in the low
whisper which became the solemn scene, said to Miss
                                              Edwardes

Edwardes, "The gentleman we passed in the passage, was Mr Musgrave, then?—He is reckoned remarkably agreable I understand.—" Miss E. answered hesitatingly—"Yes—he is very much liked by many people.—But *we* are not very intimate."—"He is rich, is not he?"—"He has about 8 or 900£ a year I beleive.—He came into possession of it, when he was very young, & my Father & Mother think it has given him rather an unsettled turn.—He is no favourite with them."—The cold & empty appearance of the Room & the demure air of the small cluster of Females at one end of it began soon to give way; the inspiriting sound of other Carriages was heard, & continual accessions of portly Chaperons, & strings of smartly-dressed girls were received, with now & then a fresh gentleman straggler, who if not enough in Love to station himself near any fair Creature seemed glad to escape into the Card-room.—Among the increasing numbers of Military Men, one now made his way to Miss Edwards, with an air of Empressément, which decidedly said to her Companion "I am Capt. Hunter."—& Emma, who could not but watch her at such a moment, saw her looking rather distressed, but by no means displeased, & heard an engagement formed for the two first dances, which made her think her Brother Sam's a hopeless case.—

Emma in the meanwhile was not unobserved, or unadmired herself.—A new face & a very pretty one, could not be slighted—her name was whispered from one party to another, & no sooner had the signal been given, by the Orchestra's striking up a favourite air, which seemed to call the young Men to their duty, & people the centre of the room, than she found herself engaged to dance with a Brother officer, introduced by Capt. Hunter.—Emma Watson was not more than of the middle height—well made & plump, with an air of healthy vigour.—Her skin was very brown, but clear, smooth and glowing—; which with a lively Eye, a sweet smile, & an open Countenance,

gave

gave beauty to attract, & expression to make that beauty improve on acquaintance.—Having no reason to be dissatisfied with her partner, the Even⁵ began very pleasantly to her; & her feelings perfectly coincided with the reiterated observation of others, that it was an excellent Ball.—The two first dances were not quite over, when the returning sound of Carriages after a long interruption, called general notice, & "the Osbornes are coming, the Osbornes are coming"—was repeated round the room.— After some minutes of extraordinary bustle without, & watchful curiosity within, the important Party, preceded by the attentive Master of the Inn to open a door which was never shut, made their appearance. They consisted of Ly. Osborne, her son Lᵈ Osborne, her daughter Miss Osborne; Miss Carr, her daughter's friend, Mʳ Howard formerly Tutor to Lᵈ Osborne, now Clergyman of the Parish in which the Castle stood, Mʳˢ Blake, a widow-sister who lived with him, her son a fine boy of 10 years old, & Mʳ Tom Musgrave; who probably imprisoned within his own room, had been listening in bitter impatience to the sound of the Music, for the last half hour. In their progress up the room, they paused almost immediately behind Emma, to receive the Comptˢ of some acquaintance, & she heard Ly. Osborne observe that they had made a point of coming early for the gratification of Mʳˢ Blake's little boy, who was uncommonly fond of dancing.—Emma looked at them all as they passed—but chiefly & with most interest on Tom Musgrave, who was certainly a genteel, good looking young man.—Of the females, Ly. Osborne had by much the finest person;—tho' nearly 50, she was very handsome, & had all the Dignity of Rank.—

Lᵈ Osborne was a very fine young man; but there was an air of Coldness, of Carelessness, even of Awkwardness about him, which seemed to speak him out of his Element in a Ball room. He came in fact only because it was judged expedient for him to please the Borough—he was not fond

of

of Women's company, & he never danced.—Mr Howard was
an agreable-looking Man, a little more than Thirty.—

At the conclusion of the two Dances, Emma found herself, she knew not how, seated amongst the Osborne set;
& she was immediately struck with the fine Countenance
& animated gestures of the little boy, as he was standing
before his Mother, wondering when they should begin.—
"You will not be surprised at Charles's impatience, said
Mrs Blake, a lively pleasant-looking little Woman of 5 or
6 & 30, to a Lady who was standing near her, when you
know what a partner he is to have. Miss Osborne has been
so very kind as to promise to dance the two 1st dances with
him."—"Oh! yes—we have been engaged this week. cried
the boy. & we are to dance down every couple."—On the
other side of Emma, Miss Osborne, Miss Carr, & a party
of young Men were standing engaged in very lively consul-
tation—& soon afterwards she saw the smartest officer of
the sett, walking off to the Orchestra to order the dance,
while Miss Osborne passing before her, to her little expecting Partner hastily said—"Charles, I beg your pardon for
not keeping my engagement, but I am going to dance these
two dances with Col^n Beresford. I know you will excuse
me, & I will certainly dance with you after Tea." And
without staying for an answer, she turned again to Miss
Carr, & in another minute was led by Col. Beresford to
begin the set. If the poor little boy's face had in it's happiness been interesting to Emma, it was infinitely more so
under this sudden reverse;—he stood the picture of disappointment, with crimson'd cheeks, quivering lips, & eyes
bent on the floor. His mother, stifling her own mortification, tried to sooth his, with the prospect of Miss Osborne's
second promise;—but tho' he contrived to utter with an
effort of Boyish Bravery "Oh! I do not mind it"—it was
very evident by the unceasing agitation of his features that
he minded it as much as ever.—Emma did not think, or
reflect;—she felt & acted—. "I shall be very happy to
dance

CHARLES AND HARRIET
children of Sir George Cornewall of Moccas
By John Downman, signed and dated 1790

dance with you Sir, if you like it." said she, holding out
her hand with the most unaffected good humour.—The
Boy in one moment restored to all his first delight—looked
joyfully at his Mother and stepping forwards with an
honest & simple Thank you Maam was instantly ready to
attend his new acquaintance.—The Thankfulness of M^{rs}
Blake was more diffuse;—with a look, most expressive of
unexpected pleasure, & lively Gratitude, she turned to her
neighbour with repeated & fervent acknowledgements of
so great & condescending a kindness to her boy.—Emma
with perfect truth could assure her that she could not be
giving greater pleasure than she felt herself—& Charles
being provided with his gloves & charged to keep them on,
they joined the Set which was now rapidly forming, with
nearly equal complacency.—It was a Partnership which c^d
not be noticed without surprise. It gained her a broad
stare from Miss Osborne & Miss Carr as they pased her in
the dance. "Upon my word Charles you are in luck, (said
the former as she turned him) you have got a better partner
than me"—to which the happy Charles answered "Yes."—
Tom Musgrave who was dancing with Miss Carr, gave her
many inquisitive glances; & after a time Ld Osborne himself came & under pretence of talking to Charles, stood
to look at his partner.—Tho' rather distressed by such
observation, Emma could not repent what she had done,
so happy had it made both the boy & his Mother; the latter
of whom was continually making opportunities of addressing her with the warmest civility.—Her little partner she
found, tho' bent cheifly on dancing, was not unwilling to
speak, when her questions or remarks gave him anything
to say; & she learnt, by a sort of inevitable enquiry that
he had two brothers & a sister, that they & their Mama all
lived with his Uncle at Wickstead, that his Uncle taught
him Latin, that he was very fond of riding, & had a horse
of his own given him by Ld Osborne; & that he had been
out once already with Ld Osborne's Hounds.—At the end
of

of these Dances Emma found they were to drink tea;—
Miss E. gave her a caution to be at hand, in a manner
which convinced her of Mrs E.'s holding it very important
to have them both close to her when she moved into the
Tearoom; & Emma was accordingly on the alert to gain her
proper station. It was always the pleasure of the company
to have a little bustle & croud when they thus adjourned
for refreshment;—the Tearoom was a small room within
the Cardroom, & in passing thro' the latter, where the
passage was straightened by Tables, Mrs E. & her party
were for a few moments hemmed in. It happened close by
Lady Osborne's Cassino Table; Mr Howard who belonged
to it spoke to his Nephew; & Emma on perceiving herself
the object of attention both to Ly. O. & him, had just
turned away her eyes in time, to avoid seeming to hear
her young companion delightedly whisper aloud "Oh!
Uncle, do look at my partner. She is so pretty!" As they
were immediately in motion again however Charles was
hurried off without being able to receive his Uncle's suf-
frage.—On entering the Tearoom, in which two long Tables
were prepared, Ld Osborne was to be seen quite alone at
the end of one, as if retreating as far as he could from the
Ball, to enjoy his own thoughts, & gape without restraint.
—Charles instantly pointed him out to Emma—"There's
Lord Osborne—Let you & I go & sit by him.—"No, no,
said Emma laughing you must sit with my friends."

Charles was now free enough to hazard a few questions
in his turn. "What o'clock was it?"—"Eleven."—
"Eleven!—And I am not at all sleepy. Mama said I
should be asleep before ten.—Do you think Miss Osborne
will keep her word with me, when Tea is over?" "Oh!
yes.—I suppose so."—tho' she felt that she had no better
reason to give than that Miss Osborne had *not* kept it
before.—"When shall you come to Osborne Castle?"—
"Never, probably.—I am not acquainted with the family."
"But you may come to Wickstead & see Mama, & she can
take

take you to the Castle.—There is a monstrous curious stuff'd Fox there, & a Badger—anybody would think they were alive. It is a pity you should not see them."—

On rising from Tea, there was again a scramble for the pleasure of being first out of the room, which happened to be increased by one or two of the card parties having just broken up & the players being disposed to move exactly the different way. Among these was Mr Howard—his sister leaning on his arm—& no sooner were they within reach of Emma, than Mrs B. calling her notice by a friendly touch, said "Your goodness to Charles, my dear Miss Watson, brings all his family upon you. Give me leave to introduce my Brother—Mr H." Emma curtsied, the gentleman bowed—made a hasty request for the honour of her hand in the next two dances, to which as hasty an affirmative was given, & they were immediately impelled in opposite directions.—Emma was very well pleased with the circumstance;—there was a quietly-chearful, gentlemanlike air in Mr H. which suited her—& in a few minutes afterwards, the value of her Engagement increased, when as she was sitting in the Cardroom somewhat screened by a door, she heard Ld Osborne, who was lounging on a vacant Table near her, call Tom Musgrave towards him & say, "Why do not you dance with that beautiful Emma Watson?—I want you to dance with her—& I will come & stand by you."—"I was determining on it this very moment my Lord, I'll be introduced & dance with her directly."— "Aye do—& if you find she does not want much Talking to, you may introduce me by & bye."—"Very well my Lord—. If she is like her Sisters, she will only want to be listened to.—I will go this moment. I shall find her in the Tea room. That stiff old Mrs E. has never done tea."—Away he went—Ld Osborne after him—& Emma lost no time in hurrying from her corner, exactly the other way, forgetting in her haste that she left Mrs Edwardes behind.—"We had quite lost you—said Mrs E.— who

followed

followed her with Mary, in less than five minutes.—If you
prefer this room to the other, there is no reason why you
should not be here, but we had better all be together."
Emma was saved the Trouble of apologizing, by their being
joined at the moment by Tom Musgrave, who requesting
Mrs E. aloud to do him the honour of presenting him to
Miss Emma Watson, left that good Lady without any
choice in the business, but that of testifying by the coldness of her manner that she did it unwillingly. The honour
of dancing with her, was solicited without loss of time—&
Emma, however she might like to be thought a beautiful
girl by Lord or Commoner, was so little disposed to favour
Tom Musgrave himself, that she had considerable satisfaction in avowing her prior Engagement.—He was evidently surprised & discomposed.—The stile of her last
partner had probably led him to beleive her not overpowered with applications.—"My little friend Charles
Blake, he cried, must not expect to engross you the whole
evening. We can never suffer this—It is against the rules
of the Assembly—& I am sure it will never be patronised
by our good friend here Mrs E.; She is by much too nice a
judge of Decorum to give her license to such a dangerous
Particularity."—"I am not going to dance with Master
Blake Sir." The Gentleman a little disconcerted, could
only hope he might be more fortunate another time—&
seeming unwilling to leave her, tho' his friend Ld Osborne
was waiting in the Doorway for the result, as Emma with
some amusement perceived—he began to make civil enquiries after her family.—"How comes it, that we have
not the pleasure of seeing your Sisters here this Evening?
—Our Assemblies have been used to be so well treated by
them, that we do not know how to take this neglect."—
"My eldest Sister is the only one at home—& she could not
leave my Father"—"Miss Watson the only one at home!
—You astonish me!—It seems but the day before yesterday that I saw them all three in this Town. But I am
afraid

afraid I have been a very sad neighbour of late. I hear
dreadful complaints of my negligence wherever I go, &
I confess it is a shameful length of time since I was at
Stanton.—But I shall *now* endeavour to make myself
amends for the past."—Emma's calm curtsey in reply
must have struck him as very unlike the encouraging
warmth he had been used to receive from her Sisters, &
gave him probably the novel sensation of doubting his own
influence, & of wishing for more attention than she bestowed. The dancing now recommenced; Miss Carr being
impatient to *call*, everybody was required to stand up—
& Tom Musgrave's curiosity was appeased, on seeing M^r
Howard come forward and claim Emma's hand—"That
will do as well for me"—was Ld Osborne's remark, when
his friend carried him the news—& he was continually at
Howard's Elbow during the two dances.—The frequency
of his appearance there, was the only unpleasant part of
her engagement, the only objection she could make to
Mr Howard.—In himself, she thought him as agreable as
he looked; tho' chatting on the commonest topics he had
a sensible, unaffected, way of expressing himself, which
made them all worth hearing, & she only regretted that he
had not been able to make his pupil's Manners as unexceptionable as his own.—The two dances seemed very short,
& she had her partner's authority for considering them
so.—At their conclusion the Osbornes & their Train were
all on the move. "We are off at last, said his Lordship to
Tom—How much longer do *you* stay in this Heavenly
place?—till Sunrise?"—"No faith! my Lord, I have had
quite enough of it. I assure you—I shall not shew myself
here again when I have had the honour of attending Ly.
Osborne to her Carriage. I shall retreat in as much secrecy
as possible to the most remote corner of the House, where
I shall order a Barrel of Oysters, & be famously snug."
"Let us see you soon at the Castle; & bring me word
how she looks by daylight."—Emma & Mrs Blake parted

as

as old acquaintance, & Charles shook her by the hand & wished her "goodbye" at least a dozen times. From Miss Osborne & Miss Carr she received something like a jerking curtsey as they passed her; even Ly. Osborne gave her a look of complacency—& his Lordship actually came back after the others were out of the room, to "beg her pardon", & look in the window seat behind her for the gloves which were visibly compressed in his hand.—

As Tom Musgrave was seen no more, we may suppose his plan to have succeeded, & imagine him mortifying with his Barrel of Oysters, in dreary solitude—or gladly assisting the Landlady in her Bar to make fresh Negus for the happy Dancers above. Emma could not help missing the party, by whom she had been, tho' in some respects unpleasantly, distinguished, & the two Dances which followed & concluded the Ball, were rather flat, in comparison with the others.—Mr E. having play'd with good luck, they were some of the last in the room—"Here we are, back again I declare—said Emma sorrowfully, as she walked into the Dining room, where the Table was prepared, & the neat Upper maid was lighting the Candles—"My dear Miss Edwards—how soon it is at an end!—I wish it could all come over again!—" A great deal of kind pleasure was expressed in her having enjoyed the Even^g so much—& Mr Edwards was as warm as herself, in praise of the fullness, brilliancy & Spirit of the Meeting. tho' as he had been fixed the whole time at the same Table in the same Room, with only one change of chairs, it might have seemed a matter scarcely perceived.—But he had won 4 rubbers out of 5, & everything went well. His daughter felt the advantage of this gratified state of mind, in the course of the remarks & retrospections which now ensued, over the welcome soup.—"How came you not to dance with either of the Mr Tomlinsons, Mary?—said her Mother. "I was always engaged when they asked me." "I thought you were to have stood up with Mr James, the last two dances; Mrs Tomlinson

Tomlinson told me he was gone to ask you—& I had heard you say two minutes before that you were *not* engaged."— "Yes—but—there was a mistake—I had misunderstood— I did not know I was engaged.—I thought it had been for the 2 Dances after, if we staid so long—but Capt. Hunter assured me it was for those very Two.—"

"So, you ended with Capt. Hunter Mary, did you?" said her Father. And who did you begin with?" "Capt. Hunter." was repeated, in a very humble tone—"Hum!— That is being constant however. But who else did you dance with?" "Mr Norton, & Mr Styles." "And who are they?" "Mr Norton is a Cousin of Capt. Hunter's."— "And who is Mr Styles?" "One of his particular friends," —"All in the same Reg^t added Mrs E.—Mary was surrounded by Red coats the whole Even^g. I should have been better pleased to see her dancing with some of our old Neighbours I confess.—" "Yes, yes, we must not neglect our old Neighbours—. But if these soldiers are quicker than other people in a Ball room, what are young Ladies to do?" "I think there is no occasion for their engaging themselves so many Dances beforehand, Mr Edwards."— "No—perhaps not—but I remember my dear when you & I did the same."—Mrs E. said no more, & Mary breathed again.—A great deal of goodhumoured pleasantry followed —& Emma went to bed in charming Spirits, her head full of Osbornes, Blakes & Howards.—

The next morn^g brought a great many visitors. It was the way of the place always to call on Mrs E. on the morn^g after a Ball, & this neighbourly inclination was increased in the present instance by a general spirit of curiosity on Emma's account, as Everybody wanted to look again at the girl who had been admired the night before by Ld Osborne.—

Many were the eyes, & various the degrees of approbation with which she was examined. Some saw no fault, & some no Beauty—. With some her brown skin was the
annihilation

annihilation of every grace, & others could never be persuaded that she were half so handsome as Eliz: Watson
had been ten years ago.—The mornˢ passed quietly away
in discussing the merits of the Ball with all this succession of Company—& Emma was at once astonished by
finding it Two o'clock, & considering that she had heard
nothing of her Father's Chair. After this discovery she had
walked twice to the window to examine the Street, & was
on the point of asking leave to ring the bell & make
enquiries, when the light sound of a Carriage driving up
to the door set her heart at ease. She stepd again to the
window—but instead of the convenient but very un-smart
Family Equipage perceived a neat Curricle.—Mr Musgrave
was shortly afterwards announced;—& Mrs Edwards put
on her very stiffest look at the sound.—Not at all dismayed
however by her chilling air, he paid his Compts to each of
the Ladies with no unbecoming Ease, & continuing to
address Emma, presented her a note, which he had the
honour of bringing from her Sister; But to which he must
observe that a verbal postscript from himself wd be
requisite.—"

The note, which Emma was beginning to read rather *before* Mrs Edwards had entreated her to use no ceremony,
contained a few lines from Eliz: importing that their Father
in consequence of being unusually well had taken the
sudden resolution of attending the Visitation that day, &
that as his Road lay quite wide from R., it was impossible
for her to come home till the following mornˢ, unless the
Edwardses wd send her which was hardly to be expected, or
she cd meet with any chance conveyance, or did not mind
walking so far.—She had scarcely run her eye thro' the
whole, before she found herself obliged to listen to Tom
Musgrave's farther account. "I received that note from
the fair hands of Miss Watson only ten minutes ago, said
he—I met her in the village of Stanton, whither my good
Stars prompted me to turn my Horses heads—she was at
that

that moment in quest of a person to employ on the Errand, & I was fortunate enough to convince her that she could not find a more willing or speedy Messenger than myself—. Remember, I say nothing of my Disinterestedness.—My reward is to be the indulgence of conveying you to Stanton in my Curricle.—Tho' they are not written down, I bring your Sister's Orders for the same.—" Emma felt distressed; she did not like the proposal—she did not wish to be on terms of intimacy with the Proposer—& yet fearful of encroaching on the Edwardes', as well as wishing to go home herself, she was at a loss how entirely to decline what he offered—Mrs E. continued silent, either not understanding the case, or waiting to see how the young Lady's inclination lay. Emma thanked him—but professed herself very unwilling to give him so much trouble. "The Trouble was of course, Honour, Pleasure, Delight. What had he or his Horses to do?"—Still she hesitated. "She beleived she must beg leave to decline his assistance—she was rather afraid of the sort of carriage—. The distance was not beyond a walk.—" Mrs E. was silent no longer. She enquired into the particulars—& then said "We shall be extremely happy Miss Emma, if you can give us the pleasure of your company till tomorrow—but if you can not conveniently do so, our Carriage is quite at your Service, & Mary will be pleased with the opportunity of seeing your Sister."—This was precisely what Emma had longed for; & she accepted the offer most thankfully; acknowledging that as Eliz: was entirely alone, it was her wish to return home to dinner.—The plan was warmly opposed by their Visitor. "I cannot suffer it indeed. I must not be deprived of the happiness of escorting you. I assure you there is not a possibility of fear with my Horses. You might guide them yourself. *Your Sisters* all know how quiet they are; They have none of them the smallest scruple in trusting themselves with me, even on a Race Course.—Beleive me—added he lowering his voice

—You

—*You* are quite safe, the danger is only *mine*."—Emma was not more disposed to oblige him for all this.—"And as to Mrs Edwardes' carriage being used the day after a Ball, it is a thing quite out of rule I assure you—never heard of before—the old Coachman will look as black as his Horses—. Won't he Miss Edwards?"—No notice was taken. The Ladies were silently firm, & the gentleman found himself obliged to submit.

"What a famous Ball we had last night!—he cried, after a short pause. How long did you keep it up, after the Osbornes & I went away?"—"We had two dances more." —"It is making it too much of a fatigue I think, to stay so late.—I suppose your Set was not a very full one."— "Yes, quite as full as ever, except the Osbornes. There seemed no vacancy anywhere—& everybody danced with uncommon spirit to the very last."—Emma said this—tho' against her conscience.—"Indeed! perhaps I might have looked in upon you again, if I had been aware of as much; —for I am rather fond of dancing than not.—Miss Osborne is a charming girl, is not she?" "I do not think her handsome." replied Emma, to whom all this was cheifly addressed. "Perhaps she is not critically handsome, but her Manners are delightful. And Fanny Carr is a most interesting little creature. You can imagine nothing more *naive* or *piquante*; & What do you thing of Ld Osborne Miss Watson?" "That he would be handsome even, tho' he were *not* a Lord—& perhaps—better bred; More desirous of pleasing, & shewing himself pleased in a right place.—" "Upon my word, you are severe upon my friend!—I assure you Ld Osborne is a very good fellow.—" "I do not dispute his virtues—but I do not like his careless air.—" "If it were not a breach of confidence, replied Tom with an important look, perhaps I might be able to win a more favourable opinion of poor Osborne.—" Emma gave him no Encouragement, & he was obliged to keep his friend's secret.—He was also obliged to put an end to his visit—for

M^rs

Mrs Edwards having ordered her Carriage, there was no
time to be lost on Emma's side in preparing for it.—Miss
Edwards accompanied her home, but as it was Dinner hour
at Stanton, staid with them only a few minutes,—"Now
my dear Emma, said Miss W., as soon as they were alone,
you must talk to me all the rest of the day, without stopping, or I shall not be satisfied. But first of all Nanny
shall bring in the dinner. Poor thing!—You will not dine
as you did yesterday, for we have nothing but some fried
beef.—How nice Mary Edwards looks in her new pelisse!—
And now tell me how you like them all, & what I am to say
to Sam. I have begun my letter, Jack Stokes is to call for
it tomorrow, for his Uncle is going within a mile of Guilford the next day.—" Nanny brought in the dinner;—"We
will wait upon ourselves, continued Eliz: & then we shall
lose no time.—And so, you would not come home with
Tom Musgrave?"—"No. You had said so much against
him that I could not wish either for the obligation, or
the Intimacy which the use of his Carriage must have
created—. I should not even have liked the appearance of
it.—" "You did very right; tho' I wonder at your forbearance, & I do not think I could have done it myself.—He
seemed so eager to fetch you, that I could not say no, tho'
it rather went against me to be throwing you together, so
well as I knew his Tricks;—but I did long to see you, & it
was a clever way of getting you home; Besides it won't do
to be too nice.—Nobody could have thought of the Edwards' letting you have their Coach,—after the Horses
being out so late.—But what am I to say to Sam?"—"If
you are guided by me, you will not encourage him to think
of Miss Edwards.—The Father is decidedly against him,
the Mother shews him no favour, & I doubt his having any
interest with Mary. She danced twice with Capt. Hunter,
& I think shews him in general as much Encouragement
as is consistent with her disposition, & the circumstances
she is placed in.—She once mentioned Sam, & certainly
with

with a little confusion—but that was perhaps merely oweing to the consciousness of his liking her, which may very
probably have come to her knowledge."—"Oh! dear Yes
—she has heard enough of that from us all. Poor Sam!—
He is out of luck as well as other people.—For the life of
me Emma, I cannot help feeling for those that are cross'd
in Love.—Well—now begin, & give me an account of
everything as it happened.—" Emma obeyed her—& Eliz:
listened with very little interruption till she heard of M^r H.
as a partner.—"Dance with Mr H.—Good Heavens! You
don't say so! Why—he is quite one of the great & Grand
ones;—Did not you find him very high?" "His manners
are of a kind to give *me* much more Ease & confidence than
Tom Musgrave's." "Well—go on. I should have been
frightened out of my wits, to have had anything to do
with the Osborne's set."—Emma concluded her narration.
—"And so, you really did not dance with Tom M. at all?—
But you must have liked him, you must have been struck
with him altogether."—"I do *not* like him, Eliz:—. I allow
his person & air to be good—& that his manners to a certain
point—his address rather—is pleasing.—But I see nothing
else to admire in him.—On the contrary, he seems very
vain, very conceited, absurdly anxious for Distinction, &
absolutely contemptible in some of the measures he takes
for becoming so.—There is a ridiculousness about him
that entertains me—but his company gives me no other
agreable Emotion." "My dearest Emma!—You are like
nobody else in the World.—It is well Margaret is not by.—
You do not offend *me*, tho' I hardly know how to beleive
you. But Marg^t w^d never forgive such words." "I wish
Marg^t could have heard him profess his ignorance of her
being out of the Country; he declared it seemed only two
days since he had seen her.—" "Aye—that is just like
him. & yet this is the Man, she *will* fancy so desperately
in love with her.—He is no favourite of mine, as you well
know, Emma;—but you must think him agreable. Can
you

you lay your hand on your heart, & say you do not?"—
"Indeed I can, Both Hands; & spread to their widest
extent."—"I should like to know the Man you *do* think
agreable." "His name is Howard." "Howard! Dear me.
I cannot think of *him*, but as playing cards with Ly Osborne, & looking proud.—I must own however that it *is*
a releif to me, to find you can speak as you do, of Tom
Musgrave; my heart did misgive me that you would like
him too well. You talked so stoutly beforehand, that I was
sadly afraid your Brag would be punished.—I only hope
it will last;—& that he will not come on to pay you much
attention; it is a hard thing for a woman to stand against
the flattering ways of a Man, when he is bent upon pleasing
her.—" As their quietly-sociable little meal concluded,
Miss Watson could not help observing how comfortably it
had passed. "It is so delightful to me, said she, to have
Things going on in peace & goodhumour. Nobody can tell
how much I hate quarrelling. Now, tho' we have had
nothing but fried beef, how good it has all seemed.—I wish
everybody were as easily satisfied as you—but poor Marg^t
is very snappish, & Penelope owns she had rather have
Quarrelling going on, than nothing at all."—Mr Watson
returned in the Evening, not the worse for the exertion of
the day, & consequently pleased with what he had done,
& glad to talk of it, over his own Fireside.—

Emma had not foreseen any interest to herself in the
occurrences of a Visitation—but when she heard Mr Howard spoken of as the Preacher, & as having given them
an excellent Sermon, she could not help listening with
a quicker Ear.—"I do not know when I have heard a Discourse more to my mind—continued Mr W. or one better
delivered.—He reads extremely well, with great propriety
& in a very impressive manner; & at the same time without
any Theatrical grimace or violence.—I own, I do not like
much action in the pulpit—I do not like the studied air
& artificial inflexions of voice, which your very popular

M &

& most admired Preachers generally have.—A simple delivery is much better calculated to inspire Devotion, & shews a much better Taste.—Mr H. read like a scholar & a gentleman."—"And what had you for dinner Sir?"—said his eldest Daughter.—He related the Dishes & told what he had ate himself. "Upon the whole, he added, I have had a very comfortable day; my old friends were quite surprised to see me amongst them—& I must say that everybody paid me great attention, & seemed to feel for me as an Invalid.—They would make me sit near the fire, & as the partridges were pretty high, Dr Richards would have them sent away to the other end of the Table, that they might not offend Mr Watson—which I thought very kind of him.—But what pleased me as much as anything was Mr Howard's attention;—There is a pretty steep flight of steps up to the room we dine in—which do not quite agree with my gouty foot—& Mr Howard walked by me from the bottom to the top, & would make me take his arm.—It struck me as very becoming in so young a Man, but I am sure I had no claim to expect it; for I never saw him before in my Life.—By the bye, he enquired after one of my Daughters, but I do not know which. I suppose you know among yourselves."—

On the 3^d day after the Ball, as Nanny at five minutes before three, was beginning to bustle into the parlour with the Tray & the Knife-case, she was suddenly called to the front door, by the sound of as smart a rap as the end of a riding-whip c^d give—& tho' charged by Miss W. to let nobody in, returned in half a minute, with a look of awkward dismay, to hold the parlour door open for Ld Osborne & Tom Musgrave.—The surprise of the young Ladies may be imagined. No visitors would have been welcome at such a moment; but such visitors as these—such a one as Ld Osborne at least, a nobleman & a stranger, was really distressing.—He looked a little embarrassed himself,—as,

on

on being introduced by his easy, voluble friend, he mut-
tered something of doing himself the honour of waiting
on Mr Watson.—Tho' Emma could not but take the
compliment of the visit to herself, she was very far from
enjoying it. She felt all the inconsistency of such an
acquaintance with the very humble stile in which they were
obliged to live; & having in her Aunt's family been used
to many of the Elegancies of Life, was fully sensible of all
that must be open to the ridicule of Richer people in her
present home.—Of the pain of such feelings, Eliz: knew
very little;—her simpler Mind, or juster reason saved her
from such mortification—& tho' shrinking under a general
sense of Inferiority, she felt no particular Shame.—M^r
Watson, as the Gentlemen had already heard from Nanny,
was not well enough to be down stairs;—With much concern they took their seats—Ld. Osborne near Emma, & the
convenient Mr Musgrave in high spirits at his own importance, on the other side of the fireplace with Eliz^th.—*He*
was at no loss for words;—but when Ld. Osborne had
hoped that Emma had not caught cold at the Ball, he had
nothing more to say for some time, & could only gratify his
Eye by occasional glances at his fair neighbour.—Emma
was not inclined to give herself much trouble for his Entertainment—& after hard labour of mind, he produced the
remark of it's being a very fine day, & followed it up with
the question of, "Have you been walking this morning?"
"No, my Lord. We thought it too dirty." "You should
wear half-boots."—After another pause, "Nothing sets off
a neat ankle more than a half-boot; nankin galoshed with
black looks very well.—Do not you like Half-boots? "Yes
—but unless they are so stout as to injure their beauty,
they are not fit for Country walking."—"Ladies should
ride in dirty weather.—Do you ride?" "No my Lord."
"I wonder every Lady does not.—A woman never looks
better than on horseback.—" "But every woman may not
have the inclination, or the means." "If they knew how
                                                    much

much it became them, they would all have the inclination, & I fancy Miss Watson—when once they had the inclination, the means w^d soon follow."—"Your Lordship thinks we always have our own way.—*That* is a point on which Ladies & Gentle^n have long disagreed—But without pretending to decide it, I may say that there are some circumstances which even *Women* cannot controul.—Female Economy will do a great deal my Lord, but it cannot turn a small income into a large one."—Ld Osborne was silenced. Her manner had been neither sententious nor sarcastic, but there was a something in it's mild seriousness, as well as in the words themselves which made his Lordship think;— and when he addressed her again, it was with a degree of considerate propriety, totally unlike the half-awkward, half-fearless stile of his former remarks.—It was a new thing with him to wish to please a woman; it was the first time that he had ever felt what was due to a woman, in Emma's situation.—But as he wanted neither Sense nor a good disposition, he did not feel it without effect.—"You have not been long in this Country I understand, said he in the tone of a Gentle^n. I hope you are pleased with it."— He was rewarded by a gracious answer, & a more liberal full veiw of her face than she had yet bestowed. Unused to exert himself, & happy in contemplating her, he then sat in silence for some minutes longer, while Tom Musgrave was chattering to Elizth, till they were interrupted by Nanny's approach, who half opening the door & putting in her head, said "Please Ma'am, Master wants to know why he be'nt to have his dinner."—The Gentlemen, who had hitherto disregarded every symptom, however positive, of the nearness of that Meal, now jumped up with apologies, while Elizth called briskly after Nanny "to tell Betty to take up the Fowls."—"I am sorry it happens so—she added, turning good-humouredly towards Musgrave—but you know what early hours we keep.—" Tom had nothing to say for himself, he knew it very well, & such honest simplicity

simplicity, such shameless Truth rather bewildered him.—
Ld Osborne's parting Comp^ts took some time, his inclination
for speech seeming to increase with the shortness of the
term for indulgence.—He recommended Exercise in defiance of dirt—spoke again in praise of Half-boots—begged
that his Sister might be allow'd to send Emma the name
of her Shoemaker—& concluded with saying, "My Hounds
will be hunting this Country next week—I beleive they
will throw off at Stanton Wood on Wednesday at 9 o'clock.
—I mention this, in hopes of y^r being drawn out to see
what's going on.—If the morning's tolerable, pray do us
the honour of giving us your good wishes in person.—

The Sisters looked on each other with astonishment,
when their Visitors had withdrawn. "Here's an unaccountable Honour! cried Eliz: at last. Who would have thought
of Ld Osborne's coming to Stanton.—He is very handsome
—but Tom Musgrave looks all to nothing, the smartest &
most fashionable Man of the two. I am glad he did not say
anything to me; I w^d not have had to talk to such a great
Man for the world. Tom was very agreable, was not he?—
But did you hear him ask where Miss Penelope & Miss
Marg^t were, when he first came in?—It put me out of
patience.—I am glad Nanny had not laid the Cloth however, it w^d have looked so awkward;—just the Tray did not
signify.—" To say that Emma was not flattered by L^d
Osborne's visit, would be to assert a very unlikely thing,
& describe a very odd young Lady; but the gratification
was by no means unalloyed; His coming was a sort of
notice which might please her vanity, but did not suit her
pride, & she w^d rather have known that he wished the visit
without presuming to make it, than have seen him at
Stanton.—Among other unsatisfactory feelings it once
occurred to her to wonder why Mr Howard had not taken
the same privilege of coming, & accompanied his Lordship
—but she was willing to suppose that he had either known
nothing about it, or had declined any share in a measure
which

which carried quite as much Impertinence in it's form as Goodbreeding.—M^r W was very far from being delighted, when he heard what had passed;—a little peevish under immediate pain, & ill disposed to be pleased, he only replied—"Phoo! Phoo!—What occasion could there be for Ld O.'s coming. I have lived here 14 years without being noticed by any of the family. It is some foolery of that idle fellow T. Musgrave. I cannot return the visit.—*I* would not if I could." And when T. Musgrave was met with again, he was commissioned with a message of excuse to Osborne Castle, on the too-sufficient plea of Mr Watson's infirm state of health.—

A week or ten days rolled quietly away after this visit, before any new bustle arose to interrupt even for half a day, the tranquil & affectionate intercourse of the two Sisters, whose mutual regard was increasing with the intimate knowledge of each other which such intercourse produced.—The first circumstance to break in on this serenity, was the receipt of a letter from Croydon to announce the speedy return of Margaret, & a visit of two or three days from M^r & Mrs Robert Watson, who undertook to bring her home & wished to see their Sister Emma.—It was an expectation to fill the thoughts of the Sisters at Stanton, & to busy the hours of one of them at least—for as Jane had been a woman of fortune, the preparations for her entertainment were considerable, & as Eliz: had at all times more good will than method in her guidance of the house, she could make no change without a Bustle.—An absence of 14 years had made all her Brothers & Sisters Strangers to Emma, but in her expectation of Margaret there was more than the awkwardness of such an alienation; she had heard things which made her dread her return; & the day which brought the party to Stanton seemed to her the probable conclusion of almost all that had been comfortable in the house.—Robert Watson was an Attorney at Croydon, in a good way of Business; very

well

well satisfied with himself for the same, & for having married the only daughter of the Attorney to whom he had been Clerk, with a fortune of six thousand pounds.— Mrs Robt was not less pleased with herself for having had that six thousand pounds, & for being now in possession of a very smart house in Croydon, where she gave genteel parties, & wore fine cloathes.—In her person there was nothing remarkable; her manners were pert and conceited. —Margaret was not without beauty; she had a slight, pretty figure, & rather wanted Countenance than good features; —but the sharp & anxious expression of her face made her beauty in general little felt.—On meeting her long-absent Sister, as on every occasion of shew, her manner was all affection & her voice all gentleness; continual smiles & a very slow articulation being her constant resource when determined on pleasing.—

She was now so "delighted to see dear, dear Emma" that she could hardly speak a word in a minute.—"I am sure we shall be great friends"—she observed, with much sentiment, as they were sitting together.—Emma scarcely knew how to answer such a proposition—& the manner in which it was spoken, she could not attempt to equal. Mrs R. W. eyed her with much familiar curiosity & Triumphant Compassion;—the loss of the Aunt's fortune was uppermost in her mind, at the moment of meeting;—& she cd. not but feel how much better it was to be the daughter of a gentleman of property in Croydon, than the neice of an old woman who threw herself away on an Irish Captain.— Robert was carelessly kind, as became a prosperous Man & a brother; more intent on settling with the Post-Boy, inveighing against the Exorbitant advance in Posting, & pondering over a doubtful halfcrown, than on welcoming a Sister, who was no longer likely to have any property for him to get the direction of.—"Your road through the village is infamous, Eliz:; said he, worse than ever it was. By Heaven! I would endite it if I lived near you. Who is

Surveyor

Surveyor now?"—There was a little neice at Croydon, to be fondly enquired after by the kind-hearted Elizabeth, who regretted very much her not being of the party.— "You are very good—replied her Mother—& I assure you it went very hard with Augusta to have us come away without her. I was forced to say we were only going to Church & promise to come back for her directly.—But you know it would not do, to bring her without her maid, & I am as particular as ever in having her properly attended to." "Sweet little Darling!—cried Marg^t—It quite broke my heart to leave her.—" "Then why was you in such a hurry to run away from her? cried Mrs R.—You are a sad shabby girl.—I have been quarrelling with you all the way we came, have not I?—Such a visit as this, I never heard of!—You know how glad we are to have any of you with us—if it be for months together.—& I am sorry, (with a witty smile) we have not been able to make Croydon agreable this autumn."—"My dearest Jane—do not over-power me with your Raillery.—You know what induce-ments I had to bring me home,—spare me, I entreat you—. I am no match for your arch sallies.—" "Well, I only beg you will not set your Neighbours against the place.—Per-haps Emma may be tempted to go back with us, & stay till Christmas, if you don't put in your word."—Emma was greatly obliged. "I assure you we have very good society at Croydon.—I do not much attend the Balls, they are rather too mixed,—but our parties are very select & good.—I had seven Tables last week in my Drawingroom. Are you fond of the Country? How do you like Stanton?" —"Very much"—replied Emma, who thought a compre-hensive answer, most to the purpose.—She saw that her Sister in law despised her immediately.—Mrs R. W. was indeed wondering what sort of a home Emma c^d possibly have been used to in Shropshire, & setting it down as certain that the Aunt could never have had six thousand pounds.—"How charming Emma is!—" whispered Marg^t

to

to Mrs Robert in her most languishing tone.—Emma was quite distress'd by such behaviour;—& she did not like it better when she heard Marg^t 5 minutes afterwards say to Eliz: in a sharp quick accent, totally unlike the first— "Have you heard from Pen. since she went to Chichester? —I had a letter the other day.—I don't find she is likely to make anything of it. I fancy she'll come back 'Miss Penelope' as she went.—"

Such, she feared would be Margaret's common voice, when the novelty of her own appearance were over; the tone of artificial Sensibility was not recommended by the idea.—The Ladies were invited upstairs to prepare for dinner. "I hope you will find things tolerably comfortable Jane"—said Eliz^th as she opened the door of the spare bed-chamber.—"My good creature, replied Jane, use no ceremony with me, I intreat you. I am one of those who always take things as they find them. I hope I can put up with a small apartment for two or three nights, without making a peice of work. I always wish to be treated quite "en famille" when I come to see you—& now I do hope you have not been getting a great dinner for us.—Remember we never eat suppers."—"I suppose, said Marg^t rather quickly to Emma, you & I are to be together; Eliz^th always takes care to have a room to herself."—"No— Eliz^th gives me half her's."—"Oh!—(in a soften'd voice, & rather mortified to find she was not ill used) "I am sorry I am not to have the pleasure of your company—especially as it makes me nervous to be much alone."

Emma was the first of the females in the parlour again; on entering it she found her brother alone.—"So Emma, said he, you are quite the Stranger at home. It must seem odd enough to you to be here.—A pretty peice of work your Aunt Turner has made of it!—By Heaven! A woman should never be trusted with money. I always said she ought to have settled something on you, as soon as her Husband died." "But that would have been trusting *me* with

with money, replied Emma, & *I* am a woman too.—" "It might have been secured to your future use, without your having any power over it now.—What a blow it must have been upon you!—To find yourself, instead of heiress of 8 or 9000 £, sent back a weight upon your family, without a sixpence.—I hope the old woman will smart for it." "Do not speak disrespectfully of her—She was very good to me; & if she has made an imprudent choice, she will suffer more from it herself, than *I* can possibly do." "I do not mean to distress you, but you know every body must think her an old fool.—I thought Turner had been reckoned an extraordinary sensible, clever man.—How the Devil came he to make such a will?"—"My Uncle's sense is not at all impeached in my opinion, by his attachment to my Aunt. She had been an excellent wife to him. The most Liberal & enlightened Minds are always the most confiding. —The event has been unfortunate, but my Uncle's memory is if possible endeared to me by such a proof of tender respect for my Aunt."—"That's odd sort of Talking!— He might have provided decently for his widow, without leaving every thing that he had to dispose of, or any part of it at her mercy."—"My Aunt may have erred—said Emma warmly—she *has* erred—but my Uncle's conduct was faultless. I was her own Neice, & he left to herself the power & the pleasure of providing for me."—"But un-luckily she has left the pleasure of providing for you, to your Father, & without the power.—That's the long & the short of the business. After keeping you at a distance from your family for such a length of time as must do away all natural affection among us & breeding you up (I suppose) in a superior stile, you are returned upon their hands with-out a sixpence." "You know, replied Emma struggling with her tears, my Uncle's melancholy state of health. —He was a greater Invalid than my father. He c^d not leave home." "I do not mean to make you cry.—said Robt rather softened—& after a short silence, by way of changing the

the subject, he added—" I am just come from my Father's
room, he seems very indifferent. It will be a sad break-up
when he dies. Pity, you can none of you get married!—
You must come to Croydon as well as the rest, & see what
you can do there.—I beleive if Marg^t had had a thousand
or fifteen hundred pounds, there was a young man who w^d
have thought of her." Emma was glad when they were
joined by the others; it was better to look at her Sister in
law's finery than listen to Robert, who had equally irritated
& greived her.—Mrs Robert exactly as smart as she had been
at her own party, came in with apologies for her dress—
" I would not make you wait, said she, so I put on the first
thing I met with.—I am afraid I am a sad figure.—My
dear Mr W.—(to her husband) you have not put any fresh
powder in your hair."—" No—I do not intend it.—I think
there is powder enough in my hair for my wife & sisters.— "
" Indeed you ought to make some alteration in your dress
before dinner when you are out visitting, tho' you do not
at home." "Nonsense."—" It is very odd you should not
like to do what other gentlemen do. Mr Marshall & M^r
Hemmings change their dress every day of their Lives
before dinner. And what was the use of my putting up
your last new Coat, if you are never to wear it."—" Do be
satisfied with being fine yourself, & leave your husband
alone."—To put an end to this altercation, & soften the
evident vexation of her sister in law, Emma (tho' in no
Spirits to make such nonsense easy) began to admire her
gown.—It produced immediate complacency.—" Do you
like it?—said she.—I am very happy.—It has been excessively admired;—but sometimes I think the pattern too
large.—I shall wear one tomorrow that I think you
will prefer to this.—Have you seen the one I gave
Margaret?"—

Dinner came, & except when Mrs R. looked at her husband's head, she continued gay & flippant, chiding Elizth
for the profusion on the Table, & absolutely protesting
against

against the entrance of the roast Turkey—which formed the only exception to "You see your dinner".—"I do beg & entreat that no Turkey may be seen today. I am really frightened out of my wits with the number of dishes we have already. Let us have no Turkey I beseech you."— "My dear, replied Eliz. the Turkey is roasted, & it may just as well come in, as stay in the Kitchen. Besides if it is cut, I am in hopes my Father may be tempted to eat a bit, for it is rather a favourite dish." "You may have it in my dear, but I assure you I shan't touch it."—

Mr Watson had not been well enough to join the party at dinner, but was prevailed on to come down & drink tea with them.—"I wish we may be able to have a game of cards tonight," said Eliz. to Mrs R. after seeing her father comfortably seated in his arm chair.—"Not on my account my dear, I beg. You know I am no card player. I think a snug chat infinitely better. I always say cards are very well sometimes, to break a formal circle, but one never wants them among friends." "I was thinking of it's being something to amuse my father, answered Elizth—if it was not disagreable to you. He says his head won't bear Whist —but perhaps if we make a round game he may be tempted to sit down with us."—"By all means my dear Creature. I am quite at your service. Only do not oblige me to chuse the game, that's all. *Speculation* is the only round game at Croydon now, but I can play anything.—When there is only one or two of you at home, you must be quite at a loss to amuse him—why do not you get him to play at Crib-bage?—Margaret & I have played at Cribbage, most nights that we have not been engaged."—A sound like a distant Carriage was at this moment caught; everybody listened; it became more decided; it certainly drew nearer.—It was an unusual sound in Stanton at any time of the day, for the Village was on no very public road, & contained no gentleman's family but the Rector's.—The wheels rapidly approached;—in two minutes the general expectation was

answered

answered; they stopped beyond a doubt at the garden gate
of the Parsonage. "Who could it be?—it was certainly
a postchaise.—Penelope was the only creature to be
thought of. She might perhaps have met with some unexpected opportunity of returning."—A pause of suspense
ensued.—Steps were distinguished, first along the paved
Footway which led under the windows of the house to the
front door, & then within the passage. They were the steps
of a Man. It could not be Penelope. It must be Samuel.—
The door opened, & displayed Tom Musgrave in the wrap
of a Travellor.—He had been in London & was now on his
way home, & he had come half a mile out of his road merely
to call for ten minutes at Stanton. He loved to take people
by surprise, with sudden visits at extraordinary seasons;
& in the present instance had had the additional motive
of being able to tell the Miss Watsons, whom he depended
on finding sitting quietly employed after tea, that he was
going home to an 8 o'clock dinner.—As it happened however, he did not give more surprise than he received, when
instead of being shewn into the usual little sitting room,
the door of the best parlour a foot larger each way than
the other was thrown open, & he beheld a circle of smart
people whom he c^d not immediately recognise arranged
with all the honours of visiting round the fire, & Miss
Watson sitting at the best Pembroke Table, with the best
Tea things before her. He stood for a few seconds, in silent
amazement.—"Musgrave!"—ejaculated Margaret in a
tender voice.—He recollected himself, & came forward,
delighted to find such a circle of Friends, & blessing his
good fortune for the unlooked-for Indulgence.—He shook
hands with Robert, bowed & smiled to the Ladies, & did
everything very prettily; but as to any particularity of
address or Emotion towards Margaret, Emma who closely
observed him, perceived nothing that did not justify Eliz.'s
opinions tho' Margaret's modest smiles imported that she
meant to take the visit to herself.—He was persuaded
without

without much difficulty to throw off his greatcoat, & drink tea with them. "For whether he dined at 8 or 9, as he observed, was a matter of very little consequence."—and without seeming to seek, he did not turn away from the chair close to Margaret which she was assiduous in providing him.—She had thus secured him from her Sisters—but it was not immediately in her power to preserve him from her Brother's claims, for as he came avowedly from London, & had left it only 4. hours ago, the last current report as to public news, & the general opinion of the day must be understood, before Robert could let his attention be yeilded to the less national, & important demands of the Women.—At last however he was at liberty to hear Margaret's soft address, as she spoke her fears of his having had a most terrible, cold, dark dreadful Journey.—"Indeed you should not have set out so late.—" "I could not be earlier, he replied. I was detained chatting at the Bedford, by a friend.—All hours are alike to me.—How long have you been in the Country Miss Marg^t?"—"We came only this morn^g.—My kind Brother & Sister brought me home this very morn^g.—'Tis singular is not it?" "You were gone a great while, were not you? a fortnight I suppose?"—"*You* may call a fortnight a great while Mr Musgrave, said Mrs Robert smartly—but *we* think a month very little. I assure you we bring her home at the end of a month, much against our will." "A month! have you really been gone a month! 'tis amazing how Time flies.—" "You may imagine, said Marg^t in a sort of Whisper, what are my Sensations in finding myself once more at Stanton. You know what a sad visitor I make.—And I was so excessively impatient to see Emma;—I dreaded the meeting, & at the same time longed for it.—Do you not comprehend the sort of feeling?"—"Not at all, cried he aloud. I could never dread a meeting with Miss Emma Watson,—or any of her Sisters." It was lucky that he added that finish.—"Were you speaking to me?"—said Emma, who

who had caught her own name.—"Not absolutely—he answered—but I was thinking of you,—as many at a greater distance are probably doing at this moment.— Fine open weather Miss Emma!—Charming season for Hunting." "Emma is delightful, is not she?—whispered Marg^t. I have found her more than answer my warmest hopes.—Did you ever see anything more perfectly beautiful?—I think even *you* must be a convert to a brown complexion."—He hesitated; Margaret was fair herself, & he did not particularly want to compliment her; but Miss Osborne & Miss Carr were likewise fair, & his devotion to them carried the day. "Your Sister's complexion, said he at last, is as fine as a dark complexion can be, but I still profess my preference of a white skin. You have seen Miss Osborne?—she is my model for a truly feminine complexion, & she is very fair."—"Is she fairer than me?"— Tom made no reply.—"Upon my Honour Ladies, said he, giving a glance over his own person, I am highly endebted to your Condescension for admitting me, in such Dishabille into your Drawing room. I really did not consider how unfit I was to be here or I hope I should have kept my distance. Ly. Osborne would tell me that I were growing as careless as her son, if she saw me in this condition."— The Ladies were not wanting in civil returns; & Robert Watson stealing a veiw of his own head in an opposite glass,—said with equal civility, "You cannot be more in dishabille than myself.—We got here so late, that I had not time even to put a little fresh powder in my hair."— Emma could not help entering into what she supposed her Sister in law's feelings at that moment.—When the Tea-things were removed, Tom began to talk of his Carriage— but the old Card Table being set out, & the fish & counters with a tolerably clean pack brought forward from the beaufit by Miss Watson, the general voice was so urgent with him to join their party, that he agreed to allow himself another quarter of an hour. Even Emma was pleased

that

that he would stay, for she was beginning to feel that
a family party might be the worst of all parties; & the
others were delighted.—"What's your Game?"—cried he,
as they stood round the Table.—"Speculation I beleive,
said Elizth—My Sister recommends it, & I fancy we all like
it. I know *you* do, Tom."—"It is the only round game
played at Croydon now, said Mrs Robert—we never think
of any other. I am glad it is a favourite with you."—
"Oh! me! cried Tom. Whatever you decide on, will be
a favourite with *me*.—I have had some pleasant hours at
Speculation in my time—but I have not been in the way
of it now for a long while.—Vingt-un is the game at Osborne
Castle; I have played nothing but Vingt-un of late. You
would be astonished to hear the noise we make there.—
The fine old, lofty Drawing-room rings again. Ly Osborne
sometimes declares she cannot hear herself speak.—Ld
Osborne enjoys it famously—he makes the best Dealer
without exception that I ever beheld—such quickness &
spirit! he lets nobody dream over their cards—I wish you
could see him overdraw himself on both his own cards—it
is worth anything in the World!"—"Dear me!—cried
Marg^t why should not we play at vingt un?—I think it is
a much better game than Speculation. I cannot say I am
very fond of Speculation." Mrs Robert offered not another
word in support of the game.—She was quite vanquished,
& the fashions of Osborne-Castle carried it over the fashions
of Croydon.—"Do you see much of the Parsonage family
at the Castle, Mr Musgrave?—" said Emma, as they were
taking their seats.—"Oh! yes—they are almost always
there. Mrs Blake is a nice little good-humoured Woman,
she & I are sworn friends; & Howard's a very gentlemanlike good sort of fellow!—You are not forgotten I assure
you by any of the party. I fancy you must have a little
cheek-glowing now & then Miss Emma. Were you not
rather warm last Saturday about 9 or 10 o'clock in the
Even^g—? I will tell you how it was.—I see you are dieing
to

to know.—Says Howard to Ld Osborne—" At this interesting moment he was called on by the others, to regulate the
game & determine some disputable point; & his attention
was so totally engaged in the business & afterwards by the
course of the game as never to revert to what he had been
saying before;—& Emma, tho' suffering a good deal from
Curiosity, dared not remind him.—He proved a very useful
addition to their Table; without him, it w^d have been a
party of such very near relations as could have felt little
Interest, & perhaps maintained little complaisance, but his
presence gave variety & secured good manners.—He was
in fact excellently qualified to shine at a round Game; &
few situations made him appear to greater advantage. He
played with spirit, & had a great deal to say & tho' with
no wit himself, c^d sometimes make use of the wit of an
absent friend; & had a lively way of retailing a common-
place, or saying a mere nothing, that had great effect at
a Card Table. The ways, & good Jokes of Osborne Castle
were now added to his ordinary means of Entertainment;
he repeated the smart sayings of one Lady, detailed the
oversights of another, & indulged them even with a copy
of Ld Osborne's stile of overdrawing himself on both cards.
—The Clock struck nine, while he was thus agreeably occupied; & when Nanny came in with her Master's Bason of
Gruel, he had the pleasure of observing to Mr Watson that
he should leave him at supper, while he went home to
dinner himself.—The Carriage was ordered to the door—&
no entreaties for his staying longer c^d now avail,—for he
well knew, that if he staid he must sit down to supper in
less than ten minutes—which to a Man whose heart had
been long fixed on calling his next meal a Dinner, was quite
insupportable.—On finding him determined to go, Marg^t
began to wink & nod at Eliz^th to ask him to dinner for the
following day; & Eliz. at last not able to resist hints, which
her own hospitable, social temper more than half seconded,
gave the invitation. "Would he give Robt the meeting,
they

they sh^d be very happy." "With the greatest pleasure"
—was his first reply. In a moment afterwards—"That is
if I can possibly get here in time—but I shoot with L^d
Osborne, & therefore must not engage—You will not think
of me unless you see me."—And so, he departed, delighted
with the uncertainty in which he had left it.—

Marg^t in the joy of her heart under circumstances, which
she chose to consider as peculiarly propitious, would willingly have made a confidante of Emma when they were
alone for a short time the next morn^g; & had proceeded
so far as to say—"The young man who was here last night
my dear Emma & returns today, is more interesting to me,
than perhaps you may be aware—" but Emma pretending
to understand nothing extraordinary in the words, made
some very inapplicable reply, & jumping up, ran away from
a subject which was odious to her feelings.—

As Marg^t would not allow a doubt to be repeated of Musgrave's coming to dinner, preparations were made for his
Entertainment much exceeding what had been deemed
necessary the day before; and taking the office of super-
intendance intirely from her sister, she was half the morning in the Kitchen herself directing & scolding.—After a
great deal of indifferent Cooking, & anxious Suspense however they were obliged to sit down without their Guest.—
T. Musgrave never came, & Marg^t was at no pains to conceal her vexation under the disappointment, or repress the
peevishness of her Temper—. The Peace of the party for
the remainder of that day, & the whole of the next, which
comprised the length of Robert & Jane's visit, was continually invaded by her fretful displeasure, & querulous
attacks.—Eliz. was the usual object of both. Marg^t had
just respect enough for her B^r & S^r's opinion, to behave
properly by *them*, but Eliz. & the maids c^d never do anything right—& Emma, whom she seemed no longer to
think

think about, found the continuance of the gentle voice beyond her calculation short. Eager to be as little among them as possible, Emma was delighted with the alternative of sitting above, with her father, & warmly entreated to be his constant Comp^n each Even^g—& as Eliz. loved company of any kind too well, not to prefer being below, at all risks, as she had rather talk of Croydon to Jane, with every interruption of Marg^t's perverseness, than sit with only her father, who frequently c^d not endure Talking at all, the affair was so settled, as soon as she could be persuaded to beleive it no sacrifice on her Sister's part.—To Emma, the exchange was most acceptable, & delightful. Her father, if ill, required little more than gentleness & silence; &, being a Man of Sense and Education, was if able to converse, a welcome companion.—

In *his* chamber, Emma was at peace from the dreadful mortifications of unequal Society, & family Discord—from the immediate endurance of Hard-hearted prosperity, low-minded Conceit, & wrong-headed folly, engrafted on an untoward Disposition.—She still suffered from them in the Contemplation of their existence; in memory & in prospect, but for the moment, she ceased to be tortured by their effects.—She was at leisure, she could read & think,—tho' her situation was hardly such as to make reflection very soothing. The Evils arising from the loss of her Uncle, were neither trifling, nor likely to lessen; & when Thought had been freely indulged, in contrasting the past & the present, the employment of mind, the dissipation of unpleasant ideas which only reading could produce, made her thankfully turn to a book.—The change in her home society, & stile of Life in consequence of the death of one friend and the imprudence of another had indeed been striking.—From being the first object of Hope & Solicitude of an Uncle who had formed her mind with the care of a Parent, & of Tenderness to an Aunt whose amiable temper had delighted to give her every indulgence, from being the

Life

Life & Spirit of a House, where all had been comfort &
Elegance, & the expected Heiress of an easy Independance,
she was become of importance to no one, a burden on
those, whose affection she c^d not expect, an addition in an
House, already overstocked, surrounded by inferior minds
with little chance of domestic comfort, & as little hope of
future support.—It was well for her that she was naturally
chearful;—for the Change had been such as might have
plunged weak spirits in Despondence.—

She was very much pressed by Robert & Jane to return
with them to Croydon, & had some difficulty in getting
a refusal accepted; as they thought too highly of their own
kindness & situation, to suppose the offer could appear in
a less advantageous light to anybody else.—Elizth gave
them her interest, tho' evidently against her own, in
privately urging Emma to go—"You do not know what
you refuse Emma—said she—nor what you have to bear
at home.—I would advise you by all means to accept the
invitation, there is always something lively going on at
Croydon, you will be in company almost every day, & Robt
& Jane will be very kind to you.—As for me, I shall be no
worse off without you, than I have been used to be; but
poor Marg^t's disagreable ways are new to *you*, & they
would vex you more than you think for, if you stay at
home.—" Emma was of course un-influenced, except to
greater esteem for Elizth, by such representations—& the
Visitors departed without her.—

From the second edition (1871) of the Memoir, p. 364:

*When the author's sister, Cassandra, showed the manuscript of
this work to some of her nieces, she also told them something of the
intended story; for with this dear sister—though, I believe, with no
one else—Jane seems to have talked freely of any work that she*
                                                              might

might have in hand. Mr. Watson was soon to die; and Emma to become dependent for a home on her narrow-minded sister-in-law and brother. She was to decline an offer of marriage from Lord Osborne, and much of the interest of the tale was to arise from Lady Osborne's love for Mr. Howard, and his counter affection for Emma, whom he was finally to marry.

'SANDITON'

The title 'Sanditon' was given to the untitled, uncompleted manuscript by the Austen family, although according to a family tradition Jane Austen had intended to call this novel 'The Brothers'. In the 1871 *Memoir*, which gives extracts amounting to about one-sixth of the total manuscript, it is termed 'The Last Work'. The manuscript (now in the library of King's College, Cambridge) is a first draft, heavily corrected and revised. From dates on the manuscript we know that Jane Austen began work on it on 17 January 1817, abandoning it two months later, on 18 March, in her last illness.

A full record of the manuscript alterations is given in the text of *Sanditon* edited by R. W. Chapman, Oxford, 1925.

[B. C. S.]

CHAPTER 1

A Gentleman & Lady travelling from Tunbridge towards that part of the Sussex Coast which lies between Hastings & E. Bourne, being induced by Business to quit the high road, & attempt a very rough Lane, were overturned in toiling

toiling up its' long ascent half rock, half sand.—The accident happened just beyond the only Gentleman's House near the Lane—a House, which their Driver on being first required to take that direction, had conceived to be necessarily their object, & had with most unwilling Looks been constrained to pass by—. He had grumbled & shaken his shoulders so much indeed, and pitied & cut his Horses so sharply, that he might have been open to the suspicion of overturning them on purpose (especially as the Carriage was not his Masters own) if the road had not indisputably become considerably worse than before, as soon as the premises of the said House were left behind—expressing with a most intelligent portentous countenance that beyond it no wheels but cart wheels could safely proceed. The severity of the fall was broken by their slow pace & the narrowness of the Lane, & the Gentleman having scrambled out & helped out his companion, they niether of them at first felt more than shaken & bruised. But the Gentleman had in the course of the extrication sprained his foot—& soon becoming sensible of it, was obliged in a few moments to cut short, both his remonstrance to the Driver & his congratulations to his wife & himself—& sit down on the bank, unable to stand.—"There is something wrong here, said he—putting his hand to his ancle—But never mind, my Dear—(looking up at her with a smile)— It c^d not have happened, you know, in a better place.— Good out of Evil—. The very thing perhaps to be wished for. We shall soon get releif.—*There*, I fancy lies my cure" —pointing to the neat-looking end of a Cottage, which was seen romantically situated among wood on a high Eminence at some little Distance—"Does not *that* promise to be the very place?"—His wife fervently hoped it was— but stood, terrified & anxious, neither able to do or suggest anything—& receiving her first real comfort from the sight of several persons now coming to their assistance. The accident had been discerned from a Hayfield adjoining the House

House they had passed—& the persons who approached, were a well-looking Hale, Gentlemanlike Man, of middle age, the Proprietor of the Place, who happened to be among his Haymakers at the time, & three or four of the ablest of them summoned to attend their Master—to say nothing of all the rest of the field, Men, Women & Children—not very far off.—Mr Heywood, such was the name of the said Proprietor, advanced with a very civil salutation—much concern for the accident—some surprise at any body's attempting that road in a Carriage—& ready offers of assistance. His courtesies were received with Good-breeding & gratitude & while one or two of the Men lent their help to the Driver in getting the Carriage upright again, the Travellor said—"You are extremely obliging Sir, & I take you at your word.—The injury to my Leg is I dare say very trifling, but it is always best in these cases to have a surgeon's opinion without loss of time; and as the road does not seem at present in a favourable state for my getting up to his house myself, I will thank you to send off one of these good People for the Surgeon." "The Surgeon Sir!—replied Mr Heywood—I am afraid you will find no surgeon at hand here, but I dare say we shall do very well without him."—"Nay Sir, if *he* is not in the way, his Partner will do just as well—or rather better—. I w^d rather see his Partner indeed—I would prefer the attendance of his Partner.—One of these good people can be with him in three minutes I am sure. I need not ask whether I see the House; (looking towards the Cottage) for excepting your own, we have passed none in this place, which can be the Abode of a Gentleman."—Mr H. looked very much astonished—& replied—"What Sir! are you expecting to find a Surgeon in that Cottage?—We have neither Surgeon nor Partner in the Parish I assure you."—"Excuse me Sir—replied the other. I am sorry to have the appearance of contradicting you—but though from the extent of the Parish or some other cause you may not be aware of the fact

fact;—Stay—Can I be mistaken in the place?—Am I not in Willingden?—Is not this Willingden?" "Yes Sir, this is certainly Willingden." "Then Sir, I can bring proof of your having a Surgeon in the Parish—whether you may know it or not. Here Sir—(taking out his Pocket book—) if you will do me the favour of casting your eye over these advertisements, which I cut out myself from the Morning Post & the Kentish Gazette, only yesterday morn⁸ in London—I think you will be convinced that I am not speaking at random. You will find it an advertisement Sir, of the dissolution of a Partnership in the Medical Line—in your own Parish—extensive Business—undeniable Character—respectable references—wishing to form a separate Establishment—You will find it at full length Sir"—offering him the two little oblong extracts.—"Sir—said Mr Heywood with a good humoured smile—if you were to shew me all the Newspapers that are printed in one week throughout the Kingdom, you wd not persuade me of there being a Surgeon in Willingden,—for having lived here ever since I was born, Man & Boy 57 years, I think I must have *known* of such a person, at least I may venture to say that he has not *much Business*—To be sure, if Gentlemen were to be often attempting this Lane in Post-chaises, it might not be a bad speculation for a Surgeon to get a House at the top of the Hill.—But as to that Cottage, I can assure you Sir that it is in fact—(inspite of its spruce air at this distance—) as indifferent a double Tenement as any in the Parish, and that my Shepherd lives at one end, & three old women at the other." He took the peices of paper as he spoke—& having looked them over, added—"I beleive I can explain it Sir.—Your mistake is in the place.—There are two Willingdens in this Country—& your advertisements refer to the other—which is Great Willingden, or Willingden Abbots, & lies 7 miles off, on the other side of Battel—quite down in the Weald. And *we* Sir—(speaking rather proudly) are not in the Weald."—"Not *down* in the

Weald

Weald I am sure Sir, replied the Traveller, pleasantly. It
took us half an hour to climb your Hill.—Well Sir—I dare
say it is as you say, & I have made an abominably stupid
Blunder.—All done in a moment;—the advertisements did
not catch my eye till the last half hour of our being in
Town;—when everything was in the hurry & confusion
which always attend a short stay there—One is never
able to complete anything in the way of Business you know
till the Carriage is at the door—and accordingly satisfying
myself with a breif enquiry, & finding we were actually to
pass within a mile or two of a *Willingden*, I sought no
farther . . . My Dear—(to his wife) I am very sorry to have
brought you into this Scrape. But do not be alarmed about
my Leg. It gives me no pain while I am quiet,—and as soon
as these good people have succeeded in setting the Car^{ge} to
rights & turning the Horses round, the best thing we can do
will be to measure back our steps into the Turnpike road
& proceed to Hailsham, & so Home, without attempting
anything farther.—Two hours take us home, from Hailsham—And when once at home, we have our remedy at
hand you know.—A little of our own Bracing Sea Air will
soon set me on my feet again.—Depend upon it my Dear,
it is exactly a case for the Sea. Saline air & immersion will
be the very thing.—My sensations tell me so already."—
In a most friendly manner Mr Heywood here interposed,
entreating them not to think of proceeding till the ancle
had been examined, & some refreshment taken, & very
cordially pressing them to make use of his House for both
purposes.—"We are always well stocked, said he, with all
the common remedies for Sprains & Bruises—& I will
answer for the pleasure it will give my Wife & daughters
to be of service to you & this Lady in every way in their
power."—A twinge or two, in trying to move his foot
disposed the Travellor to think rather more as he had done
at first of the benefit of immediate assistance—& consulting his wife in the few words of "Well my Dear, I beleive
it

it will be better for us."—turned again to M^r H— & said—
"Before we accept your Hospitality Sir,—& in order to do
away with any unfavourable impression which the sort of
wild goose-chace you find me in, may have given rise to—
allow me to tell you who we are. My name is Parker.—M^r
Parker of Sanditon; this Lady, my wife Mrs Parker.—
We are on our road home from London;—*My* name perhaps—tho' I am by no means the first of my Family, holding Landed Property in the Parish of Sanditon, may be
unknown at this distance from the Coast—but Sanditon
itself—everybody has heard of Sanditon,—the favourite—
for a young & rising Bathing-place, certainly the favourite
spot of all that are to be found along the coast of Sussex;—
the most favoured by Nature, & promising to be the most
chosen by Man."—"Yes—I have heard of Sanditon. re-
plied Mr H.—Every five years, one hears of some new place
or other starting up by the Sea, & growing the fashion.—
How they can half of them be filled, is the wonder! *Where*
People can be found with Money or Time to go to them!—
Bad things for a Country;—sure to raise the price of Provisions & make the Poor good for nothing—as I dare say
you find, Sir." "Not at all Sir, not at all—cried Mr Parker
eagerly. Quite the contrary I assure you.—A common idea
—but a mistaken one. It may apply to your large, over-
grown Places, like Brighton, or Worthing, or East Bourne
—but *not* to a small Village like Sanditon, precluded by its
size from experiencing any of the evils of Civilization, while
the growth of the place, the Buildings, the Nursery
Grounds, the demand for every thing, & the sure resort
of the very best Company, those regular, steady, private
Families of thorough Gentility & Character, who are a
blessing everywhere, excite the industry of the Poor and
diffuse comfort & improvement among them of every
sort.—No Sir, I assure you, Sanditon is not a place——"
"I do not mean to take exceptions to *any* place in particular Sir, answered Mr H.—I only think our Coast is too full

of

of them altogether—But had we not better try to get you"
——"Our Coast too full"—repeated Mr P.—On that point
perhaps we may not totally disagree;—at least there are
enough. Our Coast is abundant enough; it demands no
more.—Every body's Taste & every body's finances may
be suited—And those good people who are trying to add
to the number, are in my opinion excessively absurd, &
must soon find themselves the Dupes of their own fallacious
Calculations.—Such a place as Sanditon Sir, I may say
was wanted, was called for.—Nature had marked it out—
had spoken in most intelligible Characters—The finest,
purest Sea Breeze on the Coast—acknowledged to be so—
Excellent Bathing—fine hard Sand—Deep Water 10 yards
from the Shore—no Mud—no Weeds—no slimey rocks—
Never was there a place more palpably designed by Nature
for the resort of the Invalid—the very Spot which Thousands seemed in need of.—The most desirable distance
from London! One complete, measured mile nearer than
East Bourne. Only conceive Sir, the advantage of saving
a whole Mile, in a long Journey. But Brinshore Sir, which
I dare say you have in your eye—the attempts of two or
three speculating People about Brinshore, this last Year,
to raise that paltry Hamlet, lying, as it does between a
stagnant marsh, a bleak Moor & the constant effluvia of
a ridge of putrifying sea weed, can end in nothing but their
own Disappointment. What in the name of Common Sense
is to *recommend* Brinshore?—A most insalubrious Air—
Roads proverbially detestable—Water Brackish beyond
example, impossible to get a good dish of Tea within
3 miles of the place—& as for the Soil—it is so cold &
ungrateful that it can hardly be made to yeild a Cabbage.
—Depend upon it Sir, that this is a faithful Description of
Brinshore—not in the smallest degree exaggerated—& if
you have heard it differently spoken of——" "Sir, I never
heard it spoken of in my Life before, said Mr Heywood.
I did now know there was such a place in the World."
                                                    You

"You did not!—There my Dear—(turning with exultation to his Wife)—you see how it is. So much for the Celebrity of Brinshore!—This Gentleman did not know there was such a place in the World.—Why, in truth Sir, I fancy we may apply to Brinshore, that line of the Poet Cowper in his description of the religious Cottager, as opposed to Voltaire —"*She*, never heard of half a mile from home."—"With all my Heart Sir—Apply any Verses you like to it—But I want to see something applied to your Leg—& I am sure by your Lady's countenance that she is quite of my opinion & thinks it a pity to lose any more time—And here come my Girls to speak for themselves & their Mother. (two or three genteel looking young Women followed by as many Maid servants, were now seen issueing from the House)— I began to wonder the Bustle should not have reached *them*.—A thing of this kind soon makes a Stir in a lonely place like ours.—Now Sir, let us see how you can be best conveyed into the House."—The young Ladies approached & said every thing that was proper to recommend their Father's offers; & in an unaffected manner calculated to make the Strangers easy—And as M^rs P— was exceedingly anxious for relief—and her Husband by this time, not much less disposed for it—a very few civil scruples were enough—especially as the Carriage being now set up, was discovered to have received such Injury on the fallen side as to be unfit for present use.—Mr Parker was therefore carried into the House, and his Carriage wheeled off to a vacant Barn.—

CHAPTER 2

THE acquaintance, thus oddly begun, was neither short nor unimportant. For a whole fortnight the Travellors were fixed at Willingden; Mr. P.'s sprain proving too serious for him to move sooner.—He had fallen into very good hands. The Heywoods were a thoroughly respectable family, &

every

every possible attention was paid in the kindest & most
unpretending manner, to both Husband & wife. *He* was
waited on & nursed, & *she* cheered & comforted with unremitting kindness—and as every office of Hospitality &
friendliness was received as it ought—as there was not more
good will on one side than Gratitude on the other—nor any
deficiency of generally pleasant manners on either, they
grew to like each other in the course of that fortnight,
exceedingly well.—Mr Parker's Character & History were
soon unfolded. All that he understood of himself, he
readily told, for he was very openhearted;—& where he
might be himself in the dark, his conversation was still
giving information, to such of the Heywoods as could
observe.—By such he was perceived to be an Enthusiast;
—on the subject of Sanditon, a complete Enthusiast.—
Sanditon,—the success of Sanditon as a small, fashionable
Bathing Place was the object, for which he seemed to
live. A very few years ago, & it had been a quiet Village
of no pretensions; but some natural advantages in its
position & some accidental circumstances having suggested
to himself, & the other principal Land Holder, the probability of its' becoming a profitable Speculation, they had
engaged in it, & planned & built, & praised & puffed, &
raised it to a Something of young Renown—and Mr Parker
could now think of very little besides.—The Facts, which
in more direct communication, he laid before them were
that he was about 5 & 30—had been married,—very happily
married 7 years—& had 4 sweet Children at home;—that
he was of a respectable Family, & easy though not large
fortune;—no Profession—succeeding as eldest son to the
Property which 2 or 3 Generations had been holding &
accumulating before him;—that he had 2 Brothers and 2
Sisters—all single & all independant—the eldest of the two
former indeed, by collateral Inheritance, quite as well
provided for as himself.—His object in quitting the high
road, to hunt for an advertising Surgeon, was also plainly
stated

stated;—it had not proceeded from any intention of spraining his ancle or doing himself any other Injury for the good of such Surgeon—nor (as Mr H. had been apt to suppose) from any design of entering into Partnership with him—; it was merely in consequence of a wish to establish some medical Man at Sanditon, which the nature of the Advertisement induced him to expect to accomplish in Willingden.—He was convinced that the advantage of a medical Man at hand w^d very materially promote the rise & prosperity of the Place—w^d in fact tend to bring a prodigious influx;—nothing else was wanting. He had *strong* reason to beleive that *one* family had been deterred last year from trying Sanditon on that account—& probably very many more—and his own Sisters who were sad Invalids, & whom he was very anxious to get to Sanditon this Summer, could hardly be expected to hazard themselves in a place where they could not have immediate medical advice.—Upon the whole, Mr P. was evidently an aimable, family-man, fond of Wife, Child^n, Brothers & Sisters—& generally kind-hearted;—Liberal, gentleman-like, easy to please;—of a sanguine turn of mind, with more Imagination than Judgement. And Mrs P. was as evidently a gentle, amiable, sweet tempered Woman, the properest wife in the World for a Man of strong Understanding, but not of capacity to supply the cooler reflection which her own Husband sometimes needed, & so entirely waiting to be guided on every occasion, that whether he were risking his Fortune or spraining his Ancle, she remained equally useless.—Sanditon was a second Wife & 4 Children to him —hardly less Dear—& certainly more engrossing.—He could talk of it for ever.—It had indeed the highest claims;— not only those of Birthplace, Property, and Home,—it was his Mine, his Lottery, his Speculation & his Hobby Horse; his Occupation his Hope & his Futurity.—He was extremely desirous of drawing his good friends at Willingden thither; and his endeavours in the cause, were as grateful

&

& disinterested, as they were warm.—He wanted to secure
the promise of a visit—to get as many of the Family as his
own house w^d contain, to follow him to Sanditon as soon
as possible—and healthy as they all undeniably were—
foresaw that every one of them w^d be benefited by the sea.
—He held it indeed as certain, that no person c^d be really
well, no person, (however upheld for the present by fortui-
tous aids of exercise & spirits in a semblance of Health)
could be really in a state of secure & permanent Health
without spending at least 6 weeks by the Sea every year.—
The Sea air & Sea Bathing together were nearly infallible,
one or the other of them being a match for every Disorder,
of the Stomach, the Lungs or the Blood; They were anti-
spasmodic, anti-pulmonary, anti-sceptic, anti-bilious & anti-
rheumatic. Nobody could catch cold by the Sea, Nobody
wanted Appetite by the Sea, Nobody wanted Spirits, Nobody wanted Strength.—They were healing, softing, re-
laxing—fortifying & bracing—seemingly just as was wanted
—sometimes one, sometimes the other.—If the Sea breeze
failed, the Sea-Bath was the certain corrective;—& where
Bathing disagreed, the Sea Breeze alone was evidently
designed by Nature for the cure.—His eloquence however
could not prevail. M^r & M^rs H— never left home. Marrying
early & having a very numerous Family, their movements
had been long limitted to one small circle; & they were
older in Habits than in Age.—Excepting two Journeys to
London in the year, to receive his Dividends, Mr H. went
no farther than his feet or his well-tried old Horse could
carry him, and Mrs Heywood's Adventurings were only now
& then to visit her Neighbours, in the old Coach which had
been new when they married & fresh lined on their eldest
Son's coming of age 10 years ago.—They had very pretty
Property—enough, had their family been of reasonable
Limits to have allowed them a very gentlemanlike share
of Luxuries & Change—enough for them to have indulged
in a new Carriage & better roads, an occasional month at
Tunbridge

Tunbridge Wells, & symptoms of the Gout and a Winter at Bath;—but the maintenance, Education & fitting out of 14 Children demanded a very quiet, settled, careful course of Life—& obliged them to be stationary and healthy at Willingden. What Prudence had at first enjoined, was now rendered pleasant by Habit. They never left home, & they had a gratification in saying so.—But very far from wishing their Children to do the same, they were glad to promote *their* getting out into the World, as much as possible. *They* staid at home, that their Children *might* get out;—and while making that home extremely comfortable, welcomed every change from it which could give useful connections or respectable acquaintance to Sons or Daughters. When Mr & Mrs Parker therefore ceased from soliciting a family-visit, and bounded their veiws to carrying back one Daughter with them, no difficulties were started. It was general pleasure & consent.—Their invitation was to Miss Charlotte Heywood, a very pleasing young woman of two and twenty, the eldest of the Daughters at home, & the one, who under her Mother's directions had been particularly useful & obliging to them; who had attended them most, & knew them best.—Charlotte was to go,—with excellent health, to bathe & be better if she could—to receive every possible pleasure which Sanditon could be made to supply by the gratitude of those she went with—& to buy new Parasols, new Gloves, & new Broches, for her sisters & herself at the Library, which Mr P. was anxiously wishing to support.—All that Mr Heywood himself could be persuaded to promise was, that he would send everyone to Sanditon, who asked his advice, & that nothing should ever induce him (as far ⟨as⟩ the future could be answered for) to spend even 5 shillings at Brinshore.—

CHAPTER

CHAPTER 3

EVERY Neighbourhood should have a great Lady.—The great Lady of Sanditon, was Lady Denham; & in their Journey from Willingden to the Coast, Mr Parker gave Charlotte a more detailed account of her, than had been called for before.—She had been necessarily often mentioned at Willingden,—for being his Colleague in Speculation, Sanditon itself could not be talked of long, without the introduction of Lady Denham & that she was a very rich old Lady, who had buried two Husbands, who knew the value of Money, was very much looked up to & had a poor Cousin living with her, were facts already well known, but some further particulars of her history & her Character served to lighten the tediousness of a long Hill, or a heavy bit of road, and to give the visiting Young Lady a suitable Knowledge of the Person with whom she might now expect to be daily associating.—Lady D. had been a rich Miss Brereton, born to Wealth but not to Education. Her first Husband had been a Mr Hollis, a man of considerable Property in the Country, of which a large share of the Parish of Sanditon, with Manor & Mansion House made a part. He had been an elderly Man when she married him;—her own age about 30.—Her motives for such a Match could be little understood at the distance of 40 years, but she had so well nursed & pleased Mr Hollis, that at his death he left her everything—all his Estates, & all at her Disposal. After a widowhood of some years, she had been induced to marry again. The late Sir Harry Denham, of Denham Park in the Neighbourhood of Sanditon had succeeded in removing her & her large Income to his own Domains, but he c^d not succeed in the veiws of permanently enriching his family, which were attributed to him. She had been too wary to put anything out of her own Power—and when on Sir Harry's Decease she returned again to her own House at Sanditon, she was said to have

N   made

made this boast to a friend "that though she had *got* nothing but her Title from the Family, still she had *given* nothing for it."—For the Title, it was to be supposed that she had married—& Mr P. acknowledged there being just such a degree of value for it apparent now, as to give her conduct that natural explanation. "There is at times said he—a little self-importance—but it is not offensive;—& there are moments, there are points, when her Love of Money is carried greatly too far. But she is a goodnatured Woman, a very goodnatured Woman,—a very obliging, friendly Neighbour; a chearful, independant, valuable character.—and her faults may be entirely imputed to her want of Education. She has good natural Sense, but quite uncultivated.—She has a fine active mind, as well as a fine healthy frame for a Woman of 70, & enters into the improvement of Sanditon with a spirit truly admirable—though now & then, a Littleness *will* appear. She cannot look forward quite as I would have her—& takes alarm at a trifling present expence, without considering what returns it *will* make her in a year or two. That is—we think *differently*, we now & then, see things *differently*, Miss H.— Those who tell their own Story you know must be listened to with Caution.—When you see us in contact, you will judge for yourself."—Lady D. was indeed a great Lady beyond the common wants of Society—for she had many Thousands a year to bequeath, & three distinct sets of People to be courted by; her own relations, who might very reasonably wish for her Original Thirty Thousand Pounds among them, the legal Heirs of Mr Hollis, who must hope to be more endebted to *her* sense of Justice than he had allowed them to be to *his*, and those Members of the Denham Family, whom her 2^d Husband had hoped to make a good Bargain for.—By all of these, or by Branches of them, she had no doubt been long, & still continued to be, well attacked;—and of these three divisions, Mr P. did not hesitate to say that Mr Hollis' Kindred were the *least*

in

in favour & Sir Harry Denham's the *most*.—The former he
beleived, had done themselves irremediable harm by expressions of very unwise & unjustifiable resentment at the time
of Mr. Hollis's death;—the Latter, to the advantage of
being the remnant of a Connection which she certainly
valued, joined those of having been known to her from
their Childhood, & of being always at hand to preserve
their interest by reasonable attention. Sir Edward, the
present Baronet, nephew to Sir Harry, resided constantly
at Denham Park; & M^r P— had little doubt, that he & his
Sister Miss D— who lived with him, w^d be principally
remembered in her Will. He sincerely hoped it.—Miss
Denham had a very small provision—& her Brother was
a poor Man for his rank in Society. "He is a warm friend
to Sanditon—said Mr Parker—& his hand w^d be as liberal
as his heart, had he the Power.—He would be a noble
Coadjutor!—As it is, he does what he can—& is running
up a tasteful little Cottage Ornèe, on a strip of Waste
Ground Lady D. has granted him, which I have no doubt
we shall have many a Candidate for, before the end even
of *this* Season." Till within the last twelvemonth, M^r P.
had considered Sir Edw: as standing without a rival, as
having the fairest chance of succeeding to the greater part
of all that she had to give—but there was now another
person's claims to be taken into the account, those of the
young female relation, whom Lady D. had been induced
to receive into her Family. After having always protested
against any such Addition, and long & often enjoyed the
repeated defeats she had given to every attempt of her
relations to introduce this young Lady, or that young Lady
as a Companion at Sanditon House, she had brought back
with her from London last Michaelmas a Miss Brereton,
who bid fair by her Merits to vie in favour with Sir Edward,
and to secure for herself & her family that share of the
accumulated Property which they had certainly the best
right to inherit.—Mr Parker spoke warmly of Clara
                                              Brereton

Brereton, & the interest of his story increased very much
with the introduction of such a Character. Charlotte
listened with more than amusement now ;—it was solicitude
& Enjoyment, as she heard her described to be lovely,
amiable, gentle, unassuming, conducting herself uniformly
with great good sense, & evidently gaining by her innate
worth, on the affections of her Patroness.—Beauty, Sweetness, Poverty & Dependance, do not want the imagination
of a Man to operate upon. With due exceptions—Woman
feels for Woman very promptly & compassionately. He
gave the particulars which had led to Clara's admission at
Sanditon, as no bad exemplification of that mixture of
Character, that union of Littleness with Kindness with
Good Sence with even Liberality which he saw in Lady
D.— After having avoided London for many years, principally on account of these very Cousins, who were continually writing, inviting & tormenting her, & whom she
was determined to keep at a distance, she had been obliged
to go there last Michaelmas with the certainty of being
detained at least a fortnight.—She had gone to an Hotel—
living by her own account as prudently as possible, to defy
the reputed expensiveness of such a home, & at the end
of three Days calling for her Bill, that she might judge of
her state.—Its' amount was such as determined her on
staying not another hour in the House, & she was preparing
in all the anger & perturbation which a beleif of very gross
imposition *there*, & an ignorance of where to go for better
usage, to leave the Hotel at all hazards, when the Cousins,
the politic & lucky Cousins, who seemed always to have
a spy on her, introduced themselves at this important
moment, & learning her situation, persuaded her to accept
such a home for the rest of her stay as their humbler house
in a very inferior part of London, c^d offer.—She went; was
delighted with her welcome & the hospitality & attention
she received from every body—found her good Cousins the
B—— beyond her expectation worthy people—& finally

                                                        was

was impelled by a personal knowledge of their narrow
Income & pecuniary difficulties, to invite one of the girls
of the family to pass the Winter with her. The invitation
was to *one*, for six months—with the probability of another
being then to take her place;—but in *selecting* the one,
Lady D. had shewn the good part of her Character—for
passing by the actual *daughters* of the House, she had
chosen Clara, a Neice—, more helpless & more pitiable of
course than any—a dependant on Poverty—an additional
Burthen on an encumbered Circle—& one, who had been
so low in every worldly veiw, as with all her natural endow-
ments & powers, to have been preparing for a situation
little better than a Nursery Maid.—Clara had returned
with her—& by her good sence & merit had now, to all
appearance secured a very strong hold in Lady D.'s regard.
The six months had long been over—& not a syllable was
breathed of any change, or exchange.—She was a general
favourite;—the influence of her steady conduct & mild,
gentle Temper was felt by everybody. The prejudices
which had met her at first in some quarters, were all dissipated. She was felt to be worthy of Trust—to be the very
companion who w^d guide & soften Lady D—who w^d enlarge
her mind & open her hand.—She was as thoroughly amiable
as she was lovely—& since having had the advantage of
their Sanditon Breezes, that Loveliness was complete.

CHAPTER 4.

"AND whose very snug-looking Place is this?"—said Charlotte, as in a sheltered Dip within 2 miles of the Sea, they
passed close by a moderate-sized house, well fenced &
planted, & rich in the Garden, Orchard & Meadows which
are the best embellishments of such a Dwelling. "It seems
to have as many comforts about it as Willingden."—"Ah!
—said Mr P.—This is my old House—the house of my
Forefathers—the house where I & all my Brothers & Sisters
                                                    were

were born & bred—& where my own 3 eldest Children were
born—where Mrs P. & I lived till within the last 2 years—
till our new House was finished.—I am glad you are pleased
with it.—It is an honest old Place—and Hillier keeps it in
very good order. I have given it up you know to the Man
who occupies the cheif of my Land. *He* gets a better House
by it—& I, a rather better situation!—one other Hill brings
us to Sanditon—modern Sanditon—a beautiful Spot.—
Our Ancestors, you know always built in a hole.—Here
were we, pent down in this little contracted Nook, without
Air or Veiw, only one mile & 3 q^rs from the noblest expanse
of Ocean between the South foreland & the Land's end, &
without the smallest advantage from it. You will not
think I have made a bad exchange, when we reach Trafalgar House—which by the bye, I almost wish I had not
named Trafalgar—for Waterloo is more the thing now.
However, Waterloo is in reserve—& if we have encouragement enough this year for a little Crescent to be ventured
on—(as I trust we shall) then, we shall be able to call it
Waterloo Crescent—& the name joined to the form of the
Building, which always takes, will give us the command
of Lodgers—. In a good Season we sh^d have more applications than we could attend to."—"It was always a very
comfortable House—said Mrs Parker—looking at it through
the back window with something like the fondness of
regret.—And such a nice Garden—such an excellent Garden." "Yes, my Love, but *that* we may be said to carry
with us.—*It* supplies us, as before, with all the fruit &
vegetables we want; & we have in fact all the comfort of
an excellent Kitchen Garden, without the constant Eyesore
of its formalities; or the yearly nuisance of its decaying
vegetation.—Who can endure a Cabbage Bed in October?"
"Oh! dear—yes.—We are quite as well off for Gardenstuff
as ever we were—for if it is forgot to be brought at any
time, we can always buy what we want at Sanditon-House.
—The Gardiner there, is glad enough to supply us—. But
it

it was a nice place for the Children to run about in. So Shady in Summer!" "My dear, we shall have shade enough on the Hill & more than enough in the course of a very few years;—The Growth of my Plantations is a general astonishment. In the mean while we have the Canvas Awning, which gives us the most complete comfort within doors—& you can get a Parasol at Whitby's for little Mary at any time, or a large Bonnet at Jebb's—and as for the Boys, I must say I w^d rather *them* run about in the Sunshine than not. I am sure we agree my dear, in wishing our Boys to be as hardy as possible."—"Yes indeed, I am sure we do—& I will get Mary a little Parasol, which will make her as proud as can be. How Grave she will walk about with it, and fancy herself quite a little Woman.— Oh! I have not the smallest doubt of our being a great deal better off where we are now. If we any of us want to bathe, we have not a q^r of a mile to go.—But you know, (still looking back) one loves to look at an old friend, at a place where one has been happy.—The Hilliers did not seem to feel the Storms last Winter at all.—I remember seeing Mrs Hillier after one of those dreadful Nights, when *we* had been literally rocked in our bed, and she did not seem at all aware of the Wind being anything more than common." "Yes, yes—that's likely enough. *We* have all the Grandeur of the Storm, with less real danger, because the Wind meeting with nothing to oppose or confine it around our House, simply rages & passes on—while down in this Gutter—nothing is known of the state of the Air, below the Tops of the Trees—and the Inhabitants may be taken totally unawares, by one of those dreadful Currents which do more mischief in a Valley, when they *do* arise than an open Country ever experiences in the heaviest Gale.—But my dear Love—as to Gardenstuff;—you were saying that any accidental omission is supplied in a moment by Ly D.'s Gardiner—but it occurs to me that we ought to go elsewhere upon such occasions—& that old Stringer

&

& his son have a higher claim. I encouraged him to set up
—& am afraid he does not do very well—that is, there has
not been time enough yet.—He *will* do very well beyond
a doubt—but at first it is Uphill work; and therefore we
must give him what Help we can—& when any Vegetables
or fruit happen to be wanted—& it will not be amiss to
have them often wanted, to have something or other forgotten most days;—Just to have a nominal supply you
know, that poor old Andrew may not lose his daily Job—
but in fact to buy the cheif of our consumption of the
Stringers.—" "Very well my Love, that can be easily
done—& Cook will be satisfied—which will be a great
comfort, for she is always complaining of old Andrew now,
& says he never brings her what she wants.—There—now
the old House is quite left behind.—What is it, your
Brother Sidney says about it's being a Hospital?" "Oh!
my dear Mary, merely a Joke of his. He pretends to advise
me to make a Hospital of it. He pretends to laugh at my
Improvements. Sidney says any thing you know. He has
always said what he chose of & to us, all. Most Families
have such a member among them I beleive Miss Heywood.
—There is a someone in most families privileged by superior
abilities or spirits to say anything.—In ours, it is Sidney;
who is a very clever Young Man,—and with great powers
of pleasing.—He lives too much in the World to be settled;
that is his only fault.—He is here & there & every where.
I wish we may get him to Sanditon. I should like to have
you acquainted with him.—And it would be a fine thing
for the Place!—Such a young Man as Sidney, with his neat
equipage & fashionable air,—You & I Mary, know what
effect it might have: Many a respectable Family, many
a careful Mother, many a pretty Daughter, might it secure
us, to the prejudice of E. Bourne & Hastings."—They
were now approaching the Church & real village of Sanditon, which stood at the foot of the Hill they were afterwards to ascend—a Hill, whose side was covered with the

Woods

Woods & enclosures of Sanditon House and whose Height
ended in an open Down where the new Build^{gs} might soon
be looked for. A branch only, of the Valley, winding more
obliquely towards the Sea, gave a passage to an inconsiderable Stream, & formed at its mouth, a 3^d Habitable
Division, in a small cluster of Fisherman's Houses.—The
Village contained little more than Cottages, but the Spirit
of the day had been caught, as Mr P. observed with delight
to Charlotte, & two or three of the best of them were
smartened up with a white Curtain & "Lodgings to let"—,
and farther on, in the little Green Court of an old Farm
House, two Females in elegant white were actually to be
seen with their books & camp stools—and in turning the
corner of the Baker's shop, the sound of a Harp might be
heard through the upper Casement.—Such sights & sounds
were highly Blissful to Mr P.—Not that he had any personal concern in the success of the Village itself; for considering it as too remote from the Beach, he had done
nothing there—but it was a most valuable proof of the
increasing fashion of the place altogether. If the *Village*
could attract, the Hill might be nearly full.—He antici-
pated an amazing Season.—At the same time last year,
(late in July) there had not been a single Lodger in the
Village!—nor did he remember any during the whole
Summer, excepting one family of children who came from
London for sea air after the hooping Cough, and whose
Mother would not let them be nearer the shore for fear of
their tumbling in.—"Civilization, Civilization indeed!—
cried M^r P—, delighted—. Look my dear Mary—Look at
William Heeley's windows.—Blue Shoes, & nankin Boots!
—Who w^d have expected such a sight at a Shoemaker's in
old Sanditon!—This is new within the Month. There was
no blue Shoe when we passed this way a month ago.—
Glorious indeed!—Well, I think I *have* done something in
my Day.—Now, for our Hill, our health-breathing Hill.—"
In ascending, they passed the Lodge-Gates of Sanditon
House

House, & saw the top of the House itself among its Groves. It was the last Building of former Days in that line of the Parish. A little higher up, the Modern began; & in crossing the Down, a Prospect House, a Bellevue Cottage, & a Denham Place were to be looked at by Charlotte with the calmness of amused Curiosity, & by Mr P. with the eager eye which hoped to see scarcely any empty houses.—More Bills at the Window than he had calculated on;—and a smaller shew of company on the Hill—Fewer Carriages, fewer Walkers. He had fancied it just the time of day for them to be all returning from their Airings to dinner—But the Sands & the Terrace always attracted some—. and the Tide must be flowing—about half-Tide now.—He longed to be on the Sands, the Cliffs, at his own House, & everywhere out of his House at once. His Spirits rose with the very sight of the Sea & he c^d almost feel his Ancle getting stronger already.—Trafalgar House, on the most elevated spot on the Down was a light elegant Building, standing in a small Lawn with a very young plantation round it, about an hundred yards from the brow of a steep, but not very lofty Cliff—and the nearest to it, of every Building, excepting one short row of smart-looking Houses, called the Terrace, with a broad walk in front, aspiring to be the Mall of the Place. In this row were the best Milliner's shop & the Library—a little detached from it, the Hotel & Billiard Room—Here began the Descent to the Beach, & to the Bathing Machines—& this was therefore the favourite spot for Beauty & Fashion.—At Trafalgar House, rising at a little distance behind the Terrace, the Travellers were safely set down, & all was happiness & Joy between Papa & Mama & their Children; while Charlotte having received possession of her apartment, found amusement enough in standing at her ample Venetian window, & looking over the miscellaneous foreground of unfinished Buildings, waving Linen, & tops of Houses, to the Sea, dancing & sparkling in Sunshine & Freshness.—

CHAPTER

Eastbourne.

Pl. 9.

F. Chesham fe.

From an engraving by Francis Chesham in *The Watering and Sea-Bathing Places*, 1808

CHAPTER 5.

WHEN they met before dinner, Mr P. was looking over Letters.—"'Not a Line from Sidney!—said he.—He is an idle fellow.—I sent him an account of my accident from Willingden, & thought he would have vouchsafed me an Answer.—But perhaps it implies that he is coming himself. —I trust it may.—But here is a Letter from one of my Sisters. *They* never fail me.—Women are the only Correspondents to be depended on.—Now Mary, (smiling at his Wife)—before I open it, what shall we guess as to the state of health of those it comes from—or rather what w^d Sidney say if he were here?—Sidney is a saucy fellow, Miss H.—And you must know, he will have it there is a good deal of Imagination in my two Sisters' complaints— but it really is not so—or very little—They have wretched health, as you have heard us say frequently, & are subject to a variety of very serious Disorders.—Indeed, I do not beleive they know what a day's health is;—& at the same time, they are such excellent useful Women & have so much energy of Character that, where any Good is to be done, they force themselves on exertions which to those who do not thoroughly know them, have an extraordinary appearance.—But there is really no affectation about them. They have only weaker constitutions & stronger minds than are often met with, either separate or together.— And our Youngest B^r—who lives with them, & who is not much above 20, I am sorry to say, is almost as great an Invalid as themselves.—He is so delicate that he can engage in no Profession.—Sidney laughs at him—but it really is no Joke—tho' Sidney often makes me laugh at them all inspite of myself.—Now, if he were here, I know he w^d be offering odds, that either Susan Diana or Arthur w^d appear by this letter to have been at the point of death within the last month."—Having run his eye over the Letter, he shook his head & began—: "No chance of seeing them

them at Sanditon I am sorry to say.—A very indifferent
account of them indeed. Seriously, a very indifferent
account.—Mary, you will be quite sorry to hear how ill
they have been & are.—Miss H., if you will give me leave,
I will read Diana's Letter aloud.—I like to have my friends
acquainted with each other—& I am afraid this is the only
sort of acquaintance I shall have the means of accomplishing between you.—And I can have no scruple on Diana's
account—for her Letters shew her exactly as she is, the
most active, friendly, warmhearted Being in existence, &
therefore must give a good impression." He read.—"My
dear Tom, We were all much greived at your accident, & if
you had not described yourself as fallen into such very
good hands, I sh^d have been with you at all hazards the
day after the rec^{pt} of your Letter, though it found me
suffering under a more severe attack than usual of my old
greivance, Spasmodic Bile & hardly able to crawl from my
Bed to the Sofa.—But how were you treated?—Send me
more Particulars in your next.—If indeed a simple Sprain,
as you denominate it, nothing w^d have been so judicious
as Friction, Friction by the hand alone, supposing it could
be applied *instantly*.—Two years ago I happened to be
calling on Mrs Sheldon when her Coachman sprained his
foot as he was cleaning the Carriage & c^d hardly limp into
the House—but by the immediate use of Friction alone
steadily persevered in, (& I rubbed his Ancle with my own
hand for six Hours without Intermission)—he was well
in three days.—Many Thanks my dear Tom, for the kindness with respect to us, which had so large a share in bringing on your accident—But pray never run into Peril again,
in looking for an Apothecary on our account, for had you
the most experienced Man in his Line settled at Sanditon,
it w^d be no recommendation to us. We have entirely done
with the whole Medical Tribe. We have consulted Physician after Phy^n in vain, till we are quite convinced that
they can do nothing for us & that we must trust to our

own

own knowledge of our own wretched Constitutions for any releif.—But if you think it advisable for the interest of the *Place*, to get a Medical Man there, I will undertake the commission with pleasure, & have no doubt of succeeding. —I could soon put the necessary Irons in the fire.—As for getting to Sanditon myself, it is quite an Impossibility. I grieve to say that I dare not attempt it, but my feelings tell me too plainly that in my present state, the Sea air w^d probably be the death of me.—And neither of my dear Companions will leave me, or I w^d promote their going down to you for a fortnight. But in truth, I doubt whether Susan's nerves w^d be equal to the effort. She has been suffering much from the Headache and Six Leaches a day for 10 days together releived her so little that we thought it right to change our measures—and being convinced on examination that much of the Evil lay in her Gum, I persuaded her to attack the disorder there. She has accordingly had 3 Teeth drawn, & is decidedly better, but her Nerves are a good deal deranged. She can only speak in a whisper—and fainted away twice this morning on poor Arthur's trying to suppress a cough. He, I am happy to say is tolerably well—tho' more languid than I like—& I fear for his Liver.—I have heard nothing of Sidney since your being together in Town, but conclude his scheme to the I. of Wight has not taken place, or we should have seen him in his way.—Most sincerely do we wish you a good Season at Sanditon, & though we cannot contribute to your Beau Monde in person, we are doing our utmost to send you Company worth having; & think we may safely reckon on securing you two large Families, one a rich West Indian from Surry, the other, a most respectable Girls Boarding School, or Academy, from Camberwell.— I will not tell you how many People I have employed in the business—Wheel within wheel.—But Success more than repays.—Yours most affec^{ly}—&c" "Well—said Mr P.—as he finished. Though I dare say Sidney might find
                                                                        something

something extremely entertaining in this Letter & make us laugh for half an hour together I declare *I* by myself, can see nothing in it but what is either very pitiable or very creditable.—With all their sufferings, you perceive how much they are occupied in promoting the Good of others!—So anxious for Sanditon! Two large Families—One, for Prospect House probably, the other, for N⁰ 2. Denham Place—or the end house of the Terrace, —& extra Beds at the Hotel.—I told you my Sisters were excellent Women, Miss H——." "And I am sure they must be very extraordinary ones.—said Charlotte. I am astonished at the chearful style of the Letter, considering the state in which both Sisters appear to be.—Three Teeth drawn at once!—frightful!—Your Sister Diana seems almost as ill as possible, but those 3 Teeth of your Sister Susan's, are more distressing than all the rest.—" "Oh!— they are so used to the operation—to every operation—& have such Fortitude!—" "Your Sisters know what they are about, I dare say, but their Measures seem to touch on Extremes.—I feel that in any illness, *I* should be so anxious for Professional advice, so very little venturesome for myself, or any body I loved!—But then, *we* have been so healthy a family, that I can be no Judge of what the habit of self-doctoring may do.—" "Why to own the truth, said Mrˢ P.—I *do* think the Miss Parkers carry it too far sometimes—& so do you my Love, you know.—You often think they wᵈ be better, if they wᵈ leave themselves more alone—& especially Arthur. I know you think it a great pity they shᵈ give *him* such a turn for being ill.—" "Well, well—my dear Mary—I grant you, it *is* unfortunate for poor Arthur, that, at his time of Life he shᵈ be encouraged to give way to Indisposition. It *is* bad;—it *is* bad that he should be fancying himself too sickly for any Profession— & sit down at 1 & 20, on the interest of his own little Fortune, without any idea of attempting to improve it, or of engaging in any occupation that may be of use to himself

or

or others.—But let us talk of pleasanter things.—These two large Families are just what we wanted—But—here is something at hand, pleasanter still—Morgan, with his "Dinner on Table."—

CHAPTER 6.

THE Party were very soon moving after Dinner. Mr P. could not be satisfied without an early visit to the Library, & the Library Subscription book, & Charlotte was glad to see as much, & as quickly as possible, where all was new. They were out in the very quietest part of a Watering-place Day, when the important Business of Dinner or of sitting after Dinner was going on in almost every inhabited Lodging;—here & there a solitary Elderly Man might be seen, who was forced to move early & walk for health—but in general, it was a thorough pause of Company, it was Emptiness & Tranquillity on the Terrace, the Cliffs, & the Sands.—The Shops were deserted—the Straw Hats & pendant Lace seemed left to their fate both within the House & without, and Mrs Whitby at the Library was sitting in her inner room, reading one of her own Novels, for want of Employment.—The List of Subscribers was but commonplace. The Lady Denham, Miss Brereton, M^r & M^{rs} P—— Sir Edw: Denham & Miss Denham, whose names might be said to lead off the Season, were followed by nothing better than—Mrs Mathews — Miss Mathews, Miss E. Mathews, Miss H. Mathews.—D^r & Mrs Brown—Mr Richard Pratt.—Lieut: Smith R.N. Capt: Little,—Lime-house.—Mrs Jane Fisher. Miss Fisher. Miss Scroggs.—Rev: Mr Hanking. Mr Beard—Solicitor, Grays Inn.—Mrs Davis. & Miss Merryweather.—Mr P. could not but feel that the List was not only without Distinction, but less numerous than he had hoped. It was but July however, & August & September were the Months;—And besides, the promised large Families from Surry & Camberwell,

were

were an ever-ready consolation.—Mrs Whitby came forward without delay from her Literary recess, delighted to see Mr Parker again, whose manners recommended him to every body, & they were fully occupied in their various Civilities & Communications, while Charlotte having added her name to the List as the first offering to the success of the Season, was busy in some immediate purchases for the further good of Every body, as soon as Miss Whitby could be hurried down from her Toilette, with all her glossy Curls & smart Trinkets to wait on her.—The Library of course, afforded every thing; all the useless things in the World that c^d not be done without, & among so many pretty Temptations, & with so much good will for Mr P. to encourage Expenditure, Charlotte began to feel that she must check herself—or rather she reflected that at two & Twenty there c^d be no excuse for her doing otherwise—& that it w^d not do for her to be spending all her Money the very first Evening. She took up a Book; it happened to be a vol: of *Camilla*. She had not *Camilla*'s Youth, & had no intention of having her Distress,—so, she turned from the Drawers of rings & Broches repressed farther solicitation & paid for what she bought.—For her particular gratification, they were then to take a Turn on the Cliff— but as they quitted the Library they were met by two Ladies whose arrival made an alteration necessary, Lady Denham & Miss Brereton.—They had been to Trafalgar House, & been directed thence to the Library, & though Lady D. was a great deal too active to regard the walk of a mile as any thing requiring rest, & talked of going home again directly, the Parkers knew that to be pressed into their House, & obliged to take her Tea with them, would suit her best,—& therefore the stroll on the Cliff gave way to an immediate return home.—" No, no, said her Ladyship— I will not have you hurry your Tea on my account.—I know you like your Tea late.—My early hours are not to put my Neighbours to inconvenience. No, no, Miss Clara

&

& I will get back to our own Tea.—We came out with no
other Thought.—We wanted just to see you & make sure of
your being really come—, but we get back to our own Tea."
—She went on however towards Trafalgar House & took
possession of the Drawing room very quietly—without
seeming to hear a word of Mrs P.'s orders to the Servant
as they entered, to bring Tea directly. Charlotte was fully
consoled for the loss of her walk, by finding herself in company with those, whom the conversation of the morn^g had
given her a great curiosity to see. She observed them well.
—Lady D. was of middle height, stout, upright & alert in
her motions, with a shrewd eye, & self-satisfied air—but
not an unagreeable Countenance—& tho' her manner was
rather downright & abrupt, as of a person who valued herself on being free-spoken, there was a good humour & cordiality about her—a civility & readiness to be acquainted
with Charlotte herself, & a heartiness of welcome towards
her old friends, which was inspiring the Good will, she
seemed to feel;—And as for Miss Brereton, her appearance so completely justified Mr P.'s praise that Charlotte
thought she had never beheld a more lovely, or more
Interesting young Woman.—Elegantly tall, regularly
handsome, with great delicacy of complexion & soft Blue
eyes, a sweetly modest & yet naturally graceful Address,
Charlotte could see in her only the most perfect representation of whatever Heroine might be most beautiful &
bewitching, in all the numerous vol:^s they had left behind
them on Mrs Whitby's shelves.—Perhaps it might be partly
oweing to her having just issued from a Circulating Library
—but she c^d not separate the idea of a complete Heroine
from Clara Brereton. Her situation with Lady Denham
so very much in favour of it!—She seemed placed with her
on purpose to be ill-used. Such Poverty & Dependance
joined to such Beauty & Merit, seemed to leave no choice
in the business.—These feelings were not the result of any
spirit of Romance in Charlotte herself. No, she was a very
                                                    sober-minded

sober-minded young Lady, sufficiently well-read in Novels
to supply her Imagination with amusement, but not at all
unreasonably influenced by them; & while she pleased
herself the first 5 minutes with fancying the Persecutions
which *ought* to be the Lot of the interesting Clara, especially in the form of the most barbarous conduct on Lady
Denham's side, she found no reluctance to admit from
subsequent observation, that they appeared to be on very
comfortable Terms.—She c^d see nothing worse in Lady
Denham, than the sort of oldfashioned formality of always
calling her *Miss Clara*—nor anything objectionable in the
degree of observance & attention which Clara paid.—On
one side it seemed protecting kindness, on the other grateful & affectionate respect.—The Conversation turned entirely upon Sanditon, its present number of Visitants & the
Chances of a good Season. It was evident that Lady D.
had more anxiety, more fears of loss, than her Coadjutor.
She wanted to have the Place fill faster, & seemed to have
many harassing apprehensions of the Lodgings being in
some instances underlet.—Miss Diana Parker's two large
Families were not forgotten. "Very good, very good, said
her Ladyship.—A West Indy Family & a school. That
sounds well. That will bring Money."—"No people spend
more freely, I beleive, than W. Indians." observed M^r
Parker.—"Aye—so I have heard—and because they have
full Purses, fancy themselves equal, may be, to your old
Country Families. But then, they who scatter their Money
so freely, never think of whether they may not be doing
mischeif by raising the price of Things—And I have heard
that's very much the case with your West-injines—and if
they come among us to raise the price of our necessaries
of Life, we shall not much thank them Mr Parker."—"My
dear Madam, They can only raise the price of consumeable
Articles, by such an extraordinary Demand for them &
such a diffusion of Money among us, as must do us more
Good than harm.—Our Butchers & Bakers & Traders in
                                                    general

general cannot get rich without bringing Prosperity to
us.—If *they* do not gain, our rents must be insecure—& in
proportion to their profit must be ours eventually in the
increased value of our Houses." "Oh!—well.—But I
should not like to have Butcher's meat raised, though—&
I shall keep it down as long as I can.—Aye—that young
Lady smiles I see;—I dare say she thinks me an odd sort
of a Creature,—but *she* will come to care about such
matters herself in time. Yes, Yes, my Dear, depend upon
it, you will be thinking of the price of Butcher's meat in
time—tho' you may not happen to have quite such a Servants Hall full to feed, as I have.—And I do beleive *those*
are best off, that have fewest Servants.—I am not a Woman
of Parade, as all the World knows, & if it was not for what
I owe to poor Mr Hollis's memory, I should never keep up
Sanditon House as I do;—it is not for my own pleasure.—
Well Mr Parker—and the other is a Boarding school, a
French Boarding School, is it ?—No harm in that.—They'll
stay their six weeks.—And out of such a number, who
knows but some may be consumptive & want Asses milk
—& I have two Milch asses at this present time.—But
perhaps the little Misses may hurt the Furniture.—I hope
they will have a good sharp Governess to look after
them.—" Poor Mr Parker got no more credit from Lady D.
than he had from his Sisters, for the Object which had
taken him to Willingden. "Lord! my dear Sir, she cried,
how could you think of such a thing? I am very sorry you
met with your accident, but upon my word you deserved
it.—Going after a Doctor!—Why, what sh^d we do with
a Doctor here? It w^d be only encouraging our Servants &
the Poor to fancy themselves ill, if there was a D^r at hand.
—Oh! pray, let us have none of the Tribe at Sanditon. We
go on very well as we are. There is the Sea & the Downs
& my Milch-Asses—& I have told Mrs Whitby that if any
body enquires for a Chamber-Horse, they may be supplied
at a fair rate—(poor Mr Hollis's Chamber-Horse, as good

as

as new)—and what can People want for more?—Here have
I lived 70 good years in the world & never took Physic
above twice—and never saw the face of a Doctor in all my
Life, on my *own* account.—And I verily beleive if my poor
dear Sir Harry had never seen one neither, he w^d have
been alive now.—Ten fees, one after another, did the Man
take who sent *him* out of the World.—I beseech you M^r
Parker, no Doctors here."—The Tea things were brought
in.—"Oh! my dear Mrs Parker—you should not indeed—
why would you do so? I was just upon the point of wishing you good Evening. But since you are so very neighbourly, I beleive Miss Clara & I must stay."——

CHAPTER 7.

THE popularity of the Parkers brought them some visitors
the very next morning;—amongst them, Sir Edwd Denham
& his Sister, who having been at Sanditon H— drove on
to pay their Compliments; & the duty of Letter-writing
being accomplished, Charlotte was settled with Mrs P.—
in the Drawing room in time to see them all.—The Denhams were the only ones to excite particular attention.
Charlotte was glad to complete her knowledge of the family
by an introduction to them, & found them, the better half
at least—(for while single, the *Gentleman* may sometimes
be thought the better half, of the pair)—not unworthy
notice.—Miss D. was a fine young woman, but cold & reserved, giving the idea of one who felt her consequence with
Pride & her Poverty with Discontent, & who was immediately gnawed by the want of an handsomer Equipage than
the simple Gig in which they travelled, & which their
Groom was leading about still in her sight.—Sir Edwd was
much her superior in air & manner;—certainly handsome,
but yet more to be remarked for his very good address &
wish of paying attention & giving pleasure.—He came into
the room remarkably well, talked much—& very much to
Charlotte

Charlotte, by whom he chanced to be placed—& she soon
perceived that he had a fine Countenance, a most pleasing
gentleness of voice, & a great deal of Conversation. She
liked him.—Sober-minded as she was, she thought him
agreable, & did not quarrel with the suspicion of his finding her equally so, which *would* arise from his evidently
disregarding his Sisters' motion to go, & persisting in
his station & his discourse.—I make no apologies for my
Heroine's vanity.—If there are young Ladies in the World
at her time of Life, more dull of Fancy & more careless of
pleasing, I know them not, & never wish to know them.—
At last, from the low French windows of the Drawing room
which commanded the road & all the Paths across the
Down, Charlotte & Sir Edw: as they sat, could not but
observe Lady D. & Miss B. walking by—& there was
instantly a slight change in Sir Edw:'s countenance—with
an anxious glance after them as they proceeded—followed
by an early proposal to his Sister—not merely for moving,
but for walking on together to the Terrace—which altogether gave an hasty turn to Charlotte's fancy, cured her
of her halfhour's fever, & placed her in a more capable
state of judging, when Sir Edw: was gone, of *how* agreable
he had actually been.—"Perhaps there was a good deal
in his Air & Address; And his Title did him no harm."
She was very soon in his company again. The first object
of the Parkers, when their House was cleared of mornᵍ
visitors was to get out themselves;—the Terrace was the
attraction to all;—Every body who walked, must begin
with the Terrace, & there, seated on one of the two Green
Benches by the Gravel walk, they found the united Denham Party;—but though united in the Gross, very distinctly divided again—the two superior Ladies being at
one end of the bench, & Sir Edw: & Miss B. at the other.—
Charlotte's first glance told her that Sir Edw:'s air was
that of a Lover.—There could be no doubt of his Devotion
to Clara.—How Clara received it, was less obvious—but
she

she was inclined to think not very favourably; for tho'
sitting thus apart with him (which probably she might not
have been able to prevent) her air was calm & grave.—
That the young Lady at the other end of the Bench was
doing Penance, was indubitable. The difference in Miss
Denham's countenance, the change from Miss Denham
sitting in cold Grandeur in Mrs Parker's Draw^g-room to be
kept from silence by the efforts of others, to Miss D. at
Lady D.'s Elbow, listening & talking with smiling attention or solicitous eagerness, was very striking—and very
amusing—or very melancholy, just as Satire or Morality
might prevail.—Miss Denham's Character was pretty well
decided with Charlotte. Sir Edward's required longer
Observation. He surprised her by quitting Clara immediately on their all joining & agreeing to walk, & by addressing his attentions entirely to herself.—Stationing himself
close by her, he seemed to mean to detach her as much as
possible from the rest of the Party & to give her the whole
of his Conversation. He began, in a tone of great Taste
& Feeling, to talk of the Sea & the Sea shore—& ran with
Energy through all the usual Phrases employed in praise
of their Sublimity, & descriptive of the *undescribable* Emotions they excite in the Mind of Sensibility.—The terrific
Grandeur of the Ocean in a Storm, its glassy surface in
a calm, its' Gulls & its Samphire, & the deep fathoms of
its' Abysses, its' quick vicissitudes, its' direful Deceptions,
its' Mariners tempting it in Sunshine & overwhelmed by
the sudden Tempest, All were eagerly & fluently touched;
—rather commonplace perhaps—but doing very well from
the Lips of a handsome Sir Edward,—and she c^d not but
think him a Man of Feeling—till he began to stagger her
by the number of his Quotations, & the bewilderment of
some of his sentences.—"Do you remember, said he,
Scotts' beautiful Lines on the Sea?—Oh! what a description they convey!—They are never out of my Thoughts
when I walk here.—That Man who can read them un-
moved

moved must have the nerves of an Assassin!—Heaven defend me from meeting such a Man un-armed."—"What description do you mean?—said Charlotte. I remember none at this moment, of the Sea, in either of Scotts' Poems." —"Do not you indeed?—Nor can I exactly recall the beginning at this moment—But—you cannot have forgotten his description of Woman.—

"Oh! Woman in our Hours of Ease—"

Delicious! Delicious!—Had he written nothing more, he w^d have been Immortal. And then again, that unequalled, unrivalled address to Parental affection—

"Some feelings are to Mortals given
With less of Earth in them than Heaven" &c

But while we are on the subject of Poetry, what think you Miss H. of Burns Lines to his Mary?—Oh! there is Pathos to madden one!—If ever there was a Man who *felt*, it was Burns.—Montgomery has all the Fire of Poetry, Wordsworth has the true soul of it—Campbell in his pleasures of Hope has touched the extreme of our Sensations—"Like Angel's visits, few & far between." Can you conceive any thing more subduing, more melting, more fraught with the deep Sublime than that Line?—But Burns—I confess my sence of his Pre-eminence Miss H.—If Scott *has* a fault, it is the want of Passion.—Tender, Elegant, Descriptive—but *Tame*.—The Man who cannot do justice to the attributes of Woman is my contempt.—Sometimes indeed a flash of feeling seems to irradiate him—as in the Lines we were speaking of—"Oh! Woman in our hours of Ease"—. But Burns is always on fire.—His Soul was the Altar in which lovely Woman sat enshrined, his Spirit truly breathed the immortal Incence which is her Due.—" "I have read several of Burn's Poems with great delight, said Charlotte as soon as she had time to speak, but I am not poetic enough

enough to separate a Man's Poetry entirely from his Character;—& poor Burns's known Irregularities, greatly interrupt my enjoyment of his Lines.—I have difficulty in
depending on the *Truth* of his Feelings as a Lover. I have
not faith in the *sincerity* of the affections of a Man of his
Description. He felt & he wrote & he forgot." "Oh! no
no—exclaimed Sir Edw: in an extasy. He was all ardour
& Truth!—His Genius & his Susceptibilities might lead
him into some Aberrations—But who is perfect?—It were
Hyper-criticism, it were Pseudo-philosophy to expect from
the soul of high toned Genius, the grovellings of a common
mind.—The Coruscations of Talent, elicited by impas-
sioned feeling in the breast of Man, are perhaps incompatible with some of the prosaic Decencies of Life;—nor
can you, loveliest Miss Heywood—(speaking with an air
of deep sentiment)—nor can any Woman be a fair Judge
of what a Man may be propelled to say, write or do, by
the sovereign impulses of illimitable Ardour." This was
very fine;—but if Charlotte understood it at all, not very
moral—& being moreover by no means pleased with his
extraordinary stile of compliment, she gravely answered
"I really know nothing of the matter.—This is a charming
day. The Wind I fancy must be Southerly." "Happy,
happy Wind, to engage Miss Heywood's Thoughts!—"
She began to think him downright silly.—His chusing to
walk with her, she had learnt to understand. It was done
to pique Miss Brereton. She had read it, in an anxious
glance or two on his side—but why he sh^d talk so much
Nonsense, unless he could do no better, was un-intelligible.
—He seemed very sentimental, very full of some Feelings
or other, & very much addicted to all the newest-fashioned
hard words—had not a very clear Brain she presumed, &
talked a good deal by rote.—The Future might explain
him further—but when there was a proposition for going
into the Library she felt that she had had quite enough
of Sir Edw: for one morn^g, & very gladly accepted Lady D.'s
invitation

invitation of remaining on the Terrace with her.—The
others all left them, Sir Edw: with looks of very gallant
despair in tearing himself away, & they united their agre-
ableness—that is, Lady Denham like a true great Lady,
talked & talked only of her own concerns, & Charlotte
listened—amused in considering the contrast between her
two companions.—Certainly, there was no strain of doubtful Sentiment, nor any phrase of difficult interpretation in
Lady D's discourse. Taking hold of Charlotte's arm with
the ease of one who felt that any notice from her was an
Honour, & communicative, from the influence of the same
conscious Importance or a natural love of talking, she
immediately said in a tone of great satisfaction—& with
a look of arch sagacity—"Miss Esther wants me to invite
her & her Brother to spend a week with me at Sanditon
House, as I did last Summer—But I shan't.—She has
been trying to get round me every way, with her praise of
this, & her praise of that; but I saw what she was about.—I
saw through it all.—I am not very easily taken-in my Dear."
Charlotte c^d think of nothing more harmless to be said,
than the simple enquiry of—"Sir Edward & Miss Denham?"—"Yes, my Dear. *My young Folks*, as I call them
sometimes, for I take them very much by the hand. I
had them with me last Summer about this time, for a
week; from Monday to Monday; and very delighted &
thankful they were.—For they are very good young People
my Dear. I w^d not have you think that I *only* notice them,
for poor dear Sir Harry's sake. No, no; they are very
deserving themselves, or trust me, they w^d not be so much
in *my* Company.—I am not the Woman to help any body
blindfold.—I always take care to know what I am about
& who I have to deal with, before I stir a finger.—I do not
think I was ever over-reached in my Life; & That is a good
deal for a Woman to say that has been married twice.—
Poor dear Sir Harry (between ourselves) thought at first
to have got more.—But (with a bit of a sigh) He is gone,
&

& we must not find fault with the Dead. Nobody could live happier together than us—& he was a very honourable Man, quite the Gentleman of ancient Family.—And when he died, I gave Sir Edwd his Gold Watch.—" She said this with a look at her Companion which implied its' right to produce a great Impression—& seeing no rapturous astonishment in Charlottes countenance, added quickly—"He did not bequeath it to his Nephew, my dear—It was no bequest. It was not in the Will. He only told me, & *that* but once, that he sh^d wish his Nephew to have his Watch; but it need not have been binding, if I had not chose it.—"

"Very kind indeed! very Handsome!"—said Charlotte, absolutely forced to affect admiration.—"Yes, my dear—& it is not the *only* kind thing I have done by him.—I have been a very liberal friend to Sir Edwd. And poor young Man, he needs it bad enough;—For though I am *only* the *Dowager* my Dear, & he is the *Heir*, things do not stand between us in the way they commonly do between those two parties.—Not a shilling do I receive from the Denham Estate. Sir Edw: has no Payments to make *me*. He don't stand uppermost, beleive me.—It is *I* that help *him*." "Indeed!—He is a very fine young Man;—particularly Elegant in his Address."—This was said cheifly for the sake of saying something—but Charlotte directly saw that it was laying her open to suspicion by Lady D's giving a shrewd glance at her & replying—"Yes, yes, he is very well to look at—& it is to be hoped that some Lady of large fortune will think so—for Sir Edwd *must* marry for Money. —He & I often talk that matter over.—A handsome young fellow like him, will go smirking & smiling about & paying girls compliments, but he knows he *must* marry for Money. —And Sir Edw: is a very steady young Man in the main, & has got very good notions." "Sir Edw: Denham, said Charlotte, with such personal Advantages may be almost sure of getting a Woman of fortune, if he chuses it."—This glorious sentiment seemed quite to remove suspicion.

"Aye

"Aye my Dear—That's very sensibly said cried Lady D—
And if we c^d but get a young Heiress to S! But Heiresses
are monstrous scarce! I do not think we have had an
Heiress here, or even a Co—since Sanditon has been a
public place. Families come after Families, but as far as
I can learn, it is not one in an hundred of them that have
any real Property, Landed or Funded.—An Income perhaps, but no Property. Clergymen may be, or Lawyers
from Town, or Half pay officers, or Widows with only
a Jointure. And what good can such people do anybody?
—except just as they take our empty Houses—and (between ourselves) I think they are great fools for not staying
at home. Now, if we could get a young Heiress to be sent
here for her health—(and if she was ordered to drink asses
milk I could supply her)—and as soon as she got well, have
her fall in love with Sir Edward!"—"That would be very
fortunate indeed." "And Miss Esther must marry somebody of fortune too—She must get a rich Husband. Ah!
young Ladies that have no Money are very much to be
pitied!—But—after a short pause—if Miss Esther thinks
to talk me into inviting them to come & stay at Sanditon
House, she will find herself mistaken.—Matters are altered
with me since last Summer you know—. I have Miss Clara
with me now, which makes a great difference." She spoke
this so seriously that Charlotte instantly saw in it the
evidence of real penetration & prepared for some fuller
remarks—but it was followed only by—"I have no fancy
for having my House as full as an Hotel. I should not
chuse to have my 2 Housemaids Time taken up all the
morn^g, in dusting out Bed rooms.—They have Miss Clara's
room to put to rights as well as my own every day.—If
they had hard Places, they would want Higher Wages.—"
For objections of this Nature, Charlotte was not prepared,
& she found it so impossible even to affect simpathy, that
she c^d say nothing.—Lady D. soon added, with great glee—
"And besides all this my Dear, am I to be filling my House

to

to the prejudice of Sanditon?—If People want to be by the Sea, why dont they take Lodgings?—Here are a great many empty Houses—3 on this very Terrace; no fewer than three Lodging Papers staring us in the face at this very moment, Numbers 3, 4 & 8. 8, the Corner House may be too large for them, but either of the two others are nice little snug Houses, very fit for a young Gentleman & his sister—And so, my dear, the next time Miss Esther begins talking about the dampness of Denham Park, & the Good Bathing always does her, I shall advise them to come & take one of these Lodgings for a fortnight.—Don't you think that will be very fair?—Charity begins at home you know."—Charlotte's feelings were divided between amusement & indignation—but indignation had the larger & the increasing share.—She kept her Countenance & she kept a civil Silence. She could not carry her forbearance farther; but without attempting to listen longer, & only conscious that Lady D. was still talking on in the same way, allowed her Thoughts to form themselves into such a Meditation as this.—"She is thoroughly mean. I had not expected any thing so bad.—Mr. P. spoke too mildly of her.—His Judgement is evidently not to be trusted.—His own Goodnature misleads him. He is too kind hearted to see clearly.—I must judge for myself.—And their very *connection* prejudices him.—He has persuaded her to engage in the same Speculation—& because their object in that Line is the same, he fancies she feels like him in others.—But she is very, very mean.—I can see no Good in her.—Poor Miss Brereton!—And she makes every body mean about her.— This poor Sir Edward & his Sister,—how far Nature meant them to be respectable I cannot tell,—but they are *obliged* to be Mean in their Servility to her.—And I am Mean too, in giving her my attention, with the appearance of co- inciding with her.—Thus it is, when Rich People are Sordid."—

CHAPTER

CHAPTER 8.

THE two Ladies continued walking together till rejoined
by the others, who as they issued from the Library were
followed by a young Whitby running off with 5 vols. under
his arm to Sir Edward's Gig—and Sir Edw: approaching
Charlotte, said "You may perceive what has been our
Occupation. My Sister wanted my Counsel in the selection
of some books.—We have many leisure hours, & read a
great deal.—I am no indiscriminate Novel-Reader. The
mere Trash of the common Circulating Library, I hold in
the highest contempt. You will never hear me advocating
those puerile Emanations which detail nothing but discord-
ant Principles incapable of Amalgamation, or those vapid
tissues of ordinary Occurrences from which no useful De-
ductions can be drawn.—In vain may we put them into
a literary Alembic;—we distil nothing which can add to
Science.—You understand me I am sure?" "I am not
quite certain that I do.—But if you will describe the sort
of Novels which you *do* approve, I dare say it will give me
a clearer idea." "Most willingly, Fair Questioner.—The
Novels which I approve are such as display Human Nature
with Grandeur—such as shew her in the Sublimities of
intense Feeling—such as exhibit the progress of strong
Passion from the first Germ of incipient Susceptibility to
the utmost Energies of Reason half-dethroned,—where we
see the strong spark of Woman's Captivations elicit such
Fire in the Soul of Man as leads him—(though at the risk
of some Aberration from the strict line of Primitive Obligations)—to hazard all, dare all, atcheive all, to obtain her.—
Such are the Works which I peruse with delight, & I hope I
may say, with Amelioration. They hold forth the most splendid Portraitures of high Conceptions, Unbounded Veiws,
illimitable Ardour, indomptible Decision—and even when
the Event is mainly anti-prosperous to the high-toned
Machinations of the prime Character, the potent, pervading
                                                        Hero

Hero of the Story, it leaves us full of Generous Emotions
for him;—our Hearts are paralized—. T'were Pseudo-
Philosophy to assert that we do not feel more enwraped
by the brilliancy of his Career, than by the tranquil &
morbid Virtues of any opposing Character. Our approbation of the Latter is but Eleemosynary.—These are the
Novels which enlarge the primitive Capabilities of the
Heart, & which it cannot impugn the Sense or be any Dere-
liction of the character, of the most anti-puerile Man, to
be conversant with."—"If I understand you aright—said
Charlotte—our taste in Novels is not at all the same." And
here they were obliged to part—Miss D. being too much
tired of them all, to stay any longer.—The truth was that
Sir Edw: whom circumstances had confined very much to
one spot had read more sentimental Novels than agreed
with him. His fancy had been early caught by all the impas-
sioned, & most exceptionable parts of Richardsons; & such
Authors as have since appeared to tread in Richardson's
steps, so far as Man's determined pursuit of Woman in
defiance of every opposition of feeling & convenience is
concerned, had since occupied the greater part of his literary hours, & formed his Character.—With a perversity of
Judgement, which must be attributed to his not having
by Nature a very strong head, the Graces, the Spirit, the
Sagacity, & the Perseverance, of the Villain of the Story
outweighed all his absurdities & all his Atrocities with Sir
Edward. With him, such Conduct was Genius, Fire & Feeling.—It interested & inflamed him; & he was always more
anxious for its Success & mourned over its Discomfitures
with more Tenderness than c^d ever have been contem-
plated by the Authors.—Though he owed many of his ideas
to this sort of reading, it were unjust to say that he read
nothing else, or that his Language were not formed on a
more general Knowledge of modern Literature.—He read
all the Essays, Letters, Tours & Criticisms of the day—&
with the same ill-luck which made him derive only false
                                                    Principles

Principles from Lessons of Morality, & incentives to Vice from the History of it's Overthrow, he gathered only hard words & involved sentences from the style of our most approved Writers.—

Sir Edw:'s great object in life was to be seductive.—With such personal advantages as he knew himself to possess, & such Talents as he did also give himself credit for, he regarded it as his Duty.—He felt that he was formed to be a dangerous Man—quite in the line of the Lovelaces.—The very name of Sir Edward he thought, carried some degree of fascination with it.—To be generally gallant & assiduous about the fair, to make fine speeches to every pretty Girl, was but the inferior part of the Character he had to play.— Miss Heywood, or any other young Woman with any pretensions to Beauty, he was entitled (according to his own veiws of Society) to approach with high Compliment & Rhapsody on the slightest acquaintance; but it was Clara alone on whom he had serious designs; it was Clara whom he meant to seduce.—Her seduction was quite determined on. Her Situation in every way called for it. She was his rival in Lady D.'s favour, she was young, lovely & dependant.—He had very early seen the necessity of the case, & had now been long trying with cautious assiduity to make an impression on her heart, and to undermine her Principles.—Clara saw through him, & had not the least intention of being seduced—but she bore with him patiently enough to confirm the sort of attachment which her personal Charms had raised.—A greater degree of discouragement indeed would not have affected Sir Edw:—. He was armed against the highest pitch of Disdain or Aversion.— If she could not be won by affection, he must carry her off. He knew his Business.—Already had he had many Musings on the Subject. If he *were* constrained so to act, he must naturally wish to strike out something new, to exceed those who had gone before him—and he felt a strong curiosity to ascertain whether the Neighbourhood of Tombuctoo might

might not afford some solitary House adapted for Clara's reception;—but the Expence alas! of Measures in that masterly style was ill-suited to his Purse, & Prudence obliged him to prefer the quietest sort of ruin & disgrace for the object of his Affections, to the more renowned.—

CHAPTER 9.

ONE day, soon after Charlotte's arrival at Sanditon, she had the pleasure of seeing just as she ascended from the Sands to the Terrace, a Gentleman's Carriage with Post Horses standing at the door of the Hotel, as very lately arrived, & by the quantity of Luggage taking off, bringing, it might be hoped, some respectable family determined on a long residence.—Delighted to have such good news for M^r & Mrs P., who had both gone home some time before, she proceeded for Trafalgar House with as much alacrity as could remain, after having been contending for the last 2 hours with a very fine wind blowing directly on shore; but she had not reached the little Lawn, when she saw a Lady walking nimbly behind her at no great distance; and convinced that it could be no acquaintance of her own, she resolved to hurry on & get into the House if possible before her. But the Stranger's pace did not allow this to be accomplished;—Charlotte was on the steps & had rung, but the door was not opened, when the other crossed the Lawn;—and when the Servant appeared, they were just equally ready for entering the House.—The ease of the Lady, her "How do you do Morgan?—" & Morgan's Looks on seeing her, were a moment's astonishment—but another moment brought Mr P. into the Hall to welcome the Sister he had seen from the Draw^g room, and she was soon introduced to Miss Diana Parker. There was a great deal of surprise but still more pleasure in seeing her.—Nothing c^d be kinder than her reception from both Husband and Wife. "How did she come? & with whom?—And they were so

glad

glad to find her equal to the Journey!—And that she was
to belong to *them*, was a thing of course." Miss Diana P.
was about 4 & 30,of middling height & slender;—delicate
looking rather than sickly; with an agreable face, & a very
animated eye;—her manners resembling her Brother's in
their ease & frankness, though with more decision & less
mildness in her Tone. She began an account of herself
without delay.—Thanking them for their Invitation, but
"*that* was quite out of the question, for they were all three
come, & meant to get into Lodgings & make some stay."—
"All three come!—What!—Susan & Arthur!—Susan able
to come too!—This was better & better." "Yes—we are
actually all come. Quite unavoidable.—Nothing else to be
done.—You shall hear all about it.—But my dear Mary,
send for the Children;—I long to see them."—"And how
has Susan born the Journey?—& how is Arthur?—& why
do not we see him here with you?"—"Susan has born it
wonderfully. She had not a wink of sleep either the night
before we set out, or last night at Chichester, and as this is
not so common with her as with *me*, I have had a thousand
fears for her—but she had kept up wonderfully.—had no
Hysterics of consequence till we came within sight of poor
old Sanditon—and the attack was not very violent—nearly
over by the time we reached your Hotel—so that we got
her out of the Carriage extremely well, with only Mr Wood-
cock's assistance—& when I left her she was directing the
Disposal of the Luggage, & helping old Sam uncord the
Trunks.—She desired her best Love, with a thousand re-
grets at being so poor a Creature that she c^d not come with
me. And as for poor Arthur, he w^d not have been unwilling
himself, but there is so much Wind that I did not think he
c^d safely venture,—for I am *sure* there is Lumbago hanging
about him—and so I helped him on with his great Coat &
sent him off to the Terrace, to take us Lodgings.—Miss
Heywood must have seen our Carriage standing at the
Hotel.—I knew Miss Heywood the moment I saw her

before

before me on the Down.—My dear Tom I am so glad to see
you walk so well. Let me feel your Ancle.—That's right;
all right & clean. The play of your Sinews a *very* little
affected:—barely perceptible.—Well—now for the explanation of my being here.—I told you in my Letter, of
the two considerable Families, I was hoping to secure for
you—the West Indians, & the Seminary.—" Here M^r P.
drew his Chair still nearer to his Sister, & took her hand
again most affectionately as he answered "Yes, Yes;—
How active & how kind you have been!"—"The Westindians, she continued, whom I look upon as the *most* desirable of the two—as the Best of the Good—prove to be
a Mrs Griffiths & her family. I know them only through
others.—You must have heard me mention Miss Capper,
the particular friend of *my* very particular friend Fanny
Noyce;—now, Miss Capper is extremely intimate with a
Mrs Darling, who is on terms of constant correspondence
with Mrs Griffiths herself.—Only a *short* chain, you see,
between us, & not a Link wanting. Mrs G. meant to go to
the Sea, for her Young People's benefit—had fixed on the
coast of Sussex, but was undecided as to the where, wanted
something Private, & wrote to ask the opinion of her friend
Mrs Darling.—Miss Capper happened to be staying with
Mrs D. when Mrs G.'s Letter arrived, & was consulted on
the question; *she* wrote the same day to Fanny Noyce and
mentioned it to her—& Fanny all alive for *us*, instantly
took up her pen & forwarded the circumstance to me—
except as to *Names*—which have but lately transpired.—
There was but *one* thing for *me* to do.—I answered Fanny's
Letter by the same Post & pressed for the recommendation
of Sanditon. Fanny had feared your having no house large
enough to receive such a Family.—But I seem to be spin-
ning out my story to an endless length.—You see how it
was all managed. I had the pleasure of hearing soon afterwards by the same simple link of connection that Sanditon
had been recommended by Mrs Darling, & that the Westindians

indians were very much disposed to go thither.—This was the state of the case when I wrote to you;—but two days ago;—yes, the day before yesterday—I heard again from Fanny Noyce, saying that *she* had heard from Miss Capper, who by a Letter from Mrs Darling understood that Mrs G.—has expressed herself in a letter to Mrs D. more doubtingly on the subject of Sanditon.—Am I clear?—I would be anything rather than not clear."—"Oh! perfectly, perfectly. Well?"—"The reason of this hesitation, was her having no connections in the place, & no means of ascertaining that she should have good accomodations on arriving there;—and she was particularly careful & scrupulous on all those matters more on account of a certain Miss Lambe a young Lady (probably a Neice) under her care, than on her own account or her Daughters.—Miss Lambe has an immense fortune—richer than all the rest—& very delicate health.—One sees clearly enough by all this, the *sort* of Woman Mrs G. must be—as helpless & indolent, as Wealth & a Hot Climate are apt to make us. But we are not all born to equal Energy.—What was to be done?—I had a few moments indecision;—Whether to offer to write to *you*,—or to Mrs Whitby to secure them a House?—but neither pleased me.—I hate to employ others, when I am equal to act myself—and my conscience told me that this was an occasion which called for me. Here was a family of helpless Invalides whom I might essentially serve.—I sounded Susan—the same Thought had occurred to her.—Arthur made no difficulties—our plan was arranged immediately, we were off yesterday morn^g at 6—, left Chichester at the same hour today—& here we are.—"
"Excellent!—Excellent!— cried Mr Parker.—Diana, you are unequal'd in serving your friends & doing Good to all the World.—I know nobody like you.—Mary, my Love, is not she a wonderful Creature?—Well—and now, what House do you design to engage for them?—What is the size of their family?—" "I do not at all know—replied
his

his Sister—have not the least idea;—never heard any particulars;—but I am very sure that the largest house at Sanditon cannot be *too* large. They are more likely to want a second.—I shall take only one however, & that, but for a week certain.—Miss Heywood, I astonish you.—You hardly know what to make of me.—I see by your Looks, that you are not used to such quick measures."—The words "Unaccountable Officiousness!—Activity run mad!" —had just passed through Charlotte's mind—but a civil answer was easy. "I dare say I do look surprised, said she —because these are very great exertions, & I know what Invalides both you & your Sister are." "Invalides indeed. —I trust there are not three People in England who have so sad a right to that appellation!—But my dear Miss Heywood, we are sent into this World to be as extensively useful as possible, & where some degree of Strength of Mind is given, it is not a feeble body which will excuse us—or incline us to excuse ourselves.—The World is pretty much divided between the Weak of Mind & the Strong—between those who can act & those who can not, & it is the bounden Duty of the Capable to let no opportunity of being useful escape them.—My Sister's Complaints & mine are happily not often of a Nature, to threaten Existence *immediately*— & as long as we *can* exert ourselves to be of use of others, I am convinced that the Body is the better, for the refreshment the Mind receives in doing its' Duty.—While I have been travelling, with this object in veiw, I have been perfectly well."—The entrance of the Children ended this little panegyric on her own Disposition—& after having noticed & caressed them all,—she prepared to go.—"Cannot you dine with us?—Is not it possible to prevail on you to dine with us?" was then the cry; and *that* being absolutely negatived, it was "And when shall we see you again? and how can we be of use to you?"—and Mr P. warmly offered his assistance in taking the house for Mrs G.—"I will come to you the moment I have dined, said he, & we will go about
together

together."—But this was immediately declined.—"No, my dear Tom, upon no account in the World, shall you stir a step on any business of mine.—Your Ancle wants rest. I see by the position of your foot, that you have used it too much already.—No, I shall go about my House-taking directly. Our Dinner is not ordered till six—& by that time I hope to have completed it. It is now only ½ past 4.—As to seeing *me* again today—I cannot answer for it; the others will be at the Hotel all the Even^g, & delighted to see you at any time, but as soon as I get back I shall hear what Arthur has done about our own Lodgings, & probably the moment Dinner is over, shall be out again on business relative to them, for we hope to get into some Lodgings or other & be settled after breakfast tomorrow.—I have not much confidence in poor Arthur's skill for Lodging-taking, but he seemed to like the commission.—" "I think you are doing too much, said Mr P. You will knock yourself up. You sh^d not move again after Dinner." "No, indeed you should not. cried his wife, for Dinner is such a mere *name* with you all, that it can do you no good.—I know what your appetites are.—" "My appetite is very much mended I assure you lately. I have been taking some Bitters of my own decocting, which have done wonders. Susan never eats I grant you—& just at present *I* shall want nothing; I never eat for about a week after a Journey—but as for Arthur, he is only too much disposed for Food. We are often obliged to check him."—"But you have not told me any thing of the *other* Family coming to Sanditon, said Mr P. as he walked with her to the door of the House—the Camberwell Seminary; have we a good chance of *them*?" "Oh! Certain—quite certain.—I had forgotten them for the moment, but I had a letter 3 days ago from my friend Mrs Charles Dupuis which assured me of Camberwell. Camberwell will be here to a certainty, & very soon.—*That* good Woman (I do not know her name) not being so wealthy & independant as Mrs G.—can travel & chuse for
herself

herself.—I will tell you how I got at *her*. Mrs Charles
Dupuis lives almost next door to a Lady, who has a relation
lately settled at Clapham, who actually attends the Seminary and gives lessons on Eloquence and Belles Lettres to
some of the Girls.—I got that Man a Hare from one of
Sidney's friends—and he recommended Sanditon;—Without *my* appearing however—Mrs Charles Dupuis managed
it all.—'

CHAPTER 10.

IT was not a week, since Miss Diana Parker had been told
by her feelings, that the Sea Air w^d probably in her present
state, be the death of her, and now she was at Sanditon,
intending to make some Stay, & without appearing to have
the slightest recollection of having written or felt any such
thing.—It was impossible for Charlotte not to suspect a
good deal of fancy in such an extraordinary state of health.
—Disorders & Recoveries so very much out of the common
way, seemed more like the amusement of eager Minds in
want of employment than of actual afflictions & releif.
The Parkers, were no doubt a family of Imagination &
quick feelings—and while the eldest Brother found vent
for his superfluity of sensation as a Projector, the Sisters
were perhaps driven to dissipate theirs in the invention of
odd complaints.—The *whole* of their mental vivacity was
evidently not so employed; Part was laid out in a Zeal
for being useful.—It should seem that they must either be
very busy for the Good of others, or else extremely ill themselves. Some natural delicacy of Constitution in fact, with
an unfortunate turn for Medecine, especially quack Medecine, had given them an early tendency at various times,
to various Disorders;—the rest of their sufferings was from
Fancy, the love of Distinction & the love of the Wonderful.
—They had Charitable hearts & many amiable feelings—
but a spirit of restless activity, & the glory of doing
more

more than anybody else, had their share in every exertion
of Benevolence—and there was Vanity in all they did, as
well as in all they endured.—M^r & Mrs P. spent a great part
of the Even^g at the Hotel; but Charlotte had only two or
three veiws of Miss Diana posting over the Down after
a House for this Lady whom she had never seen, & who
had never employed her. She was not made acquainted with
the others till the following day, when, being removed into
Lodgings & all the party continuing quite well, their Brother
& Sister & herself were entreated to drink tea with them.—
They were in one of the Terrace Houses—& she found
them arranged for the Even^g in a small neat Drawing room,
with a beautiful veiw of the Sea if they had chosen it,—but
though it had been a very fair English Summer-day,—not
only was there no open window, but the Sopha & the Table,
& the Establishment in general was all at the other end of
the room by a brisk fire.—Miss P— whom, remembering
the three Teeth drawn in one day, Charlotte approached
with a peculiar degree of respectful Compassion, was not
very unlike her Sister in person or manner—tho' more thin
& worn by Illness & Medecine, more relaxed in air, & more
subdued in voice. She talked however, the whole Evening
as incessantly as Diana—& excepting that she sat with
salts in her hand, took Drops two or three times from one,
out of the several Phials already at home on the Mantel-
peice,—& made a great many odd faces & contortions,
Charlotte could perceive no symptoms of illness which she,
in the boldness of her own good health, w^d not have undertaken to cure, by putting out the fire, opening the Window,
& disposing of the Drops & the salts by means of one or
the other. She had had considerable curiosity to see M^r
Arthur Parker; & having fancied him a very puny, delicate-
looking young Man, the smallest very materially of not
a robust Family, was astonished to find him quite as tall
as his Brother & a great deal Stouter—Broad made &
Lusty—and with no other look of an Invalide, than a
sodden

sodden complexion.—Diana was evidently the cheif of the family; principal Mover & Actor;—she had been on her Feet the whole Morning, on Mrs G.'s business or their own, & was still the most alert of the three.—Susan had only superintended their final removal from the Hotel, bringing two heavy Boxes herself, & Arthur had found the air so cold that he had merely walked from one House to the other as nimbly as he could,—& boasted much of sitting by the fire till he had cooked up a very good one.—Diana, whose exercise had been too domestic to admit of calculation, but who, by her own account, had not once sat down during the space of seven hours, confessed herself a little tired. She had been too successful however for much fatigue; for not only had she by walking & talking down a thousand difficulties at last secured a proper House at 8ˢ pʳ week for Mrs G.—; she had also opened so many Treaties with Cooks, Housemaids, Washer-women & Bathing Women, that Mrs G. would have little more to do on her arrival, than to wave her hand & collect them around her for choice.—Her concluding effort in the cause, had been a few polite lines of Information to Mrs G. herself—time not allowing for the circuitous train of intelligence which had been hitherto kept up,—and she was now regaling in the delight of opening the first Trenches of an acquaintance with such a powerful discharge of unexpected Obligation. Mʳ & Mrs P.— & Charlotte had seen two Post chaises crossing the Down to the Hotel as they were setting off,—a joyful sight— & full of speculation.—The Miss Ps— & Arthur had also seen something;—they could distinguish from their window that there *was* an arrival at the Hotel, but not its amount. Their Visitors answered for two Hack-Chaises.—Could it be the Camberwell Seminary?—No—No.—Had there been a 3ᵈ carriage, perhaps it might; but it was very generally agreed that two Hack chaises could never contain a Seminary.—Mʳ P. was confident of another new Family.—When they were all finally seated, after some removals to look at the

the Sea & the Hotel, Charlotte's place was by Arthur, who
was sitting next to the Fire with a degree of Enjoyment
which gave a good deal of merit to his civility in wishing
her to take his Chair.—There was nothing dubious in her
manner of declining it, and he sat down again with much
satisfaction. She drew back her Chair to have all the
advantage of his Person as a screen, & was very thankful
for every inch of Back & Shoulders beyond her pre-
conceived idea. Arthur was heavy in Eye as well as figure,
but by no means indisposed to talk;—and while the other
4 were cheifly engaged together, he evidently felt it no
penance to have a fine young Woman next to him, requiring in common Politeness some attention—as his B^r, who
felt the decided want of some motive for action, some
Powerful object of animation for him, observed with considerable pleasure.—Such was the influence of Youth &
Bloom that he began even to make a sort of apology for
having a Fire. "We sh^d not have one at home, said he, but
the Sea air is always damp. I am not afraid of any thing
so much as Damp.—" "I am so fortunate, said C. as never
to know whether the air is damp or dry. It has always
some property that is wholesome & invigorating to me.—"
"*I* like the Air too, as well as any body can; replied Arthur,
I am very fond of standing at an open Window when there
is no Wind—but unluckily a Damp air does not like *me*.—
It gives me the Rheumatism.—You are not rheumatic I
suppose?—" "Not at all." "That's a great blessing.—But
perhaps you are nervous." "No—I beleive not. I have no
idea that I am."—"*I* am very nervous.—To say the truth
Nerves are the worst part of my Complaints in *my* opinion.
My Sisters think me Bilious, but I doubt it.—" "You are
quite in the right, to doubt it as long as you possibly can,
I am sure.—" "If I were Bilious, he continued, you know
Wine w^d disagree with me, but it always does me good.—
The more Wine I drink (in Moderation) the better I am.—
I am always best of an Even^g.—If you had seen me to day
before

before Dinner, you w^d have thought me a very poor Creature.— " Charlotte could beleive it—. She kept her countenance however, & said—"As far as I can understand
what nervous complaints are, I have a great idea of the
efficacy of air & exercise for them:—daily, regular Exercise;—and I should recommend rather more of it to *you*
than I suspect you are in the habit of taking."—"Oh! I am
very fond of exercise myself—he replied—& mean to walk
a great deal while I am here, if the Weather is temperate.
I shall be out every morning before breakfast—& take
several turns upon the Terrace, & you will often see me
at Trafalgar House."—"But you do not call a walk to
Traf: H. much exercise?—" "Not, as to mere distance,
but the Hill is so steep!—Walking up that Hill, in the
middle of the day, would throw me into such a Perspiration!—You would see me all in a Bath by the time I got
there!—I am very subject to Perspiration, and there cannot
be a surer sign of Nervousness.— " They were now advancing so deep in Physics, that Charlotte veiwed the entrance
of the Servant with the Tea things, as a very fortunate
Interruption.—It produced a great & immediate change.
The young Man's attentions were instantly lost. He took
his own Cocoa from the Tray,—which seemed provided with
almost as many Teapots &c as there were persons in company, Miss P. drinking one sort of Herb-Tea & Miss Diana
another, & turning completely to the Fire, sat coddling and
cooking it to his own satisfaction & toasting some Slices of
Bread, brought up ready-prepared in the Toast rack—and
till it was all done, she heard nothing of his voice but the
murmuring of a few broken sentences of self-approbation
& success.—When his Toils were over however, he moved
back his Chair into as gallant a Line as ever, & proved that
he had not been working only for himself, by his earnest
invitation to her to take both Cocoa & Toast.—She was
already helped to Tea—which surprised him—so totally
self-engrossed had he been.—"I thought I should have
been

been in time, said he, but cocoa takes a great deal of Boil-
ing."—"I am much obliged to you, replied Charlotte—but
I *prefer* Tea." "Then I will help myself, said he.—A large
Dish of rather weak Cocoa every evening, agrees with me
better than any thing."—It struck her however, as he
poured out this rather weak Cocoa, that it came forth in
a very fine, dark coloured stream—and at the same moment, his Sisters both crying out—"Oh! Arthur, you get
your Cocoa stronger & stronger every Even^g"—, with
Arthur's somewhat conscious reply of "T*is* rather stronger
than it should be tonight"—convinced her that Arthur
was by no means so fond of being starved as they could
desire, or as he felt proper himself.—He was certainly very
happy to turn the conversation on dry Toast, & hear no
more of his sisters.—"I hope you will eat some of this
Toast, said he, I reckon myself a very good Toaster; I
never burn my Toasts—I never put them too near the Fire
at first—& yet, you see, there is not a Corner but what is
well browned.—I hope you like dry Toast."—"With a
reasonable quantity of Butter spread over it, very much—
said Charlotte—but not otherwise.—" "No more do I—
said he exceedingly pleased—We think quite alike
there.—So far from dry Toast being wholesome, *I* think it
a very bad thing for the Stomach. Without a little butter to
soften it, it hurts the Coats of the Stomach. I am sure it
does.—I will have the pleasure of spreading some for you
directly—& afterwards I will spread some for myself.—
Very bad indeed for the Coats of the Stomach—but there
is no convincing *some* people.—It irritates & acts like a
nutmeg grater.—" He could not get command of the
Butter however, without a struggle; His Sisters accusing
him of eating a great deal too much, & declaring he was
not to be trusted;—and he maintaining that he only eat
enough to secure the Coats of his Stomach;—& besides,
he only wanted it now for Miss Heywood.—Such a plea
must prevail, he got the butter & spread away for her with

an

an accuracy of Judgement which at least delighted himself; but when her Toast was done, & he took his own in hand, Charlotte c^d hardly contain herself as she saw him watching his sisters, while he scrupulously scraped off almost as much butter as he put on, & then seize an odd moment for adding a great dab just before it went into his Mouth.—Certainly, Mr Arthur P.'s enjoyments in Invalidism were very different from his sisters—by no means so spiritualized.—A good deal of Earthy Dross hung about him. Charlotte could not but suspect him of adopting that line of Life, principally for the indulgence of an indolent Temper—& to be determined on having no Disorders but such as called for warm rooms & good Nourishment.—In one particular however, she soon found that he had caught something from *them*.—"What! said he—Do you venture upon two dishes of strong Green Tea in one Even^g?—What Nerves you must have!—How I envy you.—Now, if *I* were to swallow only one such dish—what do you think it's effect would be upon me?—" "Keep you awake perhaps all night"—replied Charlotte, meaning to overthrow his attempts at Surprise, by the Grandeur of her own Conceptions.—"Oh! if that were all!—he exclaimed.—No—it acts on me like Poison and w^d entirely take away the use of my right side, before I had swallowed it 5 minutes.—It sounds almost incredible—but it has happened to me so often that I cannot doubt it.—The use of my right Side is entirely taken away for several hours!" "It sounds rather odd to be sure—answered Charlotte coolly—but I dare say it would be proved to be the simplest thing in the World, by those who have studied right sides & Green Tea scientifically & thoroughly understand all the possibilities of their action on each other."—Soon after Tea, a Letter was brought to Miss D. P— from the Hotel.—"From Mrs Charles Dupuis—said she.—some private hand."—And having read a few lines, exclaimed aloud "Well, this is very extraordinary! very extraordinary indeed!—That both
should

should have the same name.—Two Mrs Griffiths!—This is a Letter of recommendation & introduction to me, of the Lady from Camberwell—& *her* name happens to be Griffiths too.—" A few lines more however, and the colour rushed into her Cheeks, & with much Perturbation she added— "The oddest thing that ever was!—a Miss Lambe too!— a young Westindian of large Fortune.—But it *cannot* be the same.—Impossible that it should be the same."—She read the Letter aloud for comfort.—It was merely to "introduce the Bearer, Mrs G.— from Camberwell, & the three young Ladies under her care, to Miss D. P.'s notice.— Mrs G.— being a stranger at Sanditon, was anxious for a respectable Introduction—& Mrs C. Dupuis therefore, at the instance of the intermediate friend, provided her with this Letter, knowing that she c^d not do her dear Diana a greater kindness than by giving her the means of being useful.—Mrs G.'s cheif solicitude w^d be for the accomoda-tion & comfort of one of the young Ladies under her care, a Miss Lambe, a young W. Indian of large Fortune, in delicate health."—"It was very strange!—very remark-able!—very extraordinary" but they were all agreed in determ⟨in⟩ing it to be *impossible* that there should not be two Families; such a totally distinct set of people as were concerned in the reports of each made that matter quite certain. There *must* be two Families.—Impossible to be otherwise. "Impossible" & "Impossible", was repeated over & over again with great fervour.—An accidental resem-blance of Names & circumstances, however striking at first, involved nothing really incredible—and so it was settled.— Miss Diana herself derived an immediate advantage to counterbalance her Perplexity. She must put her shawl over her shoulders, & be running about again. Tired as she was, she must instantly repair to the Hotel, to investigate the truth & offer her services.—

CHAPTER

CHAPTER 11.

It would not do.—Not all that the whole Parker race could say among themselves, c^d produce a happier catastrophée than that the Family from Surry & the Family from Camberwell were one & the same.—The rich Westindians, & the young Ladies Seminary had all entered Sanditon in those two Hack chaises. The Mrs G. who in her friend Mrs Darling's hands, had wavered as to coming & been unequal to the Journey, was the very same Mrs G. whose plans were at the same period (under another representation) perfectly decided, & who was without fears or difficulties.— All that had the appearance of Incongruity in the reports of the two, might very fairly be placed to the account of the Vanity, the Ignorance, or the blunders of the many engaged in the cause by the vigilance & caution of Miss Diana P—. *Her* intimate friends must be officious like herself, & the subject had supplied Letters & Extracts & Messages enough to make everything appear what it was not. Miss D. probably felt a little awkward on being first obliged to admit her mistake. A long Journey from Hampshire taken for nothing—a Brother disappointed—an expensive House on her hands for a week, must have been some of her immediate reflections—& much worse than all the rest, must have been the sort of sensation of being less clear-sighted & infallible than she had beleived herself.— No part of it however seemed to trouble her long. There were so many to share in the shame & the blame, that probably when she had divided out their proper portions to Mrs Darling, Miss Capper, Fanny Noyce, Mrs C. Dupuis & Mrs C. D's Neighbour, there might be a mere trifle of reproach remaining for herself.—At any rate, she was seen all the following morn^g walking about after Lodgings with Mrs G.— as alert as ever.—Mrs G. was a very well-behaved, genteel kind of Woman, who supported herself by receiving such great girls & young Ladies, as wanted either Masters

for

for finishing their Education, or a home for beginning their
Displays.—She had several more under her care than the
three who were now come to Sanditon, but the others all
happened to be absent.—Of these three, & indeed of all,
Miss Lambe was beyond comparison the most important
& precious, as she paid in proportion to her fortune.—She
was about 17, half Mulatto, chilly & tender, had a maid of
her own, was to have the best room in the Lodgings, & was
always of the first consequence in every plan of Mrs G.—The
other Girls, two Miss Beauforts were just such young Ladies
as may be met with, in at least one family out of three,
throughout the Kingdom; they had tolerable complexions,
shewey figures, an upright decided carriage & an assured
Look;—they were very accomplished & very Ignorant,
their time being divided between such pursuits as might
attract admiration, & those Labours & Expedients of
dexterous Ingenuity, by which they could dress in a stile
much beyond what they *ought* to have afforded; they were
some of the first in every change of fashion—& the object
of all, was to captivate some Man of much better fortune
than their own.—Mrs G. had preferred a small, retired
place, like Sanditon, on Miss Lambe's account—and the
Miss Bs—, though naturally preferring any thing to Small-
ness & Retirement, yet having in the course of the Spring
been involved in the inevitable expense of six new Dresses
each for a three days visit, were constrained to be satisfied
with Sanditon also, till their circumstances were retreived.
There, with the hire of a Harp for one, & the purchase of
some Drawing paper for the other & all the finery they
could already command, they meant to be very economical,
very elegant & very secluded; with the hope on Miss Beau-
fort's side, of praise & celebrity from all who walked within
the sound of her Instrument, & on Miss Letitia's, of curiosity & rapture in all who came near her while she sketched
—and to Both, the consolation of meaning to be the most
stylish Girls in the Place.—The particular introduction of

M^rs

Mrs G. to Miss Diana Parker, secured them immediately an acquaintance with the Trafalgar House-family, & with the Denhams;—and the Miss Beauforts were soon satisfied with "the Circle in which they moved in Sanditon" to use a proper phrase, for every body must now "move in a Circle",—to the prevalence of which rototory Motion, is perhaps to be attributed the Giddiness & false steps of many.—Lady Denham had other motives for calling on Mrs G. besides attention to the Parkers.—In Miss Lambe, here was the very young Lady, sickly & rich, whom she had been asking for; & she made the acquaintance for Sir Edward's sake, & the sake of her Milch asses. How it might answer with regard to the Baronet, remained to be proved, but as to the Animals, she soon found that all her calculations of Profit w^{d} be vain. Mrs G. would not allow Miss L. to have the smallest symptom of a Decline, or any complaint which Asses milk c^{d} possibly releive. "Miss L. was under the constant care of an experienced Physician;—and his Prescriptions must be their rule"—and except in favour of some Tonic Pills, which a Cousin of her own had a Property in, Mrs G. did never deviate from the strict Medecinal page.—The corner house of the Terrace was the one in which Miss D. P. had the pleasure of settling her new friends, & considering that it commanded in front the favourite Lounge of all the Visitors at Sanditon, & on one side, whatever might be going on at the Hotel, there c^{d} not have been a more favourable spot for the seclusions of the Miss Beauforts. And accordingly, long before they had suited themselves with an Instrument, or with Drawing paper, they had, by the frequency of their appearance at the low Windows upstairs, in order to close the blinds, or open the Blinds, to arrange a flower pot on the Balcony, or look at nothing through a Telescope, attracted many an eye upwards, & made many a Gazer gaze again.—A little Novelty has a great effect in so small a place; the Miss Beauforts, who w^{d} have been nothing at Brighton, could

not

not move here without notice;—and even Mr Arthur
Parker, though little disposed for supernumerary exertion,
always quitted the Terrace, in his way to his Brothers by
this corner House, for the sake of a glimpse of the Miss
Bs—, though it was $\frac{1}{2}$ a q^r of a mile round about, & added
two steps to the ascent of the Hill.

CHAPTER 12.

CHARLOTTE had been 10 days at Sanditon without seeing
Sanditon House, every attempt at calling on Lady D.
having been defeated by meeting with her beforehand.
But now it was to be more resolutely undertaken, at a
more early hour, that nothing might be neglected of attention to Lady D. or amusement to Charlotte.—" And if you
should find a favourable opening my Love, said Mr P. (who
did not mean to go with them)—I think you had better
mention the poor Mullins's situation, & sound her Ladyship
as to a Subscription for them. I am not fond of charitable
subscriptions in a place of this kind—It is a sort of tax
upon all that come—Yet as their distress is very great & I
almost promised the poor Woman yesterday to get something done for her, I beleive we must set a subscription on
foot—& therefore the sooner the better,—& Lady Denham's
name at the head of the List will be a very necessary beginning.—You will not dislike speaking to her about it, Mary?"
—" I will do whatever you wish me, replied his Wife—but
you would do it so much better yourself. I shall not know
what to say."—" My dear Mary, cried he, it is impossible you
can be really at a loss. Nothing can be more simple. You
have only to state the present afflicted situation of the
family, their earnest application to me, & my being willing
to promote a little subscription for their releif, provided it
meet with her approbation.— " "The easiest thing in the
World—cried Miss Diana Parker who happened to be calling on them at the moment—. All said & done, in less time
than

than you have been talking of it now.—And while you are on the subject of subscriptions Mary, I will thank you to mention a very melancholy case to Lady D. which has been represented to me in the most affecting terms.—There is a poor Woman in Worcestershire, whom some friends of mine are exceedingly interested about, & I have undertaken to collect whatever I can for her. If you w^d mention the circumstance to Lady Denham!—Lady Denham *can* give, if she is properly attacked—& I look upon her to be the sort of Person who, when once she is prevailed on to undraw her Purse, would as readily give 10^Gs as 5.—And therefore, if you find her in a Giving mood, you might as well speak in favour of another Charity which I & a few more, have very much at heart—the establishment of a Charitable Repository at Burton on Trent.—And then,— there is the family of the poor Man who was hung last assizes at York, tho' we really *have* raised the sum we wanted for putting them all out, yet if you *can* get a Guinea from her on their behalf, it may as well be done.—" "My dear Diana! exclaimed Mrs P.— I could no more mention these things to Lady D.— than I c^d fly."—"Where's the difficulty?—I wish I could go with you myself—but in 5 minutes I must be at Mrs G.— to encourage Miss Lambe in taking her first Dip. She is so frightened, poor Thing, that I promised to come & keep up her Spirits, & go in the Machine with her if she wished it—and as soon as that is over, I must hurry home, for Susan is to have Leaches at one oclock—which will be a three hours business,—therefore I really have not a moment to spare—besides that (between ourselves) I ought to be in bed myself at this present time, for I am hardly able to stand—and when the Leaches have done, I dare say we shall both go to our rooms for the rest of the day."—"I am sorry to hear it, indeed; but if this is the case I hope Arthur will come to us."—"If Arthur takes my advice, he will go to bed too, for if he stays up by himself, he will certainly eat & drink more than he ought;
but

—but you see Mary, how impossible it is for me to go with you to Lady Denham's."—"Upon second thoughts Mary, said her husband, I will not trouble you to speak about the Mullins's.—I will take an opportunity of seeing Lady D. myself.—*I* know how little it suits you to be pressing matters upon a Mind at all unwilling."—*His* application thus withdrawn, his sister could say no more in support of hers, which was his object, as he felt all their impropriety & all the certainty of their ill effect upon his own better claim.—Mrs P. was delighted at this release, & set off very happy with her friend & her little girl, on this walk to Sanditon House.—It was a close, misty morn^g, & when they reached the brow of the Hill, they could not for some time make out what sort of Carriage it was, which they saw coming up. It appeared at different moments to be everything from the Gig to the Pheaton,—from one horse to 4; & just as they were concluding in favour of a Tandem, little Mary's young eyes distinguished the Coachman & she eagerly called out, "T'is Uncle Sidney Mama, it is indeed." And so it proved.—Mr Sidney Parker driving his Servant in a very neat Carriage was soon opposite to them, & they all stopped for a few minutes. The manners of the Parkers were always pleasant among themselves—& it was a very friendly meeting between Sidney & his sister in law, who was most kindly taking it for granted that he was on his way to Trafalgar House. This he declined however. "He was just come from Eastbourne, proposing to spend two or three days, as it might happen, at Sanditon—but the Hotel must be his Quarters—He was expecting to be joined there by a friend or two."—The rest was common enquiries & remarks, with kind notice of little Mary, & a very well-bred Bow & proper address to Miss Heywood on her being named to him—and they parted, to meet again within a few hours.—Sidney Parker was about 7 or 8 & 20, very good-looking, with a decided air of Ease & Fashion, and a lively countenance.—This adventure afforded agreable

able discussion for some time. Mrs P. entered into all her Husband's joy on the occasion, & exulted in the credit which Sidney's arrival w^d give to the place. The road to Sanditon H. was a broad, handsome, planted approach, between fields, & conducting at the end of a q^r of a mile through second Gates into the Grounds, which though not extensive had all the Beauty & Respectability which an abundance of very fine Timber could give.—These Entrance Gates were so much in a corner of the Grounds or Paddock, so near one of its Boundaries, that an outside fence was at first almost pressing on the road—till an angle *here*, & a curve *there* threw them to a better distance. The Fence was a proper Park paling in excellent condition; with clusters of fine Elms, or rows of old Thorns following its line almost every where.—*Almost* must be stipulated—for there were vacant spaces—& through one of these, Charlotte as soon as they entered the Enclosure, caught a glimpse over the pales of something White & Womanish in the field on the other side;—it was something which immediately brought Miss B. into her head—& stepping to the pales, she saw indeed—& very decidedly, in spite of the Mist; Miss B— seated, not far before her, at the foot of the bank which sloped down from the outside of the Paling & which a narrow Path seemed to skirt along;— Miss Brereton seated, apparently very composedly—& Sir E. D. by her side.—They were sitting so near each other & appeared so closely engaged in gentle conversation, that Ch. instantly felt she had nothing to do but to step back again, & say not a word.—Privacy was certainly their object.—It could not but strike her rather unfavourably with regard to Clara;—but hers was a situation which must not be judged with severity.—She was glad to perceive that nothing had been discerned by Mrs Parker; If Charlotte had not been considerably the tallest of the two, Miss B.'s white ribbons might not have fallen within the ken of *her* more observant eyes.—Among other points of moralising

moralising reflection which the sight of this Tete a Tete produced, Charlotte c^d not but think of the extreme difficulty which secret Lovers must have in finding a proper spot for their stolen Interveiws.—Here perhaps they had thought themselves so perfectly secure from observation! —the whole field open before them—a steep bank & Pales never crossed by the foot of Man at their back—and a great thickness of air, in aid—. Yet here, she had seen them. They were really ill-used.—The House was large & handsome; two Servants appeared, to admit them, & every thing had a suitable air of Property & Order.—Lady D. valued herself upon her liberal Establishment, & had great enjoyment in the order and the Importance of her style of living.—They were shewn into the usual sitting room, well-proportioned & well-furnished;—tho' it was Furniture rather originally good & extremely well kept, than new or shewey—and as Lady D. was not there, Charlotte had leisure to look about, & to be told by Mrs P. that the whole-length Portrait of a stately Gentleman, which placed over the Mantlepeice, caught the eye immediately, was the picture of Sir H. Denham—and that one among many Miniatures in another part of the room, little conspicuous, represented Mr Hollis.—Poor Mr Hollis!—It was impossible not to feel him hardly used; to be obliged to stand back in his own House & see the best place by the fire constantly occupied by Sir H. D.

IV. Plan* of a Novel, according to hints from various quarters

THE manuscript of the 'Plan' (now in the Pierpont Morgan Library) is an undated fair copy, probably written in 1816. Extracts of the work appeared in the 1871 *Memoir*. The first complete text was the edition by R. W. Chapman, Oxford, 1926.

The 'Plan' is a burlesque, part-literary, part-private, whose immediate occasion was Jane Austen's correspondence in 1815–16 with the Revd. James Stanier Clarke, Librarian to the Prince Regent (see *Letters of Jane Austen*, edited R. W. Chapman, Oxford, 1952; and *Literary Manuscripts*, ch. 5). [B.C.S.]

SCENE to be in the Country, Heroine the Daughter of a [1]Clergyman, one who after having lived much in the World had retired from it, & settled in a Curacy, with a very small fortune of his own.—He, the most excellent Man that can be imagined, perfect in Character, Temper & Manners—without the smallest drawback or peculiarity to prevent his being the most delightful companion to his Daughter from one year's end to the other.—Heroine a [2]faultless Character herself—, perfectly good, with much tenderness & sentiment, & not the least [3]Wit—very highly [4]accomplished, understanding modern Languages & (generally speaking) everything that the most accomplished young Women learn, but particularly excelling in Music— her favourite pursuit—& playing equally well on the Piano Forte & Harp—& singing in the first stile. Her Person, quite beautiful—[5]dark eyes & plump cheeks.—Book to open with the description of Father & Daughter—who are

* The notes to the *Plan*, here printed as footnotes, are JA's own marginalia. [1] Mr. Gifford. [2] Fanny Knight. [3] Mary Cooke. [4] Fanny K. [5] Mary Cooke.

to

to converse in long speeches, elegant Language—& a tone
of high, serious sentiment.—The Father to be induced, at
his Daughter's earnest request, to relate to her the past
events of his Life. This Narrative will reach through the
greatest part of the 1st vol.—as besides all the circumstances of his attachment to her Mother & their Marriage,
it will comprehend his going to sea as [1]Chaplain to a
distinguished Naval Character about the Court, his going
afterwards to Court himself, which introduced him to
a great variety of Characters & involved him in many
interesting situations, concluding with his opinion of the
Benefits to result from Tythes being done away, & his
having buried his own Mother (Heroine's lamented Grandmother) in consequence of the High Priest of the Parish
in which she died, refusing to pay her Remains the respect
due to them. The Father to be of a very literary turn, an
Enthusiast in Literature, nobody's Enemy but his own—
at the same time most zealous in the discharge of his
Pastoral Duties, the model of an [2]exemplary Parish Priest.
—The heroine's friendship to be sought after by a young
Woman in the same Neighbourhood, of [3]Talents & Shrewd-
ness, with light eyes & a fair skin, but having a considerable
degree of Wit, Heroine shall shrink from the acquaintance.—From this outset, the Story will proceed, & contain
a striking variety of adventures. Heroine & her Father
never above a [4]fortnight together in one place, *he* being
driven from his Curacy by the vile arts of some totally
unprincipled & heart-less young Man, desperately in love
with the Heroine, & pursuing her with unrelenting passion
—no sooner settled in one Country of Europe than they
are necessitated to quit it & retire to another—always
making new acquaintance, & always obliged to leave them.
—This will of course exhibit a wide variety of Characters—
but there will be no mixture; the scene will be for ever
shifting from one Set of People to another—but All the

[1] Mr. Clarke.   [2] Mr. Sherer.   [3] Mary Cooke.   [4] Many critics.
[1]Good

[1]Good will be unexceptionable in every respect—and there will be no foibles or weaknesses but with the Wicked, who will be completely depraved & infamous, hardly a resemblance of Humanity left in them.—Early in her career, in the progress of her first removals, Heroine must meet with the Hero—all [2]perfection of course—& only prevented from paying his addresses to her, by some excess of refinement.—Wherever she goes, somebody falls in love with her, & she receives repeated offers of Marriage—which she always refers wholly to her Father, exceedingly angry that [3]*he* sh^d not be first applied to.—Often carried away by the anti-hero, but rescued either by her Father or the Hero—often reduced to support herself & her Father by her Talents & work for her Bread;—continually cheated & defrauded of her hire, worn down to a Skeleton, & now & then starved to death—. At last, hunted out of civilized Society, denied the poor Shelter of the humblest Cottage, they are compelled to retreat into Kamschatka where the poor Father, quite worn down, finding his end approaching, throws himself on the Ground, & after 4 or 5 hours of tender advice & parental Admonition to his miserable Child, expires in a fine burst of Literary Enthusiasm, intermingled with Invectives again⟨st⟩ Holder's of Tythes.—Heroine inconsolable for some time—but afterwards crawls back towards her former Country—having at least 20 narrow escapes of falling into the hands of Anti-hero—& at last in the very nick of time, turning a corner to avoid him, runs into the arms of the Hero himself, who having just shaken off the scruples which fetter'd him before, was at the very moment setting off in pursuit of her.—The Tenderest & completest Eclaircissement takes place, & they are happily united.—Throughout the whole work, Heroine to be in the most [4]elegant Society & living in high style. The name of the work *not* to be [5]*Emma*—but of the same sort as [6]S & S. and P & P.

[1] Mary Cooke.   [2] Fanny Knight.   [3] Mrs. Pearse of Chilton-Lodge.
[4] Fanny Knight.   [5] Mrs. Craven.   [6] Mr. H. Sanford.

V. Opinions of *Mansfield Park*

THE 'Opinions of *Mansfield Park*' and 'Opinions of *Emma*' are collections of comments gathered and transcribed by Jane Austen from her correspondence, from hearsay, and from remarks passed on to her by members of the family. Neither manuscript is dated. The *Mansfield Park* 'Opinions' are those of the novel's earliest readers and date from 1814 and 1815; the *Emma* 'Opinions' probably belong to 1816.   [B.C.S.]

"WE certainly do not think it as a *whole*, equal to P. & P.—but it has many & great beauties. Fanny is a delightful Character! and Aunt Norris is a great favourite of mine. The Characters are natural & well supported, & many of the Dialogues excellent.—You need not fear the publication being considered as discreditable to the talents of it's Author." F. W. A.[1]

Not so clever as P. & P.—but pleased with it altogether. Liked the character of Fanny. Admired the Portsmouth Scene.—Mr K.[2]—

Edward & George.[3]—Not liked it near so well as P. & P. —Edward admired Fanny—George disliked her.—George interested by nobody but Mary Crawford.—Edward pleased with Henry C.—Edmund objected to, as cold & formal.— Henry C.s going off with Mrs R.—at such a time, when so much in love with Fanny, thought unnatural by Edward.—

Fanny Knight.—Liked it, in many parts, very much indeed, delighted with Fanny;—but not satisfied with the end—wanting more Love between her & Edmund—&

[1] Francis William Austen.
[2] JA's brother Edward Austen (Knight 1812).
[3] Edward Knight's sons.

could

could not think it natural that Edm^d. sh^d. be so much attached to a woman without Principle like Mary C.—or promote Fanny's marrying Henry.—

Anna[1] liked it better than P. & P.—but not so well as S. & S.—could not bear Fanny.—Delighted with Mrs Norris, the scene at Portsmouth, & all the humourous parts.—

Mrs James Austen, very much pleased. Enjoyed Mrs Norris particularly, & the scene at Portsmouth. Thought Henry Crawford's going off with Mrs Rushworth, very natural.—

Miss Clewes's objections much the same as Fanny's.—

Miss Lloyd preferred it altogether to either of the others. —Delighted with Fanny.—Hated Mrs Norris.—

My Mother—not liked it so well as P. & P.—Thought Fanny insipid.—Enjoyed Mrs Norris.—

Cassandra—thought it quite as clever, tho' not so brilliant as P. & P.—Fond of Fanny.—Delighted much in Mr Rushworth's stupidity.—

My Eldest Brother[2]—a warm admirer of it in general.— Delighted with the Portsmouth Scene.

Edward[3]—Much like his Father.—Objected to Mrs Rushworth's Elopement as unnatural.

Mr B. L.[4]—Highly pleased with Fanny Price—& a warm admirer of the Portsmouth Scene.—Angry with Edmund for not being in love with her, & hating Mrs Norris for teazing her.—

Miss Burdett—Did not like it so well as P. & P.

Mrs James Tilson—Liked it better than P. & P.

Fanny Cage—did not much like it—not to be compared to P. & P.—nothing interesting in the Characters—Language poor.—Characters natural & well supported—Improved as it went on.—

---

[1] Anna Lefroy, JA's niece.   [2] James.
[3] James Edward Austen (-Leigh 1837), JA's biographer.
[4] Benjamin Lefroy.

M^r

M^r & Mrs Cooke—very much pleased with it—particularly with the Manner in which the Clergy are treated.—Mr Cooke called it "the most sensible Novel he had ever read."—Mrs Cooke wished for a good Matronly Character.—

Mary Cooke—quite as much pleased with it, as her Father & Mother; seemed to enter into Lady B.'s character, & enjoyed Mr Rushworth's folly. Admired Fanny in general; but thought she ought to have been more determined on overcoming her own feelings, when she saw Edmund's attachment to Miss Crawford.—

Miss Burrel—admired it very much—particularly Mrs Norris & Dr Grant.—

Mrs Bramstone—much pleased with it; particularly with the character of Fanny, as being so very natural. Thought Lady Bertram like herself.—Preferred it to either of the others—but imagined *that* might be her want of Taste—as she does not understand Wit.—

Mrs Augusta Bramstone—owned that she thought S & S. —and P. & P. downright nonsense, but expected to like M P. better, & having finished the 1st vol.—flattered herself she had got through the worst.

The families at Deane—all pleased with it.—Mrs Anna Harwood delighted with Mrs Norris & the green Curtain.

The Kintbury Family[1]—very much pleased with it;—preferred it to either of the others.—

Mr Egerton the Publisher—praised it for it's Morality, & for being so equal a Composition.—No weak parts.

Lady Rob: Kerr wrote—"You may be assured I read every line with the greatest interest & am more delighted with it than my humble pen can express. The excellent delineation of Character, sound sense, Elegant Language & the pure morality with which it abounds, makes it a most desirable as well as useful work, & reflects the highest honour &c. &c.—Universally admired in Edinburgh, by all the *wise ones*.—Indeed, I have not heard a single fault given to it."—

---

[1] Fowle.

Miss

Miss Sharpe—"I think it excellent—& of it's good sense & moral Tendency there can be no doubt.—Your Characters are drawn to the Life—so *very, very* natural & just—but as you beg me to be perfectly honest, I must confess I prefer P & P."—

Mrs Carrick.—"All who think deeply & feel much will give the Preference to Mansfield Park."

Mr J. Plumptre.—"I never read a novel which interested me so very much throughout, the characters are all so remarkably well kept up & so well drawn, & the plot is so well contrived that I had not an idea till the end which of the two w^d marry Fanny, H. C. or Edm^d. Mrs Norris amused me particularly, & Sir Thos is very clever, & his conduct proves admirably the defects of the modern system of Education."—Mr J. P. made *two* objections, but only one of them was remembered, the want of some character more striking & interesting to the generality of Readers, than Fanny was likely to be.—

Sir James Langham & Mr H. Sanford, having been told that it was much inferior to P. & P.—began it expecting to dislike it, but were very soon extremely pleased with it—& I *believe*, did not think it at all inferior.—

Alethea Bigg.—"I have read M P. & heard it very much talked of, very much praised, I like it myself & think it very good indeed, but as I never say what I do not think, I will add that although it is superior in a great many points in my opinion to the other two Works, I think it has not the Spirit of P & P., except perhaps the *Price* family at Portsmouth, & they are delightful in their way."—

Charles[1]—did not like it near so well as P. & P.—thought it wanted Incident.—

Mrs Dickson.—"I have bought M P.—but it is not equal to P. & P.—

Mrs Lefroy—liked it, but thought it a mere Novel.—

[1] JA's brother Charles John.

M^{rs}

Mrs Portal—admired it very much—objected cheifly to Edmund's not being brought more forward.—

Lady Gordon wrote "In most novels you are amused for the time with a set of Ideal People whom you never think of afterwards or whom you the least expect to meet in common life, whereas in Miss A–s works, & especially in M P. you actually *live* with them, you fancy yourself one of the family; & the scenes are so exactly descriptive, so perfectly natural, that there is scarcely an Incident or conversation, or a person that you are not inclined to imagine you have at one time or other in your Life been a witness to, born a part in, & been acquainted with."

Mrs Pole wrote, "There is a particular satisfaction in reading all Miss A—s works—they are so evidently written by a Gentlewoman—most Novellists fail & betray themselves in attempting to describe familiar scenes in high Life, some little vulgarism escapes & shews that they are not experimentally acquainted with what they describe, but here it is quite different. Everything is natural, & the situations & incidents are told in a manner which clearly evinces the Writer to *belong* to the Society whose Manners she so ably delineates." Mrs Pole also said that no Books had ever occasioned so much canvassing & doubt, & that everybody was desirous to attribute them to some of their own friends, or to some person of whom they thought highly.—

Adm^l. Foote—surprised that I had the power of drawing the Portsmouth-Scenes so well.—

Mrs Creed—preferred S & S. and P & P.—to Mansfield Park.

Opinions of *Emma*

Captⁿ. Austen.[1]—liked it extremely, observing that though there might be more Wit in P & P—& an higher Morality in M P—yet altogether, on account of it's peculiar air of Nature throughout, he preferred it to either.

Mrs F. A.[2]—liked & admired it very much indeed, but must still prefer P. & P.

Mrs J. Bridges—preferred it to all the others.

Miss Sharp—better than M P.—but not so well as P. & P.—pleased with the Heroine for her Originality, delighted with M^r K—& called Mrs Elton beyond praise.—dissatisfied with Jane Fairfax.

Cassandra—better than P. & P.—but not so well as M. P.—

Fanny K.[3]—not so well as either P. & P. or M P.—could not bear *Emma* herself.—Mr Knightley delightful.—Should like J. F.—if she knew more of her.—

M^r & Mrs J. A.[4]—did not like it so well as either of the 3 others. Language different from the others; not so easily read.—

Edward[5]—preferred it to M P.—*only*. —Mr K. liked by every body.

Miss Bigg—not equal to either P & P.—or M P.—objected to the sameness of the subject (Match-making) all through.—Too much of Mr Elton & H. Smith. Language superior to the others.—

My Mother—thought it more entertaining than M P.—but not so interesting as P. & P.—No characters in it equal to Ly Catherine & Mr Collins.—

[1] Francis William; his brother Charles is below.
[2] Francis's wife. [3] Knight.
[4] James Austen. [5] James Edward (as p. 432).

Miss

Miss Lloyd[1]—thought it as *clever* as either of the others, but did not receive so much pleasure from it as from P. & P—& M P.—

M^rs & Miss Craven—liked it very much, but not so much as the others.—

Fanny Cage—liked it very much indeed & classed it between P & P.—& M P.—

Mr Sherer—did not think it equal to either M P—(which he liked the best of all) or P & P.—Displeased with my pictures of Clergymen.—

Miss Bigg—on reading it a second time, liked Miss Bates much better than at first, & expressed herself as liking all the people of Highbury in general, except Harriet Smith—but c^d not help still thinking *her* too silly in her Loves.

The family at Upton Gray—all very much amused with it. —Miss Bates a great favourite with Mrs Beaufoy.

M^r & Mrs Leigh Perrot—saw many beauties in it, but c^d not think it equal to P. & P.—Darcy & Eliz^th had spoilt them for anything else.—Mr K. however, an excellent Character; Emma better luck than a Matchmaker often has.—Pitied Jane Fairfax—thought Frank Churchill better treated than he deserved.—

Countess Craven—admired it very much, but did not think it equal to P & P.—which she ranked as the very first of it's sort.—

Mrs Guiton—thought it too natural to be interesting.

Mrs Digweed—did not like it so well as the others, in fact if she had not known the Author, could hardly have got through it.—

Miss Terry—admired it very much, particularly Mrs Elton.

Henry Sanford—very much pleased with it—delighted with Miss Bates, but thought Mrs Elton the best-drawn Character in the Book.—Mansfield Park however, still his favourite.

[1] Martha.

Mr

Mr Haden—*quite* delighted with it. Admired the Character of Emma.—

Miss Isabella Herries—did not like it—objected to my exposing the sex in the character of the Heroine—convinced that I had meant M^{rs} & Miss Bates for some acquaintance of theirs—People whom I never heard of before.—

Miss Harriet Moore—admired it very much, but M. P. still her favourite of all.—

Countess Morley—delighted with it.—

Mr Cockerelle—liked it so little, that Fanny w^d not send me his opinion.—

Mrs Dickson—did not much like it—thought it *very* inferior to P. & P.—Liked it the less, from there being a Mr. & Mrs Dixon in it.—

Mrs Brandreth—thought the 3^d vol: superior to anything I had ever written—quite beautiful!—

Mr B. Lefroy—thought that if there had been more Incident, it would be equal to any of the others.—The Characters quite as well drawn & supported as in any, & from being more everyday ones, the more entertaining.—Did not like the Heroine so well as any of the others. Miss Bates excellent, but rather too much of her. M^r & Mrs Elton admirable & John Knightley a sensible Man.—

Mrs B. Lefroy—rank'd *Emma* as a composition with S & S. —not so *Brilliant* as P. & P—nor so *equal* as M P.— Preferred Emma herself to all the heroines.—The Characters like all the others admirably well drawn & supported—perhaps rather less strongly marked than some, but only the more natural for that reason.—Mr Knightley Mrs Elton & Miss Bates her favourites.— Thought one or two of the conversations too long.—

Mrs Lefroy—preferred it to M P—but liked M P. the least of all.

Mr

Mr Fowle—read only the first & last Chapters, because he had heard it was not interesting.—

Mrs Lutley Sclater—liked it very much, better than M P— & thought I had "brought it all about very cleverly in the last volume."—

Mrs C. Cage wrote thus to Fanny—"A great many thanks for the loan of *Emma*, which I am delighted with. I like it better than any. Every character is thoroughly kept up. I must enjoy reading it again with Charles. Miss Bates is incomparable, but I was nearly killed with those precious treasures! They are Unique, & really with more fun than I can express. I am at Highbury all day, & I can't help feeling I have just got into a new set of acquaintance. No one writes such good sense. & so very comfortable.

Mrs Wroughton—did not like it so well as P. & P.—Thought the Authoress wrong, in such times as these, to draw such Clergymen as Mr Collins & Mr Elton.

Sir J. Langham—thought it much inferior to the others.—

Mr Jeffery (of the Edinburgh Review) was kept up by it three nights.

Miss Murden—certainly inferior to all the others.

Capt. C. Austen[1] wrote—"Emma arrived in time to a moment. I am delighted with her, more so I think than even with my favourite Pride & Prejudice, & have read it three times in the Passage."

Mrs D. Dundas—thought it very clever, but did not like it so well as either of the others.

---

[1] Charles John.

VI. Verses

For JA's letter in verse of 26 July 1809 see *Letters*. For verses incidental to her juvenilia see above, pp. 5, 9, 10, 34, 50, 74, 174.

To the Memory of Mrs. Lefroy

Mrs. Lefroy was Anne, 1749–1804, sister of Sir Samuel Egerton Brydges and wife of Isaac Peter George Lefroy, Rector of Ashe. Ashe is very near Steventon, and JA was devoted to her friend, who was killed by a fall from her horse. See Brydges, *Autobiography*, ii. 41, *Memoir* ch. 3.

The author of the *Memoir* printed the following eleven quatrains 'not for their merits as poetry, but to show how deep and lasting was the impression made by the older friend on the mind of the younger'.

1.

The day returns again, my natal day;
    What mix'd emotions in my mind arise!
Beloved Friend; four years have passed away
    Since thou wert snatched for ever from our eyes.

2.

The day commemorative of my birth,
    Bestowing life, and light, and hope to me,
Brings back the hour which was thy last on earth.
    O! bitter pang of torturing memory!

3.

Angelic woman! past my power to praise
    In language meet thy talents, temper, mind,
Thy solid worth, thy captivating grace,
    Thou friend and ornament of human kind.

But

4.

But come, fond Fancy, thou indulgent power;
   Hope is desponding, chill, severe, to thee:
Bless thou this little portion of an hour;
   Let me behold her as she used to be.

5.

I see her here with all her smiles benign,
   Her looks of eager love, her accents sweet,
That voice and countenance almost divine,
   Expression, harmony, alike complete.

6.

Listen! It is not sound alone, 'tis sense,
   'Tis genius, taste, and tenderness of soul:
'Tis genuine warmth of heart without pretence,
   And purity of mind that crowns the whole.

7.

She speaks! 'Tis eloquence, that grace of tongue,
   So rare, so lovely, never misapplied
By her, to palliate vice, or deck a wrong:
   She speaks and argues but on virtue's side.

8.

Hers is the energy of soul sincere;
   Her Christian spirit, ignorant to feign,
Seeks but to comfort, heal, enlighten, cheer,
   Confer a pleasure or prevent a pain.

9.

Can aught enhance such goodness? yes, to me
   Her partial favour from my earliest years
Consummates all: ah! give me but to see
   Her smile of love! The vision disappears.

                                       'Tis

10.

'Tis past and gone. We meet no more below.
    Short is the cheat of Fancy o'er the tomb.
Oh! might I hope to equal bliss to go,
    To meet thee, angel, in thy future home.

11.

Fain would I feel an union with thy fate:
    Fain would I seek to draw an omen fair
From this connection in our earthly date.
    Indulge the harmless weakness. Reason, spare.

Two more stanzas were published in Messrs. Sotheby's catalogue 25 April 1934, with a facsimile of the MS. The quotation about Johnson is adapted from Boswell, at 20 Dec. 1784. I do not know who owns either MS. of this piece.

At Johnson's Death, by Hamilton 'twas said,
    "Seek we a substitute—Ah! vain the plan,
No second best remains to Johnson dead—
    None can remind us even of the Man."

So we of thee—unequalled in thy race,
    Unequall'd thou, as he the first of Men.
Vainly we search around thy vacant place,
    We ne'er may look upon the like again.

Mock Panegyric on a Young Friend

Memoir ch. 5. The author believed 'that all this nonsense was nearly extempore'.

1.

In measured verse I'll now rehearse
    The charms of lovely Anna:
And, first, her mind is unconfined
    Like any vast savannah.

Ontario's

2.

Ontario's lake may fitly speak
   Her fancy's ample bound:
Its circuit may, on strict survey
   Five hundred miles be found.

3.

Her wit descends on foes and friends
   Like famed Niagara's Fall;
And travellers gaze in wild amaze,
   And listen, one and all.

4.

Her judgment sound, thick, black, profound,
   Like transatlantic groves,
Dispenses aid, and friendly shade
   To all that in it roves.

5.

If thus her mind to be defined
   America exhausts,
And all that's grand in that great land
   In similes it costs—

6.

Oh how can I her person try
   To image and portray?
How paint the face, the form how trace
   In which those virtues lay?

7.

Another world must be unfurled,
   Another language known,
Ere tongue or sound can publish round
   Her charms of flesh and bone.

Mr.

Mr. Gell and Miss Gill

The manuscript (present location unknown) of this poem is reproduced in the 1870 *Memoir* (facing p. 122).   [B. C. S.]

On reading in the Newspaper, the Marriage of "Mr. Gell of Eastbourne to Miss Gill."

> Of Eastbourne Mr. Gell
> From being perfectly well
> Became dreadfully ill
> For the love of Miss Gill.
>
> So he said with some sighs
> "I'm the slave of your *eyes*.
> Oh! restore if you please
> By accepting my *ease*."
>
> J. A.

A Middle-aged Flirt

Memoir ch. 5. *Maria* was substituted for *Camilla*, sc. Wallop (q.v. in Index to *Letters*. See note on Letter 74. 1).

On the marriage of a middle-aged Flirt with a Mr. Wake, whom, it was supposed, she would scarcely have accepted in her youth.

> Maria, good-humoured, and handsome, and tall,
> For a husband was at her last stake;
> And having in vain danced at many a ball,
> Is now happy to *jump at a Wake*.

Verses given with a Needlework Bag to Mrs. James Austen

Memoir ch. 5.

> This little bag, I hope, will prove
> To be not vainly made;
> For should you thread and needles want,
> It will afford you aid.

And,

And, as we are about to part,
    'T will serve another end:
For, when you look upon this bag,
    You'll recollect your friend.

Lines to Martha Lloyd

Who had hoped that a Mr. Best would escort her to Harrogate.
Life 1913, 70.

Oh! Mr. Best, you're very bad
    And all the world shall know it;
Your base behaviour shall be sung
    By me, a tuneful poet.

You used to go to Harrogate
    Each summer as it came,
And why, I pray, should you refuse
    To go this year the same?

The way's as plain, the road's as smooth,
    The posting not increased,
You're scarcely stouter than you were,
    Not younger, Sir, at least.
        &c., &c.

Verses to Rhyme with 'Rose'

Brabourne, *Letters* ii. 341. Lord Brabourne printed, as 'enclosed in one of the *Letters* of 1807', four sets of verses on this theme, by 'Mrs. Austen, Miss Austen, Miss Jane Austen and Mrs. Elizabeth Austen' (i.e. Edward Austen's (Knight) wife, who died in that year). JA's are these:

Happy the lab'rer in his Sunday clothes!
In light-drab coat, smart waistcoat, well-darn'd hose,
And hat upon his head, to church he goes;
As oft, with conscious pride, he downward throws
A glance upon the ample cabbage rose
That, stuck in button-hole, regales his nose,

                  He

He envies not the gayest London beaux.
In church he takes his seat among the rows,
Pays to the place the reverence he owes,
Likes best the prayers whose meaning least he knows,
Lists to the sermon in a softening doze,
And rouses joyous at the welcome close.

On Sir Home Popham's Sentence, April 1807

Brabourne, ii. 344, 'enclosed in the same letter' as the preceding. Home Riggs Popham was court-martialled for having withdrawn his squadron from the Cape of Good Hope without orders, and was severely reprimanded. His case, which he argued ably, won him sympathy, and his career was hardly prejudiced. He was promoted rear-admiral in 1814 and became K.C.B. in 1815 (*D.N.B.*). JA's interest might be personal. Popham lived at Sonning, Berkshire, where her aunt's husband Dr. Cooper was Rector.

Of a Ministry pitiful, angry ⟨? and⟩ mean,
A gallant commander the victim is seen.
For promptitude, vigour, success, does he stand
Condemn'd to receive a severe reprimand!
To his foes I could wish a resemblance in fate:
That they, too, may suffer themselves, soon or late,
The injustice they warrant. But vain is my spite,
They cannot *so* suffer who never do right.

To Miss Bigg with some Pockethandkerchiefs

Brabourne, ii. 344. Miss Bigg was Catherine, who in Oct. 1808 married Herbert Hill. Their son Herbert married Southey's daughter Bertha. The late Ernest de Selincourt found the verses, signed 'J. A. Augt 26, 1808', in an album that had belonged to Bertha Hill.

To Miss Bigg, previous to her Marriage, with some Pocket handkerchiefs I had hemmed for her.

Cambrick! with grateful blessings would I pay
The pleasure given me in sweet employ :—

Long

Long may'st thou serve my Friend without decay,
And have no tears to wipe, but tears of joy!—

On the same occasion, but not sent.

Cambrick! thou'st been to me a good,
And I would bless thee if I could.
Go, serve thy mistress with delight,
Be small in compass, soft and white;
Enjoy thy fortune, honour'd much
To bear her name and feel her touch;
And that thy worth may last for years,
Slight be her colds, and few her tears.

On the Universities

I have a note that this piece was sold at Sotheby's 27 Nov.—
year not known, but before 1921. The autograph is now in
the Henry W. and Albert A. Berg collection of the NewYork
Public Library.

No wonder that Oxford and Cambridge profound
    In Learning and Science so greatly abound
Since some *carry* thither a little each day
    And we meet with so few that *bring any away*.[1]

On a Headache

MS. (from the collection described in *T.L.S.* 14 Jan. 1926) in
the Pump Room at Bath.

When stretch'd on one's bed
With a fierce-throbbing head,
Which precludes alike thought or repose,
How little one cares
For the grandest affairs
That may busy the world as it goes!

How

[1] A false attribution; Mr. Mosley of Caius College points out that
J. A. must have copied the lines from *Elegant Extracts* (c. 1789 or
a later edition).

How little one feels
For the waltzes and reels
Of our Dance-loving friends at a Ball!
How slight one's concern
To conjecture or learn
What their flounces or hearts may befall.

How little one minds
If a company dines
On the best that the Season affords!
How short is one's muse
O'er the Sauces and Stews,
Or the Guests, be they Beggars or Lords.

How little the Bells,
Ring they Peels, toll they Knells,
Can attract our attention or Ears!
The Bride may be married,
The Corse may be carried
And touch nor our hopes nor our fears.

Our own bodily pains
Ev'ry faculty chains;
We can feel on no subject beside.
Tis in health and in ease
We the power must seize
For our friends and our souls to provide.

Lines on Maria Beckford

MS. (from the collection described in *T.L.S.* 14 Jan. 1926) in
the Winchester City Museum. For Maria Beckford see *Letters*.
The late Lt.-Col. Satterthwaite of Alton told me that his house
there was once Dr. Newnham's.

I've a pain in my head
    Said the suffering Beckford,
To her Doctor so dread.
    Oh! What shall I take for't?

Said

Said this Doctor so dread
  Whose name it was Newnham
For this pain in your head
  Ah! what can you do Ma'am?

Said Miss Beckford, suppose
  If you think there's no risk,
I take a good Dose
  Of calomel brisk.

What a praiseworthy notion,
  Replied Mr. Newnham.
You shall have such a potion
  And so will I too Ma'am.
      Feb. 7. 1811.

' *I am in a Dilemma* '

Letters, p. 278. The context seems to suggest that this and the piece following are original, not quoted.

'I am in a Dilemma, for want of an Emma',
  Escaped from the Lips, of Henry Gipps.

For the gentleman's escape see Gipps in Index to *Letters*.

On the Weald of Kent Canal Bill

Letters, p. 279. See the piece preceding.

  Between Session and Session
  The first Prepossession
  May rouse up the Nation,
  And the villainous Bill
  May be forced to lie still
  Against Wicked Men's Will.

Charades

Charades written a hundred years ago by Jane Austen and her family, 1895, includes three by her. For two surviving MSS. of family charades or riddles see R. W. Chapman, *Critical Bibliography*, 1953, No. 31. One of these MSS. belonged to Cassandra. None of its contents is ascribed to any author; but there is no reason to assume that any of it is by JA.

For the solutions see p. 457.

I

When my first is a task to a young girl of spirit,
And my second confines her to finish the piece,
How hard is her fate! but how great is her merit,
If by taking my whole she effects her release!

II

Divided, I'm a gentleman
    In public deeds and powers ;
United, I'm a monster, who
    That gentleman devours.

III

You may lie on my first by the side of a stream,
    And my second compose to the nymph you adore,
But if, when you've none of my whole, her esteem
    And affection diminish—think of her no more!

Venta

The MS., initialled 'J. A.', of verses on Winchester Races and St. Swithun, sold at Sotheby's, 3 May 1948, lot 266, and now the property of Mr. T. Edward Carpenter, came from a collection (inherited by descendants of Charles Austen) of letters and other relics (mainly by or belonging to Jane Austen) the greater part of which had been described at length in *T.L.S.* 14 Jan.

1926. This creates a presumption that the verses are hers. But they are dated 'Written at Winchester on Tuesday the 15th July 1817' (St. Swithun's day), and it does not seem probable that she could have composed four-and-twenty lines of verse within three days of her death. There is a possibility that the lines are in the hand of James Austen and were composed by him ; he is known to have written verses. Anything of his would normally be preserved by his descendants the Austen-Leighs. But he was 'in frequent attendance' on his sister in her last illness, and might well leave the MS. in College Street. The two hands are very similar.

The authors of *Jane Austen's Sailor Brothers* (1906, p. 272) published the verses as hers. But it may be significant that the authors of the 1870 *Memoir* and of the *Life*, 1913, all of whom had access to this collection, ignored them.

P.S. In writing this note I strangely overlooked the evidence of Henry Austen's *Biographical Notice* prefixed to *NA and P*, 1818: 'The day preceding her death [in fact she died 18 July] she composed some stanzas replete with fancy and vigour.' That no doubt settles the question.

Venta

Written at Winchester on Tuesday the 15th July 1817

When Winchester races first took their beginning
It is said the good people forgot their old Saint
Not applying at all for the leave of St. Swithin
And that William of Wykham's approval was faint.

The races however were fix'd and determin'd
The company met & the weather was charming
The Lords & the Ladies were sattin'd & ermin'd
And nobody saw any future alarming.

But when the old Saint was inform'd of these doings
He made but one spring from his shrine to the roof
Of the Palace which now lies so sadly in ruins
And thus he address'd them all standing aloof.

Oh,

Oh, subjects rebellious, Oh Venta depraved
When once we are buried you think we are dead
But behold me Immortal.—By vice you're enslaved
You have sinn'd & must suffer.—Then further he said

These races & revels & dissolute measures
With which you're debasing a neighbouring Plain
Let them stand—you shall meet with your curse in your
  pleasures
Set off for your course, I'll pursue with my rain.

Ye cannot but know my command in July.
Henceforward I'll triumph in shewing my powers,
Shift your race as you will it shall never be dry
The curse upon Venta is July in showers.

           J. A.

On Capt. Foote's Marriage with Miss Patton

Edward James Foote was a friend of the Austen family. His
marriage to Mary Patton took place in 1803.   [B.C.S.]

Thro' the rough ways of Life, with a patten your Guard,
May you safely and pleasantly jog.
May the ring never break, nor the knot prove too hard,
Nor the Foot find the Patten a Clog.

VII. Prayers

In the collection described in *Times Lit. Supplt.* 14 Jan. 1926 were three prayers, preserved in two manuscripts. The first MS. is inscribed 'Prayers composed by my ever dear sister Jane', and the paper has a watermark dated 1818; JA died in 1817. The hand is probably—almost certainly?—Cassandra's. The second MS. has no clue to its date; it is partly in a hand which I think may be Henry Austen's, partly in a hand which has been thought by experts to be JA's own.

The prayers were first published by Mr. William Matson Roth at the Colt Press of San Francisco in 1940. The edition includes a facsimile of the page thought to be partly in JA's hand. Since it is printed throughout in capitals I have not been able to reproduce the capitals of the MS.

I

Give us grace almighty father, so to pray, as to deserve to be heard, to address thee with our hearts, as with our lips. Thou art every where present, from thee no secret can be hid. May the knowledge of this, teach us to fix our thoughts on thee, with reverence and devotion that we pray not in vain.

Look with mercy on the sins we have this day committed and in mercy make us feel them deeply, that our repentance may be sincere, & our resolution steadfast of endeavouring against the commission of such in future. Teach us to understand the sinfulness of our own hearts, and bring to our knowledge every fault of temper and every evil habit in which we have indulged to the discomfort of our fellow-creatures, and the danger of our own souls. May we now, and on each return of night, consider how the past day has been spent by us, what have been our prevailing
thoughts

thoughts, words and actions during it, and how far we can acquit ourselves of evil. Have we thought irreverently of thee, have we disobeyed thy commandments, have we neglected any known duty, or willingly given pain to any human being? Incline us to ask our hearts these questions oh! God, and save us from deceiving ourselves by pride or vanity.

Give us a thankful sense of the blessings in which we live, of the many comforts of our lot; that we may not deserve to lose them by discontent or indifference.

Be gracious to our necessities, and guard us, and all we love, from evil this night. May the sick and afflicted, be now, and ever thy care; and heartily do we pray for the safety of all that travel by land or by sea, for the comfort & protection of the orphan and widow and that thy pity may be shewn upon all captives and prisoners.

Above all other blessings oh! God, for ourselves and our fellow-creatures, we implore thee to quicken our sense of thy mercy in the redemption of the world, of the value of that holy religion in which we have been brought up, that we may not, by our own neglect, throw away the salvation thou hast given us, nor be Christians only in name. Hear us almighty God, for his sake who has redeemed us, and taught us thus to pray. Our Father which art in heaven &c.

II

Almighty God! Look down with mercy on thy servants here assembled and accept the petitions now offered up unto thee. Pardon oh! God the offences of the past day. We are conscious of many frailties; we remember with shame and contrition, many evil thoughts and neglected duties; and we have perhaps sinned against thee and against our fellow-creatures in many instances of which we have no remembrance. Pardon oh God! whatever thou hast seen amiss in us, and give us a stronger desire of resisting

resisting every evil inclination and weakening every habit
of sin. Thou knowest the infirmity of our nature, and the
temptations which surround us. Be thou merciful, oh
heavenly Father! to creatures so formed and situated. We
bless thee for every comfort of our past and present existence, for our health of body and of mind and for every
other source of happiness which thou hast bountifully
bestowed on us and with which we close this day, imploring
their continuance from thy fatherly goodness, with a more
grateful sense of them, than they have hitherto excited.
May the comforts of every day, be thankfully felt by us, may
they prompt a willing obedience of thy commandments
and a benevolent spirit toward every fellow-creature.

Have mercy oh gracious Father! upon all that are now
suffering from whatsoever cause, that are in any circumstance of danger or distress. Give them patience under
every affliction, strengthen, comfort and relieve them.

To thy goodness we commend ourselves this night beseeching thy protection of us through its darkness and
dangers. We are helpless and dependent; graciously preserve us. For all whom we love and value, for every friend
and connection, we equally pray; however divided and far
asunder, we know that we are alike before thee, and under
thine eye. May we be equally united in thy faith and fear,
in fervent devotion towards thee, and in thy merciful
protection this night. Pardon oh Lord! the imperfections
of these our prayers, and accept them through the media-
tion of our blessed saviour, in whose holy words, we further
address thee; our Father &c.

III

Father of Heaven! whose goodness has brought us in
safety to the close of this day, dispose our hearts in fervent
prayer. Another day is now gone, and added to those, for
which we were before accountable. Teach us almighty
father

father, to consider this solemn truth, as we should do, that we may feel the importance of every day, and every hour as it passes, and earnestly strive to make a better use of what thy goodness may yet bestow on us, than we have done of the time past.

Give us grace to endeavour after a truly Christian spirit to seek to attain that temper of forbearance and patience of which our blessed saviour has set us the highest example; and which, while it prepares us for the spiritual happiness of the life to come, will secure to us the best enjoyment of what this world can give. Incline us oh God! to think humbly of ourselves, to be severe only in the examination of our own conduct, to consider our fellow-creatures with kindness, and to judge of all they say and do with that charity which we would desire from them ourselves.

We thank thee with all our hearts for every gracious dispensation, for all the blessings that have attended our lives, for every hour of safety, health and peace, of domestic comfort and innocent enjoyment. We feel that we have been blessed far beyond any thing that we have deserved; and though we cannot but pray for a continuance of all these mercies, we acknowledge our unworthiness of them and implore thee to pardon the presumption of our desires.

Keep us oh! Heavenly Father from evil this night. Bring us in safety to the beginning of another day and grant that we may rise again with every serious and religious feeling which now directs us.

May thy mercy be extended over all mankind, bringing the ignorant to the knowledge of thy truth, awakening the impenitent, touching the hardened. Look with compassion upon the afflicted of every condition, assuage the pangs of disease, comfort the broken in spirit.

More particularly do we pray for the safety and welfare of our own family and friends wheresoever dispersed, beseeching thee to avert from them all material and lasting evil of body or mind; and may we by the assistance of thy

holy

holy spirit so conduct ourselves on earth as to secure an eternity of happiness with each other in thy heavenly kingdom. Grant this most merciful Father, for the sake of our blessed saviour in whose holy name and words we further address thee. Our Father which art in heaven &c.

Solution of the Charades (p. 450)

1. Hemlock. II. Agent. III. Bank Note.

NOTES

12. Mr. Johnson's Masquerade seems to be a parody of the Harrel family masquerade in Fanny Burney's *Cecilia*, 1782 (I. bk. 2, ch. 3). [B.C.S.]

15. *Grandison*, Vol. IV, Letter 3: Sir Charles 'never suffers his servants to deny him, when he is at home'. See also p. 186.

18. *From Words*. This is from James Merrick's *The Camelion*, which JA found in her copy (we know she had one) of Dodsley's *Collection of Poems*, Vol. 5, 1758.

49. *those celebrated Comedies* ... Neither of the titles is known outside this context, so possibly they are two pieces of Jane Austen's own composition, 'celebrated' by their performance or reading at Steventon, yet for some reason not transcribed into any of the three notebooks. [B.C.S.]

50. *The more free*. Not traced.

55. *The Mystery*. The conversation in scene ii, made up of hints and mysteries, may be modelled on a similarly satirical passage in Sheridan, *The Critic* (II. i.), a play which Jane Austen refers to in the 'History of England' (p. 147). [B.C.S.]

65. *Badroulbadour*. She is Badroulboudour in the English version of Galland's French, e.g. 1789, iv. 10.
Which is the Man. By Hannah Cowley, 1782.

76. *Love and Friendship*. This title is a familiar phrase in eighteenth-century literature. Jane Austen would certainly have known it in *Sir Charles Grandison*, 1754, v. 74–75; in David Garrick, *Bon Ton* (1775, p. 8 in the 1776 edition), performed by the Austens at Steventon in 1787 or 1788; and in a contribution by Henry Austen to his own Oxford periodical *The Loiterer*, no. 27, 1 August 1789. [B.C.S.]
Deceived in Freindship. Not traced.

86. *We fainted* ... Probably an allusion to *The Critic* (III. i), the stage direction 'They faint alternately in each other's arms'. [B.C.S.]

A BAROUCHE-LANDAU BY GODIOL

From *Le Beau Monde*, 1806

97. *we sate down.* This passage is a parody of Johnson's description of his sitting in Glen Shiel in *A Journey to the Western
Islands* (1775), to which book JA owed also her knowledge
of the two universities of Aberdeen (118). The 'malevolent
and contemptible' Macdonald of Macdonald Hall reflects that
Sir Alexander Macdonald ('Sir Sawny') of whose sparing
hospitality at Armadale in Skye both Johnson and Boswell
complained.

98. *Eastern Zephyr.* JA was not innocent of classical mythology
('her sister in Lucina' *Letters*, p. 329), and we may be confident that *Eastern* is a joke.

100. *Talk not to me* . . . Probably an imitation of Tilburina's
ravings in *The Critic* (III. i), although it may be a parody of
Lear's mad speeches, see especially *King Lear*, IV. vi. 97.
   just Seventeen. Perhaps a polite bow to Cassandra, who
would be seventeen in January 1791. [B.C.S.]

103. *What an illiterate villain* . . . Probably an imitation of
Joseph Surface's hypocritical protestations in *The School for
Scandal* (IV. iii). Jane Austen acted in this play. [B.C.S.]

105. *Gilpin's Tour to the Highlands.* William Gilpin, *Observations, relative chiefly to Picturesque Beauty, made in the year
1776, on Several Parts of Great Britain; particularly the High-
Lands of Scotland*, 1789. [B.C.S.]

   Stage Coach. In letter 99, to Cassandra, Tuesday? August
1814, Jane Austen writes of this, 'my own Coach between
Edinburgh & Sterling' (p. 397). [B.C.S.]

107. *our Company.* This would remind Jane Austen's family
audience of their own theatricals, held in the Rectory or in
a converted barn during her childhood. For example, *The
Rivals* was played in 1784, and we know that performances
certainly continued until 1789. The Austens, too, sometimes
had difficulty in raising a full cast (see the letters of Eliza de
Feuillide to Philadelphia Walter, *Austen Papers 1704–1856*
(1942), ed. R. A. Austen-Leigh). [B.C.S.]

109. 'Sunday' is perhaps erased in the MS. I note that 13 June
1790 *was* a Sunday.

110. *Messrs Demand & Co* . . . *£105. 0. 0.* These lines are not in
Jane Austen's hand. In 1807 Henry Austen became a partner

in the banking house of Austen, Maunde and Tilson. So possibly they were added by a member of the family. This would have kept up to date the mixture of fantasy and family history of which so much of the juvenilia are compounded. [B.C.S.]

Rakehelly Dishonor seems to be fictitious.

113. *Hervey.* Usually *Henry*, but *Henry Hervey*, p. 129.

118. The collocation of *think* and *feel* was common. Some heroines boasted their sensibility, disclaiming sense; others had both; thus Fanny Burney's Camilla (1796) 'possessed . . . the thinking and feeling mind'. But JA's use of underlines may suggest that she had been reading Boswell's *Hebrides* as well as Johnson's *Journey* (see note to p. 97) and recalled his footnote under 13 September, where he recorded that his sovereign 'thinks and feels as I do' on a delicate subject.

For the two universities see note to p. 97.

130. *Malbrook.* Properly 'Malbrouck s'en va-t-en guerre', an eighteenth-century French nursery song which became popular all over Europe. [B.C.S.]

outlandish words. Charlotte's opinion is that of her author. In a letter Jane Austen refers to 'due scraps of Italian & French' (p. 135), borrowed phrases which she uses frequently and facetiously in her letters. [B.C.S.]

139. *Shakespear's Plays.* 2 *Henry IV*, iv. v.

Shakespear's account. Henry V, iii. iv; v. ii. [B.C.S.]

140. *Edward the 4th.* This entry parodies the corresponding section in Goldsmith's *Abridgement*, 1774 (p. 155) to his *History of England*. [B.C.S.]

Edward the 4th . . . the Picture . . . In the manuscript, twelve of the thirteen sections of the 'History' are headed by medallion portraits in water-colour by Cassandra Austen. They are witty caricatures. Edward IV, described by Jane Austen as 'famous only for his Beauty and his Courage', is drawn by her sister with a coarse and stupid face. The portraits are reproduced in colour on the endpapers of the 1922 edition of *Love and Freindship* and in black and white at the end of *Volume the Second*, 1963. [B.C.S.]

140. *Jane Shore.* By Nicholas Rowe, 1714. [B.C.S.]

had time. Miss Lascelles suggesting that JA wrote this and not *had him* (as in 1922), I had further recourse to the MS., which confirms her.

141. *declared that he did* not *kill his two Nephews.* Notably by Horace Walpole in his *Historic Doubts.*

142. *Abbott of Leicester,* 1509–34. Richard Pexhill was abbot of St. Mary of the Meadows, Leicester, 1509–34.

6th of May. The only date which Goldsmith gives in the *History of England,* (1764), in his account of the eight reigns from Henry IV to Henry VIII. Jane Austen's great play of mentioning this precise date is probably a reminder of Goldsmith's 'dateless' history. [B.C.S.]

143. *Duke of Norfolk . . . cause.* This reference to Norfolk's support (and again on p. 145) may be an allusion to the way in which historical novelists represented the friendship between Norfolk and Mary as a romantic love-affair. [B.C.S.]

Delamere. The hero of *Emmeline, or the Orphan of the Castle* (1788) by Charlotte Smith. [B.C.S.]

145. *Mr Whitaker.* Probably John Whitaker, 1735–1806, author of *Mary Queen of Scots Vindicated,* 1787. Jane Austen may have been led to this work by a reference in Gilpin's Highland *Observations* (see note to p. 105), where he writes sympathetically of 'that unfortunate princess, Mary, Queen of Scots' and refers the reader to 'A late historian, Mr. Whitacre' who has 'thrown the guilt on Elizabeth' (i. 92, and note). [B.C.S.]

146. *one . . . now but young.* Francis William Austen, 1774–1865, the fifth son, at this time a midshipman on board the *Perseverance.* In the event, his signs of promise were fulfilled: he became Admiral of the Fleet. [B.C.S.]

153. *Ride where you may.* 'Laugh where we must, be candid where we can.' *Essay on Man,* Ep. i. 15.

167. *Yes I'm in love.* JA owed her knowledge of W. Whitehead's 'The *Je ne scai quoi*', which she quotes again in *MP* ii. 12, to Vol. II of Dodsley's *Poems* (1748–58), her copy of

which she had to relinquish with Steventon (Letter of 21 May 1801).

> 'Yes, I'm in love, I feel it now,
> And Cælia has undone me.'

170. *Rowling.* Fanny's father (JA's brother Edward, later Knight) lived at Rowling in East Kent until *c.* Oct. 1798 (Brabourne, *Letters*, 1884, i. 149).

186. *Sir Charles Grandison's.* Mr. A. D. McKillop in an admirable article (*Notes and Queries*, 196.20, 29 Sept. 1951, 428) remarks that 'a reader would have to know the action of that story pretty well' (but we knew she did!) 'to refer casually to Sir Charles's zealous attendance on the injured and the ill'. See also p. 15.

189. *On his return home . . .* From this point onwards, manuscript pages 21–27, there is a distinct change in the hand and the ink in which 'Evelyn' is written. Moreover, there are significant orthographical and stylistic features pointing to outside authorship, possibly one of Jane Austen's young nephews or nieces who may have been allowed to try his hand at completing the story, just as happened in the case of 'Catharine' (see note to page 239). These questions of authorship are fully discussed by B. C. Southam, 'Interpolations to Jane Austen's "Volume the Third"', *Notes and Queries* (May 1962) ccvii. 185–7. [B.C.S.]

191. *Westgate Buildings.* The connotation of this address will be familiar to readers of *Persuasion*.

199. *Emmeline . . . Ethelinde.* See s.v. Charlotte Smith in Index IV. Grasmere is described at the beginning and end of *Ethelinde*.

205. *Barbadoes.* Mrs. Musgrove in *Persuasion* is similarly ignorant of our possessions in the West Indies.

206. *to sea.* JA's first intention on p. 203 was 'sent to Sea' which she changed to 'got into the Army'; she failed to alter the second place.

232. *note.* This refers to the *Explanation of the Catechism* by Thomas Secker, 1809. [B.C.S.]

239. Beginning 'Kitty continued' to the end of 'Catharine', the manuscript hand is different, probably not Jane Austen's. [B.C.S.]

240. *Halifax.* A slip for Barlow, see p. 204.

242. *Tantôt . . . oppresse.* Not traced.

321. *Guildford* was substituted in the MS. for Dorking. At p. 338 JA failed to replace R. by D. Perhaps her original intention was Dorking and Reigate, for which she substituted Guildford and D (i.e. Dorking).

338. *R.* This may be a survival of an original intention to place the Watsons' village near Reigate.

356. *the Bedford.* Where John Thorpe was equally at home.

370. *Cowper. Truth* 327 :

> Just knows, and knows no more, her Bible true—
> A truth the brilliant Frenchman never knew ; . . .
> He prais'd, perhaps, for ages yet to come ;
> She never heard of half a mile from home.

390. *Camilla.* Fanny Burney's heroine was nine at the outset of the story.

397. *either of Scott's Poems.* Sir Edward goes on to quote *Marmion* and *The Lady of the Lake.* JA had forgotten *The Lay of the Last Minstrel*, which she had quoted in *MP*, and perhaps ignored *The Field of Waterloo*, which her brother had borrowed in 1815.

427. *of Man.* The MS. has 'by Man'.

INDEXES

ABBREVIATIONS

i, ii, iii: Volumes the First, Second, Third

    Su: Lady Susan
    W: The Watsons
    Sa: Sanditon

INDEX I (1)

CHARACTERS IN 'CATHARINE'

The characters in the other Juvenilia are not indexed

INDEX I (2)

CHARACTERS IN 'LADY SUSAN'

Martin, Sir James (245), m. Lady Susan Vernon, q.v.

Smith, Charles, 264.

Summers, Miss, schoolmistress in Wigmore St., 246.

Vernon, Lady Susan, d. of an unnamed peer; widow of — Vernon, formerly of V. Castle, Staffordshire (249, 251); of 10 Wigmore St. (245), and, later, Upper Seymour St. (298); *c.* 35 (251); m. Sir

James Martin (312). Her o.d. Frederica Susanna (274), 16 (266, 274), m. Reginald De Courcy, q.v.

Vernon, Charles, of Churchill, Sussex, y.b. of Lady Susan's first husband (249), m. Catherine De Courcy, q.v., 'children in abundance' including Frederic (250), Catherine (277).

Wilson, Lady Susan's maid, 284.

INDEX I (3)

CHARACTERS IN 'THE WATSONS'

Beresford, Colonel, 330.

Betty, maid at the Watsons', 346.

Blake, *see* Howard.

Carr, 'Fanny' (340), friend of Miss Osborne, 329.

Curtis, surgeon of Guildford, 321.

Edward(e)s, Mr. and Mrs., of 'D. in Surry' (*see* Watson); their d. Mary, twenty-two, 322; 'at least' £10,000, 321.

Harding, 'old Dr.' of Chichester, 317.

Hemmings, Mr., of Croydon, 353.

Howard, Rev. —, 'clergyman of the Parish (Wickstead) in which the Castle stood', 329; 'a little more than Thirty', 330; m. Emma Watson, q.v. (363); his widowed sister — Blake, 35 or 36 (329, 330); her son Charles, 10 (329) and other children (331).

Hunter, Captain, 320 (m. Mary Edwards?).

James, Mr. Watson's coachman, 319.

Marshall, Mr., of Croydon, 353.

Musgrave, Tom, 'a great flirt', 318; '8 or 900 £ a year', 328.

Nanny, maid at the Watsons', 344.

Norton, Mr., of Capt. Hunter's regiment, 337.

O'Brien, *see* Turner.

Osborne, Lord, of O. Castle, Surry; his mother 'nearly 50' and unmarried sister, 329.

Purvis, —, did not marry Elizabeth Watson, 316.

Richards, Rev. Dr., 344.

Shaw, Mrs., of Chichester, 317.

Stokes, Jack, 341.

Styles, Mr., of Capt. Hunter's regiment, 337.

Tomlinson, banker of D. (*see* Watson); his wife and sons, — and James, 322, 336.

Turner: Emma Watson's widowed aunt in Shropshire, m. (2) Captain O'Brien (315, 321, 326).

Watson, (? Rev., 343–4) —, of Stanton (317), a village near 'D. in Surry' (315, &c.) or 'R' (338, *see* note)—presumably Dorking and Reigate; widower (315); his sons Robert, attorney of Croydon (348), m. Jane — (£6,000, 321); their d. Augusta (350); Sam, surgeon of Guildford (320, 321); his daughters

INDEX I (4)

CHARACTERS IN 'SANDITON'

INDEX II
REAL PERSONS

The Kings and Queens of England (Vol. II) are omitted. References to
Letters *mean that further information will be found in the indexes to
my edition*

INDEX III

PLACES

Feigned places are distinguished by inverted commas

INDEX IV

AUTHORS AND BOOKS

A list, nearly complete, of all literary allusions in J A's works and her letters will be found in my current edition of N.A. and P., p. 295